OPERATION FLOWER PETAL

SHELLEY MUNRO

MUNRO PRESS

Operation Flower Petal

Print ISBN: 978-1-99-106351-9
Digital ISBN: 978-0-9951395-6-5

Editor: Evil Eye Editing

Cover: Kim Killion, The Killion Group, Inc.

Munro Press, New Zealand.

First Munro Press electronic publication February 2021

First Munro Press print publication May 2024

DEDICATION

For Paul, my partner in crime and fellow adventurer.

INTRODUCTION

He falls for her...literally.

Since her husband's murder, Ada Buckingham's life has comprised one calamity after another, and the hits keep coming, yet each day, she picks herself up and begins again.

Military man Matt Townsend, AKA Frog, expects a challenging assignment when he agrees to train soldiers in tough country terrain. The rules: stay away from the old lady's flowers and notify her of days or nights with *flash-bang*.

Easy, right?

On arrival via parachute, he plummets into the lady's flowers. The sexy spitfire who confronts him isn't the maiden aunt-type he imagined, but man, she intrigues and entices him, and he's eager to learn more.

Matt is quick to insert himself into her life, and his mission evolves once he learns something is hinky and dangerous in the world of Ada. While he fell arse over teakettle, Ada is slower to believe or trust, but Matt is confident in his charm and brings his A-game. Now all he needs to do is keep her safe.

You will love this latest addition to the Military Men series because it contains a charming, confident, and audacious soldier known for his singing voice—not!—and a brave and determined heroine with a love of flowers. You'll also find skullduggery in a country town, danger, and gossip aplenty. Sit back with a glass of wine and enjoy the romantic adventure.

CHAPTER 1

BLACK LETTER DAY

ADELAIDE BUCKINGHAM'S HAND TIGHTENED on her phone. She bit her bottom lip and listened to the gloating voices of Greg's parents.

"We received a copy of the profit-and-loss from the accountant. You made another loss," her mother-in-law crowed. "Only two-and-a-half years before the land reverts to a true Buckingham."

Tears filled her eyes, and she swallowed hard. Ada—as her family and friends called her—started to reply before pressing her lips together. Speaking her mind wouldn't help. The best way to honor Greg was to keep working.

"Flowers! I've never heard of anything so stupid in all my life," her father-in-law muttered. "Greg would turn in his grave if he knew what you were doing to our land."

Still, Ada didn't justify the changes she'd made or the way she'd pivoted her plans to give herself a better chance of making Greg's farming dream come true.

"I'm glad you received the accounts. I guess I'll speak to you next year." She got the words out without crying and disconnected the call. Their glee and malicious triumph in her failure became more difficult with each passing year. She had to make her flower-growing enterprise work. It was her last chance, and she'd put every last dollar into the change, every bit of energy, every last hope.

Ada picked up the glass of juice she'd poured herself and took a sip. Her gaze settled on the next piece of bad news—the day's mail.

A strangled yowl wrenched Ada from her death stare at the envelopes. She grimaced and peered out the window. Country commotion. The racket shouldn't disturb her any longer, yet she jumped every time she heard a weird noise. When she spotted nothing out of place, she turned back to the white envelopes on her kitchen counter.

Waiting. Unopened.

Lurking pieces of evil ready to jump out at her like a jack-in-a-box.

It didn't take much to guess the top one's contents since the sender had emblazoned their symbol plus their return postal address on the front—her copy of the farm accounts.

The second envelope had Ada holding back a scream and her stomach turning rock hard.

The yowl sounded again, closer this time. The stressed call had Ada leaping to her feet and taking the one stride necessary to reach her front entrance. Calling up every scrap of bravery, she wrenched open the door and padded onto her wooden deck. It took long seconds for her gaze to adjust to the dark. She scanned the shadows, uneasy at the out-of-place cry, but determined not to act like a nervous city-girl—the label her husband's family had saddled her with after she'd married their son.

Greg hadn't cared Ada couldn't spout the finer points of a Romney sheep or whistle a sheepdog. He'd loved her, and she'd returned the sentiment until the day he'd died, murdered by a mystery assailant almost three years ago.

When the distressed cry came for a third time, she pinpointed the direction and spotted faint movement.

"A cat," she whispered, her tense shoulders relaxing. Laughing at her nerves, she slipped back inside. In her tiny house's compact kitchen, she pulled a bottle of milk from her fridge and located an old bowl. Some idiot had tired of their pet and dumped it in the countryside. Nothing much surprised Ada these days, although she wondered how the cat had turned up in her backyard. Her land sat at the end of a long valley, sandwiched between the Moewai River and the range of mountains behind. Access for her and her neighbors was via a no-exit road, which ended at her property.

Ada set the bowl outside and retreated to her house and her pile of mail.

"Damn and blast." She swooped forward, plucked up the letter from the bank, and ripped it open. Although her hands trembled, Ada scanned the note from the loan's manager. Hot tears filled her eyes while anger pumped through her veins. She tightened her grip, the paper wrinkling under the pressure.

"Greg, if you were here," she gritted out, "I would murder you myself."

Then shame swamped her, and her shoulders slumped.

Greg had dreamed of farming sheep rather than embracing the family dairy farm legacy, and thanks to the generous help of his aunt, he'd inherited this block of land. A shudder slipped down her spine at the memory of the family blowup and what she called the *disowning*. Unfortunately, the inheritance came with strings, but she and Greg had discussed the risk, agreed on the plan.

Greg hadn't gone with full disclosure.

"I'm sorry," she whispered because talking to her dead

husband assuaged her loneliness. "You would've told me, eventually. We would've worked out the problems." But even as she uttered the words, irritation flickered inside her.

Greg had left her standing in a heap of sheep doo-doo.

Until she'd received the first communication from the bank six months ago, she hadn't known of the loan. It wasn't from their local Moewai bank. After her initial shock, she'd managed the funds to cover the final interest installment plus part of the principal, but the balance was due in full in two months. Not only could she not repay the rest, but because of the will stipulating her tenure of the land, the property wasn't hers free and clear until she made a profit. Selling any part of it was impossible.

When she and Greg had taken possession of the land, the goal of making a profit within eight years had seemed easy. After Greg's murder, she'd stood her ground, and the judge had agreed with her. Legally, she had two more years to make a profit. If she failed, the land returned to Greg's family, and she'd walk away with nothing.

And didn't they enjoy reminding her of the fact?

Each year, they gloated over the negative income figures and the bottom line.

Hot tears stung her eyes, and she flung the crumpled letter on her counter. Sniffing, she reached for the third letter. This one came from the New Zealand Army, although what they wanted, she had no idea.

Ada ripped open the envelope and read the request on the single sheet of paper.

Dear Greg,

Re: Army Training Exercise

You approached us several years ago with an offer of your land should we require it for one of our training exercises. I've tried ringing the cell number you gave me at the time of our meeting, and this is the last resort since I couldn't find a way of contacting you online.

Ada paused in her reading and frowned at the letter. The man—a Captain Jacob Massey—couldn't have known Greg well if he'd missed her husband's murder. She continued reading.

We would like to use your high country to conduct training exercises for our troops. I understand you have a working farm, and this will cause an interruption in your farming endeavors, so we are offering payment of one thousand dollars per day for one month. At this stage, we are undecided about the time the exercises will continue. We think three weeks, but it will not be longer than one month.

If you agree with us using your land, please call the number below to discuss the same.

Yours faithfully,

Captain Jacob Massey

Ada hissed out her breath, hope surging through her to replace the helplessness she'd experienced since she'd first learned of the loan her husband had taken out without telling her. A thousand dollars a day. Three weeks. Wow! That was twenty-one thousand dollars. While she owed the bank fifty-thousand dollars, this was a fantastic start.

A lifeline.

She had her emergency fund of five thousand dollars, plus if she harvested her flowers, dried, and packed them ready to sell, she might manage a few more thousand. It might be enough for the bank to consider refinancing.

It was too late to call the captain, but she'd do it in the morning. Bolstered by the opportunity, she decided she was hungry.

As she constructed a ham and cheese sandwich, she

glanced out the window. A dark shape slinked toward the bowl of milk. Ada froze, holding her breath when the cat sniffed the contents, then lapped at the offering. She smiled, relieved both of them were having a better end to their day.

With another smile of approval, she turned on the radio and listened to the talk-back station. The callers discussed local affairs. At present, politics was popular since the elections were in a few months. Ada settled into her comfortable chair while she focused on mindful breathing. It usually helped, but this evening her problems kept leaping from her locked mental box and circling back to give her a hard time.

What if the bank manager didn't agree to a partial payment? Everyone—her local bank manager and Greg's family—had pooh-poohed her fledgling business selling dried flowers as confetti. She'd continued anyway, inspired by a television special she'd watched.

"Don't get too far ahead of yourself, Adelaide Buckingham," she whispered.

First, she'd speak to the army man. She yawned but sensed she wouldn't sleep, not with her busy mind. With a sigh, Ada pulled out the folder holding the mockups for her label designs.

She sifted through her three choices. Keep it simple, she

decided. With that in mind, she discarded the busiest of the three designs. The other two were appealing, but the color combination of one drew her more.

With that decided, she powered up her laptop and used the same motif on her fledgling website. She tweaked her homepage and reread her 'about' page. Bland and uninspiring, it lacked the emotion necessary to grab the attention of brides and wedding planners.

Ada discarded her copy and started again.

I love flowers. When my husband died, I needed to make significant changes. I'm a city girl with a love of plants and gardening, so I sold the sheep—a silly animal I found challenging to deal with due to my lack of experience—and searched for another way to make the farm productive. After watching a reality show on television where couples visit properties with an eye to moving to the country, the show's special interest feature snared my attention. It detailed a farmer who'd diversified and grown flowers. He dried the flowers and produced a natural, environmentally friendly confetti, popular with brides, the church ministers, and the local council because cleanup was minimal compared to paper confetti or rice.

The idea stuck with me. It intrigued me, and after

researching the flowers available in New Zealand, I chose to grow delphiniums. They're perfect for the climate and suit the rich soil here at Moewai.

Moewai Flowers was born.

Ada reread what she'd written. Better. Much better. When she yawned again, she checked her watch. Almost midnight.

In her bedroom, she pulled on an oversize T-shirt and crawled into bed. She must've dozed because she awoke with her heart racing. The cat yowled.

Ada swallowed and cocked her head. Was someone whispering? No, it was the wind. She fumbled with her light and checked the time. Five-thirty. She exhaled. Her alarm would wail in half an hour, anyway.

After dressing in her old clothes and making tea, she slipped outside to sit on her deck. The birds sang and tweeted their dawn chorus, and she intended to enjoy the show. Her backside had almost hit the seat cushion when she noticed the writing in scarlet paint emblazoned across the wall of her shed.

Leave or face the wrath.

Ada cursed and went to call the cops.

Again.

CHAPTER 2

MATT FALLS FOR ADA

MATT TOWNSEND KNOCKED ON his boss's door and paused for an invitation to enter.

"Ah, Matt," the grizzled man said. "Perfect timing. Have a seat."

Now that Matt—also known to his friends and fellow officers as Frog—had retired from active service in the New Zealand Special Air Service, he'd slipped into a trainer's role. Although he thought he'd miss the action, he'd found he preferred the slower pace and the fact no one shot at him daily.

"What's up, boss?"

"We've received the go-ahead for another training mission. It's down country at a place called Moewai. Ever heard of it?"

Matt shook his head. "No."

"It's a country town close to Eketāhuna in the lower North Island."

Matt shrugged. "My brother-in-law is from Eketāhuna."

His boss tapped his fingers on his desk and pulled out a file. "We're calling the training exercise Operation Flower Petal."

Matt barely controlled his splutter of astonishment. "Pardon?"

His boss's face lit up with enjoyment. "Ada Buckingham, the landowner, grows flowers to turn into wedding confetti."

"I can see how training in a paddock of flowers might challenge our men."

The boss's eyes twinkled, and a dimple popped into view.

Matt's brows rose. "What aren't you telling me?"

"Details." His boss opened the manila folder. "We will restrict the military exercises to the farm's hill country, and we must stay away from the flowers. Also, we are to contact Ms. Buckingham when we're using live ammunition or anything that goes *bang-bang*."

"*Bang-bang*?" Matt parroted. "Is that a new technical

term?"

His boss chuckled. "Ms. Buckingham's phone number is in the file. Ring her if you intend to make noise."

"I can do that. Anything else?"

"Keep out of her way and away from her flowers. Do that, and she told me she'd be happy. The rest of the op details are in the folder. I know we've discussed the program, but my secretary has included everything in here. Questions?"

"No, I'm happy with the mission statement and what we want to achieve," Matt said.

"Excellent. I'm interested to see what our newer men can do."

"They're fit and capable. I'd be surprised if the soldiers didn't excel." The exercises they'd devised *should* test the men because he had a gut feeling this lot would see action soon.

Two weeks later, Matt tossed the pack containing his clothes and supplies on the back of a utility vehicle. The other two trainers followed suit, then the three dozen men going through the training exercise loaded their packs. One of his trainers pulled the canvas top over the luggage and sealed it securely.

"See you soon," he said. Minutes later, he drove off.

"Right." Matt blew a whistle. "We're off for a run. Ten

kilometers," he ordered. "Followed by one lap around the obstacle course."

His men knew better than to grumble, but Matt guessed they'd presumed today would be an easy one. Unfortunately for them, the flight was brief. Matt wanted the luggage and supplies to arrive first.

Matt and his soldiers boarded a plane five hours later for the quick hop to Moewai. Except, they weren't landing in the traditional way. Their arrival would be via parachute.

"Remember, the object is to land within the marked zone. The soldier or soldiers who land closest to the target get to relax instead of cooking dinner tonight. Keep away from the lady's flowers."

One man snorted. "Is that why we got landed with the name Operation Flower Petal?" He rolled his eyes. "That is gonna look great on our training records."

Several of the men whooped, and Matt grinned.

"As long as you don't land in the flowers, we'll be golden. Gear up for the jump. We leave as soon as everyone is ready." Matt donned his parachute, using his typical methodical actions, double-checking as he went. Once satisfied, he ran a practiced eye over his soldiers. They were experienced jumpers, having done this hundreds of times during basic and training exercises. Most of this group had jumped into hot spots, and he had full confidence in their abilities.

There was the usual joking when the plane took off. Matt settled back and closed his eyes while listening to the ribald teasing and gossip flowing around the cabin.

It seemed mere minutes passed before the guy assigned to help with the jump shook him awake. Matt rose and prepared for the exit. After their run and the obstacle course this morning, he'd drilled them on the jump site and told them what to expect.

"Right," Matt called. The cold air buffeted him, flapping his clothes and chilling his skin. "Who's first?"

"Me." A beefy soldier stepped forward, enthusiasm glinting in his eyes.

"Right," Matt said. "Go."

The soldier leaped without hesitation, swiftly followed by the rest of the group.

Matt met the gaze of the guy helping. "Thanks!" Then he, too, leaped from the plane. As always, pure adrenaline shot through him. The wind whipped his hair as he fell. He scanned the land below, both to check on his soldiers and to orientate himself. Parachutes filled the sky, and two men hooted.

Matt pulled his cord, and his body jerked upward as his chute opened. He noticed he and one soldier were off course after jumping last from the plane.

Then he groaned because of the blaze of color in the paddock below them—the blue, the pink, the purple, and the white were strips of boldness against the landscape. Beyond, the river flowed in a silver ribbon, cutting through the land as it headed toward the Tasman Sea.

As his chute drifted lower, Matt attempted to maneuver, but a gust of wind caught him and his stray soldier. Matt cursed under his breath.

This was gonna make him real popular with the old lady property owner.

He attempted to change his trajectory but to no avail. His man experienced the same problem, but he landed to the right of the flowers.

Matt wasn't so lucky.

Chapter 3

Spitfire Alert

Ada heard the plane fly overhead and stopped work to walk outside. She glimpsed the cat before she lifted her gaze to search for the aircraft. Without hesitation, men or women leaped out, one after the other. She shuddered. No way would she ever jump from a plane, even if there was a parachute attached to her back.

Her phone rang, and after a glance at the screen, she answered. "Hi, Sherry."

"Oh, Ada," her neighbor said. "Are you all right? The grapevine says you had trouble at your place last night. Everyone was talking about it today."

"Huh, that didn't take long," Ada said, thinking the mailman had a big mouth. "I'm fine. Someone spray-painted the side of my shed. I took pics and sent them to the local cop. He's been out to take photos too."

"You didn't hear anything?" Sherry asked, concern in her voice.

"Not a thing." Ada's skin crawled at the idea of people creeping around her property. The cop had suggested she get a dog, and she was seriously considering this recommendation.

"I'm so sorry. Bart and I had friends over for a barbecue. It was a lovely evening we sat outside until late. Sound travels at night, so I'm certain we would've noticed anything untoward."

"It's not your fault. I've reported the vandalism, and that's all I can do at this stage. Although it's frustrating. I don't know why they're victimizing me. I keep to myself and never cause trouble."

Sherry cleared her throat, and everything inside Ada went cold.

No, please don't mention what I think you're going to say.

"Do you think this is something to do with Greg's murder?"

"No," Ada said in a sharp voice. She was tired of the gossip and the innuendos and the well-meaning people who kept telling her she needed to move on. After all, it had been three years. Greg wouldn't want her to be unhappy.

"I'm sorry," Sherry said in a small voice. "You have so much trouble at your place."

"Not really," Ada corrected. "The cop I spoke with thinks my problem is teenagers acting stupid. He's more worried about the thefts in the district. Did you hear? George Carole's prize yearling bulls have vanished, and the cop told me Meredith and Paul Jones had a quad bike spirited away last night."

"There was talk at the farmers' market today," Sherry said.

Ada turned when someone shouted. "I've gotta go, Sherry. Thanks for calling." She cut Sherry off mid-sentence and started running. "Hey! Hey, you! Don't land in my flowers. Don't!" she screeched.

But it was too late.

The parachutist landed in her pink delphiniums.

Ada marched over to a second man who had missed the flowers and was packing his parachute.

"Your boss assured me you'd stay away from my flowers," she snapped. "You have the entire run of the hill section. The only place I stated was out of bounds were my flower fields."

"I know." The man pulled a face. "I'm sorry. A gust of wind caught us. We tried to miss your flowers. Frog, especially."

Ada glared at the hapless man who was trying to stand and crushing more of her delphiniums. "Stop moving," she snapped. "You're making things worse."

The man froze before turning to gaze at her. "I'm so sorry," he said in a pleasant baritone. "The wind ripped over the ridge and dragged us off course. The rest of my team landed in the jump zone."

"Do you realize the damage you've caused?" Ada suddenly felt off-balance.

The man not only had a sexy voice, but he was gorgeous. Tall with broad shoulders. Short, but not too short brown hair. Bright blue eyes. Facial hair that skimmed his chin and framed his mouth...

Muttering under her breath, she ripped her gaze off him and focused on the damage he'd inflicted on her poor flowers. The man and his parachute had flattened dozens of stems. If she worked quickly, she could harvest the blooms before the plants died. Because one glance told her there was no fixing this catastrophe.

"I'm sorry," the man said. "I'll do anything I can to fix the damage."

"It's too late," Ada snapped, incensed over again. Was it too much to ask one thing?

One. Thing.

The man studied the flowers and frowned. "I truly am sorry."

Ada glared at him, her mind busily working on a way to get him out of her flowers without inflicting more damage.

Matt tried to stop staring at the irate woman glowering at him as if he'd committed murder. He hated upsetting anyone, but this truly hadn't been his fault. She was lucky Hemi hadn't landed in her flower patch too.

"Frog, what next?" Hemi asked. "Can you pick up your chute and hand it to us, so it doesn't crush any more of the lady's flowers?"

"Ada Buckingham," the woman snapped.

Matt felt his eyes widen. This was Ada Buckingham? He'd pictured a little old lady. This woman looked younger than him. Perhaps late twenties to his early thirties. She wore her long black hair tied in a ponytail, and it gleamed with health. Her eyes were a light blue or gray. He couldn't tell from where he stood. Her black brows were determined slashes above her eyes while she had a smattering of freckles across the bridge of her nose. His gaze wandered over her stubborn chin to her chest and upper torso, encased in a T-shirt with the words *Hot Babe* emblazoned on the front.

The fabric lovingly hugged her shape, and it was a busty

one. Matt hissed out a sigh. She was beautiful and just his type. Not that she'd give him a second chance now that he'd crushed her flowers.

"Frog. Also known as Matt Townsend." Matt raised his chute a bit at a time, wincing when the flowers didn't spring back to their former position. He inhaled and didn't get a floral perfume at all. "Why don't these plants smell like flowers?"

"Delphiniums don't have a scent. I grow them for their petals."

"Oh," he said, none the wiser from her explanation.

"What do you do with the petals?" Hemi asked, saving Matt from asking.

"I dry them and sell them as confetti." Ada eyed his chute as he gathered it into his hands.

"I'll come closer to take the chute weight," Hemi said.

Matt grimaced, studying the surrounding ground. Hell, he'd done a job on these blooms.

"Wait," Ada demanded. "Let me pick the flowers before you trample them." She scooted in front of Hemi and bent over, rapidly picking the flower heads rather than the stems. She used her jumper as a container, making several trips before she'd retrieved most of the blooms between Matt and where she and Hemi stood.

Matt caught Hemi studying Ada's backside and winged

his soldier a warning glare. Hemi grinned and shifted closer to Ada. He whipped off his T-shirt to reveal a muscular and tattooed chest. From what Matt saw, she didn't even blink when Hemi told her he'd hold the flowers in his shirt while she picked.

That she was still angry, he had no doubt. Her stiff shoulders and low mutters told him of her fury. Once again, he wondered how he could fix this. When he came up blank, he asked her.

"What can I do to make this right?"

She straightened and met his gaze. He steeled himself against the punch of heat that struck him. It still packed a wallop.

Typically, he never had problems pulling a bird when he wanted one.

This woman looked as if she might tell him to piss off. Now wasn't the right time to ask her out for a drink or dinner.

"I'm short of workers," she said finally. "The people I'd organized to come next weekend are picking elsewhere instead."

Hell, her day sounded as if it had been as crappy as his.

An idea came to him. "How many do you need?"

"As many as I can get," she replied. "But at least twenty to thirty. That means I'll get the entire area picked in one day, or enough that I can finish the rest on my own. I intend to pick tomorrow since the weather forecast is better than today."

Matt nodded in acknowledgment. "Will those flowers still make decent confetti?"

"Yes," she said.

"Good, my men and I will help you pick for a couple of hours each day this week, and I think I can rustle up a few people for the weekend. Not the number you want, but it will be a start. It might be enough if we pick flowers for you during the week."

She glanced at Hemi, who was staring at Frog open-mouthed. Ada straightened. "What time will you be here?"

"We need to conduct the exercises we've planned for the soldiers, but we should finish by four if we start early. That way, we can pick from four until six. On the nights where we have exercises, we'll pick before we start."

"Ah, boss," Hemi said.

Matt shot him a stern gaze, and Hemi thankfully shut up. "We'll discuss it back at camp. Ada, can I move now? My legs are turning numb."

She scanned the flowers in front of him, plucked more blossoms before nodding. "Yes."

Matt placed his feet with care as he made his way

toward where Hemi and Ada waited. Hemi accepted his parachute and walked to a clear space where he efficiently rolled it up.

Matt's radio buzzed. "Yeah," he said, not taking his gaze off Ada. The woman was natural and sexy with no artifice about her.

"Where are you?"

"Gust of wind took us. It's going to take Hemi and me a while to hike up to the campsite."

A chuckle came, and Matt knew he and Hemi were in for a world of teasing once they arrived at camp.

"We'll expect the camp set up and our dinner ready when we get there." Matt ended the call. He picked his way out of the last of the mangled flowers—not a straightforward task with his big boot-clad feet.

Ada scrutinized his progress, and Matt had to work to withhold his amusement at her aggravated huff. She was cute in her indignation, and it made his mind wander to other, more intimate encounters. Curiosity raised its head. How would she look in the throes of passion?

"When are you leaving?" Ada asked pointedly.

Matt grinned at her. "Outstayed our welcome?"

She tensed then, but he caught the wobble of her bottom lip. When he scrutinized her closer, he noticed the shiny, liquid glint in her eyes. Crap, he had a sister. He knew what the glisten meant. Matt hesitated and came to a decision. He'd back off and let her regroup. Meantime, he'd do a little snooping and hope like hell they had cell phone coverage at their campsite.

"Ms. Buckingham, I—"

"Mrs. Buckingham."

Matt's stomach fell. It figured the first woman to interest him in months had a husband stashed in the background. "I apologize. Mrs. Buckingham, I'll be in touch regarding the days we intend to use live ammunition as promised."

"What about the flower picking?"

Matt withheld his amusement, pleased to see her feistiness had trumped her imminent tears. "Is it too soon to pick tomorrow?"

"That would work—as long as it doesn't rain. Picking in the afternoon works best for me."

Matt imagined informing his men of this surprise challenge and groaned inwardly. "I doubt if any of my soldiers have experience in flower picking."

"Experience isn't necessary," Ada said in a cool voice. "All I need is for my workers to have a smidgen of intelligence and the ability to follow orders."

"Is four too late?"

"Slightly earlier if you can manage, but four is

acceptable. Now, if you would excuse me, I need to process these petals. Goodbye." With the abrupt farewell, she turned and stalked away with Hemi's T-shirt full of flowers.

"Hope you've got a spare shirt," Matt murmured.

"No problem, Frog. I'll steal yours since you're the one who crushed the little lady's flowers."

Chapter 4

Archie Claims an Owner

Ada stomped to her shed. "Stupid bloody man. Avoiding my flowers wasn't asking for too much."

Thankfully, Ada had added an extra thousand onto the first offer, and the army man hadn't quibbled. Irritation flared in her anew as she pulled open the shed and turned on the lights. At least the vandals hadn't gained access. If they'd trashed her drying machine, her hopes for staying afloat would've died a quick death. She would've lost the land she and Greg had struggled to keep.

A faint meow had her glancing at the door. A tortoiseshell cat in black, yellow, and patches of orange hovered in the open doorway.

"Ah, you've gathered enough bravery to show yourself,"

Ada said to the cat.

Instead of advancing, he planted his butt and watched her warily. Ada shrugged and turned her attention back to the flowers. Although the soldier had crushed the plants, the petals were salvageable.

She spent the next half hour separating the pink petals and placing them on wire mesh racks. Once done, she stacked the frames into her drying machine and set the timer for four hours.

While she'd been working, the cat had ambled closer. Ada pretended to ignore the animal but spied on its movements. The feline wasn't skinny or mangy. In fact, the cat appeared in decent condition, which meant some idiot had dumped it because their pet had become an inconvenience. It happened way too often for her liking. She'd seen six chooks running around at the main road turnoff, but the poultry disappeared as fast as they'd arrived. Either a hawk had snared them, or a local had grabbed them for the dinner pot. The latter wouldn't surprise her since she'd had a dozen chickens, and they'd vanished one by one. She had detected no disturbances but doubted a hawk capable of opening her chicken coop without leaving a mess of feathers.

When she didn't shout at the cat, it padded closer, and to her delight, the feline brushed against her calves and issued a purr. She continued to ignore the creature and cleared her workspace instead, deciding it would be best to let the cat become comfortable before trying to pet it.

Next, she checked her large flower bins were clean and water-free. A pulse of excitement pumped through her because this was the start of her new business. Tonight, she'd make her website live and step into the future. Time to book the advertising in the magazines and websites she'd researched. With the wedding season about to kick off—brides adored their spring and summer weddings—she hoped to take advantage of the surge in business.

A car pulled into her driveway, and Ada pulled a face. She'd had enough of people today.

"*Yoo-hoo!* Ada! Are you in there?"

Sherry.

Ada pasted on a smile and walked out to greet her neighbor. The woman was well-meaning and beloved throughout the district, but Ada didn't feel like dealing with her cheerfulness right now. Too bad. It seemed she wouldn't get what she wanted today.

"Ah, there you are," Sherry said in a bright voice. A pocket-sized woman, she carried a cane basket, which held a plastic container. If Ada had to guess, Sherry had brought either biscuits or a cake since her neighbor was an enthusiastic baker. "You sounded off when I spoke to you earlier. I thought I'd visit to cheer you up. I can guess at some of your angst." She gestured at the spray-painted message adorning Ada's shed.

"Yes," Ada said, anger bursting through again. If she ever caught the culprits, she'd forget herself and use the boxing skills her father had taught her as a teenager.

Sherry limped toward Ada, her gait awkward because of a childhood accident, which had led to a bad break. The injury had never healed properly, despite subsequent operations.

Instinct had Ada wanting to offer help, but she knew better. Sherry was famously independent and a hard worker. She single-handedly ran the successful farmers' market and gave tirelessly of herself for local charity work. If someone required aid, Sherry was the first to offer her services.

"I have a banana loaf. It's still warm from the oven," Sherry said, her golden-brown eyes glowing with good humor. She flicked a long strand of caramel-colored hair off her cheek. "A slice with butter will go perfectly with tea."

Ada knew a hint when she heard one. "Thank you, Sherry. That's very thoughtful of you. Would you like to join me for a cup of tea?"

"That would be lovely." Sherry smoothed her floral dress and adjusted the pale blue shawl she wore on her shoulders.

"Okay. Let me shut my shed, and I'll make that tea. Why don't you wait on the deck, or you can go inside if you want a comfortable seat? The house is unlocked."

The breeze disordered Sherry's long hair, and she brushed a lock off her face and smiled, looking much younger than her correct age of forty-three. "You won't take long. I'll wait for you."

Ada shrugged and reentered her shed. She checked the time left on the drier. It would stop automatically, but she eagerly awaited the final product. She'd trialed cornflowers in both pink and blue, and she'd also dried hydrangea and rose petals. This was the first time she'd processed her delphiniums.

"Okay, kitty," she murmured. "Time for you to go outside." She made a shooing motion with her hands, and the cat lifted its nose and sauntered from the shed. The second it cleared the doorway, the cat hissed, its back arching and fur expanding outward until the animal doubled in size.

Ada hurried outside to see what had upset her new arrival. She discovered the cat and Sherry eyeing each other with abject horror.

"Oh, I'm sorry," Ada said. "Do you not like cats?"

Sherry backed up and almost tripped when her foot caught on an uneven patch. She windmilled her arms to regain her balance.

"Are you okay?" Ada asked.

"I'm sorry. It's not that I dislike cats. I'm allergic. Always have been. When did you get a cat?"

"It's a stray," Ada said. "Come on. I'll make you that cup of tea. It sounds as if we could both do with one."

"Has the cat been inside? I'd hate to start wheezing. My eyes swell and water continuously. Then I sneeze. It's not a pretty sight, and it always takes me days to recover."

"But you're not allergic to other animals?" Ada led the way, and Sherry limped after her.

"No, just cats," Sherry said. "Your house is so cute. A tiny house wouldn't suit me—not with my three men, but it's adorable."

Ada nodded and let her mind drift since they'd had this conversation before. Married to Bart, the local stock agent, Sherry had two adult sons in their twenties. According to Sherry, the sons were messy, and a tiny house with its nifty storage and fold-out units wouldn't work when the men in her life didn't pick up after themselves.

"I'm not sure where the cat has wandered outside. You'd better sit inside out of the way of any cat hair." Ada led her neighbor inside and gestured at a seat.

Sherry sank down with a gusty exhalation. "I've been on the go since six this morning."

Ada reached for her kettle. "Oh?"

"Yes, Bart is busy with a private stock sale at a farm near Eketāhuna. Craig started a two-week-long training course at the bank. I'm sure I've mentioned my oldest son's appalling timekeeping. A disaster when this course is important to his advancement opportunities."

"That's good," Ada said, more for something to say. She'd never taken to Sherry's two sons. Not long after Greg's death, Craig had hit on her. Not that she'd ever tell Sherry. She'd dealt with the persistent Craig, thanks to her father's training. Eddie, the youngest, was plain strange and creepy. Lately, he'd asked her out whenever he saw her. Rumors circulated the district, and the word was one shouldn't turn their back on Eddie. She understood because if she spent too much time in his vicinity, her nape prickled.

"Eddie is having woman problems. A girl from the district who he used to date is telling everyone she's pregnant with Eddie's child."

"Oh, dear." Ada wisely refrained from adding more.

"Yes. There was another reason I came to visit you." Sherry paused.

Ada poured the boiling water into her china teapot. "Oh?"

"I've been searching for another person to sell flowers. You've turned me down before, but I wondered if you'd reconsider. I understand if you sell your flowers, you won't have the petals to dry, but you'll have the income immediately. Surely that's an advantage?"

An excellent point. The plants in the area where the soldier had landed would likely die anyway. Perhaps she should try selling a few buckets of flowers. They wouldn't go to waste since she could harvest the unsold stems for her confetti. "All right. When is the next market?"

"I have a mid-week market the day after tomorrow. My normal flower seller cannot attend because of a date clash with another event."

"All right," Ada said with her customary decisiveness. "I'll do it."

"What about the weekend market?"

"I'll give you a tentative yes, but it will depend on how successful I am at the mid-week one. How much is the charge?"

"Fifty dollars," Sherry said. "But you're doing me a favor by stepping in, so I'll do you a deal. You can have the stall for twenty dollars."

Ada had one last twenty-dollar note in her wallet, which

meant economizing on food if she didn't sell many flowers. She straightened her shoulders. She would do this. "Do I pay you now or on the day?"

Sherry beamed. "On the morning is perfect, dear."

"What time does the market start?"

"It goes from ten until two, although many stallholders pack up early if they sell out of produce. I suggest you arrive by nine-thirty at the latest. There is a special parking area for stallholders, which is close for unloading your flowers."

Ada sliced and buttered the banana loaf. She placed it on the breakfast bar she used as a table along with a plate and napkin. Next, she poured Sherry's tea into a china mug and handed it over. This wasn't the first time Sherry had arrived with food and a silent demand for tea, so she'd learned her neighbor enjoyed black tea with two teaspoons of sugar. Ada shunted the sugar bowl closer to Sherry.

"Thank you."

Ada poured herself a milky mug of tea and claimed the second chair.

"Have some loaf, dear. You work hard and need the calories."

"Thank you," Ada said again.

"Do you have any idea who tagged your shed?"

Ada's mouth flatlined. "No."

"You're not having a good time of it, are you, dear? Do you think you've picked up a stalker?"

"What? No!" Ada said firmly. "The experts decided my house fire was an electrical fault, and the local cop told me several farmers and businesses within the town area have suffered problems with graffiti this week. It's more a case of bad luck."

Sherry leaned over and patted her hand. "You have more than your fair share."

The blast of emotion that struck when someone alluded to Greg came, but time had turned it bittersweet. "I'm fine," Ada stated with determination and changed the subject. "Do you know the location of my stall?"

"The position you're filling is between a cheese-seller and a kebab stall. I'll be there to take care of any problems. I'll give you directions once you pop into the office to pay me."

"Thanks."

"Are you intending to clean off the paint? Wise heads suggest if you leave graffiti in place, it attracts more."

Ada ground her teeth together, then took a sip of tea to hide her grimace. She swallowed a mouthful of tea and one more before attempting to reply. "Yes, I'll scrub it off when I get time."

"Craig and Eddie will help. They won't mind."

"Thanks for the offer. I'll see how I go. Besides, I'm sure Craig and Eddie are busy with their own things."

"But it's up so high. How will you manage?" Sherry asked, her neat brows arching in surprise.

"Sherry, it's a point of pride with me to attempt tasks myself. It's not as if I can afford to pay for help."

Sherry frowned. "There is such a thing as too much pride."

"I think we should agree to disagree." Ada smiled to negate her rejection of Sherry's suggestion.

"Who were those men I saw as I drove up?"

Ada's mind shot straight to Matt—or Frog as the other man had called him. She'd wondered where the nickname had come from and wished she'd felt she could ask. Maybe she'd learn when he returned to pick flowers.

If he returned.

Sherry cleared her throat, making Ada realize she'd zoned out.

"The army is running training exercises on my farm. The terrain of my hill country is perfect for stretching the soldiers physically."

"How nice," Sherry said. "It's a wonder I hadn't learned of the training exercise."

"It's a recent thing," Ada hastened to add. "I doubt many people in the area know. The army man I spoke to requested that I not speak about it. They don't want looky-loos turning up to get in the way."

"Understandable," Sherry said. "I hope they're paying you. You should lease the land. Or better still, sell it. You're too young to struggle this way."

Ada concealed her irritation by sipping her tea. "I have a long-term plan. One Greg and I made together."

"But Greg isn't here."

Ada's phone rang with perfect timing. "Please excuse me, Sherry. I need to answer this."

Sherry stood and smoothed the creases from her dress. She plucked her shawl from the chair back and arranged it around her shoulders. "It's time for me to go. I have a busy day."

"Thanks for dropping by." Ada swiped the face of her phone. She didn't recognize the number, but the interruption thrilled her, given the timing. "Just a moment," she said to her caller.

"You go ahead," Sherry said. "You can drop my container off later."

"Thanks again," Ada said to Sherry. "Hello."

"Is this a bad time?" a masculine voice asked.

She recognized the owner immediately—the soldier. "No, my visitor is leaving. How can I help you, Mr. Townsend?"

"Matt," he said firmly. "Part of our deal while using your land is to notify you when we're using live ammunition."

Ada's throat turned dry, and she swallowed hard, the thought of gunfire thrusting her into the past. She cleared her throat with a tiny cough. "Tomorrow?"

"To help you with your flowers, we're changing our schedule around. We're doing a night exercise this evening and early morning in which we'll be making noise."

"You're not blowing up my land?"

"No, we don't need to use explosives. The grenades we'll be throwing are about commotion and smoke rather than desecration."

"And you'll return the land to the state it was before you arrived?"

"Yes, those were the terms of the deal we signed with you."

Ada tapped her finger against her thigh. "Thank you for letting me know. What time will you arrive?"

"Between four and five. We'll pick for two hours then leave."

"That's acceptable," Ada said.

Although she'd originally planned to pick her field of flowers in a short time, this way might be better. She could dry flowers each night and set up a production cycle.

"I'll see you tomorrow. Thank you for ringing." She

disconnected the call and left her tiny house, closing the door behind her. With long strides, she headed for her drying shed. Her gaze skimmed the graffiti, and she pursed her lips.

She had an old tub of white paint in her shed, leftover from when she'd painted her tiny house exterior. Her ladder would reach. Yeah, she'd take care of the lurid red paint as soon as she bagged her existing confetti. The farmers' market would be the perfect place to test a local market for her product. Every bit of cash she earned would go toward repaying Greg's loan.

She still had two months before the loan was due, and she refused to surrender without a fight.

CHAPTER 5

HOW TO PICK FLOWERS

ADA BALANCED ON THE top rung of her ladder, dipped her roller into the white paint, and ran it over the red writing. Despite her plans, she hadn't managed the task the previous day, and now, she observed the result with pleased satisfaction. Although the red showed through, and she'd need another coat, a lightness pulsed in her chest as she completed her task. Determination to carry on fueled her, despite the hurdles she faced. She ignored the slight tremor in her hand, a remnant of the gunfire that had echoed through the hills during the soldiers' exercise.

The explosive sounds might've ceased hours ago, but every shot had shoved her mind back to her husband and his murder. She'd heard gunshots then but had thought little of the harsh cracks because Greg often let his friends come rabbit shooting. The rabbits were pests, and shooting helped to keep them under control. Now, every time she identified gunfire or any sound resembling a weapon discharge, her mind jerked back to Greg's death.

Stress, according to her doctor.

A human reaction.

But knowing why she reacted and what provoked her didn't help much. *Gah!* She had to stop thinking about this. She focused on her painting and concentrated fiercely on each glide of her paint roller. Even better, the words were no longer legible.

"Take that, you ratfink bastard," she muttered.

"Who is a ratfink bastard?" a masculine voice asked with distinct interest.

Ada jerked, the roller coating her hand with a layer of white paint. Her can slipped, and the ladder wobbled.

"What the devil are you doing?" This time the voice sounded irritated.

Ada righted her balance, redistributed her weight, and slowly turned to glower at the man—no, the group of men—who stood watching. "What does it look like I'm doing?"

"Painting?"

"Give the man a prize."

Several of the men chuckled.

"Why are you painting? Can't someone do it for you?" Matt asked. "Your husband?"

"My husband is dead. Not that it's any of your business. I wanted to cover the graffiti. It offended my eyes every time I walked outside."

"Fair enough," he said. "Why don't I hold the ladder? My men will wait while you paint, then you can come and show us what you want us to do."

Ada stared at him for a microsecond. His expression told her nothing. Finally, she jerked her head in a brief nod. "I need to move the ladder. I-I can explain what to do with the flowers so you can get started." Ada clambered down and squeezed past him because he'd taken it upon himself to steady the ladder. She caught a whiff of greenery, sweat, and man and slowed her steps.

"Something wrong?" Matt asked, cocking his head.

Ada shook away the stupid and hustled to her shed where she stored buckets for the flowers. She handed one to each man, then strode to her field. She stopped at the end of a row of pale pink delphiniums and waited for the men to crowd around. "Picking flowers is easy. Let me show you." She plucked the head of an open flower and dropped it into the nearest bucket. "Leave the flowers that aren't open yet. I'll harvest them during the next pick.

If you're on a pink row, please only pick pink flowers. I need to keep the colors separate. Half of you can start on this row, and the others can start on the purple. Any questions?"

"No, that's clear," Hemi said, answering for everyone.

"Excellent," Ada said. "I'll watch for a while to make sure you listened before I return to my painting."

Good-natured chuckles filled the air, but Ada still observed with an eagle eye. Although they wore a uniform, they looked the worse for wear. Mud splattered their trousers and boots, and the nearest man had a rip in the back of his shirt. Each man sported stubble. She watched them for another three or four minutes. They chatted and joked as they picked flowers, thankfully following her instructions.

She strode back to her shed and met Matt walking toward her.

"The painting is finished," he said. "I'll do another layer to cover the red paint fully before I leave."

"I could've done it," she snapped.

"You could," he said instantly, soothing some of her ire. "But I'm taller and was here. Why don't you just accept the help and pick flowers instead?"

"I—thank you." He was right. *Unfortunately*. Ada turned back toward her flowers, conscious of the man walking beside her.

No, not walking.

He prowled, the silence between them full of something charged. She swallowed, willing herself not to glance at him. What the devil was wrong with her? She'd been around men, both before and after Greg's death. Before Greg's murder, she hadn't looked at another man because he had been *it* for her. Afterward, misery had buried her too much even to consider anyone else. That was why this awareness of this man—Matt Townsend—was so disconcerting.

"I missed your job description. Can you run through it for me?" His deep voice washed over her, then came a long pause. "Ada?"

She shook herself. "Sorry, I have a lot of things on my mental to-do list. Yes, I'll show you." She grabbed two buckets from the pile of spares and handed one to Matt.

She started on a row of deep pink flowers and demonstrated how to pick.

"That's easy enough."

"It is," she agreed. "But it becomes tedious after a while." Ada left Matt to harvest flowers and started on the next row.

Unfortunately, it was close to Matt, and the man muddied her mind.

She wasn't thinking. Her skin prickled, ultra-awareness of him driving her to distraction. Ada huffed out a breath as she plucked flowers and dropped them into her bucket.

"Something wrong?" he asked.

"I told you I'm busy."

"Do you know who painted the graffiti on your wall?"

This time her sigh held aggravation. "Believe me, if I caught them, I'd insist on charges. This is the second time I've had graffiti scrawled on my shed."

"Did they break into your shed? Did you hear them?"

"No, to both questions." A meow from her right gave her a reason to focus on something other than Matt. "Hey, kitty," she murmured. To her delight, the cat came straight to her and rubbed against her legs.

"You're not totally alone out here," Matt said.

The cat wandered over to Matt and rubbed against his legs too.

Traitor. Ada gave him a stink-eye, but he didn't notice since he'd crouched to pet the cat. The stray allowed that too, much to her chagrin.

Ada continued picking while she forced her attention to tomorrow's market stall. She should've asked Sherry how many flowers she thought she might sell. A ball-park figure. She'd have to guess. As to price, she'd have to think on that too.

A thought occurred. She'd ring around several florists and ask how much she'd need to pay for a bouquet of delphiniums. She'd pretend she was buying one and go from there. Pleased with the solution, she picked as fast as she could, practice making her quicker and more efficient than the men. She reached the end of the row and started picking back toward Matt. Once she'd filled her bucket, she carried it to her shed, left her bucket of flowers there, and grabbed her cell phone from where she'd left it on the kitchen counter.

She did an internet search and found four florists in the region.

After noting telephone numbers and running an eye over the arrangements on their websites, she numbered the businesses in order of preference. Then, she rang the first one on her list and went through her spiel. By the time she'd finished, she had an average price.

That chore sorted, she returned to her flower field. To her surprise, several of the men were speedy pickers. She scanned the rows they'd already picked and discovered their work was perfect.

"Have you done this before?" she asked the closest soldier.

"Yep. Worked in horticulture during my student days. A few of us did," a skinny man with a bald head said. "Do you have more buckets?"

"Sure," Ada replied. "There are a few over there." She gestured at the three remaining buckets. "I'll take these flowers back to my shed and bring back the empties."

"I can help and act as a runner," Matt said. "That way, you could start the next part of your process."

"How many rows do you want us to pick?" the skinny man asked.

"Just this band of pale pink flowers and the purple," Ada said. "That will give me tonight to start the drying process."

"You're doing this by yourself?" Matt asked.

"Yes." Ada strode to the full buckets of flowers, each step bouncy and high-energy. Exhilaration ran through her, along with an accompanying warmth and the urge to pump her fist into the air.

Matt trailed her, but she ignored him, preferring to dwell on her elation. *Yes!* She was moving on to the next step. After the bad luck that dogged her—Greg's murder, their house destroyed in a fire, and now the pickers unable to come, this day counted as a victory. Yes, she'd need to work late into the night, but the sooner she could get her product readied for sale, the quicker the money would start rolling in.

Matt carried four buckets, two in each hand, and Ada

oversaw him to make certain he didn't bruise any of the petals. The man took care without her having to warn him, and this sent a tingle of appreciation through her. She immediately thrust away the physical awareness and lengthened her steps to get to her shed.

She set down her buckets and opened the enormous doors to let in the natural light. Ada retrieved two of the buckets and lifted them into the special holders.

"Do you want all the flowers there?" Matt asked.

She turned to find him standing close behind her, and her heart did a weird little change-up in reaction. "Ah, yes, please." She stood aside to allow the big man room to maneuver. Once he'd emptied each of the buckets, he gathered them together.

"I'll bring back the next full ones. It seems my boys have hidden talents."

Ada nodded, wanting to bounce in her excitement. "They're much faster than I thought they'd be. At this rate, it won't take them two hours to pick the flowers. Is the picking cutting into your training time?"

Matt grinned, taking his face from handsome and attractive to arresting. Ada blinked and had to think hard for a second to focus on what she'd asked him.

"We're still training. My boys ran most of the way, and we'll run a different route on the way back to camp. The flower picking is their rest time."

"How long will you be here? The man I spoke with wasn't positive."

"Two weeks at least. Perhaps more if the training goes well. This lot will ship out, and another group arrives," Matt said. "My two helpers and I will stay to train each lot of soldiers they send us. The brass may decide a third group of soldiers would benefit."

"From what I could gather, Greg approached the army a while ago. How come the army decided to train their men here all of a sudden?"

Matt smiled. "We like to change up things and keep the men on edge. Most of them have experienced the terrain and the areas we've used in the past. The brass wanted to throw them something new so we can do training on cliffs and hilly country that's more like what we'd see in the hot spots around the world."

"I see."

"Well, I'd better get these empty buckets back to my men, seeing as they're over-achievers."

The moment Matt disappeared, Ada used precious seconds to take deep breaths. Her hand trembled, but it had nothing to do with firearms and loud noises. This time it was because of a man. Ada took another breath and forced herself to focus. Gradually, the tremors subsided, and she settled into the routine of separating the petals. Like picking, this was a laborious process. She worked automatically, her fingers flying while she contemplated which flowers to sell at the market.

Matt appeared without warning, and she was proud of herself for not leaping off her seat or giving in to her start. "The boys are finishing the row." Several soldiers followed him with full buckets of flowers.

"We can help you with that part, since the picking didn't take long."

Ada started to demur, but then her practical side stepped forward. Thankfully. "Even if you could do half of the flowers before you need to go, it will save me time."

Matt nodded. "Show the boys what to do, and you do something else."

"Are you sure?" Ada asked. "These men didn't sign up for work with flowers."

"It makes a change, Miss Ada," one of the Māori boys commented.

Several of his friends agreed with him.

"We don't get to stand in one place or sit while we're training. Frog is a hard taskmaster," one said.

Ada showed them what to do and started filling the drying racks. By the time the men had to leave, she'd racked most of the petals, and the remaining flowers wouldn't take long to process. She turned to Matt and his men. "Thank you so much for your help today. You've saved me hours of work."

"It's the least we can do after I landed in your flower field," Matt said.

"I thought Hemi did the dirty deed," one soldier said. "He told us it wasn't, but I didn't believe him."

Ada glanced at Matt and found him grinning again.

"We didn't think Frog would make such a mistake, not with his training," a soldier said.

"Think again." Hemi huffed indignantly. "You should've believed me."

Matt winked at Ada, then turned to his men. "Get ready to move out. We're jogging three kilometers up the valley before we begin a climbing exercise."

Someone groaned, and Matt shouted, "Anyone else groans, we'll run an extra five kilometers."

The men jogged out of her shed, leaving her alone with Matt.

"Thanks again. I appreciate your help today. It has put me ahead. I'm off to the local farmers' market tomorrow from ten until two in the afternoon. I thought I'd be half-asleep, running on determination after working throughout the night."

"Don't you have help?"

"I can't afford it at the moment. I mean, I had booked pickers, which would've made harvesting my crop doable." She frowned. "I still don't understand why they thought I'd canceled. As far as I knew, they were arriving this weekend."

"Someone canceled on your behalf?"

"Yeah, that's what they told me."

"Are there any other growers who live nearby?"

"Drying petals to make confetti is a specialist niche. No one else in the lower North Island is doing the same thing. I got the idea from watching a television show featuring a place in Shropshire, England. Ah, shouldn't you go now? Do your men know where they're going?"

"They do," Matt said. "We'll be here tomorrow, but perhaps earlier. What do we do if you're not back from the market?"

"I'd like the dark blue flowers picked tomorrow. I can leave the empty buckets outside just in case I'm held up."

"Plan." Matt's slow smile almost buckled her knees. "Tomorrow."

Ada watched him until he disappeared, shook herself free of her daydreams because really! So far, the men in her life had added to her complications. Greg had taken out the loan without mentioning it to her. Eddie kept bugging her and making her uncomfortable while the single men in the town eyed her like a juicy morsel. She wasn't ready to take a man into her life. Not even one who made her heart beat faster each time she glimpsed him.

Ada applied herself to plucking the final petals free of their stamens and preparing them for drying. Two hours later, her drying machine was humming while she wiped down her counters and washed out her buckets. She set the buckets to dry, gave her shed a last glance to check everything was in its right place and closed up for the night. She picked up three containers of dried petals—the ones she'd dried as she experimented—plus a handful of plastic bags in which to place them. After dinner, she'd pack the petals and offer them for sale—just a few as another experiment.

At the last moment, she padlocked her shed even though it was a pain in the butt. She'd put the key around her neck so she wouldn't lose it. Keep the door locked against casual intruders.

Ada didn't feel like eating but knew from experience she fared better if she didn't skip meals. She decided on a quick pasta meal with the fresh vegetables she had on hand. After dinner, Ada spent the evening packing her confetti in clear bags and arranging each packet in a basket according to color.

As was her standard practice, she made herself a cup of

peppermint tea and sat outside to listen to the night birds and insects. The cat emerged from the old blanket Ada had arranged and stalked over to her for a scratch. A purr erupted immediately, making Ada smile.

"Do you like that, fella?" She continued to stroke. "If you're going to hang around, you need a name. Hmm, a boy's name. Harry? William? Archie?"

The cat meowed at her third suggestion, and she clapped her hands, her mouth quirking at the moment of silliness.

"A royal name. Archie, it is."

She sat back in her chair and savored the peace. The cat returned to its bed and did two twirls before settling. A morepork—New Zealand's native owl—called once. Twice. The faint rumble of a vehicle interrupted the familiar evening melody. The engine growl grew louder, and she stiffened, hoping that she wasn't about to have visitors. Relief filled her when the roar cut off abruptly and didn't restart. A visitor at her neighbor's place, then.

Ada studied the front gate beyond her driveway and stood. While she usually left the gate ajar, tonight, her instincts told her to close it. The gate wasn't a huge barrier to trespassers but gave her a warning of unexpected visitors. Ada stood and pulled the gate shut, fastening the catch before she returned to gather her empty cup and retire for the night.

"Good night, Archie." She stooped to pet the animal.

Ada had a big day tomorrow and needed her sleep. As she locked her door, her thoughts drifted and detoured. Instead of her husband, Matt Townsend's rugged and handsome visage came to mind. Ada forced the wretched man back out and stomped off to have a cold shower.

She was too busy for a man, and that one had charming rascal written all over his beaming face.

Chapter 6

Market Hijinks

The next morning, Ada rose at six. She dressed hurriedly and hustled outside to pick her flowers. Ada ended up picking ten bunches of wildflowers from her experimental patch along with thirty stems of each color of delphinium, which meant she had white, blue, pink, and lilac.

Lightheartedness bubbled in her chest and a faint adrenaline rush had her ready way too early. "I might as well go now," she informed Archie.

The cat meowed and wound his way over to her, now brave enough to enter her tiny house. He rubbed against her legs and purred his satisfaction.

"Wish me luck, Archie."

After double-checking she had everything, Ada jumped into the driver's seat and drove out the gate. She'd just cleared her gateway when she recalled she'd fastened it shut the previous evening. Ada slammed on the brakes. Horror flooded her as she regarded the open gate behind her. She licked her lips, her hands clenching and unclenching the wheel. There was no way the gate had opened by itself.

Ada scrutinized her surroundings, and when she couldn't see anyone, she climbed from her vehicle. She sensed nothing sinister. The normal host of birds sang in the treetops and bees buzzed as they collected nectar from her flowers. Not a single human-made sound pierced the natural harmony. Once she'd ensured she was alone, Ada walked over to the gate.

That was when she noticed a piece of paper pinned to the wood railing.

Her hand trembled as she reached for it. She tugged the paper and studied it with fixed concentration. It was blank. Why would someone tack an empty sheet of paper to her entrance? She turned it over and stilled, tension sliding through her in an icy chill.

Ada swallowed hard as she read the printed words.

You can't keep me out.

She jerked, her nostrils flaring. Someone was playing fun-for-them games. Greg's murderer? She didn't know, but she didn't intend to take chances. Instead of following her initial impulse to fling the note in the rubbish, she shut her gate and returned to her vehicle.

She had time to stop by the police station before the farmers' market.

"You're late," Sherry accused when Ada walked into the office.

"Yes, I know. I'm sorry about that." Ada didn't offer excuses since the police officer had told her to keep the note details to herself.

"Someone else scored your allocated area. They were here," Sherry said, her manner school-teacher stern.

"I understand." Ada bit her tongue instead of lashing out in frustration. This was going to be one of those days—no need for her to exacerbate the problem.

"I have a small area I use in emergencies. You can have that."

"Thank you." Ada blinked hard since fury pushed moisture to her eyes. She refused to let those tears fall. "That will be fine."

Three people walked into the office to see Sherry, and she made a tiny huffing sound as she pulled out a hand-drawn map. "Unfortunately, you can't park nearby. You'll have to carry your supplies. Will that be a problem?"

"No," Ada said through gritted teeth.

"Right. That's twenty dollars."

Ada clenched her jaw and pulled the twenty-dollar note from her pocket. "I'd like a receipt, please."

Sherry huffed again, her mood more ruffled than usual. In fact, Sherry seemed out of sorts. She scrawled a receipt for Ada and slapped it onto the counter in front of her. "Next!"

Shaking her head, Ada exited the office and almost plowed into the police officer she'd spoken to at the station only half an hour ago. His capable hands helped her to maintain her balance.

"Sorry," she muttered, her cheeks heating. "I'm in a hurry. I need to unload my flowers for my stall, but because I was late, Sherry gave away my allocated area."

"Ada, I'll help," the police officer said. "Since your tardiness was my fault."

Ada's head jerked up, and she did a double-take at his smiling eagerness. A sinking sensation came next, and she opened her mouth to tell him she could manage.

He spoke first. "You'd be doing me a favor. We've had a slew of thefts recently, and the boss sent me to check the vehicles and farm machinery at the market. Helping you will let me fit in better."

"All right," she acquiesced and gestured to her right. "My vehicle is this way."

Thankfully, the cop—Sam—didn't speak but walked at her side and nodded hello to the various locals they encountered. With Sam's help, she carried two buckets of flowers plus her signs over to her stall. It was in a far corner, but she'd make the best of it. The stalls on either side of her were open for business.

"Why don't you start selling, and I'll bring the rest of your flowers?" Sam asked.

"Are you sure?"

"You're doing me a favor here." Sam winked and strode away before she could offer her thanks.

With a shrug, Ada arranged her flowers and set out her signs. Traffic was brisk at the neighboring stalls, but not a single person stopped to study her flowers.

"No customers," Sam said when he arrived with her confetti and the last two tubs of flowers. He'd corralled another guy to carry a tub of flowers, too.

"I'm afraid not. There's time yet. Thanks for the help."

"Anytime," Sam said. "I'll take a packet of your confetti. My youngest sister is getting married next month, so it will come in handy."

"I'll give you a packet. Which color would you like?"

"The blue, but please, let me pay. I'd like to be your first customer and give you luck."

"Five dollars then," Ada said, halving the price. "Thank

you."

Sam pocketed the confetti and handed her a five-dollar note. He winked. "Back to work for me."

Ada's gaze followed him as he sauntered away. He was a nice guy, but he felt more like a brother. The army man, however. *Matt.* Every time she looked at him, her pulse lurched. On the plus side, he was here for mere weeks. All she needed to do was bolster her defenses while he was around, and once he left, she could relax. Easy-peasy.

At first, business was slow, although the neighboring stalls had lines of customers. Ada lifted her chin and stalked to the front of her flower stall to hawk her produce. "Flower. Flowers. Get your flowers here!"

Those in the nearest line stared, but Ada ignored them.

"Do you have a wedding in the family coming soon? Get your confetti here! Natural, environmentally friendly confetti. Get your wedding confetti here!"

Several young men jeered and made cat-calls and smart comments.

Ada didn't let them faze her. She plucked a bouquet from water and stalked to them. She waved the flowers in front of their startled faces. "Fought with your girlfriend? Your wife? Buy her some flowers and score brownie points."

The men guffawed, but a tall, slender man with a sleeve

of tattoos stepped forward. "How much?"

"Twenty-five dollars," she said.

"You think the flowers will work?"

"If you give them along with an apology, it means you've been thinking about the argument. Your lady will understand you don't like it when you're not speaking to each other." Ada paused, her mind ticking as she wondered what persuasion she could use next.

"Done." The man pulled out his wallet. He handed over the correct change and accepted the flowers.

"Make sure you head home soon because the flowers will do better if they're in water," Ada advised.

"I'm buying food, then leaving," the man replied. "Although the line is moving slow."

"Why don't you go to that stall there and buy fresh bread? Get cheese from the one next door. Buy a bottle of wine or cider and take your wife for a picnic down by the river after you give her the flowers."

The man checked the number of people standing in the slow-moving line and nodded. "Excellent plan. My lady is always complaining I spend more time with my mates than with her."

"Perhaps you should listen and reduce the number of visits with your mates," Ada murmured in a softer voice.

He turned to his friends. "Catch you later."

"What about the footy game?" one of his friends asked.

"I can watch the rugby on telly later," he replied. "I only have one wife." And with that, he marched over to the much shorter queue at the bread stall.

"Are any of you taking your girlfriends to the rugby?"

"No," a blond-surfer dude type snapped. "This is a bloke-only outing."

Fools. Ada turned away from them and went through her spiel again. "Confetti. Get your natural confetti here!"

A woman paused to study her prices and chose four white stems of delphinium.

Yay! Ada hurried over to tend her customer.

Two women approached her to ask about the confetti. Ada gave them each a sample pack and told them to order via her website or call her if they wanted more. She pointed at the business card attached to the sample.

"I love the idea of flower petals. The local minister told us he doesn't allow rice or paper confetti. I want to ask him about flower petals before we commit to buying your confetti," a middle-aged woman with rimless glasses and city attire said.

The younger woman standing beside her remained silent, but she'd listened carefully to Ada's marketing spiel.

"Are you getting married in the local church?"

"Yes, the Anglican church," the younger woman said.

"Well, you know where I am if you decide to purchase my confetti." Ada waved them off with a smile and served a stoop-shouldered, gray-haired gentleman who purchased delphinium stems.

While business wasn't exactly brisk, Ada made back her stall cost, plus enough to make her glad she'd attended the farmers' market.

At two, she had several stems of delphiniums left plus one pre-made bouquet and ten confetti packs. She'd drop the flowers at the office for Sherry and hope her neighbor's mood had improved since this morning. The leftover stems she could harvest, and the pre-packaged confetti was okay for the following week.

Ada packed up and carried the flowers back to her vehicle first because, knowing her luck, people would help themselves while she wasn't present. When she drew closer to her car, she noticed her vehicle was on a lean.

Of all the times to get a flat tire. She muttered under her breath and stomped closer. A vein in her forehead pulsed as she sized up the situation. All the tires appeared flatter than usual. She set aside her flowers and crouched to study the flattest one.

"Bloody hell," she muttered.

Someone had pierced the rubber with a sharp object. She wasn't certain of what, but it took a decent amount of strength for someone to shove a knife into a tire wall.

Her brief check of the others told the same story, although her tires were in different degrees of deflation. Grunting in vexation, she placed her remaining flowers inside her vehicle and cracked the windows to cool the interior. She returned to her stall to collect the rest of her things, while keeping an eye out for the local cop.

With the number of people coming and going, surely someone had noticed the vandalism. She didn't find Sam, so once she'd cleared her site, she locked her vehicle and stomped to the police station.

Why her? If she caught the culprit, she wouldn't hold back with her temper. Miserable bastard. Because it had to be a man. Ada doubted she'd have the strength to commit the crime. She pushed through the front door and found Sam at the desk. His eyes widened as he straightened and flashed her a smile. The pleased expression had her freezing inside.

No, no, *no!*

"I have a crime to report," she blurted before he could skip to flirtation. "Someone vandalized my tires. If it were just one, I would've fixed the problem and driven home. I can't with one spare and four flat tires."

Sam's brows rose. "All four?"

Ada nodded.

"I'll have to wait for my colleague to return from lunch."

Ada sniffed. "You know where I'm parked. I'll meet you there and contact the local garage to ask about repairs."

"Don't let them touch anything until I get there."

"I won't." Ada was becoming an old hand at dealing with the police.

The car park was almost empty on Ada's return, and Sherry had left, her office locked. No flowers for Sherry, then. The local mechanic arrived and surveyed her tires.

"I should have three tires in stock. I'll can deliver them and help you change the flats." He quoted a price, and Ada winced.

"Thanks, I'd appreciate that." She needed her vehicle, which meant she had to suck up the cost and economize elsewhere.

The mechanic left, and Ada sat in the shade to wait for Sam.

An hour later, he trotted into the car park. "Sorry, we had a report of a property break-in, and I had to check on that."

Ada's rebuke faded. "Was anyone hurt?"

"No, but the burglars got away with a quad bike, three chainsaws, and a ride-on lawnmower."

"I don't remember theft being such a problem when I first moved to the area," Ada said.

"It has become worse since the local freezing works closed. Many people lost their jobs."

"That's not an excuse to steal from others," Ada snapped.

"You're right," Sam said. "I'm merely commenting on when I think the problem started."

"Do you have any idea on the identity of the culprits?"

"We're following several leads," Sam said. "Now, someone has tampered with your tires."

"Yes, George Clayton has been and gone. Someone used a sharp object to pierce them. George has gone to get replacements and should return soon. He offered to help me change the flats."

"This looks like mischief rather than a crime. I'll note it and ask around. Difficult to catch the offender in this type of crime unless we find a witness."

Ada shrugged because she wasn't confident of what might come out of her mouth.

"I'll add it to your file."

Cool, she had a file. "Do you think it's the same person committing these nuisance crimes?"

"I'd go with high possibility," Sam said. "We'll get them, eventually."

"Or they'll tire of harassing me and start picking on someone else."

"That too. Keep your wits about you and watch your security. Leave nothing unlocked."

Neither of them mentioned the third possibility, although Ada thought about it, and she was sure Sam did too. The culprit might escalate and cause worse problems.

CHAPTER 7

NOSY NEIGHBORS AND FLASH-BANG

MATT AND HIS MEN arrived an hour earlier than he'd told Ada to expect them. Ada wasn't there, but she'd left the empty buckets for them. He directed his men to the rows of blue delphiniums, and they set to work.

Hemi tapped him on the shoulder over an hour later. "We're out of buckets, boss."

"I'll check if Ada is back yet. The market finished at two, so she should almost be here."

"We'll carry the full buckets to the shed," Hemi said.

His men trooped after Matt. Ada hadn't returned, and when Matt tested the shed door, he found it locked.

"I can pick that lock, Frog," a soldier offered. "That way, we're not wasting time."

Matt hesitated, weighing the consequences. "Try not to damage the lock because I don't want Ada to shout at me again. The woman in a temper is a force to reckon with."

"You frightened of a little ole woman?" someone called. Several hooted.

"Frog is interested in her," another dared to suggest.

"If you guys have the energy to get cheeky, I'm not working you hard enough," Matt said, and he was only half-joking.

The padlock clicked, his soldier opening the door in seconds.

Matt's brows rose.

The beefy soldier smirked. "Misspent youth."

"Right," Matt said. "Half of you go back to picking, and the rest of us will do the next stage. Remember not to bruise the petals. We don't want another lecture from Ms. Buckingham."

Matt considered calling Ada before deciding to go ahead. He didn't get the sense she was flaky or irresponsible.

He organized his men, and they set too, separating the petals from the rest of the flower. By the time they'd finished picking the row and plucking petals, Ada still hadn't arrived.

"Frog, are we going to wait?" a soldier asked.

"No, we've kept to our bargain with Ada. Besides, the training team has a special exercise planned for the morning. You'll need your sleep."

A chorus of groans followed his announcement.

Matt checked they'd tidied and left the shed interior as they'd found it. "Let's move out." He was the last to go, and he switched off the lights and padlocked the shed again.

His men set off at a brisk pace, and he jogged behind them and hollered instructions. Since this didn't take much brainpower, his mind circled to Ada. She was a strange woman. Prickly. Blunt. Yet, she was beautiful and had an inner core of strength that appealed to him. Some women would've broken under the stress of losing a husband, yet she was attempting to start a new enterprise.

He figured she was a woman of her word, so either the farmers' market had gone for longer, or something unexpected had occurred. Ada Buckingham was the last person he'd ever accuse of being flaky.

Problem was her absence worried him, and he wouldn't feel right until he learned why she hadn't turned up. Stupidly, he hadn't thought to call her. A mistake, but he'd kept thinking she'd turn up at any moment. Matt pondered his options and rubbed his neck before coming to a decision.

"Listen up! Turn right and run up the valley. Watch for rabbit holes. I don't want to haul your hairy arses out with broken ankles!"

"My arse is smooth as a baby's bottom," a wiry soldier called from the front.

Ribald comments and snickers followed this.

"Remind me later to increase the kilometers we're running tomorrow," Matt called.

As he'd expected, the comments ceased, allowing him to return to his thoughts. He couldn't call Ada until this evening since they were conducting another exercise as soon as they reached camp.

Half an hour later, they crested the last hill, giving them a view over their campsite and the valley. A farm boy, Matt could see the potential in this land. It was a pity it was sitting idle, although the land had paved the way for him to meet Ada.

The jury was out on her opinion of him.

The woman was filling his mind way too often when he should focus on his job. He had no idea why she intrigued him. Perhaps it was because she presented a mystery, and Matt was one who loved a challenge.

· ♥ · ♥ · ♥ · ♥ · ♥ ·

ADA PULLED UP IN her driveway three hours later than she'd expected. The first thing she spotted was the stack of empty buckets in front of her shed, and her shoulders slumped. She should've rung Matt to tell him she was running late. She would've done that if her stupid phone hadn't had a hissy fit. Stupid bloody thing. She needed to purchase a new phone or at least a battery but didn't have the budget.

She climbed out of her vehicle, and the cat emerged from a nearby bush. Ada stooped to pet the purring animal while pondering the best course of action. Decision made, she straightened and unpacked her vehicle. The leftover flowers were looking droopy after sitting inside the hot car. She'd pluck those petals and move on to picking until it became too dark. Then, she'd process those flowers and get up early in the morning. Plan.

Ada unlocked her shed and came to an abrupt halt on seeing the bins of blue flower petals. Giddy relief almost took her out at the knees.

Somehow, the army men had picked flowers and prepared them for drying in the time she'd been away. Somehow, they'd entered her shed and relocked it without breaking her lock. Gratitude flooded her. She dragged out one of her stools and sat in front of a container of blue petals. She slipped her hand into them and scooped up a handful, before letting them drop back into the bin.

The men... This was amazing.

Ada jumped to her feet and layered the petals on her drying racks. Once she had the blue petals going through the drying process, she processed the leftover flowers, this time mixing the colors. Half an hour later, she was in her field and picking over an already harvested row to catch the late blooms.

She noted the row of blue flowers was perfect, with only buds left on the long stems. These men she'd been lucky enough to blackmail into harvesting her flowers were quick and efficient. A fortunate break for her.

Ada completed picking in just over an hour and ambled the rest of her flower field, checking on the plants' health. While she'd grown delphiniums predominantly, she had a few rows of cornflowers and a patch of wildflowers. Everything looked healthy, with no signs of crown or root rot, and she'd need to harvest the cornflowers within the next few days.

The next morning, Ada awoke with a spring in her step. The weather forecast promised sun and cloudless skies for the week to come, and all going well, she'd harvest a significant part of her crop by then. Archie, who'd slept indoors last night, wound around her legs and meowed in a plaintive demand for food.

Ada hadn't thought to shop for cat food yesterday, but now she added this to her list before pulling out another can of tuna. Her last one. The cat didn't seem to mind, nor did he seem to be a fussy eater. She checked her phone and noted the battery had charged to ten percent and stopped. Enough to make and accept phone calls. The second she pulled her phone off the charger, it died.

"Great." She glared at her older-model phone and slapped it onto her kitchen counter before brewing a pot of tea. Her mind slipped to Matt, his virile image swaggering into her thoughts.

Gah! Why couldn't she stop thinking about the man? Greg was the one who should fill her thoughts, not this soldier impostor. Tired of men and their secrets—*looking at you, Greg*—Ada made quick work of her breakfast before filling a water bottle and heading out. Two hours later, she was busy picking mauve delphiniums and getting into a rhythm. A loud purring sound from nearby had her pausing in her picking.

"Hey, kitty. You're getting brave." The cat seemed to have adopted her, and the animal's presence made her feel less alone. She smoothed her hand along the cat's spine before continuing with her work.

Since she hadn't seen the soldiers yesterday, she wasn't

sure if the men were picking today.

A loud bang echoed through the hills without warning, and Ada jumped, almost dropping her flower bucket. Several more equally loud explosive booms reverberated through the valley, and the cat issued a loud hiss and fled toward her tiny house. Ada's arms tightened around her container, and a tremor raced down her spine.

Dammit. The soldiers had promised they'd inform her if they were doing exercises with loud charges going off. *They'd promised.*

Gritting her teeth, she continued picking, but each dull boom had her flinching, her hands trembling, and her knees knocking. Determined, she kept on with her scheduled picking while fairness had her presuming Matt had called her, and she hadn't received the message because of her stupid phone. She filled a bucket and reached for another empty pail. A forceful explosion resounded through the surrounding hills, and she pressed her lips together.

It was early afternoon when the bangs and explosions tailed off. The cat returned and chose a sunny spot where he could watch her. Although Ada's shoulders ached from picking, she took the four full buckets back to her shed and left them in the cooler to process later.

A car pulled into her driveway before she headed back to

her field.

Sherry.

The diminutive woman climbed from behind the wheel and limped toward Ada. She wore her usual floral dress, this one pale blue, and sandals, her long hair flowing over her shoulders. Sherry's left leg, which was longer than the right, dragged over the gravel and raised a dust cloud with each step. "Where have you been? I've been ringing for ages."

Ada shrugged. "My phone is charging. It's inside."

"Ada, dear. That's not safe these days. You should have your phone with you. What happens if you have an accident? Or a strange man attacks you?"

"Me?" Ada pressed her right hand to her breasts. "I'm working in the flower fields, which aren't far from the house."

"But, dear. Someone murdered Greg. You of all people should practice safety."

Ada pressed her lips together, achingly aware that Greg's murder was unsolved, and it was looking increasingly likely the culprit would never get caught. The local cops had assured her they hadn't stopped searching for her husband's murderer, but Ada was a realist. It had been three years.

"The farmers' market was busy yesterday," she said.

"Yes," Sherry said. "How did you go? Did you sell much?"

"I meant to count my takings last night, but I got busy doing other things."

"You were late."

"Yes, I had problems at home here and had to call the local police."

"Again?" Sherry's voice rose, and Ada got the sense Sherry thought she'd overreacted.

Ada didn't mention the note but moved to her afternoon calamity. "Someone slashed my tires yesterday during the farmers' market."

Sherry's brows rose. "Oh, dear. You attract trouble like a magnet."

"Tell me about it," Ada muttered.

The shots started again, echoing loudly through the hills.

Ada started and balled her hands into fists. Bloody men. If they were repeating the exercises next week, they could give her a schedule in advance, detailing the days, no, the hours they intended to fire guns or whatever soldierly ammunition they were using.

"What is that?" Sherry asked.

"I agreed to let the army use my high country for their training exercises."

Sherry's brows rose. "All the land?"

"Yes," Ada said. "I needed the money."

Sherry's face turned sympathetic, and she patted Ada's arm. "Are you having money problems, dear? You know Bart wants more land. You only have to say the word."

"My land is not for sale," Ada said through clenched teeth.

"Surely, you're not holding on to the land because of Greg?"

"No." Ada kept the truth to herself. The land wasn't hers. *Yet.* "I'm keeping the land to grow my flowers. Not for any other reason."

"You're so young," Sherry said in a gentle voice. "Don't you want children? A husband. More friends? You sequester yourself on the farm and work so hard. I worry about you."

Ada contained her impatience, knowing Sherry meant well, even though the chiding delivery made Ada want to clap her hands over her ears. "My parents tell me the same thing."

"I suppose they worry too. You've had so much bad luck. Your house burned down not long after Greg died. Then there are the other strange things happening to you. I mean, why would anyone slash your tires. Do you know who did this?"

"No one saw a thing. I'm sorry to hurry you, Sherry, but did you want something? I'm on a timeline here."

"Oh." Sherry looked taken aback but rallied fast. "Did you want me to book a stall for you for Saturday?"

"Not this weekend," she said. "I'm sure it's important to attend the market regularly, but I need to finish harvesting my crop. If it's all right, I'll start at the beginning of November."

Sherry studied her for a long moment before frowning. "I can do that, but it will mean I can't give you a stall in a prominent position. You'll have the same one I gave you yesterday or a similar position."

"That's fine," Ada said without hesitation. She'd make any stall Sherry issued her work.

"Very well, but I think you're making a mistake."

The cat slinked along the side of the shed, and Ada watched it halt on spotting Sherry. It let out a loud hiss and arched its back until it appeared double its average size.

"Is that cat still here? You shouldn't encourage it. You've no idea where it came from or where it has been. It might carry a nasty disease, or worse, fleas. Whatever you do, don't let the animal inside your house."

"I..." Ada started to say the cat had already been inside but changed her mind after seeing Sherry's expression. Honestly, sometimes her neighbor went too far with her bossiness.

"Are you positive about the stall?"

"At present, it's more important for me to harvest my crop." Because if she didn't do that, she wouldn't have a hope in hell of repaying the loan or keeping the land.

"Very well." Sherry whipped her planner from her handbag and jotted a note in her neat handwriting.

Ada smiled, attempting to smooth Sherry's ruffles. For a small woman, she liked to manage people. "Thank you for thinking of me, Sherry. You're a good neighbor, and I'm fortunate to have you living nearby."

"You're welcome, dear. Oh, look at the time. I'd better leave, or I'll be late for the council meeting." Seconds later, Sherry drove away with an airy wave.

Typically, she pushed aside Sherry's orders and what she thought Ada should or shouldn't do with her future. Yes, she'd had a lot of crummy luck, but other people did too and got past trying times. She would too.

Ada kept working until hunger, and the approaching dusk sent her inside. Archie meowed in what she was coming to recognize as his hungry cry. Strange how the cat had hissed at Sherry.

"Me, too, buddy," she said when he mewed again. "Let me carry these buckets into the shed, then we'll find something to eat."

After feeding the cat, she heated a can of soup for herself. She checked her phone and saw it had charged to ten percent again. She played her messages. One from Matt plus several missed calls from him, along with four missed calls from Sherry. There was one more, and she thought the number belonged to the bank manager. Missing that one wasn't so bad. Yeah, it was digging her head into the sand, but she was doing her best.

Her mouth split wide in a yawn, and suddenly she felt every ache and pain gathering in her shoulders. Ada yawned again and sighed because she needed to work for a few more hours. She'd known her plan to save the farm would be difficult. She'd known the physical labor and uncertainty would test her. She'd known all of that, but she'd gone ahead, anyway.

Chapter 8

Strange Lights at Midnight

During a quiet moment, Matt tried to call Ada. The call went straight to voicemail, and he didn't bother to leave a message. Instead, he returned his phone to his pocket and continued to observe the men as they ran through their current exercise.

"Move your lazy arses!" he hollered, holding back a grin when the nearest soldier glowered at him. The truth—this bunch of soldiers were top-class, and he'd needed to change up the exercises to challenge them.

"Excellent group," his fellow trainer said.

"I feel as if we need to up the difficulty," Matt said. "Any ideas?"

"We have the night tracking exercise this evening. Make

it harder."

"That's what I was thinking," Matt said with distinct slyness. "This is what I think we should do."

Later that evening, once darkness gathered in and the camp fell silent, Matt pulled on his clothes and slid from his tent. Not only was the session tonight going to be epic, but the men weren't expecting it. Matt strode to the closest tent and slapped the canvas side. "Rise and shine, ladies. Time to get moving."

He moved between the tents until all the men were awake and dressed. They crowded around him while he split them into teams and issued instructions.

There was little talk as the men pulled on their packs and slipped into the darkness in groups of four. After consulting with his two fellow trainers, he moved out to one of the positions they'd agreed would be best to watch the exercise. Matt climbed the ridge and found a post against the base of a totara tree where he was out of the wind. He sat and pulled out the flask of coffee he'd made before he left camp. The coffee was lukewarm but welcome since it would help to keep him awake.

Personally, he'd rather participate in the exercise than act as a trainer. The one downside of his retirement from the New Zealand Special Air Service. Not that he missed getting shot at in hot, dry countries.

A flash of light caught his attention, and his eyes narrowed as he followed the bob of what he guessed was a torch. Low voices carried on the night air. Not his men, because they wore night-vision goggles. He strained to listen, but nothing apart from the call of a kiwi disturbed the silence.

He followed the trajectory of the lights, which were heading to the road. A door slammed, and he identified the hum of a departing vehicle. Curious. Why would people be out here in the middle of the night? As far as he was aware, this was Ada's land. He'd ask her the next time he saw her.

Curious about her husband and his death, he'd done an internet search after their last meeting. What he'd discovered had shocked him. Someone—unknown—had murdered Ada's husband, and this knowledge had helped him to understand her caution and sometimes prickly nature.

Damn. The woman was on his mind way more than necessary. This was an essential exercise for the men. They were giving it their all, and he needed to focus. He slipped on his pair of night vision goggles and settled to await the first team.

·♥·♥·♥·♥·♥·

ADA WAS BUSY PICKING flowers, her hands moving on automatic pilot while she wondered if she should contact Sherry and ask if she could have a market stall after all.

"Ada."

She jumped and almost dropped her bucket of flowers.

"Sorry, I didn't mean to frighten you."

Ada scowled at Matt. "You shouldn't have sneaked up on me then."

Matt smiled—a wide and bright smile that had her heart beating faster. She wanted to say something smart and witty, but her mind blanked, and she stared at him with wide eyes and heat blazing in her cheeks.

Archie slipped from a row of delphiniums and trotted straight to Matt. The man stooped to scratch the cat behind his ears, taking the pressure off her. *Phew!* Saved by the cat.

Her relief didn't last for long since Matt unrolled to his full height and observed her pin-in-butterfly-specimen close. "You didn't answer your phone. I called two days ago to let you know we'd be using flash-bang equipment."

Ada screwed up her nose and pushed away the instant fear that sparked inside her. She had to get past this guilt because it wasn't healthy to cling to Greg. She knew that. The man had lied to her. No, not lied, but he'd kept secrets when they were business partners. *Life partners.*

"Hey." Matt clicked his fingers in front of her nose.

She jerked away, felt her eyes widen while her heart did that strange loop-d-loop thing that had started from the moment she'd met Matt.

She shook her head, and thankfully, the jolt re-ordered her thoughts into something that made sense. "I...ah...my phone battery died. I can only use the phone if it's plugged in, and then only now and then."

"Why didn't you get a new phone?"

"When I discover a money tree, I'll get right on that," she shot back.

He backed up a fraction. "Right. Do you want me to help?"

"Whatever." Ada returned to picking—white delphiniums today—her fingers fleet and her movements efficient. She wasn't sure how she could harvest the rest of her flowers. With half of her flowers left to pick, and the truth—she couldn't afford to pay for workers. She'd been lucky so far with the help she'd received. At least, she was building stock slowly, and yay! She'd received an order last night for two kilograms of white and pink petals.

Matt grabbed a bucket and started picking.

"Aren't you meant to be doing your soldier games?"

"We finished the training exercises last night, or rather early this morning. The group flew out at nine. Another group of soldiers will arrive on Monday morning, so I'm all yours until then."

Ada turned to face him. "I can't pay you."

"Did I ask for money?"

"No, but I thought I'd make things clear from the start."

"I figured I was still paying for landing in your flowers."

"True." The urge to smile took her by surprise.

"Have you had any more problems? Intruders autographing your shed?"

"No, nothing, thankfully. The local cops have been busy over the other side of town, according to gossip. They have several cases of stock rustling this month."

"Is that normal?" Matt asked.

"Not really. The people in this town are usually law-abiding citizens. The local cops are too busy to worry about vandalism."

"While we were doing the exercise last night—it was around two in the morning—I saw lights—one or more people with torches. Low murmurs, so I couldn't make out the words. They had a vehicle and drove off. Do you know who that might have been?"

"I own the land up there. The access road belongs to me."

"Any idea what they might've been doing?"

"None."

Matt shrugged. "I'll keep an eye out during our exercises next week."

"It's probably teenagers using my land for clandestine drinking or something like that. As long as they don't cause any problems, I won't worry."

The roar of an off-road bike broke the country serenity.

Ada straightened as the rowdy bikes drew closer and roared into her driveway. Not one bike. Two. Her stomach sank because she knew who was riding them.

Archie hissed, and his fur ruffled. He slunk into the flowers, out of sight, but his low growl still reached Ada.

Matt must've sensed something because he stopped picking and came to stand at her side. "Someone you know?"

"My neighbor's sons," Ada said in a clipped voice as Craig and Eddie sauntered toward her. They didn't spot Matt straight away but lost some of their cockiness when they did.

"Who are you?" Eddie demanded.

The Walsh boys took after their father, with both topping out at around six feet. They had black hair—tied back in a tail in Eddie's case while Craig followed the professional route, his hair cut short at the sides and longer on top. Ada guessed Craig dressed and styled himself more than his brother because of his bank job.

"I'm Ada's boyfriend." Matt moved to Ada and drew her closer to his side.

His physical presence helped her conquer the rush of anxiety she always experienced in Eddie's vicinity. She dug her hands into her pockets, bracing for their reaction.

"Boyfriend?" Eddie's tone came close to a snarl. "You never said you had a boyfriend."

Ada lifted her chin, gave off attitude. "Why would I?"

"Mum didn't know," Craig added, his blue gaze assessing and probing. "She knows everything. All the latest gossip."

"Ada and I don't see the need to share our business," Matt said.

Eddie glared at Ada. "How long have you been with him?"

"I'm a soldier with the New Zealand army. I've been away and now I'm back."

"What did you want?" Ada broke the stare-down between Eddie and Matt, drawing Eddie's attention to her. A sliver of unease tiptoed down her spine at the flash of temper in his eyes.

Once, she'd been at a party Sherry had thrown at her house. Eddie had cornered Ada when she'd gone to use the restroom. Luckily for her, two teenage girls had come along and interrupted. Eddie had backed off, stepping away from where he'd cornered her with a whispered, "Later." Ada hadn't liked the man then, and she took care to avoid him if possible.

This unannounced visit was a variation on his behavior, and she'd been lucky Matt was here.

"I came to ask you out," Eddie drawled, the quiet words more of a threat than a statement. "I didn't realize I'd be stepping on toes."

"No harm done," Matt said. "Ada and I have kept our relationship on the down-low because we weren't positive we'd maintain our long-distance romance." He winked at her, and a blast of warmth suffused her. "Now I'm back, we have no doubts about our compatibility."

"Is that right, Ada?" Eddie probed her reaction, cunning darting through those light blue eyes before his impassive features hid his emotions. "You don't seem excited by this development."

Ada jerked upright and willed herself to calm. "I don't do PDAs," she snapped. "That's not who I am, and my relationship with Matt is private."

"I thought you were madly in love with your husband," Craig contributed to the conversation. "Mum told us that's why you never date."

"You discuss me with your mother?" Ada exclaimed, horrified, although she should've become used to the gossip after Greg's murder.

"You're our neighbor. Single and attractive. We're single." Craig's gaze ran up and down her body. "Chances are you're one woman we might mention to our mother."

Eew.

Ada pressed harder against Matt, and he pressed a kiss to her temple.

Matt sent the Walsh brothers an amiable grin, although Ada sensed the explosive tension in his muscles. Up this close, it was easy to comprehend Matt's power and strength. The danger he presented that he usually hid beneath his personable charm and lazy demeanor. Matt Townsend was the perfect person to stand at her side.

"Now you know better," Matt said, using that good-boy nature. "Ada is mine." His voice hardened. "I don't like to share, and I hate it when my lady becomes upset."

He'd gauged the situation in the same way she had. She wasn't misinterpreting the threat Craig and Eddie had brought with them.

"Can't blame a guy for trying." Craig nudged his brother. "We should leave. If Ada hasn't seen her boyfriend for several months, neither of them will want us hanging around."

Eddie released a growl seconds before an agitated feline hiss filled the air.

Ada turned her head to see her adopted cat glaring at the brothers.

"I didn't know you had a cat," Eddie said with a pointed glower in his brother's direction.

"Ada is full of surprises," Matt quipped. "Thanks for stopping by." With that, he guided Ada away from the brothers and toward her house. "Let's have something to eat, sweetheart, before we start work again."

Ada hated turning her back on the brothers, and the tension never left her shoulders until the rumble of their bikes filled the air. The cat fluffed up again, hissing for a second time before it darted in front of her and Matt.

As the bikes roared away, Matt took her hand. Instead of yanking free, Ada let the contact stand and took comfort from his presence. She shuddered. If Matt hadn't been here, she wasn't sure what might have happened. She avoided Eddie as much as possible, and the brothers had never visited her in this way. She'd felt vulnerable.

"Do you have a spare room?" Matt asked once the roar of the bikes had receded.

Ada glanced at Matt. "The couch pulls out into a bed."

"That will work," Matt said. "I'm staying here tonight and over the weekend. I didn't like the way those two were eyeing you."

It hadn't been her overactive imagination then. "How?"

"Like you were a delectable treat, and they wanted to take a bite," Matt said, pulling no punches. "Could you smell the alcohol on them?"

"Truthfully, they scared me so much, I didn't take in details," Ada said. "I was concentrating on not trembling or showing a reaction to their presence. I get the sense my fear would've pleased them."

"At least you're taking the threat seriously. Have they tried this before? Hurt you? Harassed you?"

"Eddie cornered me at a party a few months ago. Two girls came along before it got too bad, and I've dodged him ever since."

"Wise move." Matt stepped onto her deck. "The one with the long hair gave off bad vibes. I think the other one reins him in, but it wouldn't surprise me if one or both of them were high from some drug they'd mixed with the alcohol. A buzz makes a man brave."

"Oh, joy," Ada muttered. "They give me the creeps on a good day. I want nothing to do with them, but it's difficult because their mother is lovely. Everyone likes her, and she does a lot for the district. The farmers' market was her brainchild, and it brings a lot of business from the surrounding towns. The locals weren't doing well before the market, but Sherry told everyone it would be excellent for business. She was right. Sherry was the first person to welcome Greg and me to the district."

Matt nodded. "Your house is small."

"That's why it's called a tiny house."

"What made you decide on this style rather than a conventional home?" He didn't wear the judgmental expression that others had shown her, so she gave him an honest answer.

"My house burned down, and the insurance payout wasn't enough to rebuild. It wasn't long after my husband died, and I was a mess. I'm a city girl and had no clue of how to run a farm. My husband and I farmed sheep. He did most of the work and planning because he had farming experience. After his death, I had no hope in hell of continuing, so Sherry's husband—he's a stock agent—helped me to sell the sheep. I used that money to start my flower business. It was the only skill I had. I'm a keen gardener and have always enjoyed growing plants."

"The stock agent—he's those guys' father?"

"Yes," Ada said. "Is a sandwich okay? I haven't gone food shopping this week." A lie since she'd been in town. Money was the problem, and at the moment, she needed to economize.

"That's fine," Matt said.

"Watch your head. Most of the interior will be fine for your height, but a couple of places might be a squeeze."

Matt grinned, and it lit up his entire face. "Thanks for the warning."

Ada shook free from the Matt spell and led the way inside. She was aware of Matt, and for a moment, she was sure he was checking out her butt. She was wrong. When she turned toward the kitchen part of her tiny house, she found him taking in the layout and contents of her home. He flashed her a cheerful beam. Her skin prickled with awareness and something else more foreign. Attraction. Lust. Yearning. A bouquet of the former.

He was her first male visitor, and she hadn't expected him to monopolize the space.

"Can I explore?"

She nibbled her bottom lip before nodding. She'd made her bed after getting out of it this morning, and she mostly picked up after herself and replaced items in her concealed storage units, but it was her home, and personal items were on show. Her stack of gardening books. Her pile of business papers and her laptop because she kept a close eye on the farm budget. Mostly outgoings at the moment, although, yay! Her first order the previous night.

"Ada?"

"What?" Her gaze shot to him, and she discovered his smile had widened. "Oh! Yes, you're welcome to take a look." She forced a friendly smile while she concealed her trembling hands behind her back. "Tell me what you think."

"I will," he promised in his husky voice.

She watched him amble toward the far end of her home and the divider that partially hid her bedroom. Her tastes were plain, but she did like her comfort with puffy pillows and high thread count sheets. Her room was restful, with muted shades of teal and steel gray.

While he explored her tiny house, she applied herself to pulling sandwich makings from the fridge. As she'd warned him, pickings were slim, but the bread was fresh, and she had plenty of lettuce from her garden to provide filler.

She sensed him walking past—a disturbance of the air, followed by a hit of his masculine scent. Although he'd been camping for a week, he didn't stink. Her mind slid to the next natural conclusion. The soldiers had cleaned up in the stream that ran through the valley and emptied into the Moewai river. A stealthy image crept into her mind, and she imagined Matt without his clothes. Immediately heat gathered in her cheeks, and her hands shook anew. *Gah!* What the heck was wrong with her?

Footsteps heralded his return. "I thought this place would be pokey, but I didn't have to duck once. I'd even fit in the shower. The storage units and how you've utilized every space is amazing. I'm impressed."

Ada set a plate of ham, cheese, and salad sandwiches on the wooden counter she used as a table. She added smaller empty plates and two cloth napkins.

"Do you take milk and sugar in your tea?" Ada was proud of her neutral tone. It was remarkable considering the rate of her heartbeat and the sporadic hand trembles.

"Just milk," he said. "I've learned to drink tea or coffee as it comes, but milk is a treat."

She nodded as if she understood when his words made her inquisitive. Given that she hated strangers questioning her, she didn't push her curiosity at him.

"How often do you go up to the area we used for training?"

Surprised, Ada glanced at him. "I haven't been up there for months."

Archie chose that moment to strut through the doorway. The cat paused on seeing Matt, stared, and continued inside. Ada half-expected more hissing, but the animal surprised her. He walked over to Matt and investigated his camo trousers. Apparently, they passed his sniff-test because the cat rubbed against Matt's legs and began some heavy-duty purring.

"You should be honored," Ada said, surprised by the cat's calm acceptance and trust. "Archie has hissed at everyone else who has visited me this week."

"I like animals. My parents had a farm when I was growing up. They've sold it since and retired to a smaller lifestyle block."

"Where do you live when you're not working?"

"I have a place on the outskirts of Pukekohe. It's peaceful, and I get my country fix, yet it's close to the city and the army base where I work."

"Who looks after it while you're away? I figure you're away from work often." She hesitated. "Is it all right for me to ask?"

"You can ask me whatever you want, but I reserve the right not to answer."

Her soft laugh surprised her, coming out of left field. She stopped smiling almost as soon as she'd started because of the way his eyes widened, and his gaze grew intent. Interested. God, he felt the same attraction she did. The desire, the interest, the subtle dance of flirtation crackled in the air between them.

Matt appeared to shake himself. "Would one of your neighbors use your stockyards?"

"What? No, I don't think so."

"I mentioned the lights and strangers on your land late last night. We haven't had rain for a week at least, but there were hoof marks in the yard as if someone had held stock there. I saw fresh droppings."

"That's interesting," Ada said. "The local farmers have complained of missing stock this week. I wonder if the thieves were using my yards to hold the stock until they decided what to do with the animals."

"It could be something innocent. Animals can wander. Using your yards might've been innocuous."

"True." Ada paused. "I should let the local cops know when I next go into town."

"It might be nothing. I'll keep an eye out for anything strange this coming week."

Ada pushed the plate of sandwiches at him. "Are you certain you want to pick flowers this afternoon?"

"I prefer to keep busy." Matt accepted a sandwich and placed it on his plate.

"Take a couple more. I intend to work you hard." She immediately wanted to recall her words because she hadn't phrased herself well.

His head lifted, and his gaze shot to hers. A tiny smile played around his lips. "Do your worst."

CHAPTER 9

THAT MAN IS MESSING WITH MY HEAD

MATT ENJOYED WORKING IN the flower field. The sun beamed down, but the heat was pleasant rather than stifling. Bees buzzed around the flowers, and birds sang from the trees and native bush surrounding the field. Even better, the beautiful Ada picked beside him. She was a woman of few words and hidden depths. Strong. She'd had to be with the curve balls life had chucked her. Funny, he'd never had problems talking to women or snagging one he set his sights on. The uniform helped—sure—but he liked women, and they seemed to gravitate to him.

Ada was a challenge, and being with her even in a platonic way made him feel alive and more self-aware than he'd been since he left active service. He hadn't been searching for a woman, but now he thought he might have found one anyway.

"Did you still want extra workers for tomorrow?" Matt asked, breaking the silence.

"Yes. I wish I knew who hired my pickers away from me," Ada said, scowling.

"You don't seem to have much luck."

Her lips formed into a grimace. "Tell me about it."

That was all it took for Matt's spidey senses to twang. This woman had suffered a lot. The murder of her husband. The fire. Pickers going AWOL, slashed tires, the graffiti on her shed. There were probably more incidences she hadn't mentioned since she wasn't the whinging type. If he added in the strangeness at her yards, the total came to someone messing with Ada on purpose. He didn't think he was jumping to conclusions, but he might run these suspicions past Josh and Dillon.

"I'm meeting with friends tomorrow. They'll help with the picking. Four willing hands plus us is better than nothing, right?"

"I couldn't ask you to do that. You should relax with your friends instead of working for me." She pushed out a sound she meant to be a laugh, but to Matt's ears it more rivaled a groan. "I'm not even paying you because I can't afford to."

"Believe me, you're doing them a favor. They like to keep busy. The weather forecast says fine, so we can catch up while enjoying the outdoors. It beats sitting around a pub."

Ada frowned, and he could tell he hadn't convinced her.

"Do me a solid," he added. "If I visit their homes, my friends let their wives trot out their single friends. They can't do that here. Besides," he said with a wink, "you're my girlfriend. I can tell them that with a straight face."

"Are you sure?"

"Yep." He'd ring Josh and ask him and Ash to bring enough food for a barbecue. They wouldn't mind.

They kept picking flowers until the sun dipped low on the horizon, and his back ached. Once they reached the end of their row, Ada straightened with a groan.

Matt averted his gaze from her rounded breasts that pushed against her tight T-shirt, and when that didn't work, he imagined his grandmother in a bikini. *Huh*. That did the trick and allowed him to relax a fraction. "Let's stop for the day. I'm hot and hungry."

"I second that," she said, her voice husky.

Matt didn't know if staying in her house, which wasn't big enough to swing a cat in—one of his grandmother's many sayings—was the best idea. Then, he recalled the hot, hungry expression of the dude with long hair. He couldn't leave her alone. This was a short-term thing, so he'd suck it up. If he could get through the tough NZSAS training, this should be a walk in the park. Another grandmotherly favorite.

The cat appeared from an unpicked row and trailed them as they strolled back to the shed with the last of the flowers they'd picked.

Ada opened the shed, and they dumped their flowers into a larger bin.

"Will you have to prepare these for drying tonight?"

Ada sucked in a cleansing breath. "Yes. I knew this part of the process would mean long days. I keep telling myself that once I get through this, the next step will be much easier. This first year is a learning experience."

"Anything you'd do differently next time?" Matt asked as Ada locked the shed.

"I'd plant the flowers so the picking was more staggered. This year, I planted everything at the same time. If I have a worker shortage in the future, staggering the crop would mean I could make do with less help. I'd plant a bigger mixture of flowers—maybe more cornflowers and try roses so I can offer a bigger range of petals. I'm learning from the inquiries I'm receiving that the brides have very individual tastes."

Matt grinned while shaking his head. He couldn't help it because what bloke thought of the minute wedding details like confetti?

Ada sent him a curious look as she toed off her boots. "What's so funny?"

"Most guys, especially the ones I work or spend time with, would never consider flower petals or confetti in their wedding plans."

It was Ada's turn to chuckle. "I get it. Weddings are mostly for women, while men are more interested in getting to the honeymoon."

She turned away to enter her house, and Matt ogled her. She wasn't skinny, but nor was she overweight. The woman worked damn hard, and he felt a sense of pride and admiration for her.

A lot of women would've given up and returned to the city. Not Ada.

She'd weighed up her resources and designed a plan that worked for her. Now, she was trying damn hard to reach her goal, despite the obstacles she faced. A man had to respect her determination.

"I'm not sure what I have for dinner."

"I'm not a fussy eater. Anything I can do to help?"

"Have a shower," she said. "I don't mean to imply you need one. It's more I thought you might enjoy hot water after camping for a week."

"I'd love a shower," Matt said.

"Right. I'll grab you a towel. I don't have any spare clothes that will fit you."

"No problem. I have clothes in my pack."

She frowned. "I didn't see you carrying anything."

"Because I set it aside when I saw your neighbors arrive."

"Oh."

"It's by the shed," he said.

"Well, I'll leave a clean towel for you then figure out what I can feed you."

"Thanks." Matt decided he'd definitely ask Josh or Dillon to bring food when they came. He could imagine the teasing he'd receive, but no problem. Now that he'd met Ada, he intended to pursue her. His job change kept him in New Zealand now, and he'd long ago tired of the single scene where one-night stands were easy.

He made the call, and as he'd predicted, Josh was in fine form. Even his sister, Ashley, got in a dig or two.

Ash snort-laughed. "I'm looking forward to meeting Ada. Flower picking sounds way more restful than wrangling politicians. I can't wait to witness my security team's reaction. Probably a similar one to when I make a rare trip to the lingerie department with them in tow."

"Yeah, I bet that's fun for them," Matt said.

"Later." Ashley hung up.

Dillon was out, but Matt spoke to Ella, who told him they were looking forward to seeing him.

"I thought we'd have a barbecue," Matt said. "Ada has one on her deck. I'll check the gas bottle and call back if we need a spare."

"Don't worry. I'll get Dillon to bring one. I'd already thought about food, so that's covered."

"Thanks, Ella. This means a lot to me."

"I can't wait to meet your Ada. Moewai isn't far from here, but I don't get out your way often. I should because rumor says the farmers' market is excellent. See you tomorrow."

Satisfied with his phone call results, he scooped up his pack and headed back to Ada. Ella had called her *your Ada*. Hell, he hadn't even kissed her yet. *Slow down, Matt.* Then he grunted because he knew himself well. Once he set himself a goal, he didn't stop.

Wait until he explained their first meeting to his sister—if Josh hadn't told her already—and how Ada had shrieked at him for flattening her flowers. Matt was still snickering at the memory when he walked inside. The scent of frying onion wafted to him, and his stomach grumbled.

"Is everything okay?" Ada asked. "You took a long

time."

"I had a couple of phone calls. Dinner smells great."

"Wait until you taste it," she said, her tone dry. "The cupboards are fairly bare. I knew I should've shopped the other day, but by the time I finished with the cops and organized replacement tires, I'd had enough."

"Don't apologize. I understand."

She shrugged off his words and jerked her head toward the bathroom. "Don't use all the hot water."

"I won't," he promised, and succumbing to instinct, he kissed her on the cheek and headed for the bathroom. He felt the weight of a stare on his back as he left and grinned. Nothing like keeping a woman off-balance.

Ada ripped her gaze off Matt's backside and blew out a breath to steady herself. This man had pushed his way into her life and slid past her defenses before she'd even realized he was coming. She wasn't sure what to think. Briefly, she considered sending him packing, but then her shoulders slumped. The man had saved her from an even nastier scene with Craig and Eddie. They'd never visited with such obvious intent, and she hated to think what might've happened if Matt hadn't arrived.

Eddie hadn't hidden his lust, and he'd acted like a thwarted child once Matt had claimed her. A shudder worked through her, and her skin crawled at the danger that had emanated from Eddie.

Then there was the flower picking. He'd worked at her side without complaint. No, she was doing the right thing in giving him a place to sleep and feeding him. She just wished she didn't feel such a potent attraction to the man. When he'd drawn her against him in that possessive manner, she'd almost swooned with the forceful lust swamping her.

Ada rifled through her freezer and pulled out a bag of frozen corn kernels and another of peas. She added the vegetables to her pan, considered Matt's size, and added more. She continued with the dinner preparations, boiling water for the pasta and turning on the oven to heat the dinner rolls she'd found in her freezer. For dessert, she'd caramelize apples and serve them with the last of the ice cream. Hopefully, that would be enough food to fill the soldier and sate her hunger. Who knew picking flowers would create such an appetite?

Matt appeared in a pair of shorts and a tight T-shirt. One glance at the freshly showered man, and she'd added another visual to her memories. Images to keep her tossing and turning late into the night. The man wore clothes, for goodness sake, but he was so big. Masculine. Quite unlike Greg, who'd been a lanky man with a runner's body.

Ada swished the vegetables and crisp bacon pieces around her pan to distract herself from staring. "I have a six-pack of beer in the fridge. Help yourself while I jump in the shower."

"Should I watch anything for you?"

"I'm about to put on the pasta, but I should be out of the shower by the time it's ready. Give it a stir. Other than that, relax. I don't have a television but put on music if you like. There is a tablet with several playlists and a BlueTooth speaker."

"I'll be fine." Matt shunted her toward the bathroom. "Go. I'll take charge of the pasta. How many cups?"

"Three," she said.

"Go." He reinforced his instruction with another push.

Ada went, her skin tingling where he'd touched her. For the first time in ages, she pictured herself with a man. Naked. "Get a grip, Ada," she muttered.

After a quick shower, that felt way too intimate because he'd been in the vicinity. Her house was small. If she called out, he'd arrive in seconds.

"Ada," she muttered, angry with herself for this...this...

Heck, she didn't know what it was, but *it* was doing her head. After giving herself a stern talking to, she reached for her fresh clothes and realized she didn't have any. The wretched man had rattled her so much, she'd forgotten to grab more. She groaned.

Great. *Just great.*

At least her towels were large because that was all she had to cover her nakedness. With a deep breath to bolster her bravery, she wrapped her towel firmly in place, shoved her dirty clothes into the hamper, and stalked from the bathroom.

Matt stilled on spotting her. His lips curved in an appreciative and sexy grin that jolted her libido and escalated her pulse rate. "Nice shoulders. Did you forget something?"

She lifted her nose and ignored his heated gaze. "I'm not used to having a man around my house."

His grin was breathtaking, and it stole her reason. She took half a step toward him before her brain jerked into gear. Holy Hannah, she had to breathe. She sucked in a hoarse breath and marched past him to reach her bedroom. Inwardly, she cursed the open-plan concept she'd embraced with her house design. Although a decorative screen concealed her as she pulled underwear from drawers, awareness turned her movements jerky. A tremor seized her, and she didn't stop shaking until she'd donned an old T-shirt and a pair of black leggings. After another deep inhalation, she padded back to the kitchen area, brushing past Matt to check the pasta.

"It's cooked," he said. "I turned off the element and was about to drain it for you."

Ada opened a cupboard and pulled out a strainer. Minutes later, she tossed vegetables and bacon through the pasta and dressed it with her favorite truffle oil. The oven timer went off, and she retrieved the dinner rolls.

"Can you grab two placemats from the drawer over there?" she asked, gesturing with her chin since she had her hands full.

Moments later, they were eating, and while Ada had suspected the dinner might be awkward, that wasn't the case. Matt chatted about the upcoming week of exercises and how happy his boss had been with the results.

"How did you persuade your friends to help pick tomorrow?" Ada asked.

"I told them I'd parachuted into your flower field, and you'd shouted at me. Then, I mentioned how you'd conned me into picking flowers to make up for the transgression. That was all the incentive they needed. They told me they looked forward to meeting the woman who'd tongue-lashed me. I met these guys during training for the NZSAS. We're not related, but they're my brothers. I'd do anything for them, and all I have to do is ask for them to return the favor. Dillon and Josh left the service before I did. Both of them got married, and they've settled down."

"Where do they live?"

"Josh lives in Auckland but travels a fair bit. Dillon, who is Josh's brother, has a farm in Eketāhuna. Dillon's wife, Ella, works for the Pūkaha Mount Bruce Wildlife Center. Actually, Ella does a lot in the community. She'd be the perfect contact for rounding up casual workers when you need them."

Ada opened her mouth to say she didn't need help, but he halted her with a raised hand.

"You're managing with a little help, but what happens if you get sick or another roadblock appears out of left field? You need to have reliable workers you can contact at short notice. Dillon's parents live in Eketāhuna. Mrs. Williams is a gracious lady who could help you. She takes part in those women's groups. You could visit, describe what you do, and mention you often need casual help. In country towns like Eketāhuna and Moewai, unemployment is high. Also, those women's groups might be a market for your confetti." He paused, his gaze intense.

"Thank you." Ada forked up a mouthful of penne pasta. "I hadn't considered that angle, and I should have."

"How do you market your product? Do you attend bridal shows?"

Ada swallowed her pasta. "Not at this stage. A stall is expensive. I sold a few confetti packets at the farmers' market, and now that I have stock to sell, my website has gone live. I've had one order so far, which I'll package after dinner."

"Do you do online advertising?" Matt asked.

She wrinkled her nose. "I'm running on a shoestring, so no."

"Your product dovetails with weddings and parties and other celebrations. Have you thought of doing a blog to highlight your product and give tips on arranging events? Take photos because your flower fields are pretty."

Ada discovered her mouth was wide open, and she snapped her teeth together while different emotions slapped her left and right. Shock. Amazement. Excitement. Admiration.

"A blog," she said finally. "That's a fantastic idea, and I should've thought of it earlier. I have a camera and have already taken heaps of photos from right through the growing process. It wouldn't take me much to do a blog post each week."

"Your first post should be about why you chose flowers and confetti," Matt said. "Share as much of your journey as you're comfortable with. People prefer authenticity."

Ada nodded while wondering how much to share. She'd think about it. Besides, the story of Greg's murder was in the public arena. "Thanks, Matt."

They did the dishes together, and it had grown dark by the time Ada decided she'd better get to work on her flowers or she'd never sleep tonight. Plus, she needed to pack the order and get it ready to courier to her customer.

"I'm going to my shed. You don't have to come," Ada said. "Relax and get some sleep."

"I won't sleep if I know you're working alone in your shed."

"I've done it before," she retorted.

"Which doesn't mean you have to continue doing it. I don't trust those two yahoos not to come back and bother you. If I help, you'll finish quicker."

Ada didn't have the energy to argue. She pulled on a coat because it got cold in the shed, donned socks and boots, and strode outside. First, she packed her order, scooping mainly white petals into bags with a touch of pink delphinium. She wrapped the cellophane bags of petals in brown paper and stuck it near the door with the order form and address details. Tomorrow, she'd zap to the post office and return before her pickers arrived. It would give her a chance to pick up groceries too.

With the order completed, she got to work separating petals and stacking racks in her drying machine. It was three hours later by the time she and Matt finished.

"We picked more flowers than I realized," she said with

a yawn.

"Are you pleased with your yield?"

"Very," she agreed, scooping up her order and locking the door behind them.

Back in her house, she found a pillow and two blankets for Matt. He stripped down to his underwear, unbothered by her presence.

"Is something wrong?" he asked, jerking her gaze from a muscled chest and abs. Her fingers tingled with the urge to touch.

She did the only thing possible for self-preservation. She fled.

"Goodnight, Ada." Matt's amused voice drifted after her.

A blast of heat rushed to her cheeks, and her hands—normally competent—did that strange tremor thing again as she disrobed. This man had wormed into her thoughts. No, not wormed. He'd parachuted like the daredevil soldier he was, and each moment she spent with him made her even more aware of her self-imposed loneliness, her longing to feel like a woman again.

CHAPTER 10

AN OFFAL SURPRISE

ADA DRAGGED HERSELF OUT of bed at six the next morning.

"Can't sleep?" Matt asked on her return.

"No," she said shortly, leaving her answer brief. What she needed was a cup of tea. She filled the kettle and prepared her teapot.

"You're not working? It's too early to pick since it's not light yet."

"I'll empty the drier and store the petals. I need to wash out the buckets and dry them ready for today. Once that's done, I'll have some toast and start picking. I have to courier my package in town, but other than that, I'll do as much picking as I can today. If we can do the first

SHELLEY MUNRO

pick on the remaining rows, then I should cope with the late-blooming flowers."

"Sweetheart, you have to rest. You're exhausted." Matt strode to her and ran his thumb over the skin beneath her eyes.

She gasped at the intimate action but couldn't retreat because he'd trapped her between the counter and his bulk.

"I understand a lot rides on you making this year a success, but you have to look after yourself too."

"I will," she gritted out, stung by his warning because he spoke the truth. He didn't know she was fighting a losing game because of the loan and Greg's parents.

A business like hers took time to establish, and the loan was a cruel blow. She still didn't understand how it had happened. Why? Why hadn't Greg told her of the loan? She guessed the fire had destroyed the official documents. Back then, not long after Greg's murder, she'd zoned out on life and floated through each day. Business papers had been the last thought on her mind.

Tired of arguing or rather discussing the subject, she poured her tea and handed another to Matt. Although it was still dark, dawn wasn't far away, and the birds were singing. She dropped onto her Adirondack deck chair to enjoy the dawn chorus.

Immediately, she almost dry-retched at a rancid stench riding on the air.

"What is that stink?" Matt demanded.

"I don't know." Ada breathed through her mouth to mitigate the putrid smell.

"Do you have an outside light?"

"It's just inside the door on the right."

Matt retreated, and seconds later, light cut through the darkness. He cursed. "Wait there."

Ada's stomach twisted while Matt stalked to the gate. He returned in minutes. "Animal intestines. Someone decorated your gate and fence."

"I didn't hear a thing."

Matt scowled. "Me neither, but I was knackered. Not much sleep in the last two days."

Ada could see not hearing the visitors bothered him. "What do I do?"

Matt shrugged. "Since neither of us heard, our best bet is to ring the local cops. I don't know if they'll want to see or if they'll be happy with photos. Do you have the local number? I'll ring them for you."

"Why is someone harassing me?" Ada demanded. "What have I done to deserve this?" Her in-laws jumped to mind. While they'd shown they were capable of cruelty, this prank wasn't their style. But they could've paid someone to do it, a tiny voice whispered in her mind. Heaven knew they coveted this land. She glanced at Matt, wondering if she should tell him. No, she decided. Family business. Private. The last thing she wanted was the knowledge to become gossip fodder.

"What about those two guys?" Matt asked. "Your neighbor's sons?"

"I rarely see them and avoid them if possible."

"Have you mentioned anything to their mother? About the way her sons are harassing you."

Ada pulled a face. "No."

"Maybe you should."

"It would be like whipping a puppy. Sherry is so nice. She's a popular lady around here because she's always helping when people need her. She expects nothing in return."

"Her sons are bullies. I've met their type before, and they don't enjoy getting bested. At least mention it to the cop so he can monitor the situation. If they're hassling you, they're probably doing the same to other women."

"Maybe," Ada said. "Why does this have to be so hard? All I want is to keep my head down and grow flowers."

"Perhaps that is what these bullies are counting on."

Ada shrugged. "I'll ring the local cops." She stood and stomped inside to get her cell phone.

"Well?" Matt asked when she returned outside.

"The cops said to email photos plus an account of what happened. Evidently, they have their hands full with several cases of stock smuggling and a rash of farm equipment burglaries. My problems fall into minor offenses."

"You start your work, and I'll take photos with my cell phone, then clear away the offal."

"What will you do with it?"

"I'll bury it. That's the best way to hide the smell."

Ada didn't argue since the thought of dealing with the putrid offal had her stomach churning. Her cup of tea bubbled inside her stomach, and for a moment, she feared it'd make a return appearance. "Thanks," she managed. "I appreciate the help."

"No problem," Matt said. "Where should I bury it?"

"There's an area on the other side of my gate. The farther away from the house, the better."

"Spade?"

"I have one in my shed." Ada retrieved the spade for Matt and left him to his gruesome task while she stored her dried petals and cleaned to prepare for the new day of picking. What sort of person did this? She settled into her duties, working on automatic. The petals were beautiful, having retained their gorgeous colors. She tipped them into clean containers and fastened the lids.

Once she'd completed her shed chores, she grabbed her pile of empty buckets and headed out to pick. She plucked pink blossoms with efficiency, and her mind wandered. She couldn't believe Craig and Eddie would do this, although each time she discarded the notion, her mind circled back. Greg's parents? No, them harassing her made little sense, either. But if they'd recruited someone else to stack the odds in their favor—

"Ada, do you want me to post your courier parcel for you? I need to pick up supplies for the training next week."

She cocked her head. "How are you going to do that? You don't have a vehicle."

"I thought I'd borrow your vehicle and drop the extra supplies at our camp before I return. I'll fill it with diesel in exchange."

"Can you pick up bread and sandwich fillings? I can give you a list."

"No problem."

She wiped her hands down her old jeans. "I'll get money."

"Nah, don't worry. You can refund me later. I'll grab your parcel and get going, so I'm back before my friends arrive."

"The keys are in the drawer with my tea towels."

"I spotted them last night," he said with a grin.

She nodded and returned to her picking, only lifting her head to stare at him when she was positive his attention was elsewhere. Her breath hissed out as her gaze landed on his butt. He was wearing his army trousers again, and a T-shirt stretched across his shoulders. Her insides tingled, and she ripped her focus away with difficulty. This man wandered through her thoughts way more than he should. She'd loved Greg with all her heart—enough to leave the excitement of Auckland to put down roots in the country. She'd learned new skills and ended up exhausted with blisters on her hands after helping with farm tasks.

She didn't have time for a man, but Matt tempted her to squeeze him into her schedule. Ada forced herself to return to work as her vehicle fired to life.

Yeah, she needed to focus on her flowers and not let a sexy, charming army man divert her from winning this land and losing everything.

· ❤ · ❤ · ❤ · ❤ · ❤ ·

MATT DROVE INTO THE country town of Moewai and parked outside the post office. He took care of Ada's courier parcel first, making sure he received a receipt and the tracking number to give to Ada later.

A police officer greeted him as he pushed through the door—a skinny dude with close-cropped black hair and piercing brown eyes. "How can I help you?"

"I'm here on behalf of Ada Buckingham. She rang earlier about the offal decorating her property entrance. I've got the photos here, but I wanted to talk to someone about the problems she's having. Someone slashed her tires the other day, sprayed graffiti on her shed, and now this. I'm betting there have been other instances. Two young men visited the other day and were pestering her when I arrived. If I hadn't turned up, things might've turned nasty."

"Sorry, who are you?"

"Ada's boyfriend," Matt said without hesitation. "I'm in the army, which means I'm away for months at a time. The entrails left at Ada's place had to come from somewhere. It wouldn't surprise me if the two young men wanted payback after I sent them off."

"Do you know who they were?"

"Ada's neighbors. The sons."

The cop's brows winged upward. "Craig and Eddie?"

"Yeah, I think those were their names."

"You're new to the neighborhood—at least I haven't seen you here before. Craig and Eddie are popular kids, and their parents are hardworking and do a lot for the district. I'm not saying you're wrong, but it would surprise me."

"Fair enough, but can you at least check their whereabouts last night? Did you find any animal carcasses? There were too many entrails to come from one animal. Ada mentioned several local farmers have reported missing stock. I'm part of the military group doing exercises on Ada's land. Two nights ago, I spotted lights at the set of yards. Heard voices. Ada doesn't own any livestock, but someone used those yards."

"Did you see anyone or animals?" the cop asked, his gaze turning sharp.

"I was too far away to get a good visual. When I checked the next morning, there were cattle tracks in the yard."

The cop jotted several notes. "We'll check it out, but we're already following several leads."

Matt nodded, getting the sense these cops had too much work and minimal staff. "Where do you want me to email these photos?"

The man rattled off an email address, and Matt sent the photos.

"Thanks," Matt said. "You'll let us know should you learn anything?"

"Yes," the cop said.

Matt strode from the police station, unsatisfied with the

man's response. While he understood there was no proof, his gut told him someone was plotting to destroy Ada or at least scare her into leaving. He should check the value of her land. Was it as simple as that? Someone wanting her land was trying to force her out?

He headed to the supermarket and stocked up on food, loading a trolley with fresh fruit and vegetables plus meat, drinks, milk, cereal, and a few sweet treats. That should be enough to feed everyone today and add to Ada's sparse stores. He figured he'd deal with her pride later. Besides, he doubted she'd shout at him in front of his friends and sister. Food shopping done, he topped the vehicle up with fuel and headed back to Ada's.

Once he'd stored the provisions, he joined Ada in the flower field. He'd thought Dillon and Josh would've been here, but he was glad they hadn't arrived yet. His grin felt a fraction evil, but he couldn't wait for Ada to meet his sister.

"Everything go okay?" Ada asked as he stepped onto the opposite side of the row to her and started picking.

"Yep. I put the receipt and the tracking number for your parcel on the counter."

"Thanks," Ada said.

"I hadn't thought I'd enjoy picking flowers, but it's restful. I enjoy the buzz of the bees and the color from the flowers. The birds. The scents. The company."

"It's not as much fun when it's raining, or the wind comes up. Then all you'd smell is my worry."

"Yeah, I get you wouldn't want the wind to flatten your plants. How did you decide on these?"

"It was very scientific." She wrinkled her nose. "I went with my heart. I've always liked delphiniums and grew them in my garden when I lived in Auckland. They grow well in the soil here, and the place in Shropshire are doing well with their delphiniums."

"What part of Auckland did you live in?"

"Mount Eden," she said. "Close to Eden Garden, which is a popular place for plant lovers. As a teenager, I had a job at the café there on the weekends and during school holidays. The people I worked with were generous with their knowledge, and I absorbed a lot. My grandmother did the rest. I inherited my green fingers from her. My parents live in an apartment in the central city, and it'd surprise me if they owned a single plant. My grandmother grew delphiniums. I knew they were excellent for confetti, so they were my first choice. I mentioned before that now I have more experience, I'll grow different species and plan to pick over a longer period rather than a concentrated harvest."

"Makes sense." He cocked his head on hearing a vehicle.

"My friends have arrived. I'll carry these buckets back to the shed and get them organized."

Ada stopped picking. "I'll come too."

"Keep working," Matt said. "Do you want me to start them on the white row?"

"Please."

"I'll bring everyone by and introduce them first. I haven't seen my sister for ages. It'll be great to catch up."

"Your sister? Did you tell me your sister was coming?"

Matt hid his grin with his hand. "I thought I did, but I didn't want to scare you." He left with a wave, but her words drifted after him.

"Why would your sister scare me?"

Matt chuckled. She was about to find out, and he couldn't wait to see her reaction.

Chapter 11

Matt's Sister is the What?

Curiosity blazed in Ada when Matt strode away, his cheerful whistle trailing in his wake. His eyes gleamed, and his body had bopped in constant motion. Excited to see his friends—that was clear. She exchanged her bucket for an empty one and continued picking. At least thoughts of Matt had driven her problems to the back of her mind.

Masculine laughter floated to her and sounds of greeting. Cheerful exclamations and Ada smiled. After a few minutes, the voices headed in her direction. She spotted the men first. They were big, and bore muscular builds, their hair coloring and physiques similar enough that she would've picked them as brothers. Everyone wore casual clothes, and Ada figured Matt had warned them to don their older gear.

"Ada, these are my friends Dillon Williams and his brother Josh."

Dillon had a well-trimmed beard, and he dipped his head in greeting. Josh stepped forward and shook her hand, his face wreathed in welcome. His dark brown hair shone in the sun, and his blue eyes sparkled with humor. He was as tall as Matt—around six-four at a guess.

"My wife, Ella," Dillon said, guiding a smiling woman with bright pink hair and equally bright clothing closer.

Josh drew the second woman forward, and Ada froze. "My wife, Ash."

"And my sister," Matt added, distinct humor coloring his voice.

Ashley Townsend, the current prime minister of New Zealand, stepped forward with a smile and offered her hand. "The minute Matt mentioned a flower farm and how he'd landed in your flowers, I had to meet you." Ashley Townsend was tall for a woman and slim. She had long, straight honey-blonde hair, and she wore it pulled back in a ponytail.

"Ah...pleased to m-meet you," Ada stuttered before shooting a glare at Matt. "Matt told me his friends were helping with my flower picking. He never said his sister was coming, nor did he mention it was you. I can't ask the prime minister to pick my flowers." She planted her hands on her hips. "That's something you should've mentioned."

Both Dillon and Josh chortled while the prime minister's grin broadened.

"We have come to pick flowers. You might even get my security men to help since it's so quiet here. You've chosen a beautiful spot. I'm a city girl these days, but I grew up on a farm. It's always a treat to get away from the job and the press. Ask Matt. I jumped at the chance to visit my big brother and have a day with family. Josh will tell you how excited I was the instant I finished speaking with Matt. Nelson. Gerry. Come here so I can introduce you to Ada."

Nelson stood at around Josh's height of six-four and held himself with a military bearing. His tan skin suggested Māori ancestry, as did his close-cut black hair and brown eyes. Gerry was a fraction shorter, which made his shoulders appear even broader. He reminded Ada of a rugby player—one of the powerful and bulky forwards—because his gray suit struggled to contain his shoulders. He had a shaved head, blue eyes, and groomed, two-day stubble on his powerful jaw.

"Ash always tells the truth." Josh winked at his wife.

Holy flaming meatballs! The prime minister of New Zealand. Ada wasn't clear what to do with this situation.

"Why don't I show everyone how to pick while you collect yourself?" Matt asked.

"My flowers. I'll do it," Ada snapped.

"Glad to see you refuse to take any of his crap," Josh said.

"I second that." The prime minister waggled her finger at her brother. "Remember, Josh and I owe you. Don't think we've forgotten the way you interfered in our lives."

Ada studied the siblings. She saw exasperation in the prime minister and smugness in Matt.

"He needs knocking down a peg," Josh said. "Ada, we're in your hands. If you show us what to do, we'll get started."

Ada pinched her inner arm. Hard. It hurt, so she figured she was awake, and this wasn't a weird dream caused by eating spicy food late at night. She handed each of the new arrivals a bucket, then stalked over to the end of the row to show what she needed them to do.

"Ashley," Nelson said in a deep voice. "Gerry and I will work on the row either side of you, so we can get to you quickly if necessary."

"Okey-doke," Ashley agreed.

"I'll work beside Frog," Josh said, and his voice held relish.

The army guys had referred to him as Frog, too, and Ada wondered at the nickname's story. She'd ask later. Right now, she needed to get these flowers picked.

It soon became clear Josh, Dillon, and Matt were close friends. They teased and joked and mentioned other army friends as they caught up with what each of them had been doing. She learned Dillon had alpacas while Josh did security work when he wasn't traveling with his wife to Wellington and overseas.

"You're having dinner with the queen?" Matt exclaimed.

Ada glimpsed Josh's expression before he broke into a grin.

"Yeah. Who'd have thought I'd get to chat with Liz and Phillip. The behind-the-scenes people have sent us pages of rules and details of the correct etiquette. It's stressful."

"But you get to go to the palace," Ella said. "I dare you to steal a teaspoon."

"No!" Ashley ordered. "Please don't dare him to do anything."

"Don't worry, sweetheart. I promised to behave. I'm representing you and New Zealand. No teaspoons." He paused. "I might, however, take a photo of the loo."

Dillon and Matt guffawed while Ashley issued a loud groan.

"Don't," she pleaded. "Do not give Josh ideas. Do not give him suggestions. And most of all, do *not* dare Josh to do anything. I'd hate to be the first prime minister to get kicked out of Buckingham Palace. Also, remember, I can place you in jail and throw away the key. I have the power and the security guards to help me."

Silence greeted Ashley's speech.

A laugh escaped Ada, and she clapped one hand over her mouth, almost dropping her picked flowers.

Matt closed the distance between them, took her bucket, and set it on the ground. "Are you siding with Ash?"

"I enjoyed seeing you speechless," Ada said. "Ashley, a masterful stroke."

"I should throw around my weight more often," Ashley said.

Ada chuckled at the mutters coming from the men and continued picking. Although she still couldn't get over the fact the prime minister was picking her flowers, this woman impressed her, even if she'd never agreed with her party's politics.

"What happens to the flowers after you've harvested them?" Ashley asked.

"Why don't you show Ashley the next stage?" Matt suggested. "We'll keep picking while you get a head start. You might get to bed earlier tonight."

"I'd love to see," Ashley said with what appeared genuine interest.

"Ashley, we'll go with you," Gerry said.

"That's fine," Ada said, bemused and unable to get past that this free labor was thanks to Matt. While the workers she'd arranged would've cleared her field in a full day, her harvest was still progressing at a sustainable pace. She'd taken the time to check the forecast. No rain on the horizon. If there were any unpicked flowers, she'd manage them on her own. "Can you carry two of the full buckets for me?"

"Sure." Ashley seized two of the buckets.

Nelson picked up two and Gerry the remaining ones.

"We'll check out the area, then one of us will return to picking," Gerry said.

Ada led the way to her shed. She pulled the keys out of her pocket and unlocked the door.

"You lock your shed during the day?" Nelson asked.

"I've had a few problems with intruders and malicious damage. The last thing I want is for someone to destroy my stock or my drying machine."

Nelson and Gerry shared a glance.

"Have you informed the police?"

"Yes, the police are supportive, but they've had other difficulties recently. Stock rustling is an enormous problem around here, and the police have prioritized the larger crimes. My challenges are minor compared to the ones the farmers are dealing with."

Nelson turned a stern expression on her. "That's not true. Someone murdered your husband. The police have never charged the culprit. Your house burned down. The police understand this, right?"

Ada swallowed hard.

"Stop, Nelson." Ashley turned to Ada and reached for her hand, giving it a quick squeeze. "I'm sorry. My men investigate the people I have dealings with, even if they're family friends. It's part of the job." Her tone was apologetic.

Ada swallowed for a second time. "It's fine." She turned on the lights and pulled the doors fully open. "I separate the petals from the green part and place the petals on the racks. Once the racks are full, I put them in the drier. I usually dry the petals overnight, then they're ready to sell as confetti. I store the finished product in dry containers, and when the orders come in, I pack and ship."

"How are the orders going?" Ashley asked.

"My website has been live for mere days. I shipped my first order this morning."

"Congratulations," Ashley said. "I love the idea of natural confetti. I bet the church committees prefer it too. No cleanup."

"Yes. I intend to blog, do some advertising, and

approach the local ministers to tell them about my product."

"What about wedding shows?"

Ada pulled a face. "I'm a sole-trader. My time is better spent working here at the farm. It's a trade-off. I can't do everything. I figured it would be better to start small and go from there."

"Fair enough. Should we start now?"

"Sure," Ada said.

"We'll be back after we check the vicinity," Nelson rumbled.

"I'll be here. Plucking petals." Ashley waited until her protection officers left before glancing at Ada. "Thanks for inviting me to help. I don't have many opportunities to relax with my friends and family."

"But you're working." Ada protested.

"*Pfff!*" Ashley gave a dismissive wave of her right hand. "This isn't difficult. It's fun. Work is reading a stack of parliamentary briefs and taking in all the information, so I can answer questions and ask intelligent ones of my own."

"Not my idea of fun," Ada agreed.

"Never mind that. Tell me before Nelson and Gerry return. How long have you been dating my brother?"

"What?" Ada gaped at Ashley, then wrested her gaze from the amused prime minister to focus on preparing white delphinium petals. "We don't know each other well."

"Matt likes you. He's never introduced me to his girlfriend before."

"I'm not his girlfriend," Ada protested.

"You don't like him?"

"Yes, I like him—"

"He's protective of you, just like Josh is with me. It's harder to recognize yourself, but after meeting and marrying Josh, I can see it with you and Matt."

"No, I—"

"Stop interrogating the poor girl," Nelson ordered.

"Where's the fun in that?" Ashley asked.

Gerry strode into the shed. "Do you smoke?"

"Me?" Ada asked. "No, I've never smoked."

"Does your brother smoke?" Gerry demanded, his piercing gaze on Ashley.

The sparkle in Ashley's eyes subsided as she took in his serious mien. Her gaze shifted to Nelson. "What's going on, boys?"

Ada sat in frozen shock caused by a combination of their weird behavior and Ashley calling her protection men *boys* in a crisp voice that held none of its previous teasing.

"I found a spot behind your house where someone has loitered for a long time, judging by the number of cigarette butts," Gerry said.

"Behind my house?" Ada asked in a faint voice. "Watching me?"

"That would be our supposition."

Ada gaped at them, her stomach a mass of knots. They meant it. They thought someone was watching her comings and goings.

"Do you know anyone who smokes?" Nelson asked. "A past boyfriend? Someone you've argued with in the past?"

"No! I don't have a boyfriend."

"Aw! Matt's your first. That's so sweet," Ashley cooed.

"Stop teasing her," Gerry said, his tone stern. "It's your brother you should target, not an innocent bystander."

"True," Ashley conceded and calmly continued preparing petals.

Ada followed suit, so she didn't have to see Nelson's or Gerry's serious expressions because they scared her rigid. Someone was spying on her. She'd sensed a frisson of something a time or two but shrugged away the horrid sensation. She hadn't wanted to believe her senses, and dwelling on bad things made the situation worse when she had no proof.

"Ada?" Nelson prompted.

"I told you I've had a few incidents I've reported to the police."

"Such as?" Ashley asked.

"Graffiti spray-painted on my shed. A note pinned to an open gate that was closed when I went to bed. And last night, someone draped offal over my fence. Matt removed it and buried it for me."

"Ada!" Ashley's sympathetic gaze brought heat and a sting to Ada's eyes. Ashley's gaze went distant for an instant, and she shuddered.

"That's terrible. I have experienced something similar, so I sympathize."

"What did the police say?" Gerry prompted.

"They have a record of each incident plus photos. To be honest, they're overworked. There is a crime wave in the area and the neighboring towns. The infringements here are nuisance ones and given low priority."

"This is so frustrating," Ashley said. "We're training more police officers, yet since times are tough, there is an element of society who take the simple way to feed their families or supply their drink or drug habits. My party and I are doing our best, but it's difficult to strike the correct balance."

"Should you be telling me this?" Ada asked. "I'm a farmer, and we traditionally vote for your opposition."

Nelson guffawed, and even Gerry grinned. Ashley shook her head and made a tsking sound.

Ada smiled briefly, then sobered. "Are these signs recent?"

"It's hard to say," Gerry said. "If you like, I can photograph the scene and remove the cigarette butts. Get Matt to check for you tomorrow to see if there are any new butts on the ground."

"Your peeping Tom sounds careless or stupid," Ashley said.

Ada shrugged, the knots in her stomach tightening. It was plain creepy, especially since she spent so much time on her own. "What would you recommend?"

"I'd clear the butts from the scene. That will work short term. Other than that, your best bet is to install cameras."

Ada breathed out her frustration. "I can't afford that." *Besides, if you don't repay the loan and make a profit, security is a moot point.* She'd lose everything, anyway. "Can you show me where they're standing?"

"Sure." Gerry gestured her to precede him. "I'll show you now."

Ada rose. "I'll be back in a moment."

Ashley waved her away. "No problem. I'll show Nelson what to do and set him to work."

As Ada followed Gerry from her shed, Nelson's rumble of complaint and Ashley's chiding laughter followed her. In contrast, apprehension made her steps wooden while

145

her pulse thudded, the sound echoing through her mind with a deafening *bang-bang-bang*.

Gerry led her across the open space between her shed and tiny house, then took the path to her washing line. He continued past her garden of hydrangeas and finally halted when he came to an old totara tree. Its trunk was wide enough to conceal an adult.

"Stop." Gerry pulled out his cell phone. He pointed out the cigarette butts and snapped several photos. There was a dozen or more littering the ground. Fear sliced through the knots filling her stomach, and for a fleeting second, she thought she might barf. From here, a person could see right into her bedroom. Watch her dress. Undress.

"That's my bedroom," Ada whispered.

"You're probably looking at a man then," Gerry said, his demeanor calm. Kind. "You'd better report this, and from now on, pull your curtains and lock your doors if you're alone."

Ada swallowed hard. "I'm alone most of the time."

"If I were you, I'd get a friend to stay with you," Gerry said.

Ada ran through her options. Sherry would stay with her if she asked. But no. That would raise too many questions. And even worse, Sherry might send one or both of her sons to keep Ada safe. No! Not an option.

"I need to work." She strode away from Gerry with straight shoulders and her chin lifted when she wanted to hide and curl up in a ball, preferably in a dark room.

This wasn't fair, and the why ate at her.

Why would someone torment her in this way? She was a decent person. Abrupt. True. And it would be right to say she was slow to build friendships. Still, after everything she'd been through—the nosy and morbid interest in her personal life, the accusations she'd killed Greg—the armor she'd constructed to protect herself was understandable.

Ada stalked into her shed and resumed work.

"Everything okay?" Ashley asked, finally.

"Everything is peachy," Ada said. "Just peachy."

Chapter 12

Matt Gets a Lecture

THE SCENT OF COOKING meat and ketchup filled the air. Matt swallowed the last of his steak and pushed away his plate. He enjoyed hanging out with his friends and sister, although Ada worried him. She'd become quieter and more withdrawn as the day progressed. She'd answer questions if anyone spoke directly to her, but something more was bothering her than the latest prank. He didn't think it was anything he'd done.

It was late afternoon, and they'd picked most of the flowers. The rest they'd pick tomorrow since Ella had promised to return with a friend to help Ada. Josh and Dillon had cranked up the barbecue, and they were all filling empty stomachs and having a well-earned beer.

"Matt," Ashley whispered.

He smiled at his little sister. Not so little or unimportant now. He was proud of her, and he was thrilled his careful planning and maneuvering had pushed Ashley and Josh together. A masterstroke. "Yes?"

"Can I have a word in private?"

"Sure." He stood and reached for his sister's hand. "Come and see Ada's wildflowers. They're pretty and would make an excellent post on your social media pages. Do you have your phone?"

"I'd love to see the wildflowers," Ashley enthused. "I've already taken photos of the flower fields and the finished dried petals."

Nelson stood to follow, and Gerry bolted down the last of his sausage and bread, prepared to trail them too.

"We're walking over there and will be within visual distance," Matt said. "Can you watch from here?"

Nelson and Gerry communicated in silence.

"Yes," Nelson said. "Don't take too long."

"Sure. What's up?" Matt asked as soon as they were out of earshot.

"Ada. Did she tell you?"

Matt stopped walking and turned to his sister. "Tell me what?"

"Nelson and Gerry did their normal sweep after they

arrived. Gerry found a spot where they believe someone watches Ada."

Anger flashed through Matt while his muscles tensed. "A peeping Tom?"

"Gerry says the spot has a direct line of sight into Ada's bedroom."

"Fuck," Matt bit off the curse, but it wasn't enough to calm the angst that slapped him. "Someone is out to rattle Ada, and judging by how quiet she's been this afternoon, they've succeeded."

"What will you do?"

"I'll stay with Ada as much as I can, but I need to conduct night exercises as part of the training."

"Could Dillon and Ella help short-term? Gerry suggested she install cameras and a security system."

"What did she say to that?"

"Nothing much," Ashley said. "She shrugged and told us she needed to get back to work. Matt, I like her. I learned her background because Nelson did his normal sweep. She's had a tough life. The murder of her husband then losing her house in a fire. It's obvious she works hard."

"I get the impression her future rests on this crop of flowers."

Ashley tipped up her head, and the corners of her mouth curled a fraction upward. "You like her."

"I do," Matt confirmed. "She's prickly and strong. Stubborn. I admire her tenacious nature. Her determination to succeed, despite the odds. She wasn't born in the country. She lived in Auckland until her marriage. Country life is new to her. Most women would've left after what she has gone through."

"Do you have a plan?" Ashley asked.

"Not yet. I'll hang around and hope like hell I can be here when she needs me. My gut says this person hasn't finished with her yet."

"Are you sleeping with her?" Ashley paused. "Matt, you can't do your usual kiss and run. Not with Ada. You can't cause her extra pain. If all you're interested in is a fling, leave now. Don't hurt her any more than you need to."

Matt's brows rose, and he glared. "Who mentioned leaving?"

"You're serious about her?" Surprise sounded in his sister's voice. "I saw you liked her, but I thought—"

"Our relationship might not have gone far yet, but I'm not here for a casual fling. I want more."

Ashley's gaze narrowed. "You haven't slept with her?"

"None of your business."

Ashley snorted. "You say that to me." She stepped closer and poked him in the chest. "After what you did to Josh and me?"

"You love Josh. Besides, I had a feeling he'd like you, and he did. I knew he'd keep you safe from your stalker. I was right, wasn't I?"

"That is beside the point. You interfered in my life. Josh's life and you were smug once everything went the way you'd planned."

Matt's good humor faded. "Fair enough, but I did it because I thought you'd be perfect for each other. I saw an opportunity and took it. Be honest. If I'd introduced you under normal circumstances, you would've been polite but walked away because of your goal to be the prime minister. You were in danger, and you needed him. Josh needed you too because he didn't have a path forward after the army."

Ashley rolled her eyes. "While there might be truth in your words, you need to cease acting smug about fixing us up without either of us being aware of your behind-the-scenes maneuvering."

"You're right," Matt said. "In fairness, Josh is a good friend, and you're my sister. I care about you both, and I wanted you to be happy. You're perfect for each other."

"Which leads me back to Ada. She's fragile."

"Ada?"

"Yeah. A person can only get up so many times before they give up."

"Ada isn't like that. She's strong."

"I see her strength, but she zones out sometimes, and the place where she goes during those moments—she's not robust there. She's here on her own, and she needs help."

That stung because he was doing his best. "I am helping Ada."

"I know, but she internalizes a lot of what is happening in her life. To me, she looks like a woman under enormous strain. I mean—this morning's offal debacle, and now she's learned she has a creeper spying on her in the privacy of her home. That person has destroyed her precious haven."

"I intend to stay with her until I have to go back for the next training session."

"Do you think Ada would let Josh stopover when you can't? He can help with practical security measures. I haven't suggested it to him yet, but he's between jobs at the moment. I'm spending the next two to three weeks in Wellington since a lot is happening with the cabinet and parliament. You'd be doing Josh and me a favor by giving him an assignment."

"Yes." Matt didn't have to consider the suggestion. Josh would protect Ada. Matt didn't even care if Josh and Ash teased the hell out of him for the next five years. When he left, he wanted to know Ada was safe while he couldn't take care of her security personally. "I'd appreciate Josh's help."

"Right. I'm heading back to Wellington tomorrow. Josh was going to stay with Ella and Dillon, but it sounds as if they'll be here to help as their farm and jobs allow."

"Thank you." Matt hugged his sister.

"I like her very much," Ashley said once she pulled away. "Don't mess up."

Matt chuckled. "No pressure."

·❤·❤·❤·❤·❤·

ONCE MATT'S FRIENDS AND sister left, Ada turned to him in gratitude. "Thank you. Everyone has helped so much today. I might have an early night."

Matt strode to her, his eyes intent and severe for once. "You should rest. It's not right for you to exhaust yourself."

"It's only short term until I make a profit. Once I've picked the bulk of the flowers, my days won't be as long."

Matt brushed a lock of black hair off her cheek and thumbed away a smudge of dirt from her chin with a tenderness that turned her breathless. "You're exhausted. Why don't we finish early? You have a shower while I cook dinner."

"I didn't get around to shopping. I'm embarrassed to admit if you hadn't purchased food, my guests would've gone hungry. How much do I owe you?"

"Unnecessary. Everyone enjoyed helping. Otherwise, they wouldn't have volunteered to come back tomorrow. I grabbed meat pies from the bakery when I bought the bread. I figured I'd heat those for dinner and make a salad or cook peas to go with them."

"You don't have to look after me." But oh, having someone fuss over her was so nice.

"You're not an imposition. I like you, Ada, and I want to get to know you better. I'd love to kiss you, but right now, you're exhausted. My efforts are better placed in feeding you and getting you to rest."

She stilled as warmth radiated across her skin. "What does that mean? The liking part, I mean." She waited anxiously for his reply, like a giddy schoolgirl in the throes of a crush.

Matt stroked her cheek, and his touch seared clear to her toes. This man was dangerous, and not just in the soldier sense. He endangered her equilibrium. She wasn't sure what to think, how to act.

"It means I'd like to kiss you again, but I'd also enjoy taking that kissing to its natural conclusion."

"Sex?" Her reply came close to a squawk.

Matt leaned closer to kiss the tip of her nose. "Hell, yes, I mean sex. You're gorgeous, and I admire you—the goals you've set for yourself and your work ethic. You're an incredible woman."

Ada frowned, but she had to force herself to make that expression. It wouldn't do for Matt to think he could win her so easily. Yet he tempted her more than any other man since Greg. She forced herself to step away and instantly hated the separation. "I...I need to think," she mumbled.

"The last thing I want is to pressure you," Matt said.

"It's not that. This is a lot," she said finally, even though he was a temptation magnet, drawing her to him without effort.

"Do you have any idea who might want to peer through your bedroom window?"

"Craig or Eddie come to mind, but as far as I know, neither of them smoke. Sherry, their mother, is very anti-smoking. She's always been outspoken, and I remember her encouraging the local council to make it illegal for smokers to stand outside their place of work during their breaks." She shrugged, rubbing her chest to release the resulting tension. Someone spying on her. Neither of her in-laws smoked and sneaking around wasn't their style. They preferred face-to-face gloating. The knowledge of the unauthorized scrutiny prickled her skin and had her longing to wash. "I don't know."

"Men you've dated?"

"Huh! Who has time for that? I spend my free time sleeping. The rest of the time, I work."

Matt cupped her cheek, lifted her chin so their gazes met. "I understand you have goals, but you can't continue working full-out. You know that, right?"

Ada jerked from his touch, annoyed even as she acknowledged his truth. She couldn't stop until she secured Greg's land. It was her way of honoring him. "It's none of your business."

Instead of taking umbrage, Matt dipped his head. "Let's eat and relax. Are you certain you don't have a telly somewhere in one of those cupboards?"

Ada had difficulty holding back her laugh. "No, if I want to watch a show, I drag out my tablet or use my laptop."

"Tablet," he said immediately. "We can share, and it'll be an excellent excuse to cuddle."

Heat roared through Ada at the intensity in his gaze. She focused on her feet to regain her equilibrium. This man. She wasn't sure what to do with him.

Matt decided for her by taking her left hand in his and dragging her toward her tiny house. She jolted a fraction at their first touch, suddenly breathless. Lordy, she hadn't felt this zing, this awareness of a man in so long, not since the early days dating Greg. She'd loved her husband and settled into country life as best she could. Their parting from his family had been tough, and the turmoil had brought them closer.

"Where did your mind go?"

"My husband."

Matt stilled, his cheerful expression wiping clean. "Do you want me to back off?"

Ada squeezed his fingers and tugged on his hand to command his attention. "That's not what I meant." She sucked in a breath to bolster her courage. "I loved my husband, and he loved me, but he's gone. The years have passed since someone killed him, and the memories aren't as sharp. It's harder to picture Greg's face. This is a roundabout way of saying I'm feeling the same pull I felt when I met Greg at a rugby after-match. I like you."

Matt's slow grin shoved her pulse into a choppy beat. A sizzle sped the length of her body, and she licked her lower lip as awareness pulsed between them.

"Most women wouldn't admit an attraction," he whispered.

"I'm not most women."

"I understand that, and that's part of my fascination with you. You don't flirt or play games." He rolled his eyes. "A lot of women chase soldiers, especially if they suspect you're in an elite squad."

"Responsibilities change a person. Before I met Greg, I was more carefree. Now, my future depends on me working hard."

"All work and no play isn't good for a body," Matt said. "That's according to my grandmother. She'll like you."

He wanted her to meet his family. She thought about that. He'd already introduced her to his sister—the prime minister. Maybe he was serious.

"My grandfather was one for spouting sayings all the time."

Ada opened the front door of her tiny house, and Matt scowled.

"You should lock your house while you're working in the paddocks. You're isolated. It's too easy for someone to sneak around, especially with so much native bush surrounding your home."

If he thought she'd argue the point, he was wrong. "You're right. I'll take more care with security. Ashley's protection guys reckon I should set up a security system. I can't afford that."

"The first year of business and money is tight. I understand," Matt said. "We'll think of something. Take a shower while I start on our meal."

"You don't have to make dinner. You've already done so

much for me today."

"I want to. Relax for ten minutes. I bought a bottle of white wine. You can have one once you've cleaned up."

"Now there's an incentive," she said. "I haven't had a glass of wine for months."

Showering while Matt was around felt as intimate as it had the previous evening. While the water poured over her head, she considered her next move. Even if this was a fling, she was walking into the relationship with her eyes wide open. She wanted him, and she'd have him for as long as he wanted her in return.

Ada wandered into the kitchen, this time fully dressed since she'd taken a change of clothes with her. Matt had the oven on, and a savory aroma wafted on the air. He also had a salad underway.

"I thought we'd keep it simple."

"Works for me," she said.

"Let me pour you a glass of wine."

"You'll find a set of wineglasses in the cupboard on your right."

"You do like white wine?"

Ada grinned, wide and honest, and full rein. "I've never met a wine I haven't liked. Most people prefer a white over a red, or vice versa. Me—I like both."

"Good to know." Matt opened her cupboard to peer

inside. He removed two glasses and filled them. He handed her one and raised the remaining one in a toast. "To a successful harvest. May you receive many online orders."

"To success and mega orders," she repeated with excitement.

"I've put on the oven timer. I should have time to have a shower before it buzzes."

She nodded. "I'll get out the place-settings."

By the time Matt returned, his hair wet, she was watching the early news on her tablet. She tried to remember when she'd last done this—relaxing with a pre-dinner drink—and couldn't recall. It told her Matt was right. She was a dull workaholic. Once she'd picked her flowers, she'd aim for better balance. Maybe she could get back to running before she started her day. Or attend the yoga class at the local gym—something she'd always wanted to try.

Her phone rang, diverting her thoughts.

She glanced at the screen and didn't recognize the number. "Hello, Ada Buckingham speaking,"

"It's Johnathon Brookes at the local police station. I understand you've had problems today, and I wanted to check in with you before I head home."

"Yes," Ada said. Usually, she didn't receive follow-up calls from the cops. She swiveled slightly to study Matt's expression. "Someone decorated my fence with offal this morning while visitors discovered an area where it appears someone has set up camp to watch my house."

"The prime minister stopped by the station this afternoon. Her protection team told me about your peeping Tom."

"Oh." She hadn't seen that coming.

"They expressed their concerns for your safety."

"I see." Well, she thought she did. Because someone in authority had championed her, the police had followed through and made contact. The adage—it wasn't what you knew but who.

"Contact us should you have any further concerns. If you require our advice regarding security measures, we'd be happy to help. Do you have anyone who can stay with you?"

"Yes," Ada said politely. Once Matt left, she'd take stock again. "Thank you."

The police officer concluded the call, and Ada stared at her phone, then shook her head.

"What's wrong?"

"Your sister stopped at the police station on the way back to Eketāhuna. She and her protection team spoke to the police about what they found today."

Matt removed her phone from nerveless fingers. After

he set it aside, he wrapped her in a hug. Ada held herself stiff before relaxing and accepting the comfort he offered.

"How are you doing?" he murmured against her hair.

"Am I in danger?"

"You'd be a fool to ignore the finding today. You need to close your curtains at night, lock your doors, and keep your house locked when you're working elsewhere. And you need to keep your phone on you at all times. Make sure it's charged. Stay aware of your surroundings instead of zoning out."

Matt made sense, yet she loathed watching everyone in her life with suspicion. She pushed back to see his face. "How do I know I can trust you?"

His gaze narrowed before he flashed her a quick grin. "Touché. You're right to question me. It means you're taking the situation seriously. But for the record, I've been back in New Zealand for a month. Before that, I was with my team in Afghanistan. I slept on your couch last night and never left your house until this morning. You might be a sound sleeper, but I promise I didn't drape intestines over your fence. You witnessed my arrival when I crashed into your flowers."

"I don't think you're the culprit," Ada said with a frown. "First, you have a lot of respect for your sister, and I doubt you'd do anything to upset her. Also, from what

I've seen, you don't smoke. I've never seen you touch a cigarette, nor do you smell like an ashtray."

"Thanks," he said, his tone dry.

"And last, you've been working with your men. I doubt you've had time to harass me."

"I haven't been alone often," Matt added.

"Which answers your question. I can rule you out because you've had chaperones."

Matt drew her nearer again and pressed a kiss to the top of her head. He tipped up her head, smiled at her, then slowly kissed her. His kiss started soft until Ada released a groan, craving more. He traced the seam of her mouth, and the second she opened for him, he took control. Driving her pleasure. Taking pleasure for himself.

A foreign sound intruded, and it took her a second to recognize the ring of her phone. Matt pulled away, and Ada tsked in protest.

"It's probably a prank call."

"What?" he said, transferring from lover to soldier in a blink. "Have you received prank calls before?"

"No, I meant telemarketing calls. I misspoke."

The phone rang again.

"Are you going to answer that?"

"Yes," Ada said and answered her phone. "Hello?"

"Ada, it's Sherry Walsh. I was about to give up! I

still have one stall site available for the farmers' market tomorrow. Are you positive you want to waste this opportunity?" Sherry sounded her normal enthusiastic self, and her cheerfulness lightened Ada's mood.

"Actually, Sherry. I have been thinking about the market. I'd love to take the empty spot for tomorrow and every weekend after that if it's available."

"Sold to my beautiful neighbor," Sherry chirped. "Ada, I'm so pleased you've changed your mind. I know your sales might've disappointed you last time, but I've been advertising the market in the local papers and on the radio. As long as the weather holds, I'm positive we'll have an exceptional turnout."

"Fantastic. I'll be there on time. Do I pay you at the office for the stall?"

"Please," Sherry said. "You've made the right decision. The market will be an additional income stream for you."

"Yes," Ada agreed. "Thanks for thinking of me."

"I'm your neighbor. We have to look after each other. I'll see you tomorrow." And with that, Sherry disconnected the call.

Ada set her phone back on the charger and turned to Matt. "I'm selling flowers at the farmers' market tomorrow and hopefully some of my confetti."

"Is it profitable?"

"I made a hundred dollars last time." She wrinkled her nose. "That didn't cover the damage to my tires, but who knows. If I can get the word-of-mouth thing going, it will be worth the time."

"When does the market start?"

"Nine. I need to be there half an hour beforehand to pay for my stall and organize my flowers. The market finishes between one and two in the afternoon. Earlier, if I sell all my stock."

"When will you pick the flowers?"

"In the morning is best."

Archie strolled from Ada's bedroom and meowed.

"I grabbed cans of cat food while I was shopping," Matt said.

"You did? Thanks, that was very thoughtful of you."

Matt shrugged. "No big deal."

Maybe not to him, but his care warmed her inside.

The timer buzzed, and Matt retreated to take the pies from the oven. "Dinner is served."

Although the pie wasn't homemade, Ada enjoyed every mouthful. They'd worked hard, and now that she'd slowed, exhaustion weighted her limbs. She helped Matt with the dishes.

"Would you like another glass of wine?" Matt asked.

"No, but I'd love a cup of tea. I usually sit outside and

listen to the night sounds."

"You won't be doing that any longer," Matt said, his voice a trifle strident.

Ada lifted her head to meet his determined gaze. "As much as I hate to agree with you, you're right. If I'm on my own, I'll be inside with the door locked."

"Good girl."

"Why do I feel as if I should wag my tail?" Ada said.

Matt grinned, and it was a punch to her heart. Man, she was in trouble. This man would leave eventually, once he completed his training sessions. But wasn't a little fun better than nothing? Yes, he'd mentioned kissing, but that didn't mean permanence.

"I'm glad you're listening to commonsense."

"Can we sit outside?"

"Yeah," Matt agreed. "I'll make tea. Stay inside until it's made, and we'll go out together. I don't want any surprises."

Ada sat on a barstool and watched Matt as he made her tea. The man was observant since he found her tea caddy without a long search.

"What sort do you want?"

"Peppermint, please."

Once he'd made the tea, he paused in the doorway, blocking Ada's outdoors access. She shoved at his shoulder.

"Wait. Check the vicinity. Clear," he said after a few minutes.

"Thank you very much," she said, aiming for sweet.

He chuckled. "I know you're capable, sweetheart. But I'm here to help."

Ada plonked onto one of her outside chairs and held out her hand for her tea. "I sit out here with Archie and plan my list of chores."

"You enjoy a ritual."

"There's nothing wrong with liking a routine."

"Defensive, much?" He sipped his tea, and his eyes twinkled, or maybe it was the moonlight highlighting his humor.

Ada yawned and clapped her hand over her mouth.

"You're exhausted."

"I am tired," she agreed.

"Finish your tea and sleep."

"It's still early," she protested.

"Doesn't matter. You want to pick your flowers early and organize what you need for your stall. If you get a decent sleep, you'll be on your game tomorrow."

"True." Ada drank more of her tea as an owl cried out. "I love hearing the morepork."

"You have a slice of heaven here."

"That's why I enjoy sitting out here after dinner. The stars are so bright, and I hear the owls' call. Archie comes out here with me, and it's peaceful."

"You won't sit out here when I'm not here or when you're alone," Matt ordered.

"I get it. I do. I'm not stupid." She spoiled her indignation with a wide yawn.

Ada finished the last of her tea and rose. "I'm heading to bed now."

Matt remained sitting on the deck and listening to the sounds of the night. An insect clicked over to his right. Archie jumped onto his lap and purred his pleasure when Matt stroked him. Somewhere in the distance, a throaty engine fired to life. The neighbors, Matt guessed.

The engine roar continued, then receded as if the vehicle was heading away from the neighbor's place.

Peace reigned as Matt finished his tea. He sat for a bit longer before standing and going inside. The cat followed and jumped onto the couch where Matt had slept the previous night.

It was quiet inside too. Ada's bedroom lay in darkness. Matt hesitated, then stripped to his boxer-briefs. Barefooted, he padded into Ada's bedroom and joined her on the bed. If she objected in the morning, he'd blame

Archie. The cat had made himself at home on the couch, and Matt hadn't wanted to disturb him.

Whether Ada would argue, he wasn't sure, but it didn't matter. He was claiming half of her double bed, and if she didn't wake to object, that was on her.

CHAPTER 13

STUD BULL RECCY

A SICKLE MOON HUNG in the sky, and it flirted with the cloud cover, making the night darker than average. Ralph Dawson stabbed the button to open the window on the passenger's side. He observed the dozing stock. The mournful cry of an owl rang out, and he shivered. "Are these the right animals?"

The man at the wheel grunted. "They're stud bulls and worth over ten-thousand dollars a head. We can nab them easily, and I have a buyer farther north who won't ask questions."

"Won't someone notice them grazing among other cattle?"

"That's the beauty of the plan—it's a secluded property.

The buyer checks his cattle several days a week. If anyone else sees the bulls amidst the herd, my buyer will play dumb. *They weren't there last time I checked my stock. I have no clue where they came from.* Meantime, most of his cows will be in calf, and the progeny will be worth a decent amount of money. That's what we're selling, which is why these bulls will go to three properties, all carefully selected. If the cops discover the bulls, we'll still make a profit. If they don't, we'll move the bulls to a second property and repeat the sequence later."

Ralph nodded his understanding. It was an innovative strategy. "Sounds like a workable plan, if we can whisk the bulls away without the owner twigging."

"That's where the rest of our scheme comes into play. We take them tomorrow night when the owner and his wife celebrate their fortieth wedding anniversary. Their kids have given them a hotel voucher for a night in Wellington and booked them a romantic dinner."

"How did you find out?"

The man tapped the side of his nose, his grin broad and confident. "Never you mind. Are you in? I need help to yard the bulls and load them onto my truck. One hour of work tops."

Ralph hesitated. He couldn't get caught and upset his wife again. She was always at him to work hard because they needed the money. "Are you positive no one will interfere? This paddock is close to the house."

His prospective boss started the vehicle and drove away from the property. "The house will be empty. The son lives at home, but he stays with his girlfriend during the weekend. He'll notice the bulls missing the next day, but tomorrow night, it will be a straightforward job. Do you want in or not?"

"Yes." Ralph didn't hesitate, even though the bold plan had butterflies loop-d-looping in his gut. He swallowed to moisten his dry mouth. "How much does the job pay?" A lot counted on the answer since he was taking a tremendous risk despite the man's assurances.

"One thousand dollars buys your help and your silence. You bring your dogs to yard the bulls and help us get them on the truck. You don't discuss this with anyone or tell anyone your destination. You don't flash money around town or start spending up large and attract attention."

"One thousand dollars?" Jubilation filled Ralph since this would take care of his gambling debt, and he'd have a little over to give to his wife. Janice would never learn of his stupidity. This was his chance to fix his mistakes, and all he needed to do was help for an hour and forget everything afterward.

"That's my last offer," the driver said in a harsh voice.

"What if I decide not to help?" Ralph bit his tongue and wished he'd remained silent. The expression on the driver's face, his sharp inhalation, told Ralph he'd blundered.

"That boy of yours who you're so proud of?"

Ralph understood a threat aimed at him. "You wouldn't!"

"Don't test my resolve. You either do the job and keep quiet, or you don't. Either way, any whisper of this plan reaches my ears or the cops, your son will face danger."

"I'll do it," Ralph blurted.

The driver's toothy smile glinted inside the dim interior of the vehicle. "Excellent. You will receive your payment once we load the bulls. Do you have questions?"

"Where should I meet you? I'll need my vehicle to bring my two dogs with me."

"I suggest you park in the same place we stopped tonight. Anything else?"

"No," Ralph said.

"Excellent. Meet us here at seven tomorrow night. It will be dark with no neighbors to see something they shouldn't."

Ralph jerked his head in compliance. "Tomorrow night at seven."

The driver headed straight to the town and dropped Ralph in the pub car park. Although tempted to grab a drink or two to steady his nerves, Ralph headed home. Janice and Scott might enjoy his company for a change. He unlocked his vehicle and climbed inside, fully sober for the first time in months.

He'd do this thing and move on. Be a better husband. A better father.

Yeah, he'd turn over a new leaf and become a man to make his wife and son proud.

CHAPTER 14

MATT MAKES HIS MOVE

MATT WOKE WITH A feminine body pressed against his back. With satisfaction, he closed his eyes again and let himself drift. He wanted to do this—wake in this manner for the rest of his life.

Incredible.

Astonishing, really.

He smiled. Crazy, since he hadn't thought he'd want to settle with one woman. Ada had altered everything, and he hadn't done anything more than kiss her.

That would change.

Soon.

He made the promise to himself even as he drifted closer to sleep.

Ada Buckingham was the woman he wanted and one he'd protect with everything he had. His woman. She just didn't know it yet.

·❤ · ❤ · ❤ · ❤ · ❤·

ADA WOKE SLOWLY, THE familiar dawn chorus dragging her from sleep.

Warmth filled her, and for once, the alarm clock wasn't wailing, yanking her from a cozy bed. Her eyes flicked open, but she didn't move a muscle as she attempted to ascertain what the extra warmth meant. The last time she'd felt this safe, this secure had been when Greg was still alive.

The thought had her stiffening. Then, she sprang off the mattress, almost face-planting when her feet tangled in the covers. She whirled, heart thumping in an adrenaline frenzy. Still in a crouch, she stared at the man lying on her bed, his blue eyes regarding her in amusement.

Ada rose to glare at him. "What are you doing?"

"The couch is too short, and Archie claimed it before I could. You sleep on one side of your bed, so I made an executive decision. Besides, I stated my intentions last night. I didn't push because I'm not a moron. But in my world, in my thoughts, wanting to kiss you, sleeping beside you, and enjoying innocent physical contact is part of the deal."

Ada blinked, part of her wanting to laugh. The man had a cheek. But he was correct. He had told her what he had in mind, and she'd agreed to his proposal. "Next time, give me a warning. Given everything happening around here, I'm a bit jumpy."

Matt propped himself up on one elbow, and the sheet fell away to reveal his chest. His splendid bare chest.

"Are you naked under there?"

"Wanna come here and find out for yourself?" A teasing smile played around his sensual lips.

"Is that a dare?"

"Do you want me to dare you?"

Ada released an inelegant snort and shook her head. She scooped up a pair of jeans and the rest of her discarded clothes from the previous evening. While part of her wanted to retreat and find privacy to finish dressing, Ada whipped off her pajama top and put on her bra. Seconds later, she pulled on a T-shirt. She replaced the pajama pants with her jeans.

Without checking his reaction, she said, "Do you want tea?"

"And toast," he said. "I'm starving."

Barefooted, she padded to the doorway.

"Like the pajamas," he murmured.

She paused, waiting to learn if he'd say more.

"Also, I enjoyed the show. Can't wait to run my hands over that silky skin of yours."

His teasing words prodded her to move while her brain stumbled over her reaction. He was pushing her, yet she didn't feel coerced, pressured, fearful, and an entire thesaurus of similar words.

Yep, the truth was she liked Matt, and he was right. He'd stated his intentions, allowing her an opportunity to reject his overture. She hadn't.

His army training had turned him into a leader, made him decisive. Yet he displayed an inherent kindness. Her grandmother would've called him a gentleman and spoken of his actions with approval. Ada nodded as she filled her kettle. If she told him no or asked him to leave, he'd respect her decision—even if her verdict contradicted what he wanted.

This made her confident in her resolve to enjoy Matt's company. Ada pulled blinds and opened curtains, letting the early morning light into her home. With each window uncovered, tension rose in her. What lurked outside to scare her today? But she found not a thing out of place.

"Nothing to see here," she murmured.

Archie meowed at the door. Ada let him outside, but instead of wandering outdoors, she scanned her driveway.

All seemed peaceful. The last of her tension seeped away as a thrush landed on her shed rooftop and burst into song.

"Any problems?"

Ada turned to smile at Matt. "I couldn't see, hear, or smell anything wrong."

"Excellent start to the day," Matt drawled. "Should I do the toast?"

"Please."

"Which flowers will you pick today? We've picked most of your delphiniums."

"I have stock ready for picking." She paused. "I might do bouquets of wildflowers and round out those with a few stems of delphiniums."

"What about your confetti? I didn't think you bagged that until you received an order."

"I've sample packs to give anyone who shows interest. Last time, I sold some, but I think samples are best. If anyone wants confetti straightaway, I can take their order and bag it for them tonight."

"Will you have time to make samples?"

"Sure, because you're going to help me."

He cracked a grin. "I might demand a payment for my help."

"Like what?" She was flirting with him. Her pulse rate did a bit of a change-up as she awaited his response.

"*Hmm*," he said as if he was considering his reply.

The unholy gleam in his eyes warned her he had something in mind already. Ada lifted her chin and retreated to take care of the tea. She pulled the milk out of the fridge and handed Matt the loaf of bread.

"I enjoy seeing the rise of your stubborn chin. The challenge in your pretty brown eyes. When we met, you acted closed off. We're good for each other, I think." He sidled closer and hip-bumped her. "You're coming out of your shell."

Ada opened her mouth to snap at him. The wretched man was teasing, prodding her into an emotional reaction. "Make the toast," she said because she didn't trust herself to respond and keep her dignity. "I'm hungry."

Matt's phone rang as the toast popped up.

"What do you want on yours? Strawberry jam or vegemite? I might have peanut butter."

"One of each," he said as he retreated to get his phone.

Ada buttered the toast and added the spreads. She was enjoying her toast and vegemite when Matt returned. He continued to speak on his phone and listen while sipping the tea she handed him.

"Great. See you later." Matt hung up. "Ella asked if it was okay if she brought a girlfriend with her. I told her yes."

"That's fine. Are you sure your brothers want to return for a second day? You told them not to come until this afternoon, right?"

"Nope. They'll be here soon. They've already left Eketāhuna."

"But I can't be here when I've promised Sherry I'll take the market stall." If she canceled now, Sherry would never repeat this opportunity.

"Do you trust me to follow your instructions?" Matt asked.

"Yes," she said without hesitation.

"Then tell me what you want to happen, and I'll supervise here. When Ella learned about the market, she said she'd go with you because she'd thought about trying a stall. She's thrilled to see how everything works. If you're agreeable, Ella will help you while we take care of picking and anything else you want us to do."

"I feel as if I'm taking advantage."

"Ada, you're doing us a favor."

"How?" she demanded because all she saw was hard work, dry hands from picking, and aching limbs.

"If you haven't noticed, Josh, Dillon, and I are soldiers. We trained and worked together. Civilian life is more difficult, and we do better if we keep busy. You're helping us to do something together. A project, if you will, while reinforcing our bonds. Believe me, working at picking flowers is a lot healthier than meeting at the pub."

Put that way, Ada understood. "I appreciate your help."

"I know," Matt said. "We wouldn't want to help you if you took us for granted. You don't."

"Thanks." She swallowed her last mouthful of toast and the dregs of her tea. "I'd better pick those flowers. I can't be late this morning. The parking lot fills up fast, and I want to park as close as possible rather than offer a vandal another go at my vehicle. Foot traffic is heavier near the market entrance."

"Go," Matt urged. "I'll clean up here before I come to help."

With a picking plan in mind, Ada gathered her clippers and went straight to her wildflower plot. By the time Matt joined her, she'd moved on to the stock.

"These flowers remind me of my grandmother," Matt said. "My father's mother. She used to grow them every summer, and walking through her garden was like entering a perfume store. She told me as a youngster she aimed to attract the bees and other insects to help her pollinate her fruit trees." He grinned. "When I used to stay with her, she'd have me climbing trees to pick the higher fruit. She broke her arm, trying to pick apples, and after that, my dad and his brother told her she had to get someone in to pick her fruit."

"Did she?"

"She mostly followed their order, but she had a mischievous streak. I think she placated them and did what she wanted when they weren't there."

"Is she still alive?"

"No, she passed away two years ago. I didn't attend her funeral because I was overseas, but man, I miss her. She was excellent at gardening. Had a green thumb for sure, but her cooking was horrid. Mum used to send me with a suitcase of snacks whenever I'd stay with her. If we visited, Mum would take food or tell Dad he was taking us out for a meal at the local pub."

Ada laughed. "I thought all grannies were fantastic cooks."

Matt shuddered. "Not mine. Ask Ashley if you don't believe me. Our other gran won awards for her baking. We ate well when we visited her."

Ada picked for several minutes, handing the stems to Matt to hold.

"What do you want us to do today?"

"Work on the last few rows of unpicked flowers, I think."

A loud moo rent the air, and Ada stiffened. "That sounded close."

"We shut the roadside gate," Matt said.

Another moo sounded, this one closer.

Matt cursed. "You finish sorting out your flowers. I'll investigate the cattle."

"Delphinium is poisonous to most animals," Ada said.

"They must be outside your property because the gate was still closed when I came out to help you." He disappeared around the corner, grunted another louder curse.

Her flowers. No. Please, not her flowers. She'd had enough bad luck. Didn't she deserve a break? Ada picked up as many flowers as she could carry, rushing to get them in water so she could help Matt.

A vehicle pulled up. A horn honked.

"Open the gate," Matt roared. "Come and help me before these bloody cows do any further damage."

Ada rounded the edge of her shed and almost dropped her armful of flowers. Three cows rushed through her unpicked flowers, crushing the plants beneath their bulky bodies. Several other animals grazed on the grassy borders.

Ella rushed to her side, her pink hair restrained in two pigtails this morning. "This is my friend, Suzie. She wanted to help. Where did the cattle come from?"

"I've no idea," Ada said, shock and anger and frustration filling her. "The gate was closed last night, and it's still shut this morning. The gate is the only way they could get into my flowers."

"I'm pleased to meet you, Ada," Suzie said. "Don't worry. The men have everything under control." Suzie had confined her black hair in a braid and donned light makeup, which enhanced the brown skin from her part-Māori heritage. Her smile was bright and friendly, and held sympathy. "I understand Ella is helping you with the farmers' market. What do you need to do to prepare your flowers? How can we help?"

Ada winced as a cow made a run for it and bowled through her flowers, trampling them underfoot. Matt soon had the animal turned around. Instead of driving them toward her gate, they were herding them to the end of her paddock. Gritting her teeth, because she couldn't fall apart in front of strangers, she said, "Can you take these flowers for me? I couldn't carry them all."

"I'll take them," Ella said. "They smell amazing."

"I'll come with you," Suzie said.

"We won't be long," Ada said to Ella. "Sorry. I haven't unlocked the shed yet."

"No problem. I'll wait."

By the time Ada returned, Matt, Dillon, and Josh had finished with the cattle.

"How did the cows get into my flowers?" Ada asked.

"Someone cut the fence. Do you recognize the cattle?" Matt asked.

"No," Ada said. "Bart, my neighbor, has yearlings and never keeps his stock to this age. I mean, he's a stock agent, so he keeps turning over his animals. Did they have brands? Did they eat my flowers?"

"They've been here for several hours, judging by the pugging on the ground. Mostly they've grazed the grass on the edges. It didn't look as if they've eaten your flowers. Rather, they've pushed their way through looking for water or grazing."

"Brilliant," Ada said in an understatement.

"Will your insurance cover this?" Suzie asked.

"No." Ada held a basic policy. It had been all she could afford, but she didn't explain. It was no one's business but her own.

"I took a photo of the cattle and will contact the local cops," Matt said.

"How bad is it?" Ada asked. "I'll call Sherry and cancel."

Matt's expression turned serious as he brushed a tear from the corner of her eye. "You've picked the flowers," he said. "Why don't you and Ella go to the market? I'll sort everything out here for you."

"But I can't let you do that," she whispered, aware of their audience.

"You can. We'll fix the fence and pick flowers for you. How about I get Suzie to pick the stems of delphinium still suitable for selling at the market?"

"But—"

"Ada, sweetheart. You don't have to do this alone. Please let us help you."

After an inner battle, Ada finally gave a clipped nod. "Thanks."

"Not necessary." Matt kissed the tip of her nose before he started issuing orders.

Ada stared after the men as they strode off to undertake their tasks.

"Do you have clippers?" Suzie asked. "I have my mission. Need clippers."

"Sure." Ada grabbed her spare pair off a shelf.

"How many flowers do you want me to pick?" Suzie asked.

"Pick as many as you can of the damaged ones," Ada said. "Once you've done that, bring them back here, and I'll let you know if we need more." Another tear ran down her cheek. Just from the brief glimpses she'd had of her flowers, she doubted many would be usable.

"What should I do?" Ella asked, sympathy filling her features.

"Um." Ada sucked in a breath to center herself. She

moved to the corner where she stored her buckets. "These are the buckets I use for my flowers. Can you fill them with flowers and add enough water to keep them looking fresh? You'll find a tap outside to the right. Once that's done, we'll load them into my vehicle. While you're doing that, I'll pack confetti samples. I should've done it last night." She pulled a face. "I knew it, but it's exhausting working all day."

"I slept well," Ella said as she set to work.

Ada took another two or three deep breaths and forced herself to focus. Confetti samples. She'd make as many as she could, given the time restraints. She checked her watch. Fifteen minutes, then they'd leave. A tear spilled free, and she brushed it away with a trace of impatience. Crying was a waste of time. It wouldn't fix this mess.

Move on. Make lemonade out of lemons, as her grandmother used to say. That's what she needed to do because if she didn't focus on the positive, Ada thought she might lose it.

CHAPTER 15

STOCK THEFTS GALORE

ADA AND ELLA PULLED up in the car park ten minutes before Ada's deadline. She found a space close to the office and felt better about the inherent security.

"I'll pay for my stall. Won't be long," Ada promised.

"Can I come with you?"

Ada shrugged. "Sure. Is this the nearest farmers' market to you?"

"Yes, we don't have one in Eketāhuna. There was discussion of starting a market, but like so many things, we had talk with no action."

Ada forced a smile. "Sounds familiar. Come on. I'll introduce you to Sherry Walsh. She's the powerhouse around here who organizes these things."

There was a short queue when they arrived, but given Sherry's efficiency, it moved fast.

"Hi, Sherry. This is my friend, Ella. She's helping on my stall today," Ada said.

Sherry's glance took in Ella with her pink hair and pigtails. "Are you from Moewai? I don't believe we've met."

"No, I live in Eketāhuna," Ella said with a smile.

"Eddie is dating a lovely girl from Eketāhuna. She had dinner with us last night," Sherry said. "That's fifty dollars today, Ada."

Ada handed over her money and stood aside for the next person. "Thanks, Sherry."

"Your spot is on the map." Sherry beamed. "Sell heaps!"

"Thanks," Ada said. The clock was ticking, and she was no closer to paying off her loan.

They detoured to Ada's vehicle and carried two flower buckets each to Ada's spot.

"Why don't you set up, and I'll collect the rest of the flowers and the confetti?" Ella suggested.

Ada smiled her thanks. "Can you grab my signs for me first? They're on the back seat."

"No problem."

Ada sold two bunches of stock before Ella arrived with her signs and her confetti samples. She sold another posy before Ella had time to bring more flowers. Ada didn't know if it was an advantageous spot or the fact she'd arrived early, but she did a brisk trade, selling out of her stock by ten. Unfortunately, the confetti samples didn't prove as popular.

"I have a suggestion," Ella said. "Why don't I take a box of the confetti and try to drum up trade? I'll be a wandering salesman while you stay with your flowers. I'll leave you a handful in case."

"Have at it," Ada said, trying not to feel discouraged.

Not long after Ella left, two women stopped to browse Ada's flowers.

"I'll take four delphinium stems," the older woman said.

While Ada wrapped the flowers for her, the two women discussed stolen cattle.

"Wayne was pissed when he discovered his cows missing. They're quiet and wouldn't break out of the paddock. Most of them were bucket-fed."

"Did he report it to the police?"

"Yes, not that I expect them to do anything. So far, four cattle farmers have missing stock. Several sheep farmers have lost entire flocks, and a pony disappeared last week. The woman who told me said the pony's owner—a child—is distraught."

Ada's ears pricked at the mention of quiet cattle. Matt

had stated they seemed unruffled, although they'd torn through her flowers at an incredible speed. Matt intended to report the cattle to the police. He'd taken photos, so if the cows turned out stolen, the cops would know. Best if she didn't mention specifics.

"The police have been busy recently, trying to track down stolen animals," Ada said.

"You'd think they'd be onto the thefts more than they are," one woman retorted. "I heard they have a similar problem in the Eketāhuna district."

Something to ask Ella. She seemed plugged into the gossip if what Dillon said was true during their teasing discussions yesterday.

Ella was away for a good hour, but Ada didn't get her hopes up because her attempted selling hadn't borne fruit so far. Ella arrived back with bright eyes, an empty box, and two coffees. "I saw you took milk yesterday, so I figured a latte would work for you."

"Thank you." Ada stared at the empty box again. "What happened to the samples?"

"I gave them out. I hovered around the coffee stall and in the area in the middle where people stop to eat their snacks or drink their coffee. Since summer is here, many people have weddings planned or know of people with upcoming weddings. I thought I could take samples home with me. Suzie and I know a few brides, and we'd be happy to champion your business. Your samples will impress our acquaintances as will knowing Suzie and I picked flowers and helped with the preparation process."

Ada stared at her dumbly, her mind so full of emotion, she wasn't confident what words would spill from her mouth.

"Here, have a coffee and accept graciously. I loved picking yesterday, and it is always fun to catch up with Dillon's brother and Ashley. I've heard lots about Frog since I met Dillon. Somehow, I thought he'd be shorter and broader. I don't know why." She grinned. "Dillon growled when I mentioned Frog is a hunk. *Oops*, slight diversion there. I was trying to say we want you to succeed, and we're happy to help. I'd like to take a few samples to the girls at work."

Ada sipped her coffee to ground herself. "Did someone say you work at the bird sanctuary?"

"I'm part-time now since I help Dillon on the farm. If you want an unpaid spokesperson for your confetti, please consider me. Your confetti is such a neat idea."

"I don't know what to say."

A woman approached to buy flowers.

"Drink your coffee," Ella said. "I've got this. Go for a walk and take a break."

Ada hesitated before deciding a walk might settle her churning emotions. Thanks to Matt, she was making friends. Valuable contacts. When she overheard two farmers discussing their missing stock, she loitered, interested to learn more.

"The police are chasing their tails," one farmer said with a trace of bitterness. "I've lost an entire flock of pedigree sheep from these brazen thieves. We were away for the weekend, but the neighbors never questioned a stock truck or strangers rounding up my sheep with the dogs they brought with them."

"Your neighbors saw the theft happen?" the second farmer said in disbelief. "And did nothing?"

"Yeah."

"Were they able to give the cops a description, at least? Or a registration number for the truck?"

"No." The farmer didn't hide his indignation. "The cops have no clue where my sheep are, or the thieves' identity, or where they might strike next. A couple of other farmers had stock stolen on the same weekend. Jock Haines lost his stud bulls last night."

Ada studied the lavender products, sympathy filling her. She understood their frustration. When the stall owner wandered toward her, Ada turned away. She scanned the stalls and drifted toward a group of chatting men. Most, she recognized as farmers. Their discussions centered on the thefts. One mentioned a district meeting to devise an action plan. Ada walked a slow circuit before heading back to her stall.

"That was fast," Ella said. "You haven't even finished your coffee."

"The farmers are discussing stock thefts. They're angry—to the point of taking matters into their own hands—saying the police aren't doing enough."

"Several customers have mentioned the thefts," Ella said.

Another customer arrived and purchased the last of the wildflowers. Ada gaped at the empty pails. "Wow! You've sold heaps."

"I love selling and talking to customers. What's going on?" Ella looked past Ada.

Ada scanned faces and noted Sherry busy talking, her hands flashing in illustration until other taller locals crowded around and blocked her from view.

"It's something big. Maybe the cops have caught the rustlers." Ada checked her watch and saw it was after midday. No wonder she was starving.

"How long are you staying? Right to the end?" Ella asked.

"Business is trailing off, and people are seeking

sustenance rather than products. Let's give it another ten minutes."

Five minutes later, a woman appeared. "Excellent! You have flowers left. I purchased a bunch last week and wanted more since we're having a party. I'll take what you have left."

Once the lady wandered off, Ada and Ella packed up. Something was going on, but Ada didn't hang around since she wanted to check on the damage to her flowers.

"Why does your husband call Matt Frog?" Ada asked to distract herself. She backed out of her parking spot and inched toward the exit, stopping often because pedestrians wandered blindly without checking for traffic.

"Matt loves to sing karaoke. Dillon tells me Matt's singing is like listening to an out-of-tune bullfrog."

"Oh," Ada said. "His speaking voice is sexy."

"Ha! I told Dillon you're a couple."

"We've kissed, but that's all. Sure, we like each other, but my life is here, and Matt will return to Auckland soon."

"A sexy fling. Makes sense."

Ada wrinkled her nose. "It's been a while for me, and I'm too busy to invest in a relationship."

"Are you too busy for friends?" Ella asked. "I'd love to keep in touch, help with the market again. If you're extra busy, I can take charge of the stall for you."

"That would be awesome!" Ada slowed on the outskirts of town, near the Dawson farm. It took fifteen minutes for the line of traffic to crawl past the Dawson driveway.

"That's an ambulance behind us," Ella said. "The siren isn't going. That's ominous."

"What?" For a few tense seconds, the vehicle's appearance thrust Ada back to the time of Greg's murder. The ambulance siren had blared during its arrival, but they'd gone silent and left, giving way to the police scene examination. "Do you think they're picking up a body or something like that?" She held her breath and waited for Ella's reply.

"It's a guess. Moewai is a small community. The story will come out before tonight."

"Along with wild rumors," Ada said in a stark voice, still remembering. Ice coated her skin, and she clutched the steering wheel, trying to thrust away the memories attempting to bury her. Her mind focused on Matt. His smile. His delectable body. His kindness. His work ethic. Slowly, her rapid breathing evened out, and blood flowed to her whitened knuckles.

The car in front of her rolled forward, and Ada was pleased to concentrate on driving. Because she either sensed Ada's emotional upheaval or was busy studying their surroundings, Ella remained quiet. The traffic crawled past the roadblock, each driver speaking to a police officer before they drove onward.

The tension snaking through her rose higher as they approached the roadblock. She opened the driver's side window and braced for a conversation with a cop she knew by sight.

"Good afternoon," the cop said. "Could you tell me where you've come from?"

"The farmers' market," Ada replied. "I have a stall there."

"What time did you travel from your home to the market?"

"Around twenty past eight. I wanted to make sure I was early this week."

"Did you see anything unusual during your drive?"

"No. A herd of cows got into my field this morning, and they trampled my flowers. I was not happy, and I'm still angry. Those cattle..." Ada trailed off, but she was certain the cop got the gist of her anger.

"Did you report this to the police?"

"Yes," Ada said. "What's happening?"

"I'm not at liberty to say," the police officer said.

"Can I go now?"

He waved her onward. Ada drove slowly, gradually picking up speed.

"Do you know the people who live there?" Ella asked.

"Not well. I've met Janice Dawson through the local women's functions my neighbor Sherry has dragged me to during the last two years. Her husband, Ralph, is a bit of a lay-about. He spends most of his time and money at the pub while Janice works two jobs to keep their son fed and clothed. Ralph works, and I don't think he beats her or the child, but he's what you'd call a weak man who lacks willpower."

"Is it possible he snapped and hurt her?"

"I don't know them well enough to speculate."

Instead of pouting at the verbal knockback, Ella smirked. "Fair enough. Forgive my curiosity. I try not to gossip, but sometimes inquisitiveness tips over into nosiness."

Ada sucked in a deep breath as she drove over the hill and down the other side. The valley extended beyond, and she glimpsed the river. "I get it. I do. You have my apology, too, because I'm ultra-sensitive to gossip. After my husband's death, rumors ran riot. One implied I'd shot Greg in cold blood and was crying innocent. Another that did the rounds was my husband and I had a threesome, and the jealous third shot Greg. Then there were the rumors of his gambling tendencies and his secret plot of drugs. His gang membership. The locals' imaginations, fueled by false stories in the press, knew no limitations."

"Oh, Ada. I'm so sorry. That must've happened while I was out of the district. That's awful and difficult to live through."

Ada's mouth twisted as she drove past the Walsh farm. Eddie pulled up at the end of the driveway and yielded to her vehicle. He blew her a kiss. She ignored him and kept her eyes on the road.

"It wasn't a great time in my life. It didn't help that Greg's parents blamed his death on me. They told everyone who'd listen that I'd caused the split between Greg and the rest of the family."

Ella reached over and squeezed Ada's hand before resettling in her seat. "That must've been incredibly difficult. Dillon's family is so supportive. I love his brother and sister, and his parents are close to their children. They accepted me without hesitation. Who is that guy? He hasn't moved his car."

Ada felt her top lip curl. "Eddie keeps asking me out. I wouldn't date him if someone paid me a thousand dollars. He came over with his older brother last week. Thank goodness Matt was there because they give me the creeps."

"But isn't Matt leaving soon?" Ella asked. "Dillon mentioned something about him training again this week."

"Yes. Don't worry. I'm used to being alone. I can look after myself." And maybe if she said that enough, she'd believe her assertion. Eddie and Craig had frightened her, and the pranks aimed at her were making her jumpier than usual. Her farm's isolation was problematic.

She couldn't give up and move because her financial future lay with the farm—unless Greg's parents won the land. She gave a half-laugh that drew Ella's attention, but Ada didn't explain her thoughts. To do that would smack of surrender. Ada intended to fight to the end, despite her fear and misgivings. She could do nothing less for Greg.

CHAPTER 16

THE POLICE QUESTION ADA

"WHAT IS THE DAMAGE?" Ada demanded the instant she spotted Matt.

Matt pulled a face. "The cattle flattened quite a few plants. We cut those stems and harvested the blossoms we could. Other than that, we've finished the picking."

Ada's brows rose. "Already?"

"Yes. The rows we worked on were light on blooms." He frowned. "It was almost as if someone had picked the row."

"That's weird," Ada said. "You mean the ones nearest to the river, right?"

"Yes," Matt confirmed.

"I walked along those rows two days ago. The stems

were full of blooms."

Dillon, who'd stood beside Matt, silent, frowned. "I noticed footprints and pointed them out to Josh. We decided you'd made the prints." He glanced at her feet. "They were a similar size to your boots."

"There might be a few of mine. It rained two nights ago, but we didn't get much rain." She puckered her brow and thought back. "The prints might've come from whoever placed the cattle there."

"Oh, someone deliberately let those cattle on your land. They cut the fence and drove the cattle through the gap. They left the animals to graze at will."

"Uncool," she muttered under her breath. "I keep to myself. If anyone has a problem they should tell me to my face instead of this clandestine bullshit stuff."

Someone laughed, and when she scanned faces, she settled on the one with the broadest grin. Matt.

"Your official description of clandestine bullshit stuff is spot-on," he said.

An inelegant snort escaped Ada. "It'd make this easier if I understood the reason behind the harassment." She shrugged away her irritation, her frustration, and straightened her shoulders. "I'd better survey the damage."

"I'm starving," Ella said. "We didn't have time to eat. Who wants sandwiches?"

Ada's steps slowed, and embarrassment swept her. "Ella, I'm a terrible hostess, and if I were paying you, the Labor Department would chase me for abusing employment rules. Let me rustle up something to eat."

"Stop," Dillon said, the discordant note in his voice making Ada freeze.

She stared at Ella's husband.

"We came yesterday because Matt asked us for help. Today, we're here because we enjoyed our day and wanted to support Frog's"—he shot Matt a glance—"friend. We're capable of organizing food, and not one of us is shy in asking for what we need. You're dealing with enough. Stop stressing."

Ella sidled closer to Dillon and squeezed his beefy arm. "What he said," she murmured. "Does anyone else want sandwiches? Is your house locked, Ada?"

"Yes, I'll get those sandwiches underway."

Ella held out her hand. "Give me the keys, and I'll find what I need. I doubt I'll get lost inside your house. It's adorably cute. Check your flowers. I know you're concerned."

"Give Ella the keys, sweetheart," Matt said. "I'll show you what we've done."

Ada handed over her keys. Ella and Suzie trotted off to the tiny house while Josh and Dillon continued preparing picked flowers for the drying process.

Matt took Ada's arm and led her away. Once they rounded the corner of the shed, he stopped walking. He smiled down at her, his eyes crinkling at the edges. "Dillon was off the mark when he called you my friend. I think of you as more, but I've told you that already."

"You're all talk," Ada muttered.

Matt flashed her a bad-boy grin. The part of himself he hid behind his good-guy persona, but now he wasn't concealing a thing. Her insides did this weird surge that was approval and panic. Did she want to unleash this man? A soldier with a big heart and equally huge dollops of determination and strength.

"Oh, sweetheart," he whispered. "You should know better than to poke the bear."

Seconds later, he'd plastered her against his hard chest with his bulky arms wrapped around her shoulders.

"Last chance to tell me you don't want this."

Ada did what she suspected was a credible impression of a fish. "I...ah..."

"Time's up."

Matt kissed her. When she'd expected aggressive and passionate, she didn't get that. Not at first. He started gentle, and the second she responded, he took the kiss up another notch. She'd always thought heroines in historical romances swooned because their corsets were too tight. Matt proved to her a kiss—his kiss—was capable of just as much damage. He explored her mouth, using lips and tongue, and even his teeth to great effect. He parted their mouths and nuzzled her neck.

A moan slipped free from her, and he laughed softly.

"For the first time, I'd be happy to see the back of my friends," Matt murmured. "I have to leave tomorrow morning to prepare the camp for the new group of soldiers."

"Tomorrow?"

"Yeah. Come on. Let me show you the damage."

"You told me it wasn't bad."

"I lied," he said, his tone grim. "I decided if you intended to fall apart, you'd prefer to do it when you were alone."

"And your friends agreed?" Her tone hovered around snide level.

He gave a curt nod.

"For future reference: my preference is for truth. Always. The bottom line is I own the land and started growing the flowers, which means I'm in charge of every facet. I have the final say. Therefore, I take the bad with the good. That means I need every scrap of information necessary to make decisions."

"Fair enough," Matt said. "From now on, I'll give you

truth, starting with the fact tonight I'll be sleeping in your bed again. This time will be different because neither of us will get much sleep. Can you deal with that?"

Ada met his direct gaze. "Yes."

"Excellent." His chuckle held a trace of wolf along with the bad-boy. "Let's do this flower thing then." He twined their fingers and led her away from the shadows behind the shed.

Ada found her knee strength challenged, and she noticed her elevated pulse rate. This man—he was dangerous to her equilibrium, but she didn't care. She figured she deserved something good in her life for a change.

As they neared her flower fields, tension slipped into her muscles.

The feel-good mood generated by Matt's kisses faded as he led her to the row end. From here, it was simple to spot the fence damage. The cows had knocked over most of the flowers at the row's end.

"Someone drove them into my flowers deliberately."

"I'm surprised we didn't wake."

"I was exhausted," she said. "But this worries me. If someone did this without us hearing the disturbance, what else can they do? I see you put the cows in the old yards. Do they have water? And what did the cops say? You contacted them for me, right?"

"The cows have water. They seem in excellent health, which means they didn't eat your flowers."

"Just trampled them."

"Yeah. Dillon read out their ear tag numbers to the cop who took the message. He told us to keep them in the yard, and they'd contact the owner for you."

"I hope it's today, otherwise I'll need to find somewhere else to put them. The cattle can't stay in the yard overnight without feed."

Matt's phone buzzed, and he pulled it out of his pocket. "Two cops have arrived. They're asking for you."

Ada scanned the broken and bent stems and the remnants of what had been a glorious display of pink delphinium. She noted Matt and his helpers had rescued the useable petals. "I think I'll yank these out and replant. Maybe more cornflowers, so I have variety in my petal colors."

"Sounds like a plan," Matt said. "Maybe we'll have time to clear the ground for you later this afternoon."

She nodded. "I'd better speak to the police."

The two police officers weren't local cops and wore suits and serious expressions.

"Ms. Buckingham?"

"Yes," Ada said. Their demeanor had her warning

antenna blaring at hurricane force.

"Detective George and Detective Conway," Detective George stated.

Both men flashed their I.D.

Detective George pursed his lips and scrutinized Ada, his blue gaze intense. His cobalt tie and navy suit matched his eyes. "Do you know a Ralph Dawson?"

"Sure, he lives about ten kilometers down the road. I don't know him well."

The two men exchanged a glance, and when they surveyed her again, both bore a sharp eagerness that had her wanting to retreat. Only Matt's silent presence kept her feet grounded.

"I know his wife better." No sooner had Ada uttered the words than she wished she'd remained quiet. Her instinct had been to fill the silence.

"Is that right?" Detective George asked, his brows rising.

"What is this about?" Matt asked.

"Who are you?" Detective George demanded.

"I'm Ada's fiancé," Matt said, not giving his name.

Ada jolted hard and feared her expression gave away this lie.

"Is that true?" Detective George asked.

Ada stiffened her backbone and went with instinct. "Yes."

"I see. And does your fiancé know of your relationship with Ralph Dawson?"

"What?" Ada gaped at the detective before shifting her gaze to Detective Conway, who observed her as if she were an interesting bug. "I don't...I haven't had a relationship with Ralph."

"Your affair ended recently. He took the break badly and after leaving a note, committed suicide this morning."

"What?" Shock kicked Ada in the gut. Ralph Dawson was a slob and not her kind of man. "But he's married with a child."

"Good of you to realize that, after the fact," Detective George said.

"If the man committed suicide, then why are you harassing my fiancée?" Matt demanded.

"That's just it," Detective George said. "Although the death looks like a suicide, we don't think he killed himself."

"You think I murdered him?" Ada asked, her voice higher than usual.

"Where were you between the hours of eleven last night and seven this morning?" Detective George asked.

"I was here," Ada said.

"Can anyone corroborate this?" Detective Conway probed.

"Matt was with me."

"Your full name?" Detective George demanded.

"Matt Townsend," Matt said.

"And were you with Ms. Buckingham during the hours we've mentioned?" Detective Conway asked. His suit was black, and his white shirt bore a coffee stain.

"Yes," Matt said with a bit of snap to his voice. "I've spent the weekend with Ada. We worked late and went to bed around ten. We were up at six because Ada needed to prepare her flowers for this morning's market."

"I don't understand. Why are you asking me this?" Ada asked.

The two cops exchanged a glance, and Detective Conway tucked away his notebook.

"We'll be in contact," Detective George said. "Don't leave town."

The pair strutted to their Ford sedan without answering her question.

"Crap." Ada stared after the departing vehicle. "I should've stayed in bed this morning."

CHAPTER 17

ADA DOESN'T GO TO BED ALONE

"WHAT DID THE COPS want?" Dillon murmured after Ada jogged inside to help Ella and Suzie.

Matt dropped onto the top step that led up to the deck since Josh and Dillon occupied the two chairs.

"Guy up the road committed suicide. He left a note saying he was having an affair with Ada. Could be wrong, but there was something about their questions that made me think there was more they weren't sharing."

"Did she have an affair with the guy?"

"Nope," Matt said instantly and without hesitation. "She didn't murder him because I've been with her since Friday night. She works damn hard. Ada slogs for a full day, comes in for dinner, and spends several more hours toiling before retiring for the night. Even if I hadn't been here to act as her alibi, I wouldn't have believed the accusation. She's straight-up. Blunt and honest."

"You like her," Josh said.

"She's mine. She might not admit it yet, but I know, and that's enough."

"You haven't known her for long," Dillon said.

Matt released a snort. "The pair of you were quick to claim your women. We're decisive. I'm worried about leaving her alone. I've got to go back to camp tomorrow morning to prepare for the next group of soldiers."

"We discussed that," Josh said. "Ashley is in Wellington for the entire week. I'll bring Mum and Dad's campervan and set up here. It beats sitting around in the capital, and I can help Ada around here. Works for both of us."

"What did Ash say?" Matt asked although he figured his sister would be cool.

"It was her suggestion. She'd prefer me to be busy," Josh said. "Nelson and Gerry will protect her. Phone sex is fine."

Matt screwed up his face. "I do not want to hear about my sister's sex life," he grumbled.

"Serves you right for jerking us around," Josh said, an unholy gleam in his blue eyes.

"As long as you watch Ada and don't get distracted. I'll

discuss it with Ada."

"Discuss what with me?" Ada set a plate of sandwiches on a wooden side table next to Dillon's chair.

Ella and Suzie carried two more plates of sandwiches. Ella handed her plate to Matt while Suzie placed hers on the table.

"We were discussing the suicide and the other things happening around here," Matt said. "I want your permission to share with Dillon and Josh."

"I should know since I'm staying with you next week," Josh said.

"You're not staying in my house," Ada snapped.

Josh grinned, not bothered by her attitude in the slightest. "I'm bringing my own house."

Ada stared at him. "What?"

"Ada." Matt reached for her hand and tugged her to the step beside him. "Something bad is going on around here. Those cops will be back because they think you had something to do with that guy's death. I know you didn't do it, which makes me suspect someone is trying to set you up. In the short time I've been here, you've had your shed spray-painted, animal guts draped on your fence, the cows in your flowers, and now the dead man."

Josh swallowed the last of his sandwich. "Perhaps these pranks tie to your husband's murder."

"All of that happened?" Suzie looked appalled. "Why aren't you a jabbering mess?"

"I am," Ada said drily. "I just hide it well."

"Have other things happened?" Dillon asked.

Ada kept her gaze lowered before saying, "Yes."

Dillon's eyes narrowed. "How many instances have you contacted the cops?"

"About half. Honestly, if I can't move my confetti, I'm finished anyway."

Ella scowled. "Things are that bad?"

"Yes. I recently discovered my husband took out a loan using the property as security. The loan is due next month. Crap," Ada said, her expression appalled. "Can we change the subject?"

"Didn't you say you'd organized pickers and someone hired them away from you?" Matt asked.

"Yes."

"Someone wants your land," Dillon stated. "They're trying to scare you away."

Matt tensed since it was an idea he'd considered before now. "Has anyone offered to purchase your farm?"

"I had a few offers after Greg died. Bart Walsh offered to buy it, and I had inquiries from several of the land agents who deal with farm sales. I told them it was too soon for a decision of that magnitude," Ada said, and it was apparent she was choosing her words carefully. Matt suspected she wasn't telling them everything.

"Did any of the prospective purchasers act upset?" Ella asked.

"There was no pushback or threats or anything like that. Bart told me he could do with more land and his offer stood if I changed my mind. He bought two hundred hectares on the other side of Moewai not long afterward. Land agents still ring me, but they're nice about it."

"That sounds like a dead-end then," Josh said. "But you need to keep reporting problems to the local cops, no matter how small. It's clear someone is harassing you on purpose."

"Maybe it's the neighbor's sons. That one with the long hair isn't right in the head. He frightened you the last time he visited. If I hadn't been here, I hate to think what would've happened," Matt said with a snap in his tone.

"Sherry mentioned Eddie is dating a girl from Eketāhuna. Honestly, Eddie doesn't have the brains to hound me in this manner," Ada said. "Scuttlebutt says he scraped by at school. Sherry celebrated when he scored his apprenticeship at the garage."

"I'll dig around next week," Josh said.

"I'll ask questions in Eketāhuna. It's surprising how gossip spreads," Dillon said.

A utility vehicle with two dogs riding on the back tray pulled into Ada's drive, and a middle-aged man with a shock of white hair uncurled from behind the wheel. A younger version of the man, this one with black hair, climbed from the passenger side of the vehicle.

"I understand you have my cattle," the man said.

Ada stood. "Jock. They're in my yards. They got into my flowers, but they seem okay. I don't think any of them ate the delphiniums."

"They're poisonous?" Jock asked.

"Very to animals," Ada said. "That's why I left the fences intact. How did your cattle get here?"

"I've no idea. Carly and I went out for dinner last night around five. The cattle were in the paddock when we left. They weren't there this morning. Are you positive they're okay? They're all in-calf and are the building blocks of the herd I'm building."

"The cattle are fine. They have water and seem content enough. How are you getting them home?"

"Tony will drive them home with the dogs. They're quiet, and he'll take it easy."

Ada gestured them to follow her. "I'll show you the yards."

"We'll say goodbye now," Dillon said, standing. "We're heading home."

"I'll call you during the week." Ella gave Ada a swift hug.

To Matt's surprise, Dillon hugged Ada too. The couple left with Suzie.

"I might as well head off too," Josh said. "I'll be here in the morning and will bring supplies to fix your fence for you. Dad has materials in the shed that will do the trick."

"Thanks, man." Matt clasped Dillon's hand and pulled him in for a man-hug. He did the same with Josh, then followed Ada and the new arrivals to get their stock.

Jock and his son examined their cattle and seemed pleased with their condition. They opened the gate and drove the ten animals along the road at an amble.

Jock thanked her again and followed his son, leaving Ada alone with Matt.

"An eventful day," she said.

"Yep, it'll be relaxing to get back to my day job."

Ada laughed, the burst of sound bringing a grin to Matt.

"Anything else we need to do today?"

"I'm going to stack the prepared petals into the drying machine and leave it going overnight. Other than that, I intend to shower and relax on the deck. I can tackle the trampled plants tomorrow."

"Works for me," Matt said.

In the past, he might've attempted seduction, but they lazed around with a beer each. Ada cooked them steak for dinner while he sorted out the salad.

"Greg hated cooking and never helped in the kitchen," Ada said.

Matt loathed the comparison to a dead man and especially one who'd had close contacts with Ada. He merely grunted.

"He took care of the outdoor stuff. I enjoy doing both."

"Then or has that changed?" Matt asked, getting an inkling of what she meant.

"Greg had unyielding opinions on the duties within a marriage. It didn't bother me then. If someone tried that now I'd react differently."

"Message received loud and clear. The flowers were your idea," he added. "You pivoted and went in a different direction to take advantage of your strengths. Why would you worry about what I think or me taking over?"

The air whooshed from Ada, and she rubbed a hand over her face. "Everything that has happened has me rattled. And..." Her gaze darted to him before dancing away again. "I like you a lot, but I'm nervous about the sex part. What if I make a mess of everything?"

"You won't," he said with certainty. "If you're worried, we could leave dinner and hit the bedroom right now. Pound those nerves away."

"Now you're making fun of me."

"Never. I fell for you, remember."

Ada let out a rude snort, and when he waggled his brows at her, she giggled.

The exuberant sound had him grinning in return. It made him realize Ada didn't laugh much. She was serious and burdened with responsibility. He figured since her husband's murder, she'd been running to keep ahead of the turmoil in her life. At that moment, he made a promise to himself. His mission was to make her happy, to help her enjoy the fun things in life.

"The steak is ready—unless you prefer it well done."

"Nope," he said. "Looks good to me."

They ate together, and Matt chatted about his upcoming training and Ada's success at the farmers' market. Once they'd finished their meal, Matt stood and cleared their dishes.

"I'll do the dishes now," Ada said.

"No." Matt stacked the dishes in the sink and put away the condiments they'd used. Then, he held out his hand, his heart thumping while he waited for Ada to give her silent consent.

The seconds while she studied him had never seemed so long.

Finally, she stood and wrapped her fingers around his.

"I'm not sure this is a great idea, but I'm doing this

anyway. I like you a lot, and I want to take this next step."

"Yes." Matt wanted to pump his fist into the air and express louder approval. With his gaze on hers, he drew her closer. He kissed her forehead and led her to the bedroom. Before he went any further, he pulled the curtains. "I might get the door too. We don't want anyone bursting in without an invitation."

"No." Her smile faded, and Matt wanted to curse.

"Be right back." Matt made good on his word and found her standing by her bed. Damn, he'd wanted her relaxed and happy. Right now, she reminded him of a possum in headlights. "You can change your mind if you like."

"No." Ada's gaze zapped to him. "I don't want to go to bed alone."

"Well, that's funny because I hate to sleep by myself."

Her gaze flew to his. "Is that why I found you in my bed?"

He grinned. "It might've been the reason."

Ada took a step toward him, and he met her halfway. He kissed her, and his world righted itself. Her scent washed over him—nothing flashy, but a delicate soap aroma that did more for him than the most trendy or sophisticated designer perfume. Her generous breasts rubbed against his chest. While she wasn't overweight, she wasn't a twig either—his past go-to type. Even now, he wasn't sure what had made him chase Ada because this *was* a pursuit on his part.

He'd taken one look at her furious face, and his heart had gone pitter-patter. Every woman he'd dated in the past had ceased to matter, replaced by the one.

Ada.

Everything inside him had settled, and he finally understood why Dillon and Josh had changed.

His lips roved her jaw and down her neck, and each soft sound she made, each groan of pleasure pleased him greatly. His fingers were clumsy as he unfastened the buttons of Ada's blouse, but the smooth, tanned skin he revealed was worth the struggle.

"You're gorgeous," he murmured. "I've tried to imagine you naked."

She lifted her head. "You have?"

"Oh yeah." Matt suspected his grin was more wolfish than admiring and reassuring. "Don't forget, I've seen you in a towel, so I had a little to work with."

"You might've seen my best bits."

Matt laughed. "The best part of you is your sexy mind, your determination, and your never-give-up attitude. I like your nose." He patted it with a forefinger. "Your faint freckles." He brushed those with his finger too. "Your curvy backside, which is mighty distracting. I told you before, I fell for you from the first. Enough talk," he said when she opened her mouth. He scooped her up easily.

"Matt, I'm too heavy to—"

Before she could finish her protest, he'd set her on the mattress, and she stared up at him with wide eyes.

He'd already drawn the curtains, and now he switched on one of her bedside lamps. No way did he want to miss a visual—something for him to take with him when he had to leave in the morning.

He winked at her. "Time to unwrap my present."

Ada huffed. "Do it fast. I don't like to wait."

"Impatient?"

"Yes. I'll get to see you too."

Curious, he asked, "Have you imagined me without clothes?"

"Why wouldn't I?"

Matt laughed, the sound exuberant and infectious. "Let me even the playing field then." He stepped back, jerked his black T-shirt over his head, and stripped off his jeans to his boxer-briefs. Also black.

Ada's brows rose. "Nice."

"Is that all I get?" He'd thought she might be shy since she was a private person and slow to trust.

"You're not naked yet," she pointed out.

"You're wearing more clothes than me."

"I can fix that." She took a step back and rapidly stripped. "I might rest now."

Matt's grin widened as she reclined on the bed, facing away from him without a hint of shyness to display that curvy backside and the sexy line of her spine.

"Challenge accepted," Matt whispered loud enough for Ada to hear. She giggled. At least he knew she wanted him since this was an implicit invitation.

Matt took one moment longer to admire the picture she made against her steel-gray covers with the soft light highlighting her curves. He plucked a strip of condoms from his jeans pocket and placed them on the nightstand. Then, he stripped off his boxer-briefs and joined Ada on the bed.

"Now, the question is where to touch you first." He waited for her reply, curious about what she'd say.

A shudder worked through her. "Everywhere."

"God, yes." Matt rolled closer and pressed his lips to her shoulder blade. Seconds later, his hand settled on her waist. He shifted his hips enough for his erection to brush her backside, and she immediately pushed against him to deepen the friction.

"Yes," he whispered, no longer in a teasing mood.

He placed a hand on her shoulder and pushed her over until she lay flat on the mattress.

She winked. "Come get me."

Matt stared at her, his avid gaze taking in her breasts' plump curves, the paler skin, and pink nipples. Her full mouth, slightly swollen after their kisses and now wreathed in a smile. Her brown eyes. His gaze drifted downward to take in the dip of her waist and the flare of her hips. She'd splayed her legs, offering just a glimpse. Matt moved over her, and before he took her lips, he whispered, "My pleasure."

CHAPTER 18

A FORMAL INTERVIEW AT THE STATION

ADA HAD NEVER ACTED with such brazen disregard for self-protection, yet something about Matt pushed her to be herself and not put on a single bit of pretense. She didn't hide or give into shyness. Neither did she pretend she didn't want him. She'd tried to ignore Matt and the attraction she'd felt for him from the day he'd turned up with his soldiers to help her pick flowers. When he'd failed to react to her rudeness, she'd started paying greater attention.

And now she'd given up fighting.

It was time to take something for herself, no matter how fleeting that might be. Matt would leave once his work here ended. Ada understood that. She understood her heart would break—just a little—but she'd survive. She understood all of this, yet she was still going ahead and grabbing pleasure and companionship with both hands.

Matt's eyes turned dark without warning before he slammed his mouth down on hers and caged her between him and the bed.

Man unleashed. *Yum.*

Ada wrapped her arms around his neck in case he got it into his brain to move now that they'd started down this road.

He lifted his head, a tiny grin playing around his sensual lips. "Chill, sweetheart. I'm not planning on going anywhere. Not even if we get an intruder outdoors."

"Good to know."

"Relax."

"This restlessness surging through me is sexual tension," she informed him. "It's your job to stamp that out and turn me into a limp kitten."

He laughed then before he kissed her again. This exchange held none of their earlier desperation. Instead, the moment their lips met, heat flared in her, and it traveled downward until it resided in the needy spot between her thighs. Her nipples grew hard, tight, and definitely tender.

As if he read her mind, or maybe she'd telegraphed her desire, one big, callused hand settled on her breast. He squeezed his palm against her nipple, giving her a little ease.

She groaned. "I ache."

"I promise to make everything better," Matt whispered.

"Less talk. More action,"

His chuckle sped another shudder through her, then to her relief, he kissed her hard and wet with tongue. Such a great kiss, it melted her.

She held on tight while he did other equally decadent things to her body. His hands coasted down her rib cage and settled on her hips while he moved his mouth across her throat. He sucked on the upper curve of one breast before his mouth hit her nipple. The way he drew on her breast was bliss. Amusement followed the thought. She—the ever-practical woman—was thinking about bliss in connection with sex.

And she was thinking other airy-fairy stuff too.

One big hand cupped her butt and squeezed, rocketing sensation in all directions. Ada moaned and clung to him in a tight embrace. Their lips met again for one of those excellent soul-destroying kisses. She parted her legs farther and wrapped them around his hips.

"You in a hurry?"

"I am now," she murmured and did some exploring

of her own with her mouth. His neck tasted faintly salty while he smelled of soap. Her soap. Her man.

At least for now.

Ada shoved away the thought and lived in the moment. She ran her fingernails down his back, his hoarse groan driving her pleasure.

His body, she discovered, was a splendid work of art. Muscles honed by his soldiering. Tight butt. Long, heavy limbs, full of power and abs she wanted to explore at closer quarters.

With that in mind, she wriggled from his embrace, intent on examining those ridges and muscles of his abs.

"No." Matt's tone held an order. He gripped her wrists to halt her investigation of his body. "I'm holding on by a thread here. I enjoy sex the same as other men, but it gets old after a while. Haven't done this for months."

Ada studied his face. He wasn't lying.

"Me neither."

"Got that, sweetheart, and that's why I want to make sure it's good for you."

That said, he released her wrists, paused a beat—she thought to make sure she intended to obey his edict—and kissed his way down her body.

Her hips lifted without volition. Cool air bathed the swollen flesh between her legs while anticipation bubbled within her like sparkling wine. As he moved even lower, his gaze connected with hers. Hot, masculine intent blazed back at her, the desire flowing from him drying her mouth. She swallowed and gulped when he bit her inner thigh. The hint of pain darted straight to her center, and one hard pulse pumped through her. His lick seconds later had her gasping.

"Matt," she whispered hoarsely, his name a desperate demand to hurry.

He chuckled. Message received loud and clear.

Just when the anticipation had turned her tense, he took one languid lick along her slit. He did this tongue swirl thing that made her gasp and her hips lift to give him better access. The second pass of his tongue pushed her closer to climax. So good. And so much quicker than usual.

"Yes," she murmured. "Yes. Right there."

He laughed against her flesh, but she wasn't sure why. Then, she didn't care because he sucked on her clit, the direct stimulation shoving her over a cliff. In free-fall, she toppled into the bubbling heat and passion, the spasms of her sex continuing for long seconds while every bit of tension in her receded.

Matt kissed her inner thigh, giving her another hint of teeth before he rose up the bed and took her into his arms. His mouth covered hers, and he kissed her senseless until all she cared about was the man in her bed. His erection left a wet trail on her upper belly, yet he did nothing to hustle them on to the next step. He touched and kissed and nibbled. He caressed and explored until he'd sussed out every one of her tender spots.

Ada drifted on a cloud of sensual heat, drowsy and replete, and willing to let him set the pace. His kisses were sublime, and she couldn't get enough of his mouth and tongue.

Matt pulled from a kiss and grabbed a condom. He sheathed himself with quick efficiency and covered her. He notched his cock at her entrance and pushed inside before halting.

"Why are you stopping?"

"I don't want to hurt you."

In lieu of an answer, Ada jerked her hips, driving Matt deeper into her body. "Please," she said simply, her gaze on his. "I don't care if you hurt me. Not that I think you will. I'm ready, and any aches and pains are welcome. Tomorrow, I'll remember this. You."

Matt withdrew, and this time pushed deeper, his cock gliding into her.

She released a deep, gratified sigh and gripped his shoulders. "More."

Matt chuckled, and in his next thrust, he filled her.

He held still for an instant and kissed her in that slow, profound way she adored.

"Feels good," Matt whispered against her ear.

"On my end, too. So fantastic. Sublime."

They rocked together, Matt's big body shuddering in her arms. She sensed he was close, but even so, he took the time to make certain she was with him. One blunt finger strummed her clit even as his thrusts became jerky. His mouth slammed down, the nip of his teeth driving her into another orgasm. The instant she pulsed around his cock, he removed his finger and pumped his hips. Harder. Faster. His breath emerged in hoarse pants.

"Feels amazing," he whispered, punctuating this with a loud groan. His hips snapped in rapid jerks, and he stilled while buried deep inside her.

Ada clung to him, her eyes closed as her breathing returned to something resembling normal.

"Sweetheart," Matt whispered. He brushed the hair from her face and kissed the corner of her mouth—a soothing kiss.

She smiled. "Thanks."

"I should thank you."

Matt kissed her again and separated their bodies. He took care of the condom and returned. Ada sank back into his arms, drawn like a magnet. She felt complete and happy with not an ounce of the tension and worries she normally experienced. Her eyes fluttered closed, and she sank into sleep.

Matt made love to her again in the early morning, or at least she thought it wasn't a dream. When she woke again, it was to a coffee scent floating through the air. She jerked upright, worried she'd woken late, but a glance reassured her it was six and her standard waking time.

Ada climbed out of bed, aware of a slight soreness but not minding. She plucked clean clothes from storage, deciding a quick shower might be in order before she started work.

"You're awake." Matt stood and stalked over to her. He kissed her good morning, his breath tasting of coffee.

"Is there enough coffee for me?"

"I'll pour you one."

"Give me five minutes," Ada said. "I need a shower."

"Don't take too long. I need to leave in fifteen minutes at the latest."

Given the time limitation, Ada didn't argue and had a speedy shower before heading back to her kitchen, now fully dressed. "Did you intend to wake me?"

"I thought you'd prefer to sleep."

"For future reference, if we do this again, wake me. Tell me you're leaving." *And kiss me goodbye,* she finished silently. *I never want to have a man leave me without saying goodbye.*

He stared at her for a moment and offered a clipped nod. He handed her a cup of coffee, prepared just as she liked it. "I'll remember. Toast?"

"Please."

He grabbed the bread and filled the two slots of the toaster. "I'll do a quick reconnoiter before I go. We don't want to miss someone loitering and waiting for me to leave."

"I'll be fine." Ada sent a prayer skyward, hoping she was speaking the truth.

"Not sure what time Josh will arrive, but let him help you. He wouldn't have volunteered to stay if he didn't mean it."

Ada frowned. "He doesn't need to sleep here."

"Please let him. For my peace of mind," Matt said. "He's a brother. I trusted him to keep my sister safe, and he'll keep you from harm too. Do it for me. Please."

Finally, Ada nodded.

"You have my phone number along with Josh's and Dillon's. Use them if you need one of us. Promise."

"Anything else?" Ada asked, letting her testiness show.

"Yes." He leaned closer to kiss her cheek. "Keep the bed warm for me. I'll be back at the weekend."

He'd told Ada this was the last week of training before he headed to Auckland. She hated to seem needy, but she'd miss him. It was going to be bad enough this week. The man had wormed under her skin, and she wasn't sure if she liked her growing desire.

"And keep out of mischief," he added.

Ada scoffed at that. Trouble followed her around like a tame puppy.

True to his word, Matt headed out fifteen minutes later, his pack on his back. Ada watched him through her kitchen window, her mind going back to that awful time of Greg's murder. At least this time, she'd kissed Matt goodbye. But somehow, it didn't make much difference.

Matt had left, and the idea she might never see him again twisted her into knots.

Ada released a gusty sigh before forcing herself into action. She locked her house and surveyed the shed before checking on her damaged flowers. For the next hour, Ada hand-pulled the trampled plants and tossed them aside. With that done, she strode back to get her rotary hoe.

A cop car halted in her driveway as she unlocked her shed. Every muscle in her body turned rigid at seeing the same detectives from yesterday. Their suits seemed more rumpled, so perhaps they'd worked through the night.

"Can I help you?" Her anxiety emerged in her unusually

squeaky voice, and she had to force down her swelling panic. The determination in their gazes didn't bode well.

"We want to question you again. At the station this time," Detective George said, his tone calm while his gaze dissected her reaction.

"Now?" Ada asked in forced exasperation. What did they want from her? What had happened overnight? "I'm busy working. Can't you ask me what you want now?"

"This is a formal interview. If you don't come willingly, we'll arrest you."

"On what charges?" Ada straightened and met their gaze with attitude. "I have done nothing wrong."

Josh pulled up in his camper van and climbed out. His brows rose at the tension sizzling in the air. "Problem?"

"They want to question me at the police station," Ada snapped, glaring at the two detectives. "They're threatening to arrest me if I don't go with them."

"What do you want to do?" Josh asked.

Her hands fisted at her sides. "I guess I'm going to the station."

"Want some company?" Josh asked.

"That's not necessary," Detective George said quickly.

"It's your right to have someone with you. If not me, a lawyer," Josh said in an even tone.

Silent hostility vibrated between the detectives and

Ada. A tangible, mutual distrust. A gut instinct that she balanced on an invisible precipice and must step with caution.

"I'd like you to sit with me." Ada fought to keep her tone even and calm. It was harassment, and none of it was fair. Matt had been with her the entire weekend, yet that didn't seem to matter to these idiots.

"Get in the back," Detective George said with a growl in his voice.

When Josh followed, Detective Conroy stepped in front of him.

"Just her. You'll need to find your own way."

With a shrug, Josh headed for the camper van. When the cop car pulled away with her in the back, Josh was busy speaking on the phone.

Ada stared out the window during the drive into town. Detective Conroy pulled up in a loading zone, and she and Detective George exited the car. When he took her elbow, Ada jerked from his touch, her anger and frustration skyrocketing when she noted the curious glances directed their way. The gossip relating to this questioning would spread like a noxious weed.

Sherry, who was leaving her office right next door to the police station, approached them. Concern furrowed her brow. "Is something wrong?" she asked in her caring way.

"Can I help?"

"A misunderstanding," Ada said through clenched teeth.

"Would you like to come to dinner tonight?" Sherry asked. "It'll be just Bart and me."

"Maybe another time," Ada replied since, although she loved Sherry to bits for her kind heart and generosity, she could be a bit of a blabbermouth.

"Hurry," Detective George ordered. "This isn't a social occasion."

"We need to wait for Josh," Ada countered, dragging her steps despite the locals' nosy interest.

"Someone will show him to the interview room."

Sherry limped closer, sympathy filling her brown eyes. "Are you certain I can't help?"

At that moment, Ada spotted Josh's campervan, and the tension in her shoulders released. Instinct insisted she needed a witness to whatever this was, and since Josh was Matt's friend, and Josh's wife was the prime minister, she trusted him to help her get through this ordeal.

Detective George guided her into the station—a nondescript reception area with mismatched chairs and faded posters attached to grimy cream walls. He gestured her along a short corridor to an interview room. The detective shoved open the door and pointed to a chair.

A fabricated table and three matching chairs sat nearby. Recording equipment filled a shelf.

"Wait there until my partner arrives."

Ada settled on the chair only to leap to her feet and pace once Detective George left the room. She hadn't even taken the time to grab her handbag, and while her phone was in her pocket, she had no idea of whom to call to extract her from this mess. She prowled several circuits of the nondescript room before footsteps approached. Quickly, Ada dropped onto a seat. Detectives George and Conroy entered the room, but there was no sign of Josh.

"We will record this conversation," Detective George took a seat on the opposite side of the table to her and read Ada her Miranda rights.

Ada's eyes widened at this, and she tugged at her T-shirt.

"Present are Ms. Ada Buckingham, Detective Steve George, and Detective Michael Conroy."

"Ms. Buckingham, please tell us how you know Ralph Dawson," Detective George said.

Ada pressed her lips together.

"Did you hear me, Ms. Buckingham?" he repeated.

"I did, but I'm not answering questions until Josh is here."

"Stopping recording at 8:43. Detective Conroy is leaving the room." Detective George clicked the machine off, and Detective Conroy walked from the interview room.

"It's in your best interests to answer our questions."

Ada let out a contemptuous snort. "You've advised me of my rights. I have the right to remain silent. I don't have to do anything."

Frustration flitted across Detective George's face before it cleared to impassive while Ada folded her hands in her lap and pretended a patience and calmness she didn't feel. Inside, anger and fear roiled like a stormy ocean. Tears itched to fall, and she batted her eyes to confine them. Everything about this situation reminded her of Greg's death. *So many prickling, upsetting emotions clawing for freedom.*

It was almost ten minutes later when Detective Conroy arrived with Josh.

The detective whispered something to his partner, and Detective George muttered an audible curse.

He glared at her, took a deep breath, and clicked on the recorder. "Interview suspended until Ms. Buckingham's lawyer is present."

Then, without another word, both detectives left the room.

"What's going on?" Ada asked Josh.

"I called Dillon, and he suggested I contact a family

friend who is a lawyer. I'm not sure what's going on here, but it's obvious they're trying to pin this murder on you. They have evidence that supports your arrest rather than believing you spent the weekend with Matt."

"I can't afford a lawyer," Ada objected, the enormous financial burden dangling over her head, bringing her out in a nervous sweat. Lord, how Greg's parents would celebrate this news.

"Don't worry. The lawyer is a friend, and he's returning a favor I did for him last year. He's Dad's friend and retired a few months ago. He doesn't mind helping after I explained everything to him. Also, you're Frog's girl, and I promised him I'd watch over you. This is me sticking to my promise."

Tears burned Ada's eyes. "Thanks."

Her lawyer showed up about half an hour later. Jeff Hoete was an older man with a full head of silver hair and dark skin proclaiming his Māori blood. He wore faded jeans and a black-and-red plaid shirt. His gumboots squeaked on the floor, and his blue eyes twinkled at her when he shook her hand. "I understand you've landed in trouble. Josh explained what he knew, but why don't you tell me the rest before I call the detectives and inform them we're ready for them."

Ada told Jeff everything. "I haven't seen Ralph Dawson

for weeks. In fact, I can remember the exact day I saw him last. It was at the local business owners' meeting on a Tuesday night at the beginning of last month. Sherry organizes it, and we have guest speakers from various organizations. We discussed security issues since we've had theft problems recently. Bart, Sherry's husband, asked if anyone had land available for grazing, and I discussed grazing options for my farm. In the end, I let the army use my land for their training since they were offering more money."

"Anything else you can add?" Jeff asked.

"Nothing I can think of."

"Right, then. We'll call the detectives back and let them ask their questions." He patted her hand. "Don't worry. We'll have you out of here in no time."

The two detectives strutted into the interview room with Detective George radiating attitude. Ada shrugged, tired of his posturing. All she wanted to do was return to her flowers.

After the formalities for the tape, Detective George started with his questions. He asked her to account for her time during the weekend. She repeated what she'd told him twice already.

"Were you having an affair with Ralph Dawson?"

"No," Ada replied in a firm voice. Jeff had told her to

answer their questions and not embellish on her answers, so she did that.

"Where were you on Saturday night?"

"At my property."

"Can anyone confirm that?"

"Matt Townsend."

The two detectives exchanged a glance, and Detective Conroy produced what looked like a letter encased in a plastic evidence bag.

"Do you recognize the signature on this sheet of paper?"

Ada accepted the bag and scanned the signature. "It looks like mine."

"Please note for the tape Ms. Buckingham has identified the letter discovered on Mr. Dawson's property," Detective George said in a dry voice.

Detective Conroy pushed a second item toward her, this one not in an evidence bag.

"For the record, we are showing Ms. Buckingham a copy of the letter." Detective George's voice held so much satisfaction fear crawled down Ada's spine. Sweat formed beneath her T-shirt. "Please read this letter, Ms. Buckingham."

Ada picked up the single sheet of paper and couldn't hide the slight tremor of her right hand. She stared at the page. The signature on the computer-printed letter resembled hers, but she'd never seen the contents, and she hadn't written it. A person might describe it as a love letter, but she'd call it erotica, and the notion she'd do any of that stuff with Ralph Dawson filled her with disgust. She'd never have an affair with a married man. *Never.*

"Did you write that letter, Ms. Buckingham?" Detective George asked.

"No, I did not."

She handed it to Jeff, who read the copy in silence, then shoved it across the table to Detective George.

The two detectives fired dozens of questions at Ada. Some she answered while others, Jeff objected to and advised her not to provide a reply.

"Is that all?" Ada finally demanded. "I want to harvest my flowers, and I can't do it while I'm here. They're forecasting rain, and the picking is time-sensitive."

The two detectives shared a glance.

"Fine, you can go, Ms. Buckingham. Please don't leave town without speaking to us. I'm sure we will have further questions."

Detective Conroy pushed away from the wall he'd been leaning against to open the door. Anger pumped through Ada, and she flayed the arrogant man with her gaze. Then, she followed Jeff from the room and out of the police station.

"Have a coffee and a sandwich with me," Jeff said. "Then I'll give you a ride back to your place. Josh told me he intended to return to your farm and pick flowers for you."

"I don't have money," Ada said. "I didn't have time to grab my wallet."

"My treat. We'll talk strategy while we eat."

Chapter 19

Matt's Unexpected Visit

THE WEEK MOVED AT the pace of a frozen alpine river. Each day, each hour, each minute, Ada half expected the detectives to arrive and arrest her. She jumped at every sound, and sleep became elusive. Josh's company was the only thing that kept her sane. That and Matt's calls. He'd rung to warn her they were firing ammunition, and she was grateful when the gunfire started.

After eight at night, she sat on her deck with Archie rubbing against her legs. Josh sat outside his camper van, talking on the phone. Probably with his wife. He made a point of calling Ashley every night. While nothing had happened, she was grateful for his presence.

Ada sipped her tea, exhausted, but she didn't have

the energy to move. Archie stiffened beneath her hand, and Josh's head shot up, and he rose, every part of him suddenly the soldier.

"It's me," Matt said, pausing in a patch of light.

Josh relaxed, as did Ada. Archie meowed and trotted over to greet Matt. Ada had noticed Archie hadn't hissed at Josh or any of her visitors apart from the Walsh family, but she'd love to give Sherry's sons a raspberry herself.

"You didn't think of calling to let us know you were coming?" Josh asked without stinting on the sarcasm.

"Sorry. Unexpected visit," Matt said. "The boys and I spotted lights on your land. Bikes too, but we were too far away to see what was happening."

Ada surged to her feet. "I want to see. Do you think they'll still be there?"

"Ada, you're dog-tired," Josh said.

Matt walked closer and pulled her into a loose embrace. He pushed aside a lock of her hair and stole a quick kiss before pulling back. "Josh is right. They've probably gone by now, but I wanted to check in case they had permission to be on your land."

"You and your men are the only ones," Ada said. "How far away were they?"

"About half an hour walk from here," Matt said.

"Let's go," Ada said. "Even if they're not still there, you

can show me their location. Maybe it's the neighbor's land rather than mine."

"Bart Walsh's land?" Josh asked.

"Yes," Ada replied. "The plots aren't square, and Bart's land dog-legs into mine at one point."

"I'm coming with you," Josh said. "Let me secure the camper van and grab my phone."

Ada switched off the lights, locked up, and retrieved her phone. She shoved her feet into a pair of gumboots. "Let's do this."

Matt grasped Ada's hand and led the way along her farm track. Once they approached the bush, they moved along the single-file path with Matt leading and Josh in the rear. It didn't take long for Ada's night vision to kick in, and the almost full moon helped their rapid ascent to the top of a hill.

"I'm impressed," Josh said once they reached the summit. "You kept up with Frog's pace easily."

"I spend most days outdoors doing physical work," Ada said, irritation burning away her fatigue.

"Stop your yakking, Josh," Matt warned. He drew Ada against his side and whispered, "We spotted the lights in that direction."

Most of the hill was in shadows, but Ada recognized the spot.

"The boundary cuts through that hill. One side belongs to me and the other to Bart and Sherry. Bart asked if he could buy this section of my land, but I told him no at the time." Besides, the land wasn't hers to sell. Determination forged through her—yet.

"Whoever was there has gone now." Josh kept his voice low.

"Have you noticed lights there before?" Ada asked.

Matt played with a lock of her hair, his fingertips running over the soft skin behind her ear. "Not in that location. The lights I spotted last week were near the yards."

Ada leaned into him, not wanting to admit to herself how much she'd missed having Matt around.

"Lights," Josh whispered.

Ada's head jerked upward, and she studied the darkened landscape. She spotted two lights. No, three before the rumble of engines drifted to her.

"They're on my land, whoever they are," Ada said.

"It looks like a vehicle or farm bikes," Josh said.

"One of each," Matt said a moment later.

The lights stopped as the three of them fell silent. The noise of engines ceased, and the lights flicked off. They waited for another ten minutes, but nothing else happened.

"What do you suppose that was about?" Josh asked.

"I don't have a clue," Ada said. "The only thing I can think of is that it's something to do with the thefts from the farms in the district."

"Someone using your land," Matt said. "Yeah, I can see how that would make sense."

"Most in the Moewai district will know I'm only using the front of my farm. I don't have animals, making it logical for people to presume I'd never visit this part of my land. I guess hiring it out to the army put a crimp in their plans."

"Anyone ask questions?" Josh asked.

"My neighbor. I don't recall if anyone else asked me directly, but this is a small town. Word gets around, especially if they see strangers."

"I noticed people staring when I strolled through town," Matt said, keeping his voice low when he spotted the lights again.

"We're too far away," Josh said.

"Doesn't matter. I'll check it out tomorrow morning," Matt promised. "I'll take photos and call you when I get a chance."

Ada frowned at the lights. "Could this have something to do with Ralph Dawson's death? The way the police were questioning me, I believe his death was murder rather than suicide." No sooner had she mentioned that than another idea presented itself—one that sent a shudder through her. "Greg was murdered up here. The area where the lights are flickering off and on isn't far from where I discovered his body."

Ada felt Matt's gaze, and she shifted a fraction, uneasy, and struggling with the surge of memories.

"The police questioned you again?"

"Twice now. Today, it was formal questioning at the station."

"But you were with me the entire time."

"Apart from when you went into town," Ada said. "I believe the locals have mentioned they saw you."

"Where were you when the cops questioned Ada?" Matt asked Josh.

"I followed her into town and called an old family friend. He's a lawyer. Jeff was with Ada when they questioned her. Whatever they suspect, they don't have enough proof to arrest Ada because they let her go home."

"Or it could be the fact I'm innocent," Ada snapped. "The lights are on the move."

They fell silent, and the three watched the illumination move away from them. Three minutes later, the last retreated and vanished.

"Were you going to tell me about the interview at the

police station?" Matt asked, breaking the silence.

"Yes. Your news and the hasty walk here distracted me," Ada said.

"If Ada hadn't told you, I would've," Josh said, and something in his tone told Ada he meant this. He'd never keep secrets from his friend.

Matt rolled to his feet and stretched. "I'd better get back to camp. Josh, can I count on you to take care of Ada?"

"Yes," Josh confirmed.

Ada bristled, irritated yet strangely touched too because having a man around the place was a valuable asset with the weird stuff happening lately.

Matt pivoted to her and reached for her hand. He clasped her fingers in his, and instantly, tingles replaced her irritation. "Stay safe, sweetheart. I'll try to visit tomorrow night, but it depends if the training goes to schedule."

"It's okay. I understand you're busy with work."

Matt took her mouth in a hot, possessive kiss. He pulled back and pressed his forehead against hers for an instant. "Take care of my girl," he said to Josh and left, fading into the shadows with nary a sound.

"Come on." Josh tapped her upper arm. "We should get a few hours of sleep, at least. My employer is a slave driver," he added. "I need to work tomorrow."

Ada huffed but fell in behind Josh. The ex-soldier

moved without hesitation but stopped now and then to listen to the background noise. Neither of them spoke during the trek back to Ada's home, giving her plenty of time to think about what those people had been doing. Foremost, people who skulked in the dark on land that didn't belong to them were up to mischief.

When they reached Ada's house, Josh stopped. "What time are we moving in the morning?"

"I'm going to the mid-week farmers' market. I need to leave here by eight-thirty at the latest. Before that, I need to bag confetti samples and pick flowers. Ella mentioned coming, but she hasn't confirmed."

"She'll be at work at the bird reserve place," Josh said.

"Right. I'd forgotten that. Ella didn't mention the mid-week market, now that I think of it."

"I can help."

"Sell flowers?"

"I didn't think I'd enjoy picking," Josh said bluntly. "Turns out, I'm appreciating the change and being outdoors instead of hanging around waiting for Ashley's meetings to end. I do security work, but I've thought it might be nice to have an interest in a landholding. That would mean I could play farmer sometimes, yet still do the odd security job and help Ash when she needs me at her back. If you ever decide you need an investor, make sure you ask me first. Ash loved it here and enjoyed the flowers. She has a green thumb when she has time." Then, with a wave, Josh headed for her tiny house. "I'll check the perimeter and make certain everything is okay before I grab some sleep. It sounds as if I have a busy day tomorrow."

Ada paused, staring after him in shock. She'd never thought of bringing in an investor. Could that be the answer to her loan repayment problem?

· ❤ · ❤ · ♥ · ❤ · ❤ ·

MATT DIDN'T DO ANY scouting until mid-morning, and even then, his time was fleeting. He set off from camp at a jog, telling his fellow trainers he needed to check on something, and he'd be back in under an hour. His sense of direction, honed by his time in the army, was infallible, and he had no difficulty finding his way to the spot where he'd spied the lights.

A shed, which he hadn't noticed because it blended, sat on the edge of a stand of trees. Distinct tire tracks led up to the locked shed. Unfortunately, he hadn't brought tools with him, and there were no windows he could peek through. He made a mental note to quiz Ada about the building because she hadn't mentioned one. He scanned the area and thought the track was relatively new. The scars on the landscape hadn't healed after the use of a digger. The dirt was a distinct orange-red. Although the area wasn't far from where he and his soldiers had camped, the soil here told of a past volcanic eruption.

He reconnoitered the area and spotted a track that curled behind the shed. He cocked his head before skulking along the undulating path and into the trees. While he noticed more tire tracks, he saw nothing else suspicious and retraced his footsteps.

As he suspected, the track joined the gravel road that eventually emerged on the main one. Interesting, although he had no bloody idea what any of this meant. For all he knew, the people who'd been here last night were trapping possums or the like.

Matt ran along the road and turned right to head back to camp. He'd call Ada tonight, not that he'd learned much. Still, his spidey senses told him this discovery might be important. He thought over everything he needed to achieve between now and the weekend and gritted his teeth. For the first time, his mission—his job—took second place, and that, he decided, was telling.

· ❤ · ❤ · ❤ · ❤ · ❤ ·

Josh was a tremendous help with picking the flowers and setting up at the farmers' market. Ada went to pay Sherry for her stall while Josh unloaded the last of the flowers and prepared her booth.

"Hi, Sherry," Ada said once she reached the front of the line. "How are things with you today?"

Sherry flashed a bright smile, but she didn't appear as happy as usual.

"You look tired," Ada added before Sherry spoke.

"I didn't sleep well. Kids," she said with a rueful shake of her head. "You think you've got rid of them, and they decide they might move home." She smiled. "How are you, dear? What did the police want with you yesterday?"

"Not much," Ada said, her tone dry. She handed over the money to pay for the stall.

"Yours is not the only trouble around." Sherry wrote out a receipt for Ada. "The Davidsons had a break-in last night. I'm not sure what the culprits stole, but Chad Davidson called the police."

Ada scowled. "That's not good."

"No." Sherry handed over the receipt and smiled at the next person in the line.

Ada was still frowning when she reached her stall.

"I need coffee," Josh said. "My shout. What do you prefer?"

"I could murder a coffee," Ada said, then winced at her words. "A latte would be great. Thanks."

"Consider it done. When I get back, you can tell me what has upset you."

Ada did a quick scan for eavesdroppers and leaned closer to Josh. "Sherry told me one of the local farmers had a theft last night. She had a queue of people waiting to pay, which meant I couldn't quiz her. Can you see if you can learn anything while you're buying coffee? There will be gossip."

He gave a curt nod and strode away while Ada busied herself with arranging her signage.

By the time Josh returned with coffee and two chocolate croissants, Ada had sold two bunches of flowers. Josh waited for her customers to leave before handing over the coffee.

"You were right," he said in an undertone. "Gossip central. People are talking about Ralph Dawson's murder." Josh scowled into his coffee.

The man was stalling. Ada could imagine the chatter since the locals would've known the police questioned her at the station. She'd been through this after Greg's murder. The scandal now couldn't be worse than that.

"Tell me," she urged. She sipped her coffee and muttered under her breath when the mouthful was hotter than she'd guessed. When Josh still hesitated, she took another more cautious sip.

"Most of the gossip suggested you had done the deed because he wouldn't leave his wife for you. The commentary was nasty."

Her fingers squeezed her cup hard enough to splash the contents over the rim. She muttered a curse and forced herself to relax. "Anything else?"

"Several locals didn't understand why the cops hadn't charged you yet. I expect your stall will be busy today since a few men and women expressed their surprise you have the nerve to show your face here."

"I see."

"Also, thieves struck two farms last night. One farmer lost a heap of power tools while another is missing two quad bikes and a golf cart."

"A golf cart?"

"Yeah. Either there is a gang hitting the properties, or they loaded the stolen gear onto a truck."

Ada tapped the side of her paper cup while she pondered. "This has been a terrible year for thefts. I've been lucky, but I don't own any large farm machinery. I own specialized equipment, and it wouldn't be easy to resell."

"You'd think the cops would be all over this," Josh said.

"Dillon will know if the thieves are hitting the farmers in Eketāhuna. I'll call him once we've finished here. *Uh-oh.* Here comes the first of the rubberneckers."

Ada straightened her shoulders. "As long as they buy flowers, I don't care. Their money will pay my bills the same as those who don't want a piece of me."

Josh chortled. "I'm the cause of additional gossip. Someone must've seen you with Frog. Half the town believes you had an affair with Ralph Dawson, and now you're here with me, and I'm wearing a wedding ring. They're not sure what to make of your exploits."

"Huh!" Ada bared her teeth in something she hoped resembled a smile when three women of varying ages pulled out of a huddle and strode toward her stall.

"Good morning, ladies," Josh said. "Can we entice you with a bunch of flowers this fine morning?"

The women smiled, and the youngest blushed a brilliant red. Not an attractive look. The instant Ada had the thought, she shoved it aside as bitchy.

The youngest woman sucked in a breath and thrust out her breasts. "I'll grab a bunch of the wildflowers, please." She sent Josh a broad smile full of flirtation. Ada watched the woman's gaze flick to Josh's wedding ring before she raised the wattage of her smile further.

Ada rolled her eyes and directed her attention to the

other women. "Can I help you?"

The two women exchanged a glance before focusing on Ada.

"Did you grow these flowers?" the older of the two asked.

The women bore a similarly shaped face, and their eyes were an identical shade of blue. One had snow-white hair in a bob, while the other had shoulder-length brown hair with pink streaks.

"Yes," Ada said. "Can I show you the delphiniums, or do you prefer cornflowers?"

"Two bunches of the delphinium, please," the younger one said. "The white ones."

The older woman who'd been staring at Josh and the youngest of the trio said, "You look familiar. Have we met before?"

Josh smilingly shook his head. "I don't think so. Although I lived in Eketāhuna for a while."

She tapped her chin with one fingertip. "Oh. I thought I'd seen you recently."

Josh shrugged off her interest with unconcern, and Ada wondered if the woman would click he was the first man. They wandered off with their flowers, and others crowded around, buying bunches of flowers as an excuse to loiter and ask nosy questions.

"How long had she been sleeping with Ralph Dawson?"

"Didn't you have any sympathy for his wife?"

"Have you lost your empathy because of your husband's murder?"

"Who is the dude staying with you?"

"Does his wife know?"

Each successive question left Ada incredulous, and she lifted her chin, meeting their rudeness with attitude. Couldn't they see she was right here?

Part of her wanted to pack up the rest of her flowers and hightail it out of there, but she gritted her teeth and pushed her blooms while attempting to ignore the increasingly offensive comments and plain nosiness.

Josh's smile faded under the onslaught. "Do you want to leave?" he asked in an undertone.

"Not until I sell my flowers. I need the money," Ada said through her bared teeth.

"Right." Josh worked harder to hawk the remaining bunches of flowers. With his charm and a ragged-at-the-edges smile, Josh sold all but one bunch of delphiniums.

"Good enough," Ada said. "I'll give these to Sherry on the way out. I've had more than enough malicious gossip."

Josh squeezed her forearm. "Small towns are the pits. None of what they're saying is true. Hold your head high and don't let them get to you."

"Thanks," Ada murmured.

Ada gave Josh her keys, and taking the last bunch of flowers, she headed for Sherry's office. Before she'd taken two steps, someone grasped her arm. Ada swung around.

"Does the prime minister know you're shacked up with her husband?" the woman from earlier asked in a loud voice.

People around them stared, and Ada drew herself up in distaste. It had been a mistake to come to the market. She'd find money another way. "What are you talking about?"

"That man is married to the prime minister of our country. I might not have voted for the woman, but I respect her, and she seems nice. She doesn't deserve this."

"Josh is my friend. That's all." Ada turned her back on the indignant woman and stalked into Sherry's office. "Sherry, I had one bunch of flowers left and thought you might like them."

"Oh! Aren't you sweet?" Sherry's brown eyes glowed with delight. "Thanks so much."

"I've got a lot to do," Ada said. "You're probably busy too."

Two men strode into the office and claimed Sherry's attention. Ada waved goodbye and left. She couldn't wait to get home and for this day to end.

CHAPTER 20

MYSTERIOUS LIGHTBULBS

WHEN THEY DROVE THROUGH the gateway—the open gate they'd closed before leaving—Josh let out a curse.

"Dammit, Frog was right to worry. Can you see anyone? Anything unusual?"

A sick sensation sloshed the coffee around in the pit of Ada's stomach. She scanned her shed, which on quick scrutiny, appeared untouched.

"Stay close to me," Josh said.

Ada slipped from behind the steering wheel, her gaze swinging left and right. As they neared her house, a loud hiss sounded from a bush. Ada started and muttered a rude word when Archie slunk from the depths of the foliage. His ruffled coat and expression screamed indignant.

"Do you see anything odd?"

Ada shook her head, irritated by this continual harassment because that's what it was—consistent bullying and intimidation designed to send her crazy. "I don't understand why someone is going to so much trouble to persecute me."

"It seems as if they're trying to force you out or at least scare you into leaving. Have you seen something you shouldn't? Or is there something about your land that makes it valuable?"

"The soil is excellent for growing flowers. Perfect. The hill country—I'm not doing the land any favors because I'm not farming it. I mentioned before I've had a few offers for the farm. The locals were certain I'd leave after Greg's death, but I had nothing back in Auckland. Most of my friends have moved on and married. They have children." She didn't mention Greg's parents and the situation with the land, although perhaps she should.

"I get it." Josh's hand whipped out to stop Ada when she went to step onto the deck.

"What's wrong?"

He directed her gaze to the three hunks of mud that had dropped off someone's footwear. Josh glanced at his boots, and they weren't muddy. Ada had worn shoes instead of her gumboots.

"That wasn't there when we left," Josh said with certainty.

"No," she agreed. "Let me change into my gumboots, then we'd better check on my flowers. The mud is the same as what I have in my fields. It's volcanic. Weirdly, my land has volcanic soil but not the neighbors'. Long ago, when a volcano erupted near here, the ash and minerals landed on my land. Strange, but excellent for flowers."

Her house door was still locked, and Ada shrugged. "Maybe it was a salesman come to call. Some people don't understand a shut gate should remain shut."

"Perhaps," Josh said, but his expression told Ada he didn't believe this suggestion any more than she did.

They found nothing out of place or unusual in the flower field, so Ada set to work picking rows they'd harvested days earlier.

She and Josh spent the rest of the day clearing the damaged plants and preparing the land for replanting, with Josh doing most of the heavy work.

Ada called a halt at six, starving because they hadn't bothered with lunch. They ate the pizza she'd cooked out on the deck and washed it down with a beer each. When Josh's phone rang, she collected the dishes and left him in privacy. The sun had set while they were eating and talking—Josh telling her about meeting Ashley and the part Matt had played in them getting together. She switched on the outside light and frowned when nothing happened. The bulb was relatively new and shouldn't have blown this quickly.

Ada was searching in her cupboard for a spare bulb when masculine voices drew her attention. Footsteps approached as she plucked the bulb free.

"Ada."

"Matt." She didn't hide her pleasure on seeing him. An instant later, she was in his arms, their mouths fused in a passionate kiss.

Matt pulled back and nuzzled her chin. "Missed you. I understand you've had excitement today."

"Yeah. Is it too much to wish for peace so I can focus on my flowers?"

"No, sweetheart. We'll sort this out. I promise."

"Yeah, if I'm not carted off to jail first," she muttered.

Matt took the bulb she was still holding from her hand. "Where does this go?"

"The outside lights aren't working. I only have one spare. Note to self—pick up more during my next shop."

"I'll change the bulb for you, then we'll have a meeting. Josh and I think you need security cameras, here and at your yards."

"I can't afford cameras, Matt. I wish I could, but I'm barely keeping my head above water as it is." It was a depiction of her growing trust in Matt that she'd even admit this shortfall to him.

"Josh works in security. I'll pay for the cameras, and if you insist, we can work out a payment plan for the future."

She nodded, but she hated this. Her business needed to produce a profit, and while it was early days for her flowers, this felt like a failure. "Thanks." She was grateful. She was, but accepting his loan felt like a backward step.

Matt came back in seconds. "The socket was empty. No bulb." Matt flicked the switch. "The other fitting doesn't have a bulb, either."

"The lights were working last night." Josh turned to Ada. "Now we know what our visitors did while we were away."

Ada gritted her teeth. "I wish they'd leave me alone."

"Those cameras are an important tool for us to catch whoever is doing this," Matt said. "Josh and I have a plan, and Dillon wants in on it too. Once I've completed this training, I'll be here for at least a month. Dillon and Josh have offered to skulk in the background watching and helping me to keep you safe."

"What about your job? Your reputation? At the market, a lady informed me I was horrid for playing around with the prime minister's husband. I told her we were friends, but I doubt she believed me."

"People can't help being idiots. I want to help you," Josh said. "Matt and I are related because of Ashley, but before that, we fought and trained together. We became brothers. We think there is something fishy going on here, and because you're Frog's woman, we're going to help you fix this. Plus, we enjoy a challenge."

Matt's woman? Was she? Ada glanced at Matt and met his gaze. She couldn't read his expression, but she got the sense he was ready to argue the point.

After Greg, she hadn't wanted to tie herself to a man again.

Happiness had felt wrong when Greg's murderer had gone unpunished and still roamed free. But would Greg want that for her? Her gaze shot to her feet as she considered this. If it had been her who died, she would've wanted Greg to move on and embrace life. She would've wanted his happiness.

The realization struck her with the force of a garden rake over the head.

Sure, she had a right to mourn, but she also had a right to be happy. Matt made her happy, and she felt as if she'd lived recently, despite the stress in her life. Decision made, she lifted her gaze. "Okay."

His approving smile did things to her insides, a pleasant hum warming her blood.

"Right," Josh said. "If we're agreed, I'm heading to the campervan to have phone sex with my gorgeous wife."

Matt growled without taking his gaze off Ada.

Josh rose with a chuckle. "My work here is done. See you in the morning."

Matt reached for her hand, the comforting squeeze melting her tension. Instantly, her body ached. She sucked in a breath, which lifted her breasts and drew Matt's attention.

"Bed," he said firmly.

She let him usher her inside. He locked the door after them and padded to the bedroom.

"I've missed you." Matt flicked on the light and stalked over to draw the curtains. "Got knocked on my arse because I was thinking about you instead of keeping my mind on the job."

"Ah, sorry?" Ada said, part of her pleased because she'd thought of him too. Constantly.

"Clothes off," Matt ordered, his fingers busy working on the buttons of his shirt. He drew the garment off, and she stared at his broad chest, the ripple of muscles as he moved.

He was down to his underwear before she'd even

started. "I better have a quick shower." He dragged down his boxer-briefs and kicked them free. She stared at his backside as he sauntered from the room and noticed it wasn't as lily-white as hers.

Thoughtful, she undressed and climbed into bed.

Matt was back before she'd thought of anything beyond what she needed to do the following day. She should check her website, her email to see if any more orders had arrived since this morning, but the sexy Matt distracted her in the best way, and she couldn't be sorry.

"Like what you see?" Matt asked.

"Yeah." Nothing less than the truth. "I missed you."

"Yeah." His sigh echoed hers. "Only two more days to go, but I don't want to discuss that." He crossed the remaining distance between the doorway and the bed with unconcern and slid beneath the covers.

Seconds later, he drew her against his chest and kissed the life out of her. Ada relaxed into his embrace and gave as much as she got.

He kissed the base of her neck where it met her shoulder and sucked hard enough for pain to zap her. She groaned, and he lifted his head, his eyes twinkling in the light cast from the single lamp on the nightstand.

"Do you mind a hint of pain?"

"I like it," she said with another groan after he repeated

the move. "It's not as if anyone is going to comment on any marks on my neck."

With a chuckle, he kissed her lightly on the mouth before his lips roved again. He kissed the tender skin behind one ear and nipped the upper swell of a breast. She exhaled, letting him touch as he liked while she ran her fingers over his shoulders, his back, and stroked his silky, albeit damp hair.

"Your breasts are gorgeous." His warm breath feathered against one nipple. "Always used to be a leg man. Your legs are stunning because you work so hard and are constantly active. But these." He squeezed a fraction, and a bolt of sensation arced toward her toes. "These are full and overflow my hands. I adore them."

He whispered and talked constantly, telling her how much he enjoyed her body and what he wanted to do to her next. Ada relaxed into the moment, kissing and caressing in return. She'd missed this intimacy, the shared laughter in the darkness, the togetherness, and the easy build of passion. Her nerves quivered while heat grew at her center.

Matt nipped her hip, and she jumped.

"Checking you're awake. You've gone quiet."

"Not asleep," she murmured. "I was thinking about how much I've missed being with a man."

Matt stilled, his gaze going to her. "I'm not a replacement, babe."

"No, I don't mean it like that. I don't think of Greg when I see you. You're very different men with distinct personalities. You're way more open than Greg was, and given your background, I would've guessed otherwise."

"Your husband kept secrets?"

"One or two," she said, the words escaping before commonsense snapped to the fore. "Sorry. I've spoiled the moment."

Matt shifted his hips, and his erection slid along the top of her thigh. "Nothing spoiled," he shared. And he set about kissing her again. This time, he didn't stop but seemed determined to crack her control. He kissed. He stroked. He pinched. Each move ratcheted up the sensual tension inside her. When he finally worked down her body, she splayed her legs without shame, silently urging him to move to the next step. He didn't disappoint.

His mouth roved.

He licked. He teased until her flesh throbbed, and her impending climax lay in wait like a cat waiting to pounce. She groaned. Ada tugged his hair, but all he did was chuckle as if he wanted to drive her crazy.

Up, up, up, she soared, then everything snapped, and lights flashed behind her closed lids as her orgasm exploded. Spasms were still striking her when Matt moved. Seconds later, he had a condom on, and he slid home.

Ada clung to his shoulders and twined her legs around his hips, encouraging him to move. He didn't disappoint her with steady strokes that pushed and retreated at an equal pace.

"You have a magic cock," she muttered.

His bark of laughter tipped her mouth into a smile. "How so?" His grin lit his expression and showed open joy and amusement.

"I'm pretty sure I'm going to come again, which is not normal for me."

"Slower or faster?" he asked.

"Everything," she said on a blissful sigh. "Everything."

His smile widened as he continued his firm, even strokes. In. Out. With each thrust, he strummed her sensitized flesh.

Ada hesitated, then reached between them to give herself the extra stimulation she needed.

"Good girl," he murmured. "A capable woman who knows what she wants. I like it," he murmured seconds before he kissed her with lips, tongue, and a hint of teeth. He increased the pace of his strokes, and the friction was perfect. She flew again, soaring in her pleasure.

Matt grunted, thrust hard, and remained embedded

inside her as he released a moan of his own. His breathing slowed, and his eyes popped open. Lazy sensuality glittered in them as he cupped her cheek and kissed her deeply. Their tongues stroked together as Ada let her legs drop to the bed.

"Wow," she whispered.

Matt pressed a butterfly kiss to her lips and parted their bodies. He stood to deal with the condom before returning to the bed and sliding in beside her.

"That was even better than I remembered," Matt said. "And I have an excellent memory."

Suddenly exhausted, Ada yawned. "Yes."

Matt laughed again, and his amusement was the last thing she recalled as she fell asleep.

She woke many hours later to the sound of birdsong. Matt no longer lay at her side, but low masculine conversation carried from the kitchen. Ada pulled a robe from the wardrobe and belted it around her waist. She grabbed clean underwear and clothes before she headed to the bathroom.

"Good morning." Josh spotted her first. He said nothing else, but one look at his handsome face told her he knew what she and Matt had been doing the previous night.

Matt turned and smiled. A panty-wetting smile, if she'd

been wearing any. He stood and walked toward her, kissing her good morning despite their audience. "Do you want coffee or tea?"

"Tea, please. I'll take a shower and be out in ten minutes."

He nodded. "Breakfast?"

"Toast and vegemite are fine."

His gaze drifted from her mouth and traveled down her neck to rest at her decolletage. A tiny grin played around his lips. "Might want to wear a T-shirt without a scoop neck today."

A blush ran through Ada, and she rolled her eyes at Matt before she escaped to the bathroom. She surveyed her neck in the bathroom mirror.

Matt had marked her, and judging by his expression, he liked that he'd done it. She hadn't told him no the previous evening, so she could hardly object to the consequences now.

With a head-shake, Ada jumped in the shower. Five minutes later, she was patting her body dry and slipping into underwear. She plastered on sunscreen and pulled on jeans and a T-shirt. She gathered her hair into her everyday high ponytail and called herself done and ready to face the day.

"Tea," Matt said when she walked into the kitchen area.

"Your toast is ready. I'll bring it outside for you. Josh is drinking his coffee out there."

"What time are you going?"

"As soon as I finish my coffee and toast."

"I have bacon and eggs. Baked beans."

"Toast is fine," Matt said. "Go and enjoy your tea."

"I'm kind of afraid to walk outside and find something wrong."

"Josh would've noticed and told me if our culprit had returned."

Ada hoped Matt was right because the sick sensation in the pit of her belly told her otherwise, and she was so tired of the constant anxiety.

There, she'd admitted it. Thanks to Matt and now Josh, she at least had the illusion of safety. Someone to help and to talk her off a ledge when she thought she was going crazy.

Ada accepted the mug of tea from Matt. She walked outside and took possession of the remaining seat.

"Nice day," Josh said. "I sent Ash some photos, and she's keen to visit again. She's stuck in a budget meeting."

"Already?" Ada said, checking her wristwatch.

"Yep. Ash works as hard as you with her meetings, press conferences, and what-not. Then there are all the parliamentary briefs she reads in bed. It's worse than toast crumbs," he grumbled with a wink to let her know he was joking.

"I liked your family a lot," Ada said.

"Wait until you meet my sister, Summer. She's hell on wheels," he said, this time shaking his head. "Summer married an ex-military man. Dillon and I didn't approve at first, but Nikolai has grown on us."

Ada sipped her tea. "I don't have siblings. Greg had an older sister." She paused because she hated the rift that had grown between Greg and his family over him branching out on his own. The fact he'd died before they'd come around made it worse, and the way they blamed Ada for the family argument. "His family don't talk to me."

"Any particular reason?" Matt asked as he handed her a plate of toast. He leaned against the deck railing and watched her over the rim of his coffee mug.

"They blamed me for Greg's leaving the family business. They had wanted him to take over the dairy farm, but Greg hated milking cows. He was more interested in sheep and creating fantastic wool to make superior garments. That was his dream, but he died before he'd started properly." Heck, she should tell them about the complications with her land, yet she hesitated still.

"The police never discovered who killed him?" Josh asked.

Ada crunched on a piece of toast and vegemite and swallowed. "The case is still open, and now and then a cop rings me to chat about the case."

"Did they have a suspect?" Matt asked.

"Not a one. It was a mystery. The cops appealed to the public for information and offered a reward, but nothing. No one came forward."

"That's tough," Josh said.

"After all this time, I doubt the cops will ever solve Greg's murder." Ada applied herself to her toast.

"What are we doing today?" Josh asked.

"I'm sowing seeds in punnets and will transplant them in the area we cleared yesterday in a few weeks. I'll do another pick of the field and process the petals together instead of keeping the colors separate. Then, I guess I'll try to fix the fence and do other repairs I've been putting off. Plus, I need to decide on an online advertising plan. Get the blog thing underway and the publicity machine rolling."

"Why don't you let me tackle the fence?" Josh asked.

Grateful for the offer because she wasn't sure how to tighten the wire, Ada said, "That would be tremendous."

Matt pushed away from the railing. "I'd better head out. Ada, we'll be using live ammunition and a bit of flash-bang. You might hear noise later this afternoon and tomorrow morning. I'll be back here on Saturday morning after everyone pulls out."

"Dillon is picking up security cameras for me," Josh said. "We'll drive up and meet you on Saturday. We can give you a lift back to Ada's once we install the cameras."

"Thanks." Matt smiled at her. "Be good. Stay safe."

Ada forced a smile. "I'll do my best."

Matt took her into his arms and kissed her. Ada clung, for some reason, close to tears. When she pulled away, she blinked hard and maintained her smile.

"Saturday," she said. "I'll be at the farmers' market again."

Matt gave her another quick kiss. "Saturday," he confirmed and walked off without a backward glance.

Not for the first time, Ada jolted back to the day of Greg's murder. A chill crawled across her skin. He'd strode off with his regular cheerful whistle. Hours later, she'd discovered him in a pool of blood.

She swallowed hard and fervently hoped the similarities weren't a bad omen. She had enough crap in her life without the guilt of losing a second man.

Chapter 21

An Offer of Money

Ada didn't hear from Matt, but Josh explained this was normal with the exercise he was running. This didn't stop her worry, but she tried to keep herself busy. They were taking a lunch break while waiting for Dillon and Ella to arrive. The alert she'd set up pinged, and she picked up her phone.

"Yay! A confetti order. It's not huge, but every order helps." She thumbed the screen and spotted an email from the bank. Immediately, her stomach hollowed out, and fear swamped her. Her hand trembled as she opened the email—a reminder the loan was due in three weeks. One hundred thousand dollars she didn't have.

"What's wrong?" Josh asked, his tone sharp.

A vehicle pulled up in the driveway, and Ada rose. "Dillon and Ella are here." Saved by their arrival.

"Great. Dillon and I can set up a concealed camera here and maybe put them up at the cattle yards earlier than we planned. My thought is the soldiers are putting a crimp in their plans. You can't see the camp from the yards, but it must be nerve-racking for your culprits if they don't know where the soldiers will turn up next." Josh followed Ada onto the deck. "Ada?"

"Yes?"

"You will tell me what put that expression of panic on your face. If Frog were here, he'd want to know. Frog is my friend, and I'm here to help."

"Money problems," Ada muttered. "You can't help. No one can help."

"Hey, Dillon. Great timing. Ada just confessed she has money problems. I figure now might be the time to discuss the plan we put together with Frog while we were fighting overseas and missing home."

Dillon shot Ada a sharp look while Ella merely appeared puzzled. In contrast, Ada wasn't sure where to point her gaze or how to react.

Finally, Dillon nodded. "We'll talk on Saturday when Frog arrives. Ada, stop acting like we stole your puppy. If you need money, Josh, Dillon, and I can help. Ella and

Ash love the flower side of your business and helped me understand the popularity of weddings and confetti and how profitable the business will be soon. But you can't grow flowers on your hill country. It makes sense for you to diversify and perhaps take on partners. Let that stew for a while."

Ada opened and closed her mouth a few times before giving him a curt nod when words failed her.

"I talked to Summer." Ella's smile brimmed with enthusiasm. "Dillon's and Josh's sister. She's pregnant with her second kid and wanted something to do. I told her about your business, and she made a ton of graphics and a list of ideas for blog posts. She also suggested places for you to advertise."

"I've just received an order," Ada blurted, her heart beating faster than expected as she tried to take in the generosity of Matt's friends. After all these years of struggling alone, even receiving the offer, the suggestion of help thrilled her, humbled her.

"Great," Ella said. "I brought my camera and would like to take more photos. I want to help and see the next stage of the process."

"We'll get to work on putting in the security cameras," Josh said.

"Thanks." Ada hesitated before squaring her shoulders.

"Make sure you give me a bill for the installation."

"No," Dillon said. "We're doing this because someone is terrorizing you. It's not right. If you insist, you can contribute toward the cameras, but Josh got a great deal on them. We're not charging you for labor, but you can feed us dinner tonight if you insist."

"That, I can do. Thanks."

"Not necessary," Dillon said in his abrupt manner.

"Show me your dried confetti," Ella suggested. "What has the bride ordered?"

"A mix of petals," Ada replied as she hustled to her shed. "The groom ordered the confetti. It's a second marriage, and both the bride and groom have grown children. He was so sweet." Even as she spoke to Ella, Ada's mind danced back to Josh's and Dillon's suggestion. She couldn't let them give her money, even though it might solve her problems and allow her to focus on making a profit.

No.

But...

Maybe she'd speak with Matt when he arrived on Saturday. Even though her relationship with him felt right, it was still of short duration. She... No, she would not stick her head in the sand. Along with being a woman, she ran a fledgling business, so she'd act with commonsense.

"Ada, are you all right?"

"Have a lot on my mind."

Ella released a snort, her pink ponytail bobbing as she clicked her fingers in front of Ada's nose.

"The sexy Matt. I can spot man-problems at fifty paces."

"Not problems exactly, but everything between us feels too new to add a discussion of my finances."

"Ah, the men's plan. Let them discuss it with you. Ask questions. It's an idea they have. You don't have to say yes."

"But what if Matt and I don't stay together? We've known each other for two weeks."

"The thing about these military men. They're used to fast decisions and trusting their gut. They take information and run with it. No hesitation. Don't worry. You'll get used to it. As for if you and Matt having merely a fling, I don't see that. I've seen the way he looks at you and you him. Even if something separates you in the future, he's a decent man. You'd still be able to work with him."

"Perhaps."

"The portion of your land you're not using interests the men. They'd use the back road, and you'd never see them unless you wanted to."

Ada's breath hitched.

Ella smiled sympathetically and patted her arm. "Don't stress. Listen to their suggestion and think about their offer. Now, show me what you do with the confetti."

Ada set up the table with her cones and her cellophane bags and labels. "He wants a mix of purple and white since that is the color scheme for the wedding. He mentioned silver too, which is a bonus since I can use these silver cones. I send the petals in the cellophane bags, and the recipients tip those into the cones when they're ready to use the confetti."

"How many bags?" Ella asked as Ada opened a tub of purple petals and another of white.

"Ten bags," Ada said. "I measure five scoops of white and five of purple into this bowl, blend them, and pack a scoop in each of the bags. I seal each bag with one of my labels. Once I'm done, I pack everything in one of these boxes."

The job took no time with Ella's help.

"What's next?" Ella asked.

"I'll put this in the house, so I don't forget to courier it to my customer, check on the boys, and pick any late blooms. Mostly the same as I'm doing every day."

"I'll help," Ella said. "I'm enjoying this. Don't forget to spend time later checking out the things Summer has designed for you. She emailed me everything, and I put it on this flash drive for you."

"I can't believe she went to so much trouble for

someone she doesn't know."

"She told me Nikolai wouldn't let her do anything, and the doctor has prescribed bed rest. Summer was going crazy."

When they locked the shed and headed back to the house, Dillon and Josh had just finished placing the cameras in position.

"We've decided we will head up to your yards and put up the cameras today," Dillon said. "We've called Matt, so he knows we're coming. I'll show you how to access the camera feed once we get back."

"I'll stay and help Ada," Ella said.

Dillon kissed his wife on the cheek, and he and Josh headed out in Dillon's vehicle. The day passed rapidly. Ella chatted about the Eketāhuna community and told her how she and Dillon met, and she'd ended up stranded by a landslide. It made Ada realize she'd missed feminine company. Sure, Sherry popped in for a cup of tea now and then, but her neighbor was such a social butterfly and busy with her community activities that it was only once a month. Ada worked so hard preparing the land and planting her flowers that she fell asleep in her chair.

Dillon and Josh arrived back.

"How did it go?" Ada asked when they stopped for afternoon tea.

"We found lots of tire tracks around your yards, considering you're not using them," Josh said.

"That's strange," Ada said. "Are you sure it's not the army men? Matt mentioned they used vehicles to bring in supplies."

"We checked with Frog. He said no. They're parking farther down the road where you have a gate leading into the paddock. They'd chosen that spot to set up camp because the stream runs through there. The men like to wash the dirt off after a training session."

Josh shook his head. "My bet is whoever owned those lights we saw the other night is responsible for the tire tracks. It was much easier to see during daylight. They're using your yards since we spotted animal tracks."

"I hate this," Ada said.

"Don't worry," Dillon said. "Show me your phone. I need to upload an app for you to check the cameras. I'll set them up to send you an alert."

"My phone isn't reliable," Ada warned. "It's working fine now, but last week it wouldn't hold a charge. It's on the list of things to replace."

"I'll check it for you." Dillon held out his hand for her phone.

"Bossy, aren't you?" Ada said dryly.

"If you stay with Matt, you'll get used to it," Ella added

to the conversation. "They're all the same. You ask Ash and Summer when you meet her."

"Not one of you pays much heed," Josh grumbled.

Ella chortled, and Ada grinned in charity. They might be bossy, but she found herself hooked because her mind kept slipping to Matt. Several times throughout the day, she thought about him. Daydreams. That told her she was in trouble and much deeper than she realized. Ada shook her head. Her romance with Greg had been fast too. It seemed decisive men did it for her.

At eleven-twenty that night, her phone woke her with a beep. She bounded upright and seized it, panic tearing through her until she realized it was the camera app alert. Dillon had warned her a bird such as a morepork would set off the camera, and the app would automatically capture a photo.

She fumbled to check the alert and examined the image. Not a bird.

A vehicle. Mud covered the number plate, and she didn't recognize the farm vehicle. A quad bike followed its registration, also indistinguishable. A helmet concealed the driver's head, and the deep shadows didn't help.

Ada scowled at the photo. Tomorrow, she'd show the men and work on a plan. After the abrupt awakening, she tossed and turned, the puzzle driving her crazy.

CHAPTER 22

CLUES BUT NO ANSWERS

MATT ARRIVED AT THE farmers' market mid-morning, and she ignored her dithering customer to give him an enthusiastic welcome.

"I missed you," Matt breathed against her ear.

"I'm so glad you're here."

Matt kissed her lips and pulled back. He studied her face before thumbing the tender skin beneath her eyes. "Didn't sleep well?"

Ada lowered her voice. "The camera caught vehicles at the yard after Josh and Dillon set them up for me. Nothing last night, but I kept waking up, thinking I heard an alert."

"Damn," Matt muttered. "I missed this. None of my men saw anything. They would've mentioned it. I asked them to keep an eye out for lights and vehicles. Did you get a number plate or identify the driver?"

"No, it's so frustrating. Difficult to tell the color from the image. It was a farm vehicle like dozens around Moewai."

"Don't worry. We'll sort out this mystery. Can you show me the footage?"

Ada pulled up the image on her phone, and Matt studied it closely.

He raised his head, his gaze narrowing. "Why is everyone staring at us?"

Ada lifted her gaze to survey the men and women standing nearby. Matt was right. They *were* staring. "It might be because they think I'm having an affair with Josh, or it could be because you're big and muscular and sexy," she teased.

"Idiots."

"It might be because they haven't seen me kissing a man, or they're curious as to why I've had two different men with me at the market." Another thought occurred. "Or it could be because the rumors about me killing Ralph Dawson in a murderous rage have gone full circle, and they're wondering if you're brave or stupid."

"You didn't kill that man. You know it. I know it, and I'm certain the cops know it too, or at least they haven't tied the evidence together to arrest you."

"Early days," Ada muttered. "With my luck, that could change."

"Don't worry. If they arrest you, I'll break you out at midnight."

Ada fluttered her lashes. "My hero."

Matt's eyes glinted as he kissed her again. "Always," he said, the loud rumble of his stomach spoiling the moment.

"I could eat," Ada said. "And I'm craving a hot pie."

"Point me in the direction, and I'll buy you one. Do you want a drink too?"

"Something cold would be great. A juice or soda. The pies are over in the corner there." Ada pointed. "Close to the local school's car wash."

"Won't be long." Matt stole another quick kiss before he strode away in pursuit of food.

Ada noticed the avid interest, the judgment, and shrugged. She couldn't control what other people thought, but she could govern her reactions. She returned to work, actively selling her flowers rather than waiting for customers to come to her.

Two young wives approached her first. Ada had noticed women arrived in pairs while the few male customers came alone. Perhaps the women felt they needed protection—safety in numbers or some such nonsense.

"How can I help you today?" Ada asked, recognizing one woman from when she attended the Women's Institute meetings while Greg was still alive. "Susan, isn't it?"

Susan uttered an awkward titter while her companion spoke, "We'd like to buy flowers. One stem, please."

"Sure," Ada said. "What color would you like?"

"Do you have red?"

Ada forced back her irritation. It was apparent she didn't have red flowers. Not a one. "No red left," she said briskly, ignoring the fact she'd never had red since delphiniums didn't come in that color. "I have pink, white, or purple."

The woman shook her head. "No, they'll clash with my color scheme."

"Who was that man?" Susan asked.

Ah, now they were getting to the point. "A friend," Ada said, keeping it vague.

"You were here with that other man on Wednesday." Susan sounded accusing now.

"Yes, another friend."

"Do your friends visit you together?" Susan's companion asked, the waggle of her eyebrows cluing Ada in on precisely what she meant.

Ada's mouth dropped open, shock hitting her with a solid wallop to the gut. "You did not suggest I have an open-door policy at my place."

"Janice, down the road, told me you were sleeping with both men," Susan said.

Ada's mouth slackened farther as she gaped at the women.

"Was that why you murdered Ralph Dawson?" Susan's friend demanded.

Ada pressed her lips together to rein in her temper. Business was slow today, and it didn't appear any new customers would save her. Finally, she snapped, "Are you really this clueless? Don't you think the cops would've arrested me if I'd killed Ralph? Move along. I don't have time for your silly questions." Ada flapped her hands at the pair and turned her attention to her buckets of flowers. She hadn't sold as many today, but she could harvest the blossoms, meaning little waste.

When she swung back, the two women were still hovering.

"Are you still here?" Ada barked at them, and to her immense satisfaction, the pair scuttled off like insects suddenly exposed to light.

Sherry limped up seconds later. "I heard that, young lady. It's no wonder you have few customers if you treat them like that."

Ada barely refrained from rolling her eyes. "They were rude first. How are you today, Sherry? I haven't been busy, but your stalls are full, and there is plenty of foot traffic. You do a wonderful job."

Sherry dimpled and tossed her long brown hair. The basket she carried on the crook of her elbow was full of fresh produce, including vegetables, cheese, and fresh bread—all purchased from the market.

"I'll take a bunch of the wildflowers, please," she said, holding out a twenty-dollar note.

Ada wrapped the flowers and gave Sherry her change.

Matt wandered back at that moment and placed his purchases on Ada's small folding table. The savory scent of cooked meat and pastry floated to her, and her stomach gave another gurgle.

"Hello," Sherry said with a bright smile.

It seemed even her neighbor wasn't immune to a sexy soldier since an appreciative smile curved Sherry's lips, and she cocked her head like a curious bird.

"Hello," Matt returned.

Sherry waited, but Matt added nothing further to the conversation.

"Sweetheart," Matt said to Ada. "I've got to eat before my stomach gnaws through to my backbone."

Ada's lips quivered as she waved him off. "Go ahead. I'll join you in a moment."

A man and woman stopped to study the flowers, plucked a pre-made bunch from a tub, and waited for Sherry to leave. Ada barely hid her amusement.

"Excuse me, Sherry. I must see to my customers."

Sherry had to give way while Ada took the dripping bunch of flowers from her customers and wrapped them. By the time Ada completed the sale, Sherry had disappeared.

"Thank you," Ada said to the couple.

"Excellent pie." Matt swallowed the last bite. "How much longer do you want to stay?" He handed her a brown paper bag containing a pie and started on another one. He swallowed his first bite, glanced around them, and lowered his voice. "Saw something interesting at the car wash."

"What?" Ada asked absently. The locals were staring again, whispering behind their hands.

"A vehicle resembling the one that activated your camera last night."

Ada's attention snapped to Matt. "Did you recognize the owner? Who was driving? Male or female?"

"I asked a woman beside me in line for the food truck. She told me it belonged to Bart Walsh, the local stock agent."

Ada stared at Matt, her mind racing. "Bart?"

"After I bought our pies, I wandered over and spoke with him. Asked him if he knew of any cattle for sale in the area."

"You didn't."

"While I was chatting with him, I noticed the mud in his tire tread. In an enormous coincidence, the soil was the same as the volcanic stuff on your land. Didn't you tell me the soil is only on your land?"

"It's true." She checked for eavesdroppers. "Are you sure?"

"That the vehicle bore the distinctive soil from your property in its tires? Oh, yeah. I'm positive."

"Why would Bart spend his nights roaming my land?"

"The vehicle might belong to him. Doesn't mean he was driving it," Matt pointed out.

"One of his sons?"

"Or he lent his vehicle to someone," Matt said. "Either knowingly or someone took it without his knowledge."

"What should I do?" Ada asked.

"We'll decide once we get back to your place," Matt said. "Too many ears around here."

"I'm not selling many flowers. I think I'll leave early today."

"Josh mentioned you needed extra cash," Matt said, his gaze going to hers.

"You men are a pack of gossips," she snapped, heat filling her cheeks.

"Josh knows I care for you, which makes it my business."

Ada muttered a few choice words under her breath. "I should tell you upfront, I loathe bossy men."

"Yeah, I believe Summer and Ella might've mentioned the same thing a time or two."

"But not your sister?"

Matt barked his amusement. "Her too. The truth is we're trained soldiers and used to taking action."

Ada issued a disgruntled sigh. "That's what Josh told me a few days ago."

Half an hour later, they were on their way back to Ada's farm.

"I can't believe Bart would be part of whatever is going on at the back of my farm," Ada said. "Bart and Sherry have always been kind to me. They checked on me after Greg died, and Sherry brought me food. I have no time for their sons, but luckily see little of them."

"Anyone might be driving his vehicle, or maybe you're mistaken, and other parts of Moewai have the volcanic soil."

"I'm not wrong," Ada said. "I know my soil. Right, say it is Bart's vehicle. What can we do?"

"We have to wait and watch. Josh and Dillon might be up for nighttime reconnoitering."

"We're thinking whatever is going on up there is something to do with the cattle thefts."

"A natural assumption, but it's better to gather the evidence before jumping to conclusions," Matt said.

"I hate this. I keep glancing over my shoulder because I feel as if eyes are boring into my back."

Matt laughed. "That's because they *are* staring at you. All that nosy interest at the market must've been annoying."

"You can say that again."

"Can you see much of your neighbor's farm from the road?" Matt asked. "I remember seeing cattle grazing when I drove past last time, but that's all."

"They built their house back from the road, and trees surround it. Sherry told me she likes her privacy and hated passersby seeing her panties and bras hanging on the clothesline." Ada snickered at Matt's expression. "You don't go around perving at laundry?"

"No." He brushed a hand across his jaw, the dark stubble rasping at the friction. He followed this up with a yawn, and she noticed his eyes were bloodshot.

"You're tired."

"A bit," he said. "I don't suppose we could cram in an afternoon nap."

"With your friends around? No." Ada pulled into her driveway and spotted Dillon, Ella, and Josh sitting on the deck, relaxing with a drink.

It made Ada glad they'd made a quick supermarket stop to grab more supplies. It was the least she could do in exchange for their help.

"How did the market do today?" Ella asked.

"Not so great. The locals were more interested in gossiping and staring at me, rather than buying flowers."

"You've picked most of the delphiniums now. Have you thought of diversifying and selling plant seedlings or making soap or bath salts? Something different for when you don't have flowers to pick."

"Not a bad idea. I wanted to experiment with lavender, and I have made soap before at a Women's Institute meeting. Fantastic idea. Thanks."

Matt sat on the steps beside Josh.

"Want a beer?" Ada asked.

"Thanks," he said.

Once she disappeared into the house with Ella, the two women discussing soap making and bath bombs, he turned to Josh and Dillon.

"I have a plan." He told them what he'd seen at the farmers' market. "I asked him how he got his vehicle that dirty, and he told me one of his sons borrowed it to go to an off-road event. If he was lying, he's a damn good one. Told me he wasn't sure where they went. The thing was, Ada is adamant the volcanic soil is only on her farm. She told me it was a quirk of the eruption."

"Given she's growing flowers, she'd know soil," Josh said thoughtfully.

"Yeah."

"Do you think Ada's problems are part of this, or are we dealing with two separate issues?" Dillon asked.

Matt slapped his hand over his mouth to hide a yawn. "No clue."

Josh sipped his beer, his brow furrowed. "Even the business with the cops was weird. Someone was feeding them the information."

"Thanks for looking after her and arranging a lawyer," Matt said.

"Family." Josh shrugged. "You would've done the same for me."

"She's feisty. Maybe too much for you to handle," Dillon said, and his voice held teasing.

Matt loved the fact his friend was more carefree and

open now that he'd hooked up with Ella. He could still be taciturn and only spoke when he had something to say, but he smiled more. "Changing the subject. We should make her an offer to use her land. The exercises went well, and I'm fairly sure the army will want to repeat the training. Ada has enough hectares to keep stock safe and run the exercises."

"We'd want to expand eventually," Josh said. "You thinking about staying here with Ada? Leaving your army job?"

"Yeah." For once, the thought of leaving the army didn't fill Matt with a sense of panic.

"Instead of renting the land out to the army, we could make a first-class obstacle course that the locals and maybe tourists can try to challenge themselves. Rugby clubs might be interested. The fire brigade. Local police," Dillon said. "The army training always includes flash-bang, which doesn't combine with stock. My alpacas hate noise."

"You guys in if Ada gives the go-ahead?" Matt asked.

"Yes," Josh said.

"Yes," Dillon seconded.

"Right. I'll speak to Ada."

Josh and Dillon shared a glance. "Ada mentioned she had money problems," Dillon said. "We've already floated the idea, and she told us she'd think about it."

The women emerged from the house carrying a plate full of sandwiches and more drinks.

"We've fixed the fence," Dillon said to Ada. "We finished ten minutes before you arrived home."

"Thank you. I can do a lot of things myself, but fencing is not one of them."

"Let us know if we can help with other things around here," Josh added. "I mean it. We prefer to keep busy."

Matt caught the expression on Ada's face—one of pleasure and confusion and a hint of not knowing what to do with the offer. He knew Josh and Dillon meant it. If they hadn't, they would've kept silent.

Matt yawned again. "Man, I'm getting too old to stay awake all night supervising soldiers. What jobs do you have for this afternoon?"

"I need to rotary hoe the field again," Ada said. "And after that, I'll pick some of my other flowers. The cornflowers and the wildflowers. I need to check the irrigation system. I think it leaks somewhere. And once I do all that, I might look at my website and implement some of the suggestions Summer has given me."

"I get to pick flowers," Ella said.

"Rotary hoe or irrigation?" Dillon asked.

"Rotary hoe," Josh said,

"I'll help you with the irrigation," Matt said to Dillon.

They knocked off work at four-thirty. Ella and Dillon headed home to feed their alpacas and told Matt they'd be back around nine.

Ada caught Matt yawning again. "Have a sleep while I cook dinner."

"I'm going to grab some shut-eye," Josh said. "This physical work has knackered me."

"I'll wake you around six-thirty for dinner," Ada said. "Go. Both of you."

Once Josh disappeared into the camper van, Matt turned to Ada. "Lie with me for a while."

"We won't sleep," Ada warned. "Later tonight. I need to get my website updated."

"A kiss then," he countered.

Ada's slow smile was a sweet balm and touched every part of him. She was his woman. He didn't hold a shred of uncertainty, but he sensed she had qualms. Matt promised himself he'd go as slow as she needed because the end prize was valuable. Priceless. He'd always known what he wanted, and Ada was worth the wait.

"I could do that." Ada slid her arms around his waist before offering her mouth.

Although he'd intended sweet, the kiss didn't turn out that way. One touch of her lips and it was like a spark igniting inside him.

Flash-bang all the way. Heat and need and want roared through him as their tongues dueled. The feel of her in his arms pushed him to the limit, and resisting the siren urge to cart her off to bed was the hardest thing he'd done in ages. They were both breathing hard when their lips parted.

"That, I didn't expect," Ada said in a shaky voice. "You have magical powers."

"We're good together." Matt kissed her cheek and dropped his arms from her shoulders. "I'll leave you to your work. You're right. If we're skulking around the place tonight, I need sleep."

"What do you think we'll find?"

Matt comprehended Ada's *we* but didn't offer an argument. He'd sensed she'd want to involve herself in any investigation, and if he put himself in her shoes, he'd like the same thing. An argument for later.

"I don't know. This situation bugs me because we have dozens of bits of information, but nothing fits together with logic." Matt yawned again.

Ada patted him on the backside. "Rest. I'll wake you later."

Matt strolled into her bedroom, stripped, and slid between the sheets. He relaxed, content with his position in Ada's bed, surrounded by her scent.

CHAPTER 23

A Neighborly Visit

Matt woke to the scent of roast chicken. He remained still, enjoying the moment and feeling heaps better after his snooze. Voices drifted from the kitchen area as Matt slid from the bed and dressed. He took a moment to tidy the bed before he joined Ada and Josh.

"Hey, sleepyhead," Ada greeted him. "Feel better?"

"Much better." Matt strode to her and stole a kiss. He didn't care who was watching or even if it looked as if he was marking his territory, because he couldn't have stopped himself if he tried.

"You have visitors," Josh said.

"I didn't think Ella and Dillon were coming back until later," Ada said.

Josh craned his neck. "It's your neighbors."

"Really? Crap. How can I look at them when I suspect they're the ones behind the cattle stealing or the other thefts in the area?"

Matt grabbed her and kissed her, stifling further speech. He didn't pull back until someone knocked on the door. Two knocks later, he lifted his head. "Focused now?"

"I can't believe you did that," Ada said, and Matt enjoyed the fire in her. She didn't blush, but her discomfort shone through in the way she shared her attention between the door and Josh.

Finally, she stared at her shoes.

"Aren't you going to answer your door?" Josh asked, his tone innocent.

Ada glowered at Josh before stomping away. Matt shared a grin with Josh before wiping his expression clean. He watched Ada's stiff shoulders as she pulled open the door.

"Sherry. Bart." There was an uncomfortable pause before she said, "How are you? We were about to have a drink. Would you like to join us?"

"That would be lovely," the woman said. Sherry. She had long brown hair with noticeable strands of gray and piercing brown eyes that Matt guessed would miss little. On the petite side, and scarcely above five feet in height, the woman still had a presence and a glorious smile.

Matt dipped his head in acknowledgment, about to speak when Ada started on introductions.

"Matt, Josh, these are my neighbors Sherry and Bart Walsh. Sherry, Bart, my friends Matt and Josh." Before any of them could say anything, Ada added, "Why don't you take a seat outside? Sherry, I'm drinking white wine. Is that okay for you? Bart, a beer?"

"Yes, please," Sherry said. "That sounds lovely."

Matt noted the woman limped as she backtracked to take possession of one of the wooden chairs on Ada's deck. Josh shook Bart's hand before Bart turned to him.

"I didn't realize you were friends with our Ada. How long have you known each other?"

"We're long-time friends," Josh answered for them. "Come and take a seat outside. Tell me about Moewai. You have such a great town. I come from Eketāhuna. Well, I mean, I grew up there."

Matt grinned inwardly at Josh's chatter. He'd learned a new skill since hanging out with Ashley. Must come in handy when she dragged him along to meet heads of state and royalty.

"I'll help with the drinks," Matt said.

"What do you suppose they want?" Ada murmured.

"Is this visit out of character?"

"Both of them together—yes. When I see Bart, it's normally at their place or around town. We chat a while, but that's it. If he's with one of his sons, I'll wave, say I'm in a hurry, and move on. Sherry is the one more likely to visit."

"Maybe I rattled him," Matt murmured.

Beside him, Ada sucked in an audible breath. "Only one way to find out."

"Steady, sweetheart. We don't want to raise their suspicions. Step softly and approach this as you would a regular neighborly visit. Steer the conversation toward local gossip. You never know when a nugget might fall into our hands—the piece to join our random snippets together."

Ada placed three beers on a tray along with a glass for Bart and two glasses of white wine. "I can do this," she muttered before straightening her shoulders, lifting the tray, and stalking outside.

Matt admired her arse as she left the kitchen. He realized he was happy in a way he hadn't been for a long time. He'd never imagined life after the army, had figured he'd stay and work his way to a desk job, but seeing how happy Josh and Dillon were, he'd wondered if there was something else for him.

Now he'd found her, and he didn't intend to let Ada go

without a fight.

Matt strode after his woman and sat on the step beside her, leaving the chairs to the visitors and Josh.

"Ada hasn't mentioned you before," Sherry said. "What do you do?"

Matt's lips quirked, and he quickly directed them into a smile and put on his game face. "I'm in the army, so Ada and I have a long-distance relationship. Josh is my brother-in-law. He's from Auckland."

"Oh." The way Sherry cocked her head, her petite build, and bright eyes reminded him even more of a bird. "You'll be leaving again soon."

Matt made a split-second decision. "On Monday. I need to get back to Auckland. I have a few days to visit my family before I return to base."

Sherry favored him with an approving smile and nod. "Family is important. While on one hand, it would be nice to have the house to ourselves, it's also fun having the boys around the place."

"If only they'd pay board," Bart groused.

Everyone laughed, and the conversation turned to local matters.

"The murder has everyone on edge." Sherry's brow crinkled in dismay. "It's all anyone has talked about at every event I've attended this week." She shot a glance at

Ada, and Matt tensed. "I understand the police questioned you."

"Yes," Ada said, and Matt wanted to cheer when she calmly sipped her wine. She answered Sherry's question but didn't give the extra detail the woman was hunting for.

"Craig mentioned he'd seen the police at your place several times. He told me a cop car passed when he was heading to work," Sherry added.

"That must've been when the cops came to check on the cattle that broke into my flowers," Ada said.

"Really?" Bart scowled. "Damn irresponsible for someone to cut a fence and drive cattle into your flower fields. You didn't see anything?"

"Not a thing," Ada said.

Matt's gaze narrowed. How had Bart known someone had cut the fence?

"It was lucky they didn't eat my flowers. The owners told me the cattle were valuable stud animals, and I would've hated for them to die, even if it wasn't my fault."

"I hate that you're alone out here. We might be neighbors, but Bart is often away for his stock agent job, and I'm not always home because of my committees and other interests," Sherry said. "What if someone attacks you instead of merely committing nuisance crimes?" She shook her head. "Why do young people find this sort of thing amusing? Believe me, I'm so thankful my two boys have turned out half decent."

"Bart, what areas do you cover for your job?" Josh asked. "Do you stick to the Moewai region or work in Eketāhuna as well?"

"The agent who lives in Eketāhuna and I work together on some sales," Bart said. "We have a large cattle sale based at the Moewai sale yards next month. The following month, we're bringing together stock from several of the local stud farms."

"How long have you been a stock agent?" Matt asked.

"Since I left school," Bart said with an expansive smile. "My dad was a mechanic, so Eddie takes after him, but my uncle had a small acreage and when there was a downturn in the economy, he worked for the local stock firm. It turned out he had a knack for it, and the local farmers trusted him. I used to tag along with him during the school holidays." He drank his beer. "I was a rabble-rouser as a teen. My parents told me I had to go out with my uncle or work with my dad. I discovered a talent for stock work. It was a turning point for me—that and meeting my Sherry."

"You didn't say what you did," Sherry said to Josh.

"I'm ex-army. Got tired of fighting in wars. I work for a hardware store up in Auckland," Josh said.

The hardware being his line of security products, some

of which they'd installed around Ashley's house. How the hell did Josh mostly get away with his anonymity, considering his marriage to the prime minister?

Matt didn't know because his brother-in-law attended the banquets and what-not without complaint. Then there had been the business with Ash's stalker. That had hit the papers, but both Ashley and Josh had kept the details close and let the police and her press office issue statements. But the end result—most people didn't recognize him, and he skated under the public radar. Matt got the feeling that neither of these two recognized Josh, who wore his holey jeans and ripped T-shirt, the stains of a hard day of work visible on his clothing.

"Ada, the reason I came," Sherry said. "I'm in charge of the stall to raise money for the local primary school. We're giving the fund an extra push because we want to build netball courts. If there is enough in the school fund after that, we're aiming to purchase more sports equipment. I wondered if you'd be willing to bake a cake for our stall."

"Sure," Ada said without hesitation. "When is it?"

"Next Friday." Sherry whipped a notebook out of the handbag that had been sitting at her feet. She jotted a note and beamed at Ada. "I know how busy you are with your flowers, but I figured since you've done most of your picking, you might have more free time."

"No problem," Ada said. "I played netball at school. Others should have the same option."

Bart and Sherry finished their drinks and turned down a second.

"We have people coming for dinner. I prepared most of the meal in advance, but I'd hate to jinx myself. Besides," Sherry said with a titter. "I'm a cheap drunk. One glass of wine is fine, but two is pushing my limits." A feline snarl drew her attention, and Sherry's countenance blanked. "You still have that cat?"

"Yes," Ada said without elaborating.

"Just as well we're leaving. I'd hate my allergies to flare up."

"I guess we won't see either of you guys again," Bart said, standing.

"Not soon." Josh rose too. "Nice to meet you both. Good luck with your cake stall."

"Thank you, Ada, for agreeing to help. If you're running short of time, you can drop your cake at my place early on Friday morning."

"Will do," Ada said. "See you at the next market."

Matt watched Sherry limp across the driveway. Bart opened the door for her and waited until she'd situated herself before closing it and rounding the vehicle.

"Does he always treat her with such deference?" Josh

asked, his voice pitched low.

"Yes, ever since I've known them. She told me he helps around the house and is an amazing husband."

Sherry waved as Bart backed up and drove away.

"Do you buy their reason for visiting?" Matt asked.

Ada shrugged. "It's true Sherry does a lot of fundraising. The locals never say a nasty word about her, which says something. I've learned they're a gossipy bunch, which is why I keep to myself. Are you leaving on Monday? I thought you were staying for longer."

"It occurred to me when they were grilling you it might be better for Josh and me to appear to leave you alone," Matt said. "We'll leave, but we'll be around. You've picked most of the flowers, right?"

"Yes. I couldn't have done it without you and the others."

"We enjoyed picking," Josh said. "I know Dillon has too. My brother wouldn't have volunteered if he disliked the task. At first, we came because Frog asked us, but after the first day, we returned because we liked you and wanted to help."

Matt watched Ada's eyes grow glassy. Her quick blink to force back her emotion.

"Well, I appreciated it. You guys got me out of a tough spot."

Matt shared a glance with Josh, and his friend gave a faint nod. A hint of nervousness twisted Matt's gut, but he shoved it away. "Ada, it's easy to see you're floundering. What if your sales are slow?"

She studied her wineglass. "I'd planned to do more pre-advertising and preparation, but the chores are endless." She lifted her head to scan him and Josh before lowering her gaze again. Her face had paled. "It doesn't matter now. I knew I'd lost before my harvest started."

"What?" Josh asked.

"Why?" Matt said at almost the same time.

"Unbeknownst to me, Greg took out a loan. Somehow, he used the farm as security, and I only learned this a few months ago."

"But your husband died a while ago," Matt said.

"The loan was for five years with the principal payment due at the end of this time."

"But what about the interest payments?" Josh asked.

Ada's mouth twisted, and Matt caught the flicker of anger in her. "Greg not only didn't tell me, but he opened a new account, and the interest payments came out of that. He must've kept it topped up and had a decent balance in there. I didn't know. Greg took care of the accounting and financial records for the farm. I didn't find the paperwork before the fire destroyed our house. The first I knew about the loan coming due was the letter I received in the mail a few months ago. It included a statement showing the original loan and a separate statement of the interest. There was even a copy of the original loan agreement with Greg's signature at the bottom."

"Did you ring the bank?" Matt asked.

"No, they'd sent all the proof with the letter setting out the original terms of payment," Ada said.

"What about refinancing?" Josh asked. "How much was the loan?"

"One hundred and fifty thousand. I paid off fifty thousand, which was all I had left in reserve. The remaining balance of the loan from the branch in Masterton might as well be one million."

"Why did you keep working? Why didn't you give up and try to sell the farm?"

Ada swallowed hard. "I don't own the land. Greg inherited the land from his aunt, but there were strings attached. He had ten years to make a profit." Ada sounded broken. "I have two-and-a-half-years left, and if I fail, the land reverts to Greg's parents."

Matt set aside his empty bottle and took Ada's glass from her hands. "Sweetheart, why didn't you say something earlier?"

"I've known you for two weeks," Ada said. "A discussion

of my problems isn't right. This is my mess, my responsibility, and I need to sort it out myself. I'm not a woman who expects a man to take care of her."

"Your in-laws have an incentive to mess with you," Matt said.

"I doubt they're responsible. The will stipulates a fair contest. If they take steps to make me fail, they'll lose the land to me. The profit clause will become void."

"Which is why reporting each nuisance to the police is important. We'll get to the bottom of this." Matt cleared his throat. "Josh, Dillon, and I were wondering if you'd agree to lease your land to us—the portion you're not using. We'd like to run sheep and develop a breed that will thrive on the hill country. We were also considering setting up an obstacle course for local groups and maybe the army to train. Why don't you let us pay off the mortgage for you as payment for using your land?"

"And I say again: we met two weeks ago. You don't know me. What if I take the money and run? Or what if I fail to make a profit and lose the land?"

Matt shook his head even as Josh laughed. He exchanged a glance with his friend and knew they were on the same wavelength. "We trust you, Ada. Besides, if you ran off, we'd still have possession of your land. Your flowers." He waggled his eyebrows. "Your petals."

Ada released an inelegant snort. "It's not as if I have anywhere to go."

"You'll take our money?" Josh asked.

"I'll consider it," she said, but her tone told Matt something else. "But again, what if I lose the land?"

"We're confident you *will* make a profit." He decided not to push her but made a mental note to ask to see the paperwork and make an appointment to see the bank manager.

"You'll make a profit," Josh agreed. "We've seen how hard you work and your orders will come because your product is excellent. What's our next move today?"

"Food." Ada sniffed and knuckled the moisture from her eyes. "If we're going to skulk around the countryside and spy on our neighbors and other trespassers, I need a full tummy. How do hamburgers sound? I have the ingredients on hand."

"Sounds good," Josh said. "What can we do to help?"

After dinner, Matt suggested Ada have a nap, but she glared at him.

"And let the pair of you creep away without me. No way!"

Matt ignored Josh's hoot since that was what he'd intended to do. The last thing he wanted was to place Ada in danger.

CHAPTER 24

THE LOAN DEBACLE

MONDAY ARRIVED WITH NONE of them any the wiser about what was going on with her farm. Ada climbed out of bed, a sense of anxiousness assailing her since their stakeout had turned into a bust. They watched in the darkness for hours but had seen nothing fiercer than an owl. She dressed rapidly and joined the men in the kitchen for a coffee.

"We'll go to the bank today to pay off the loan. Ring for an appointment with the manager," Matt said.

"Are you sure this is what you, Josh, and Dillon want to do? Don't you want to spend your money on other things?" Ada couldn't wrap her head around Matt's generosity. Josh and Dillon, too, especially when Greg's family had ignored her and pushed Greg out of their lives after he'd chosen to walk a different path. The land inheritance hadn't helped since Greg's parents had coveted the hectares by the Moewai river.

"I'm off," Josh said. "I told Ash I wanted to go to the bank with you, then I'm meeting her in Wellington. I can be back here as soon as you need me. If you and Ada learn anything else about the problems around here, contact me. Dillon, too, since he isn't far away."

"Will do," Matt said.

Josh kissed Ada's cheek before leaving with a wave. "I'll leave you to say goodbye to Ada," he said to Matt. "Don't be long."

"Are you sure you want to visit the bank?" Ada asked. She was going to miss having people around the place. Loneliness was descending on her, even though Matt and Josh hadn't left yet.

Matt cupped her cheeks and smiled at her with a gentleness that made her heart do a flip-flop. "Yes, so make that appointment."

"I will," Ada promised, even though speaking with Craig Walsh in his position as a loan officer didn't appeal.

"Text me the appointment time, and I'll meet you in Masterton." He kissed her, preventing any further conversation.

Ada sank into his kiss, admitting to herself she'd fallen for this strong, intelligent man. He made her feel safe and treasured, yet he respected her too. He asked her opinion most of the time, although, with the bank thing, he'd become plain bossy, and Josh had backed up Matt.

A horn honked outside, and Matt gentled the kiss before pulling back.

"Stay safe, and make sure you're careful with security. I'll be skulking in the background and keeping watch, but I need you to pay attention too."

"I will."

After another quick kiss, Matt jogged to the camper van and climbed into the passenger seat. Minutes later, the vehicle disappeared.

A meow sounded before Archie skulked from behind a bush and rubbed against her legs. Ada picked him up and settled in one of her outdoor chairs. Before Matt, the silence hadn't bothered her, but now it felt oppressive. Lonely. With a heavy sigh, she lifted Archie off her knee and walked inside to ring the bank.

"Hello, it's Ada Buckingham," she said once someone picked up the phone and identified themselves as being from the bank. "I'd like to see the manager about a loan and wondered if he had an appointment free for today."

"Our loan specialist is away sick, but you're in luck," the

woman chirped. "Mr. Tamaki, the manager, has just had a cancelation. Can you make it here by ten-thirty?"

"Yes. Thank you."

With three hours before her appointment, she figured she'd have time to pick and prepare the last of her wildflower patch. She texted the appointment time to Matt, locked her door, and slipped the keys into her pocket. Mindful of Matt's warning to remain alert, she scanned her paddock for signs of trouble before she focused on her picking. She took one step onto the dirt pathway that separated her rows of flowers and halted, fear lifting the hair at her nape.

A set of footprints and they weren't hers.

Neither Matt nor Josh had come down here yesterday since they'd worked on strengthening her fencing. She'd been the only person in this area since Saturday morning when she'd picked flowers for the market.

The camera hadn't sent an alert. At least she didn't think it had. She pulled out her phone and snapped a photo of the prints. Josh had told her the camera would only tell them if someone crept around her house or shed, which might be why she hadn't received an alert. Whoever had made these prints had climbed her fence or entered her property at the far end and walked back.

Anger built, and she stomped closer to her flowers. The

birds were singing, and Archie had followed her out to the flower fields, so she figured no intruders were spying on her at present.

Ada picked the flowers, and after studying the remaining buds, she decided she might pull out these plants and resow with perhaps cornflowers, or maybe she should experiment with hydrangea flowers. Yes. A challenge to take her mind off the rest of her troubles.

Aware of the passing time, Ada hastily prepared the petals and set her drier machine. That done, she took a quick shower. Ten minutes later, with her house locked, she drove to Masterton.

She spotted Matt and Josh as soon as she parked behind the supermarket.

"No problems?" Matt asked.

"I found footprints near my wildflowers," she said. "They aren't mine, and none of you walked near that area."

"Did you take photos?" Josh asked.

"Yes."

"Email them to me," Josh said. "They must've come over the fence. I'll see what I can do about setting up a couple more cameras."

"Ready for this appointment?" Matt asked.

"Yes, I brought the paperwork with me." Ada pressed

her hand against her stomach. "I'm so nervous. I had to do budgets for my flower project, but I've never spoken to this bank manager. Craig Walsh is off sick."

"Craig Walsh?" Josh asked, his tone sharp.

"Yes, he's the loan officer here."

"It'll be fine." Matt shared a speaking glance with Josh.

"Craig Walsh is a weird coincidence," Josh muttered. "Are you sure you want me at the meeting?"

"Yes," Ada said. "If you're interested in investing in the farm, you need to know the worst."

They waited for five minutes before Fred Tamaki, the bank manager, greeted them. He was an older man, bald, and dressed in a navy-blue suit. His black-rimmed glasses did little to hide the shrewd intelligence in his brown eyes.

"Ms. Buckingham." He extended his hand.

"Mr. Tamaki." Ada shook his hand and introduced Matt and Josh as friends.

"I understand you wish to discuss a loan today." He gestured them into his office. "Are you thinking of expanding?"

Ada grimaced. Why would she want to borrow more money when she couldn't pay off her existing loan? She sank onto a seat while Mr. Tamaki organized one of his staff to procure another chair for Josh.

"Mr. Tamaki, I don't understand. I've come today to

talk about paying off the existing loan. Josh and Matt are providing the capital, and we're going into partnership."

This time it was Mr. Tamaki's turn to frown in confusion. "What loan? I checked your accounts and our notes before you arrived for this meeting. You don't have a loan with us."

"Ada received a letter from the bank along with a statement showing she had a loan of one hundred and fifty thousand dollars due this month. She repaid fifty thousand, and according to the statement, she has one hundred thousand dollars left to pay. The letter indicated Greg Buckingham took out a loan before he died, and he was paying the interest from another account. Ada also paid back the overdue interest because the account her husband had left had run out of funds," Matt explained.

Mr. Tamaki sent them a blank look. He removed his glasses and pulled a white polishing cloth from his drawer. "This is most irregular. I don't suppose you have the paperwork regarding this loan. It was at this bank?"

Ada's brows furrowed. "Greg, my husband, had an account here. I have the paperwork." She pulled a folder out of her handbag and fumbled with it before she pushed it across the desk.

"A loan document." The bank manager flicked through it, his eyes widening a fraction as he studied the signatures on the last page. He pushed his glasses back on and stared at the signatures again. "It's dated almost six years ago."

"Yes." Ada tilted her head to the side and pursed her lips while her mind raced.

"The thing is, the loan officer who signed this document started working here three years ago." Mr. Tamaki reached for his keyboard and typed in a password. He navigated the screen and shook his head at what he saw.

"What's going on?" Matt demanded.

"That is what I'd like to know. Our records show your husband has never had a loan from us."

"But what about the correspondence?" Ada asked.

Matt leaned forward slightly in his chair. "You said the loan officer isn't here today?"

Mr. Tamaki hesitated. "Craig is a valuable employee. He's diligent and excellent at his job."

"So Ada's husband's account is in good standing," Matt said.

"Yes." Mr. Jones removed his glasses and polished the lenses again.

"Then what happened to the money Ada transferred to the bank?" Josh asked. "If there is no loan, she'd like it back plus the interest she paid."

Matt stood. "Plus interest on this money. I believe that is fair."

The bank manager's face contained worry lines and unease. "Can you leave the paperwork with me?"

"I suggest you take copies of everything. We'll keep the original documents. That way nothing goes missing," Matt said. "Are you sure Craig Walsh is merely sick and hasn't absconded with ill-gotten gains?"

Mr. Jones gasped, and his hands tightened on the arms of his office chair. "I'm positive this is an error."

"A costly mistake for Ada," Josh pointed out. "It has caused her considerable stress."

Ada sat frozen, unable to believe someone would do this to her. She'd fallen for a con. If she hadn't received the documentation along with the demand, she might have questioned the loan earlier. Instead, she'd paid out her hard-earned money to a thief.

"I want to inform the police," Ada said. "This is theft."

"Please don't do that. Give me time to investigate," Mr. Jones pleaded.

Ada rose. "Very well. I'll expect a call by the end of the day."

They waited while a girl copied the documents Ada had brought with her.

"What the heck?" Ada muttered as they left the bank. "How could I have fallen for such a scam? If I get my hands on Craig Walsh, I'm going to wring his scrawny neck. How could he?"

"The guy is smart. I read those documents you have," Josh said. "They look genuine. Walsh used his personal knowledge to gouge money from you. Clever, and it would've worked if Ada hadn't visited the bank manager today."

"I feel stupid," Ada muttered, unable to look at either man.

"Ada." Matt settled his two hands on her shoulders and turned her to face him. "If Craig Walsh is the culprit, he caught you when you were vulnerable and used your husband's death to drive in the nail. This was a clever scheme designed to con you." His voice roughened. "Just one of many ways to drive you off your land because from where I stand, that's the logical conclusion."

"My thoughts, too," Josh said. "If that isn't the plan, then there are lots of coincidences lined up here."

"I still feel stupid. I needed that money, and I handed it over to a...to a shyster."

"You might get your money back yet," Matt said. "The manager and his bank will want to avoid adverse publicity."

"You rattled the guy," Josh said. "He was in shock, and he can't believe a member of his staff might have pulled off a crime of this nature. I'd better get going. You coming,

Matt?"

"Yeah. Ada, I'll see you later tonight. I'll text you when I'm almost at your place and try to enter clandestinely. Okay?"

"Later. Bye, Josh. Say hello to Ashley for me." She forced a smile, and with a wave, she strode back to her car.

Once she sat in the driver's seat, she closed her eyes against the burning tears, her heart racing. Not only had she been conned, but someone had tarnished Greg's memory by making her think he'd been dishonest, making her think he'd taken out a loan without telling her. They'd been partners in all ways, yet she'd doubted him. She mentally berated herself for not trusting her husband, for thinking the worst when he couldn't defend himself. She pressed a hand to her stomach, filled with self-loathing. Remorse and guilt.

"Greg, I'm so sorry," she whispered. "Please forgive me."

The rest of the day dragged. Ada tried to work, but her skin prickled, and uneasiness swept her. No matter how many times she darted a gaze over her shoulder, she didn't spot another person. Still, her trepidation persisted the entire time she was picking and later, in her shed, preparing and placing the cornflower petals in her drier. Then, there was the guilt that filled her, her renewed grief that constricted her throat.

She gave up working outside and made her way into the haven of her home. Except, it no longer felt like a place of safety. Tension stiffened her shoulders, and finally, she called Archie inside and locked the door. If someone truly were watching her, they'd need to break into her home to get to her.

Ada considered an intruder and pulled a heavy saucepan out of the back of a cupboard.

"Now let someone try to grab me without getting a headache," she said to Archie.

The cat paused his grooming, stared at her, then continued his licking.

What the hell had she ever done to Craig Walsh?

Then, there were the vehicles that kept entering her land without permission. While the soil in Bart's tires wasn't proof of his presence on her farm, it was a clear sign his vehicle had entered her land. Ada thought back and recalled the half a dozen times loud farm bikes raced on the Walshes' property. Particularly late at night while she was sitting on her deck.

All these facts led to the Walsh family.

Surely not Sherry, but her sons. Bart, she didn't know. He might've loaned his vehicle to someone. The nuisance vandalism—well, the Walsh farm wasn't far as the crow flew. Most days, she worked hard, and exhaustion filled her by the time she crawled into bed. She slept well.

"But the watcher with the cigarette stubs," she muttered to Archie. "Tell me how that fits in."

The more she pondered her neighbors and her problems, the more the situation bugged her. She needed to snoop on her own, and now that she'd harvested most of her flowers, she had more time to reconnoiter. Yes, she'd go tonight and stake out the Walshes'.

Calmer now that she had a plan, Ada set to work, although thoughts of Greg, followed swiftly by guilt, kept intruding. She forced her mind back to work. Summer, Josh's sister, had drafted several blog posts for her and included a list of more ideas. Ada read through the first one and posted it, using the royalty-free photos Summer had also found for her. She owed Summer a huge thank you for her help because Summer had saved her hours of work. Summer had even suggested she open other social media accounts, detailing the reasons for her recommendation.

Made sense. Ada signed up for the ones Summer had mentioned and spent half an hour exploring. She posted flower photos to one and added a brief note as per another of Summer's instructions. She cross-posted her blog to some.

Last, she checked her email in the hope she'd find orders. Not a one.

Her shoulders drooped, and she cursed inwardly. Summer was right in this too. She needed an organized plan to get her advertising and word-of-mouth campaign started. She'd known her first year would be tough, and until she'd learned about the phony loan, she'd had a financial cushion to use while she found her way.

Archie rose from the chair on which he was sitting, stretched, and stalked over to where Ada sat. He rubbed against her legs before meowing. After he'd meowed for the third time, she got the message.

"All right." Ada rose, stretching. She filled Archie's bowl with biscuits before she boiled the jug for tea. With her favorite beverage in hand, she wandered out to her deck and sat, content to listen to Archie crunching on his dinner and the chirp and chatter of birds flying in to roost in the leafy green trees.

Her break wasn't as restful as usual since she kept replaying the meeting with the bank manager, and her self-loathing continued to kick her in the butt. Disgust. She had wronged Greg when she should've trusted he wouldn't do anything to put the farm at risk. He would've discussed a loan of that magnitude with her. Her shoulders rounded for an instant before she sighed and straightened to sip her tea.

While she'd been working indoors, darkness had crept

over the horizon, which told her she'd gone longer than she realized. No wonder her legs had felt stiff, and her shoulders were sore from hunching over the laptop.

Archie lifted his head without warning and stared into the darkness. Ada's gaze went in the same direction, but she nothing jumped out at her. The birds were still chattering. Archie hissed, arching his back, his gaze intent as he continued to stare into the dark shadows to her right.

It wouldn't be Matt because he'd promised to text her before he arrived. He wasn't a man to break his promises.

"Is someone there, Archie?" Ada whispered. She noticed the cat had gone tense, and his fur had puffed out. The animal's reaction had her adrenaline pumping too, her heart racing.

Ada retreated indoors. She pulled out her phone and growled under her breath when she noticed the battery had died again. The stupid thing needed replacing. After calling Archie indoors, she double-checked she'd locked the door.

She plugged in her phone, relieved it appeared to be charging. She crouched by the plug and typed in a quick text to Matt.

Are u close? Think someone is outside.

Relief filled her when her phone beeped a few seconds later.

10 mins away. Will check. Stay inside.

Ada closed her blinds so a watcher wouldn't see her with the house interior lit up like a Christmas light display. She made herself another cup of tea and forced herself to read through the other articles Summer had sent her.

The history of confetti. It was another great post, and Ada pre-scheduled it for the following week, along with the attached photos. She checked the time. Twenty minutes had elapsed. Where was Matt? This stress was not good for her.

Her phone signaled an incoming text.

At the bedroom window. Let me in?

Ada smiled and hustled to her bedroom. She opened the window and watched Matt wriggle through the gap.

"Did you find anything?"

"No, I thought I heard voices, but I didn't find anyone."

"We need to wait a bit," Ada said. "Then we're heading out on a mission of our own. I'm tired of reacting to circumstances lobbed in my direction. Tonight, I intend to investigate the Walsh family because they're part of this mess."

CHAPTER 25

NIGHTTIME RECONNAISSANCE

MATT RESTRAINED HIS AMUSEMENT because it was apparent the situation had riled his lady. "We can do that," he said once he had his reaction under control. "We should wait for at least an hour. That way, if the person watching you came from the Walsh farm, they'll have time to settle."

"Makes sense." Ada glanced down at her pale blue T-shirt. "I need cat-burglar clothes. I'll find something suitable."

"You don't have time to kiss me?" Matt teased, loving this bloodthirsty side of her. Normally, she remained stoic and kept her emotions close. Her grip had slipped its mooring tonight, and she'd fired up, ready for action.

Ada stopped mid-step and pivoted toward him. A shy

smile burst into prominence, driving off the flash of her temper. "I could do that."

"Come here," he whispered, his gaze devouring her. In the short time they'd been apart, he'd missed her. He, Josh, and Dillon had discussed the loan situation, and it seemed as if Ada had drawn the same conclusion. Craig Walsh was part of—or at least knew about—the terror campaign and bad things raining down on Ada. It was time to turn the tables and play the stalker instead of accepting the passive role. It wouldn't hurt for him and Ada to check out the situation. They'd stay at a safe distance and see what they could discover.

Ada placed her hands on Matt's shoulders. "I missed you. I'm not sure I'm pleased about that, Mr. Townsend. You fall into my life and have disrupted it ever since."

His brows lifted even as he smiled. "You don't think you've unsettled me too, Ms. Buckingham? You've turned my plans and expectations arse over teakettle, as my grandmother used to say. But instead of worrying about this change in my life, I've embraced the shift. You're beautiful and full of courage. You're a hard worker and have a brilliant plan for your life. I admire you immensely."

"You make me sound like a school ma'am character in a book."

"I hadn't finished," he said in a calm voice. "I'm crazy

about you, and I see us having a future together. Also, you're hot, and I can't get enough of your sexy body."

Ada's dark brows lifted this time. Her hands wandered his chest, and Matt held his breath, curious to see what she'd do next. So far, she'd reacted to his touch rather than taking the initiative. To his astonishment, she opened his shirt, slipping the buttons free until she could slide her fingers across his pecs. The contact of palm to chest was full of heat, and it charged through his body, sinking to his groin. Hell, he'd never reacted to another woman in this way. He wanted to love her, keep her safe. Having children with her had even wandered through his mind, and he'd never considered kids before. Not until Ada.

"I think your body is sexy, too," she said in a solemn voice. Her eyes didn't get with the program since they sparkled and reminded him of a shot of his favorite Scottish whisky. "I'd lick you all over if I could. Dip you in chocolate and settle into feast." This time her mouth quirked.

"Really?" Matt ran his hands down her back and settled them on her curvy butt. He drew their lower bodies together, letting her feel his hardness. "I could get on board with that idea."

A giggle burst from her—the sound unexpected, yet charming. He grinned at her. "We have time for a quickie before we head out. What do you say?"

If they made love, Ada might fall asleep, allowing Matt to spy on the neighbors on his own. He hated to place her in a dangerous situation, and his gut told him there was a lot here bubbling under the surface. Things they hadn't discovered yet.

Ada's smile faded, and Matt didn't hesitate. He lowered his head and kissed her. No innocent kiss, but a full-on, no-holds-barred one designed to inflame and divert her mind. She stiffened for an instant before her muscles softened. She leaned into him, and her fingernails dug into his biceps.

The bite of pain had his cock jerking, and his hips pressing harder against Ada. Sweet friction. *This woman.* Something about her had dug deep, and he never wanted to free himself. Decisiveness. Something he prided himself on and the gut instincts that directed him seldom steered him wrong. Ada was his. Josh and Dillon had teased him about falling fast and deep. Payback, according to them. He didn't care because it was nothing less than the truth.

He'd fallen under Ada's spell, and that was right where he wanted to stay.

Without breaking their kiss, he lifted her and swung her into his arms.

Ada let out a girlish *eep* before laughing, and it was

the sweetest sound. He grinned as he stalked into the bedroom. Matt placed her on the bed and rapidly divested her of her clothing and footwear. He stripped and rifled through the bedside drawer to retrieve condoms.

The entire time, he was aware of her gaze roving his body. She sighed, and when he scrutinized her, he met her smile of appreciation.

"You're great for my ego," he whispered as he stretched out beside her.

"I enjoy looking at you—your muscles. Then there is your smile. I like that too because it warms me. When you look at me, I feel loved, then I tell myself it's too soon to feel emotions that deep, that you'll leave soon for your job, and I'll be alone."

"I'm quitting the army once my term ends. Yes, I'll leave for a few months since I work at the base south of Auckland, but I'll come back during my free time, and as soon as I can, I'll be here full time. That's if you'll have me."

Ada sucked in a breath and stared at him for a long, heart-stopping moment. Matt's mouth grew dry, and his jaw clenched.

Say something, Ada. Tell me, show me you want me as much as I crave you.

"Yes," she whispered.

"Thank god," Matt muttered. "You scared me half to death. I thought you were going to tell me to take a hike, that you didn't return my feelings."

"I didn't think big, bad NZSAS soldiers experienced fear."

"Hell yeah. We're skilled at hiding it. It's all about the front. Ada, I want nothing more than to have you in my life."

"Yes," she repeated. "Now, about that quickie?"

Matt laughed, the rich sound surprising him. He reached for her and kissed her tenderly, gradually upping the passion until they were both breathing hard. He nipped the base of her neck, then soothed the sting with the lave of his tongue. Matt set a fast pace, kissing, nibbling, and licking Ada's delectable body. Her breasts. Her nipples. Her rib cage. The tender skin of her inner thighs. He swiped his tongue the length of her slit and stopped at her clit. Ada tugged at his hair and lifted her hips, urging him to action.

He stroked and licked her to climax before separating their bodies to don a condom. Seconds later, he slid into her hot, snug depths and groaned.

"This is sheer perfection," he whispered against her ear.

"It could be better yet," she grumbled, lifting into his deep stroke.

Laughing, Matt withdrew to his tip and thrust, upping the pace. He'd never felt so alive or so happy, and it was all Ada. His hips jerked as he reached for the pleasure waiting for him. A tingle started in his balls, growing and straining until the sensations became too much.

Ada's tight channel clenched around his shaft, and she released a mew of enjoyment. Matt quickened his pace, no longer holding back. Tiny spasms still rippled through Ada when his orgasm detonated through him, surging up his shaft and exploding free in a white-hot surge of passion.

Matt's breath sounded like a pump as he held Ada. He twisted their bodies and savored the peace, and Ada in his arms. This was heaven.

Ada drifted to sleep, but Matt remained awake, thinking over his future and how to fix the problems Ada was having around her farm. She was right about checking the Walshes' place, especially since their visit had been out of character. It might have been innocent, but Ada didn't think so. He didn't think it was innocuous, and neither had Josh.

Once he was certain Ada was asleep, Matt worked his limbs and torso free, helped because Ada preferred to sleep on her side. He stood and waited. When she remained silent and breathing evenly, he reached for his clothes. It was inky black in the bedroom after he'd pulled the curtains, and he bumped into the end of the bed, kicking his toe.

He cursed long and loud until he recalled he'd meant to do a clandestine escape. Matt groaned. Bloody hell. Ada had scrambled his brains, and he wasn't thinking straight.

"Matt?"

"Yeah." He rubbed his toe. It hurt like hell.

"Is it time to leave? Why didn't you turn on the light?"

More familiar with her room than him, she switched on the bedside lamp without difficulty. She took one look at him and scowled. "You weren't going to take me."

For an instant, he considered lying, but she deserved the truth. "That's true, and I would've managed it if it wasn't for that pesky bed leg."

She stared at him, her brown eyes going wide. "Are you quoting cartoon characters at me? 'I would've gotten away with it if it wasn't for those pesky kids,'" she mimicked.

Matt snorted a laugh. "I didn't think you'd catch that."

"I'm smarter than the average girlfriend. Obviously." She rolled her eyes and rose off the bed. "I'm going with you, and that's final. Craig Walsh's actions made me doubt Greg. My husband didn't deserve that, and if I'm to move on with you, I *need* to do this."

Something in her stern expression told him she'd refuse to back down, no matter what argument he used to convince her otherwise. Determination radiated from her in the set jaw, angled upward, and her intent gaze. She was no shrinking violet, content to stay home and wait for her man to deal with the troubles that came her way.

And wasn't that part of what had attracted him to her in the first place? Her no-nonsense attitude and the way she worked so hard, intent on making her new business a success and earning a profit.

Plus, she was right. She needed closure, and he'd do his best to help her.

"All right," Matt said. "But I'm the one with the experience. You'll follow my orders."

"I will," Ada promised. "I have dark clothes picked out."

And she did. She scrambled into black leggings that hugged her legs and backside and a long-sleeve black T-shirt. She donned socks and padded out to the kitchen.

"Don't turn on the lights," Matt said. "I switched off the bedroom lamp. We want our eyes to become used to the dark. Bring your phone but make sure it's on vibrate only. We don't want to warn anyone of our presence. Make sure you lock the house."

"What if someone is watching my house?"

"It's possible, which is why you're going to let me go outside first. I'll come back to get you."

"Wait," Ada said. "Let Archie outside. If he hisses, you'll

know someone is sneaking around. He has let me know most times. We can wait on the deck and pretend we're outside star-watching."

"Excellent plan." Matt nudged her and Archie out the door.

They listened for long seconds, and nothing out of the ordinary drew their attention.

"What's the best position to spy on them?" Matt asked.

"We'll climb the fence opposite my gate and walk through the bush. Bart and Sherry have large trees around their house. It should be easy enough to get close to their home."

"Right," Matt said. "Stay behind me, and if you're having trouble seeing, hold on to the waistband of my trousers. Watch your foot placement because I'd hate to announce our presence."

"Anything else?" This time she sounded tetchy.

"Yeah." He hid his grin. "If anyone spots us, I want you to find a hiding place and stay put until I return. I'll do my best to lead anyone away from you."

"Got it," she said. "Trousers. Sticks. Hide. Can we go now?"

Matt had a powerful urge to tell her this wasn't a game, but that stubborn chin of hers told him she understood the risk. He'd watched her when she'd learned someone—and the evidence pointed at Craig Walsh—had duped her of fifty thousand dollars. At first, she'd resembled a whipped puppy, then she'd gathered her anger and used it to fuel her plans. She hadn't shared them with him yet, but her trust in him was growing. She hadn't refused him, Josh, and Dillon when they'd made their suggestion to use her land. But she hadn't said yes either, and she'd admitted she had money problems and confided about the loan and the land issue. Baby steps.

"Come on," Matt said.

They walked down the driveway, and to his surprise, Ada was light on her feet. She didn't stumble around in the darkness, and unlike women from his past, she didn't chatter.

He approved since voices carried at night. A half-moon gave light, and the clouds offered changing views of the myriad stars. Over to their left, a morepork hooted, the cry haunting as it rode on the night air.

Ada tugged on his shirt once they'd walked down the road toward her neighbor's house for five minutes. She leaned closer, and he caught the lime and coconut scent of her hair.

"Climb the fence here and follow the track," she whispered into his ear. "It's a path made by their cattle. I don't think they have stock in that paddock at present, but we should be careful, anyway. It won't be much fun tripping over a sleeping cow."

Matt sniggered and strode to the fence. He vaulted over and turned to help Ada. To his surprise, she scowled and gestured for him to step out of the way. Matt followed her silent instruction, and his mouth dropped open a fraction when Ada did her own graceful jump over the fence.

Matt grinned, surprised. Yet he shouldn't be—given her competence in other areas. He crept along the track Ada had mentioned, his gaze scanning for obstacles. As the path wound into a stand of native totara, kowhai, and rimu trees, the roar of an engine cut through the gentle evening melody.

He slowed his steps. Ada tugged on his shirt again.

"The engine revving differs from other times," she explained. "Eddie works at a garage, so perhaps he tinkers with vehicles in his free time. Or, since my mind has turned suspicious, they could store stolen vehicles on their property short-term."

"Something to check out. At least they won't detect us with that racket. Do they have dogs?"

"Bart keeps three farm dogs, but the kennels are a distance from the house because Sherry had an unpleasant experience with dogs as a kid. She showed me the scar on her leg."

Matt continued along the track. The incline increased, but Ada kept up with him, and nary a complaint passed her lips. When they crested the hill, he glimpsed lights coming from the Walsh homestead. Matt slowed and cautiously traversed the slope above the driveway and garage. It sounded as if more than one person was outside, and given the hour, that seemed odd.

Ada tugged on his shirt to gain his attention. "This way," she whispered. "We'll have a better view."

Ada's insider knowledge worked to their advantage. The tree cover was better in the direction she'd guided them, and they'd be close enough to eavesdrop. Once he'd walked as close as he was comfortable with, Matt leaned against a broad tree trunk.

When Ada headed for a different one, he grasped her arm and pulled her against his side.

"I want to stand close enough for easy conversation," he murmured.

Someone revved a vehicle before the sound cut abruptly. Bart's farm vehicle arrived and pulled up in front of the house. Both Craig and Eddie sauntered out to greet their father.

"Any problems?" Eddie asked.

"No, we got the cattle away. As usual, the info was spot-on. They were grazing in the front paddock. We cut the fence, drove the stock through the break, and loaded them down the road at the neighbor's place. It's getting harder, though, because the stock losses have riled the farmers."

Ada tugged his arm, but he stilled her with a warning squeeze of her biceps. They needed to keep listening.

"You scooped up the cattle under their noses," Eddie said. "That's all that matters."

Craig laughed and muttered something Matt didn't catch.

"We can't keep doing jobs. We need to let the dust settle," Bart said. "I'm worried we're gonna make a mistake and get caught. I think it's best if we stop the plan for six months and lie low."

"Have you heard anything?" Craig asked.

"More of the same. Incensed farmers and frustrated police officers," Bart said. "I'm wondering if we should stage a theft here because that way we'd be part of the group. They're arranging a district meeting next week."

"Staging a theft here is a fantastic idea," Craig said. "Any farmer with land on a private road has suffered a theft. We're in the same position, and if the cops mark the robberies on a map, it might appear suspicious."

"Right, we'll do that," Bart agreed. "I have thirty head of steers I intended to sell, anyway. We'll truck them away tomorrow night and report them stolen the next day. Better take Sherry out to dinner that night, so you boys will have to load the truck." Bart studied the vehicle. "You need to get this gone before tomorrow, plus anything else you have in the shed for when the cops come to discuss the theft. We don't want to give them any reason to apply for a search warrant."

The more Matt learned, the more he wanted to deck these guys. They were so casual about the thefts, and it was apparent they'd been pulling this crap for a while.

"Did your mother ask where the vehicle came from?" Bart asked.

"I told her it belonged to a friend, and I was fixing it for them," Eddie said.

"Have you got somewhere else to store it?" Bart asked.

"I'll get rid of it tonight. If worse comes to worst, I can ditch it. Run it through a fence and make out kids stole it to go on a joyride."

"What about fingerprints?" Bart demanded.

Eddie held up his hands, and although it was too far away for clear vision, from the reaction, Matt presumed Eddie wore gloves.

"I've been careful, but I'll wipe down the surfaces once I'm finished," Eddie said. "Besides, we're covered with the police. Our inside man has been invaluable."

"Right," Bart said. "Don't tell your mother we're—"

A door opened with a loud squeak that reached Matt and Ada. "Are you boys going to chinwag out there all night?" Sherry called. "Supper is ready to serve."

"Sounds great, love," Bart said with barely a hesitation. "We'll be there in a few minutes."

"Make sure you are," Sherry scolded, and the door squeaked shut.

"Right," Bart said. "As soon as we've eaten, you get rid of the vehicle. Tell your mother you're meeting your mate to return the vehicle, or better yet, tell her you're going out on a late date. You know how excited she's been about your girlfriend. The pretend one. She wants grandchildren."

"Not at the expense of my freedom," Eddie retorted.

"You shouldn't have scared Ada so much," Craig said. "Then you might've gotten lucky. Mum likes Ada."

"Fuck you," Eddie said with brotherly heat.

Bart stepped between his two sons. "Can it," he snarled. "We will not upset your mother. Come on. We'll have a family supper and make her happy."

The men fell silent, and Eddie flicked off the lights that had illuminated the shed and the driveway. It took Matt a while to refocus after the bright light died. Bart and Craig disappeared into the garage. Eddie pulled down the shed door, and the area fell silent.

Matt waited a fraction longer, his gaze on the darkened shed and the faint light creeping through the thick curtains. When nothing stirred, he squeezed Ada's arm, indicating they should leave. He led the way, and she fell in behind, once again remaining silent rather than voicing the curiosity and indignation he was certain bubbled within her.

Matt had questions of his own.

They had information now, but Matt wasn't sure what they could do with it, or if it was worth going to the cops, given what they'd overheard.

CHAPTER 26

THE PLOT DEEPENS

ADA'S BRAIN BUZZED WITH the information they'd gleaned. Bart and his sons were responsible for the livestock thefts and, by the sounds of it, the stolen vehicles too. It sounded as if Sherry was in the dark. That made sense. Sherry was a popular lady and universally liked. Learning of her husband's and sons' skullduggery would distress her. Ada wondered how they'd kept this from Sherry, then answered her question. Sherry attended dozens of events and meetings. She was out several nights a week, which meant Bart and the boys could maneuver and carry out their crimes without Sherry's knowledge.

The trip back to the house seemed faster than the outward journey. Archie greeted them with a meow and slinked around their legs, purring loudly.

"I'll make sure everything is normal around your shed," Matt said. "Check your phone to see if the cameras have recorded any movement."

"All right. I'm having tea. Do you want one?"

"Sure."

Ada unlocked the door, her mind on what they'd overheard. She switched on a light and filled the jug. While this wasn't proof that the Walsh men were responsible for the nuisance pranks that had plagued her, it was a clear sign she was on their radar.

She pulled her phone out of her pocket. The battery had died again. Cursing under her breath, she plugged it in at the wall, praying it would charge. Until she earned more cash, a new phone would need to wait.

Matt came inside and locked the door after him. "Catch anything on the phone?"

"My phone battery died. It's charging, so I'll check in the morning. What do you suggest we do next?"

"I've been thinking about that," Matt said. "It's obvious at least one local cop is in on this, or they're turning a blind eye for favors or money. I was wondering if we could get one of Dillon's friends to contact Bart and tell them he has stock for sale."

"Won't he wonder why the man didn't contact the

Eketāhuna stock agent?"

"We might get around that if the property was on the boundary or close, or he could tell Bart his local agent didn't impress him, and he wants a change."

"Might work." Ada poured two cups of tea and handed one to Matt. Deciding she could do with a snack, she pulled a tin of homemade shortbread from the cupboard and offered Matt a piece. "You're suggesting the farmer requests Bart to visit him on the pretense he wants this stock sold and hope that Bart steals the cattle."

"A precise summation."

"It sounded as if Bart wanted to cut back on the thefts. What if we approached the cops in Eketāhuna? We know farmers in that area have lost stock. Do Dillon or Josh know the local police officers?"

"I'll contact Dillon tomorrow, and meantime, I'll skulk around the Walsh farm and see what else I can learn."

"You'll be careful?"

"Promise," Matt said. "I don't know why, but my mind keeps returning to the murder the cops tried to blame on you. It might have no connection, but my instincts say otherwise. If Bart and his sons are responsible, that makes them dangerous. Either way, they have a lot to lose if they're caught."

Ada sipped her tea. "I don't understand the constant

harassment. The cattle in my flower fields. The graffiti. Someone watching my property. I don't get why, and it's irking me."

"You've told me Eddie asked you out, and you refused. Perhaps your rejection brought out his vindictive side."

"It's possible. Craig targeted me for a scam. God, every time I think of that, I want to hit him."

"Call the bank manager tomorrow and tell him you've thought things over and are pressing charges," Matt suggested. "If a bank employee has committed this crime, the bank is responsible and will need to make restitution."

"Honestly, I was so angry my mind was a red haze. The money was bad enough, but they had me believing Greg had kept secrets. I-I thought the worst of Greg when he'd done nothing wrong and wasn't here to defend himself. Craig besmirched the memory of a decent man. That's what I can't forgive—the emotional hit. It eats at me."

"Understandable." Matt twined their fingers, his expression full of sympathy.

"I feel stupid," she grumbled. "For falling for the trick and not trusting Greg."

"Josh and I studied the paperwork. It looked legit. The perpetrator had access to bank stationary and your details. They knew exactly what they were doing."

"Doesn't make me feel any better." Ada drank her last

mouthful of tea and grimaced at the tea leaves that ended up inside her mouth. "I'm off to bed. I have heaps to do since I've decided to replant another section and grow another crop before summer's end. And I want to ring up the bank manager and yell and make demands."

Matt rose too. "Am I invited to your bed?"

"Yes, as long as sleep is all you have in mind. I'm not used to racing around the countryside in the wee hours of the morning. It was a weird time for them to have supper, don't you think?"

"I thought that too." Matt followed Ada into the bedroom.

A soft glow of the bedside lamp filled the room as Ada sat on the edge of the bed to remove her socks. "The one good thing to come from this is I no longer have that debt hanging over my head. I couldn't think of a next move, given I don't own the land. *Yet.* I will make a profit, dammit."

"You will. I believe in you."

Ada yawned again and tugged off her T-shirt. She rose to remove her leggings. "It's an excellent idea to speak with the Eketāhuna police."

"I'll contact Dillon as soon as we wake in the morning and ask him if he has a contact."

Ada slipped into bed naked and didn't argue when Matt

drew her near. This entire situation had discombobulated her so much she hoped she'd sleep.

The next morning, Ada woke with a kiss from Matt. Not a bad way to awaken, considering. She kissed him back, and they made love, taking their time. Afterward, they cuddled, and Ada savored the experience, relaxed and happy for a short time. Then she remembered her dastardly neighbors. Or at least, the menfolk were mean and nasty.

"Where did your mind go?" Matt murmured.

"To the Walsh men." Her hands curled to fists, and the tension broadcast to the rest of her body.

Matt kissed her cheek. "I'll put on the jug."

By the time Ada took a quick shower and dressed, Matt had a pot of tea ready and had fed Archie.

"What are your plans today?"

"I haven't changed my mind about skulking. I rang Dillon while you were in the shower and told him everything we'd discovered. He has a cop friend, and he's going to speak with him this morning." Matt's phone rang. "That's Dillon now."

Ada finished her tea and toast and picked up her phone. The charge held until she unplugged it. With a mutter, she sat on the floor and checked the camera app. The concealed camera had caught something. A vehicle that resembled Bart's farm utility. This time the number plate was partially visible.

"Matt, the camera caught a vehicle image last night."

Matt stalked over to her and studied the photo. "Can you send me a copy?"

Ada took care of that while Matt told Dillon of the fresh development. She also checked her email and pumped her fist when she spotted two separate confetti orders. Neither was big, but it was a start. Ada noted the addresses. That done, she rose and signaled to Matt that she was heading to her shed. Archie trotted after her, and she smiled as he settled for a snooze in the corner.

Once she'd packaged the orders, she picked the remaining blooms in her wildflower garden before uprooting the plants. It was time to try English lavender, and perhaps she'd prepare a corner for rose bushes. While the rose petals were too big for the cone containers, they'd be perfect for a flower girl to scatter while ambling up the aisle.

Matt sidled into her shed. "I'm trekking to your yards. Dillon is meeting me there, and we'll have a chat with the Eketāhuna cops. Did you want to speak with them, or would you prefer to stay here?"

"I need to work," Ada said. "You know everything that has happened. I'm willing to speak with the cops, should they want details from me about earlier incidents."

"Should I give Dillon's friend your number?"

"If he wants it," Ada said.

Matt kissed her goodbye and glided into the native trees.

She spent the morning working in her garden, and the honest toil drained the tension that had settled between her shoulders. Matt had helped too, and she realized she'd slowly released memories of Greg despite her troubles. Oh, they were still there, but it was the sweeter, more tender ones that lingered. A flash of guilt swamped her, cutting through her chest like a knife. She gasped, and rubbed the achy spot while sending yet another silent apology to her husband for doubting him. Tears welled in her eyes, while self-loathing tiptoed into her thoughts. She should've known. Never doubted.

Poor Greg. She'd cursed him for leaving her in this position when he had done nothing wrong. *Nothing*. He'd taken his savings and sunk it into buying his sheep, determined to secure the block of land his aunt had owned.

He'd been a good man, and he'd swept her off her feet during their first meeting at the hotel bar. She'd trusted him and her reaction to him, and their long-distance relationship had lasted a month until she'd moved to be with Greg. Her husband deserved to rest in peace, and she fervently wished the police could arrest his murderer, especially now. Greg wouldn't want her to torture herself over the loan incident. Deep down, she knew that. He'd want her to open herself to love again, but this came with bitter-sweet pain because she'd slipped in her belief of Greg's decency, his integrity.

Then there was Matt.

Two different men, but both honorable. Loving. Caring men who supported her independent nature. Greg had respected her, and she thought Matt did too.

A car roared into her driveway, and the driver stomped on the brakes, skidding a fraction on her gravel and raising dust. Ada straightened and rubbed the crook of her back.

"Ada! Where are you?"

Sherry's voice.

Ada strode toward her shed, and the moment Sherry spotted her, she limped in Ada's direction. Sherry's long hair wasn't in its regular tidy braid. In fact, it didn't appear as if Sherry had brushed her hair this morning. "Is something wrong?"

"How could you?" Sherry shrieked. "How could you do this to me?"

"Do what?" Ada halted.

"All the terrible things you told the bank manager about Craig. I thought we were friends. You could have spoken to me, discussed the matter. I knew you needed money and tried to help. This is what I get in return. You point the finger at my son, who is an honest man. The bank manager has placed him on leave and called the cops." Sherry jabbed her finger at Ada.

Ada took a cautious step back. Even though Sherry was a petite woman, scarcely above five feet, she wasn't one to mess with. "I haven't done anything." But she'd wanted to. Despite Sherry's confidence in her son, the signs pointed to Craig's guilt.

"Tell that to my son," Sherry snapped. "When I first learned Craig's news, I was furious. But now my temper has cooled, and I'm more disappointed. You've disappointed me, Ada. I thought better of you. I hope you'll learn from this, although our friendship can never be the same. Trust is easy, but once it's broken, it is more difficult to offer. You remember that. Oh, and don't bother coming to the farmers' market. I've cut down on the number of stalls. You'll understand, of course, because you're the last stallholder onboard, your stall isn't secure."

With her piece stated, Sherry marched to her car, climbed in, and drove away at a more sedate pace. Ada stared after her neighbor in shock. The loan debacle pointed directly at Craig, although the manager had indicated he'd take the next steps and communicate with her in a few days. Sherry had acted as if Ada had made up everything to get her son in trouble.

CHAPTER 27

AIM AND FIRE

MATT DIDN'T CONTACT HER. Ada tried to ring him, but her phone was only holding the charge when it felt like it. Stupid technology. The instant she plugged in her phone, it beeped several times, signaling texts from Matt.

Spoken to cops. Will tell all once I arrive home.

A later text said, **Stopping by Walsh property first.**

After working in the field for most of the day, sweat tickled Ada's skin and prickled at her nape. She jumped in the shower and changed into shorts and a T-shirt in deference to the warm evening. Afterward, she sat on the deck with an orange drink. Ice cubes tinkled as she drank.

A loud gunshot echoed through the valley without warning. Ada flinched, fear sending an arctic chill down her spine. She leaped to her feet, gaze scanning her surroundings. A flock of birds squawked and took to the air, their raucous cries punching at Ada's panic. Another two shots followed minutes later, then yawning silence.

Five anxious moments passed before the birds resettled into a tree closer to Ada. She issued a shaky laugh and resettled in her chair. Bart and his sons often shot rabbits. She should be used to the sound, but each harsh crack of a weapon shoved her back to the time when she'd discovered Greg. The blood... A shudder ran through her, and she forced her mind from the gruesome past.

Get a grip, Ada. What are you cooking for dinner?

She presumed Matt would come home, as his text promised. Ada retreated indoors to begin dinner preparations. Archie prowled inside with her and curled up on one of her cushions while she diced an onion. A quick tap sounded on her door.

Ada's hand tightened around the knife hilt.

"Ada, it's me."

"Matt." Ada hustled to the door and unlocked it to let him inside.

Blood dampened his shirt sleeve and dripped down his arm. She swayed, her fingernails gouging her palms as she fought the memories. "Matt, what happened?"

"Your neighbor happened. Eddie caught me lurking

around their shed. I don't think he saw my face, but he still fired at me."

Ada swallowed hard. "How bad is it?"

"Looks worse than it is," Matt said in an unruffled voice, and it was his composure that chipped at her fear. "He nicked me in the arm. Hurts like a bitch, but I won't die."

"All right." Ada sucked in a shaky breath. "What should I do?"

"Needs cleaning with antiseptic and a dressing to help stop the bleeding," Matt said, still calm.

Matt might be used to gunshot wounds, but she wasn't. Ada retrieved her first-aid kit, her legs trembling. While she did that, Matt stripped off his shirt and pressed a kitchen towel to the wound.

"Did you find anything?" she asked to distract herself.

"I snapped several photos before Eddie spotted me. Luckily, I heard him coming and almost made it into the trees before he started shooting."

"Did he follow? Are you sure he didn't know who he was shooting at?"

"No, his mother arrived home. He might not know my identity, but I bet he can guess since he's seen me with you."

Ada dampened a cloth and cleared the worst of the blood. To her relief, Matt was right, and the bleeding had slowed. She dabbed antiseptic liquid on the injury, surprised when Matt didn't flinch. "Did you learn anything else?"

"Dillon and I met with his cop friend. He intends to speak to his boss to see what action they can take. They're concerned by the thefts in their area and have been watching those in Moewai too. Dillon explained about the cameras and the problems you've faced. The cop came with us and took a cast of the tire tracks left last night plus photos. Dillon found a discarded ear tag. I don't know whether it had come loose or if they'd removed them from animals and dropped one."

"What's the next step? Should we report the shooting?"

"The Eketāhuna cops intend to watch Bart and his sons. I'll text Dillon about the shooting. He'll know what to tell his friend."

That sounded ominous, and Ada's stomach churned. If the bullet had been more to the right, another man she cared for would've died. She blinked hard, vulnerable at that moment, and not wanting to share. His gaze sharpened because this man was no dummy.

Ada babbled and offered a diversion. "Sherry visited and went off at me for getting Craig into trouble at his job. She had the cheek to say I'd disappointed her, and she didn't think she'd ever trust me again."

Matt muttered a curse. "But he stole from you. You're the victim here."

"I didn't bother explaining. Sherry wasn't in the mood to listen. She blamed me and reiterated how disappointed she was at my behavior and drove off in a snit. Oh, she also mentioned I could forget selling my flowers at the farmers' market." Ada pulled a face. "I'm off her Christmas card list."

"We've had an eventful day."

"Yes." She applied a dressing to the wound to keep it clean. "Are you hungry?"

"No."

"Let's go to bed and worry about this in the morning."

Matt sighed, and she thought there was relief because tension drained from his broad shoulders. "Nothing I'd like better."

$$\cdot \, \heartsuit \, \cdot \, \heartsuit \, \cdot \, \heartsuit \, \cdot \, \heartsuit \, \cdot \, \heartsuit \, \cdot$$

CRAIG FIRED A BAG of clothes into the rear of his SUV along with two bags of cash. Beside him, Eddie rearranged their gear until a tray of car parts concealed the money-filled receptacles.

Their mother limped from the front door, her lopsided gait more pronounced tonight. "Where are you going?"

Her tone was sharp, her expression one she'd aimed at them countless times during their childhood—displeasure.

Craig's stomach dropped before he pulled himself up to his full height. He wasn't a kid any longer, and his mother needed to give him respect instead of jerking him around with her emotional blackmail.

"Eddie and I are leaving before this situation becomes worse."

Eddie remained silent. Probably the best course of action since his mother might be small in stature and her patience legendary, but once her temper spiked, she was hell on wheels.

"Why?" The question emerged like gunfire.

"Ada Buckingham," Craig answered. "Ma, that's enough. We're leaving. We're not telling you where, so when the cops arrive, you can tell them you don't know our location. No lies necessary."

"But you're my sons. Where is your father? He should be here. He'd tell you running is the worst thing to do."

Eddie closed the rear of the vehicle before jogging around to the passenger seat. He climbed inside and shut the door, the slam popping their mother's attitude until she seemed to shrink in stature.

"Bye, Ma." Craig pushed aside his wave of guilt. This

was Ada's fault. If she hadn't visited the bank manager while he was away, none of this would be necessary. He'd needed a few more weeks for the fake loan to fall due, and he reckoned he could've forced Ada into selling her land to him. Unfortunately, she'd caught on to the scam, but at least he had her thousands. He smirked at the minor victory. "We'll call once we're settled."

"But where are you going?" his mother demanded.

"Best you don't know, Ma," Craig told her again and climbed behind the wheel. He started the SUV and drove away without a backward glance. He and Eddie would be all right. It was time to strike out on their own.

Eddie's phone rang before Craig reached the end of the driveway.

"Yeah." Eddie listened for a few minutes. "All right." He hung up and shifted in his seat. "How do you feel about payback? One quick detour before we leave."

Craig's brows rose and he smirked. "Works for me. Let's do it."

CHAPTER 28

AMBUSH

"I'VE RECEIVED FIVE NEW orders overnight. Five!" Ada said. "Summer has helped me so much, and she doesn't even know me."

"The Williams family are pure gold. Once you're part of their circle, they'll do anything for you. Besides, Josh is my brother-in-law. He truly is family."

Ada set down her tea and rose. "I'll pack these orders right now. I'll drive into town this afternoon to send them off."

"Where you go, I go," Matt said.

"How is your arm?"

"Bit stiff. I've had worse."

Ada shuddered. "I don't want to hear."

He tapped her on the nose. "Not gonna tell. Official secrets and all that."

Ada sniffed and reached for her phone, praying the thing would hold a charge today—at least long enough for her to fill the orders. She observed the battery icon and beamed. A lucky day.

She stalked to her shed, unlocking the door, pulling it wide open to let in the natural daylight. Her drying machine hummed as it desiccated the petals she'd prepared after breakfast.

"The first order is for twenty bags of petals. The bride wants mainly white with a hint of pink. White is popular. I thought I'd screwed up by planting too many white delphiniums, but my decision was inspired."

Matt chuckled. "Nope, you're smart. What's my mission?"

"Count out twenty cones. I send them flat, and the bride folds them into the cone shape on the day. I'll count out the clear bags ready to fill with petals."

It was fun working with Matt. He didn't grumble about flowers or women's work. In fact, he'd treated her as smart and capable from their first meeting, even when she'd berated him.

Once they'd completed the first order, Ada packed it into the courier box, and they started on the next. A foreign sound had her pausing mid-petal scoop. Her head jerked up, and her eyes widened.

"Matt." She croaked the warning about half a second too late.

Eddie slapped Matt across the back of his head with a lethal handgun, pistol-whipping the man she loved. Ada cried out and shot to her feet, every instinct urging her to run.

"Stop right there," Craig snarled, and that was when she noticed he, too, brandished a gun.

Eddie's scorching stare raked her body, and she failed to suppress her shudder. Eddie snickered, and she edged farther away. Blood welled at the back of Matt's head, and she couldn't tell if he was breathing or not.

"Eddie, handcuff the soldier. We don't want him to wake and spoil our fun." Craig's amusement didn't reach his eyes.

Ada shuddered but attempted to control her reaction when Eddie laughed.

He rubbed his groin, making certain Ada saw before he sauntered over to Matt. Eddie pulled what looked like a plastic strip from his pocket and crouched beside Matt.

When Eddie stood, Ada gulped on seeing Matt's hands restrained behind his back. Craig grabbed a coil of rope Ada kept for when she needed to stake a plant. He used a length of it to bind Matt's legs.

"Your turn." Eddie leered at Ada. He strutted toward her, and Ada recoiled until the wall halted her retreat. "There's nowhere for you to go."

Maybe so, but she didn't intend to make this easy for him. She dodged Eddie's first grab and tensed, ready to elude him again.

"Quit mucking around." Craig pointed the gun at her and fired. The boom reverberated inside the shed, and panic had Ada's heart beating so hard and fast she thought it might fly from her chest. She'd braced for pain and cried out when Craig fired a second shot.

"Two shots is all the warning you'll get. Payback because you're a stubborn bitch and refused to take our hints to sell your land and move on. Most women would've run off screaming with all the crap we dished you. *Don't move!* The next one will go straight between your eyes."

One glance at Craig told her he wasn't joking.

"Turn around," Eddie snapped. "Hands behind your back."

Ada slowly obeyed his order, gulping down breaths to remain silent, all the while fearing a bullet would slam into her back instead of the shed wall. Eddie placed the plastic band around her wrists and pulled it cruelly tight.

A ringing phone broke the taut stillness. It wasn't hers,

but she thought it might be Matt's.

"Perfect timing," Craig said. "It wouldn't do if one of you got a call out."

The ring tone ceased, and a metallic crunch sounded, which she presumed was Craig taking a hammer to Matt's phone.

"Where's your phone, Ada?" Eddie demanded.

He was so close his breath wafted across her neck. She winced, and his soft laugh mocked her. His hand reached around her body, and he unerringly found her breast. He cupped it before squeezing painfully hard. Then, he rubbed his groin against her backside, chortling when she grunted and attempted to wriggle from his touch.

"Phone," he whispered.

"On the desk."

"Good girl." He punctuated his praise with another breast grope.

Ada jerked back her leg and scored a direct hit to his kneecap. His grunt was music to her ears. His return punch in her jaw—not so much. Ada saw stars as she crumpled to the ground.

"Tie her legs, then let's go." Craig scanned her shed. "Pity that damn cat isn't here. Ma gave me grief over dumping the animal instead of drowning it like she told me."

"I told you the same thing." Eddie tied her legs with quick efficiency. He leaned over her and licked across her cheek to her ear. "We could've had so much fun together," he whispered. "But you had to fuck the soldier." He rose and kicked her in the ribs.

Fiery pain flared from the point of impact, and yet more stars burst like supernovas in her mind, and that was the last thing she remembered.

CHAPTER 29

THE PANTRY HIDEOUT

MATT WOKE WITH A hell of a headache, and it took him long moments to fathom his location. Ada's shed. The blaze of lights allowed perfect vision, despite the closed door. Or it would, once he could get his eyes to stop seeing double. He twisted and realized someone had bound his arms and legs. His memories surged back. The neighbors. The two sons. They'd jumped him and Ada.

Ada.

Crap, where was she?

He rotated his body, wincing at the pain in his ribs. It seemed as if one or both of the men had got in a kick or two once they'd knocked him out. He couldn't see Ada. Had they taken her? Damn, he'd sensed they were dangerous.

He rolled again, finding what he suspected was the remains of a phone. No way of ringing for help, then.

Adrenaline bombarded him. Fear for Ada. Luckily, his soldiering experience came to the rescue and informed him to calm the fuck down.

Deep breaths.

Calm. Center. Concentrate.

Matt followed the orders fired at his pounding head. He took a few seconds to knock back his panic, breathing as deeply as he could, given the ache in his ribs. He used his core muscles to sit upright, which gave him a better range of vision. That's when he glimpsed a pair of boots.

Ada.

Relief swept over him in a whoosh of lightheadedness until he realized those boots were motionless. His nostrils flared, and a snarl pushed past his curled lips. *The bastards.* If they'd hit her, injured her, he'd hunt down the slimy weasels and make them sorry. But first, he needed to get free. Plastic handcuffs. Strong but not infallible. He knew how to break them, and now that he was more focused, that was his next task.

Matt sucked in a huge breath and puffed it out. He repeated this several times until he was confident his soldier was in control and running the show instead of the terrified man who'd failed to protect his lady. Once he reached that place, he jerked his hands apart with as much power as he could find. The satisfying snap of the plastic band had barely registered before he was untying his bound legs and scrambling around the desk to check on Ada.

He found her sprawled on the ground, unmoving. Silent. He checked her pulse, gratified to learn it was strong.

No blood. That was good.

He checked her for other wounds and spotted her reddened and swollen jaw when he turned her. Matt untied her legs and found a pair of her clippers to deal with the plastic cuffs restraining her wrists. Once she was free, he turned her fully onto her back.

Josh and Dillon would've tried to contact him because they'd arranged to meet. He wasn't sure of the time since Craig or Eddie had stolen the watch Ashley had given him for his birthday. He loved that watch.

Matt found the door locked. Damn. They needed to escape in case the brothers returned.

A groan drew his attention back to Ada, and he hustled to her side.

"Ada," he whispered.

Her eyelashes fluttered, and tension dug into her features. Another groan escaped her.

"Ada, sweetheart. Open those pretty brown eyes of yours."

"Matt?"

"Yeah, it's me."

"What happened? Why do I have the hangover from hell?"

"Craig and Eddie Walsh jumped us. I didn't see who hit you, but one of them did. Can you sit up?" He slipped his arm around her waist, not pulling her, but allowing her to move at her pace.

"Ow. Ow. *Ow*," she muttered. "My ribs... Eddie kicked me. The bastard. When I get my hands on him, he'll be sorry. He groped me, told me how much I'd missed by hooking up with you. I wouldn't wipe my floor with him, although I'd enjoy kneeing him in the nuts."

Matt didn't comment because her anger would get her past the pain and help her to move. Yeah, he didn't comment, but he sure took note. Only a moron molested a woman, and to do it after he'd restrained her was even more reprehensible. Wait until Matt got his hands on the creep. Not a threat. *A promise.* Eddie Walsh should watch his back.

"You're bleeding," Ada said, her gaze roving his head.

Matt hadn't noticed, although now she mentioned it, he could feel blood dripping down his cheek. "Did you see what they hit me with?"

"A gun. Craig struck you from behind, then pointed the gun at me once you fell. Let me see."

He lowered his head for Ada to check his injury. Her fingers were careful as she parted his hair to better see the wound.

"There's a big lump, but the actual cut is small."

"I'll put a pad on it to stem the bleeding." He glanced around for something suitable, turning back to Ada when he heard ripping fabric. She'd torn a strip off the bottom of her T-shirt.

"It's not one hundred percent clean, but I figure it's better than nothing."

Matt folded the cloth and pressed the pad against his head. "Do you have your phone?"

She pointed at the smashed pieces on her workbench.

"Bugger," he muttered. "They smashed mine too. We'll need to walk for help." He glanced at her. "I'll go. You stay here and hide if you see anyone else."

"No," Ada snapped. "You're not going alone. We're a team. Where you go, I go."

"Where is your nearest neighbor apart from the Walsh family?"

"Five kilometers," Ada said. "And we'll walk past the Walsh property to reach them. I'm the last one on this road." Her eyes narrowed. "How about we go to the Walsh property? The boys aren't there since I got the impression they were leaving. Sherry is out most days with her activities. They have a landline. We can break in and use it to call the cops."

Matt considered her suggestion. "Plan. I'll need to break your door, so we can get out. They've locked it from the outside."

"No need. We can get out the rear door. I don't use it, but it's there for an emergency exit. Help me move this shelving at the back."

Matt took one end, and between them, they shoved the heavy shelving away from the wall. When there was enough space to squeeze through, Ada stepped behind and pushed open the concealed door.

"What's on the other side?"

"Trees. Ashley's bodyguards noticed and quizzed me about it when they got me alone."

"Those two don't miss a trick. Between them and Josh, my sister is as safe as she can be."

Ada pushed at the door again, and it grudgingly gave way with an ear-piercing squeak. Matt watched Ada squeeze through and followed, trying to ignore his pounding head.

"I'm out," Ada declared.

"Not too loud," Matt cautioned. "We don't know for sure Craig and Eddie have left."

"Sorry."

"No need to apologize. Just take care and wait until I'm out." Matt had more difficulty slithering through the same gap, and the door took a hunk of skin off before he exited.

"See or hear anyone?" he asked.

"The birds are singing, which tells me they've probably left."

Part of Matt hoped she was right while the other part wanted to use his fists on the smart-arses. At least they'd only roughed them up. Sweat beaded on his forehead as he imagined what else they could've done, especially to Ada, while he was out cold.

"Wait there, and I'll check it out." Matt disappeared before she could protest. She'd probably follow him. Mere moments later, he glanced over his shoulder and saw he was right. He scowled.

Ada lifted her chin in silent challenge. He sighed and continued his stealthy approach to Ada's tiny house. Someone had kicked in the door and trashed the place.

A horrified croak emerged from Ada, and she pushed past him to survey the wreckage of her home. When she turned to him, tears streamed down her face. He hadn't seen her cry before, not through the harassment and other problems. He'd seen her angry. He'd seen her dispirited, but her crying pierced him straight through the heart.

With two long strides, he was at her side. He drew her into his arms and buried his face in her fragrant hair. Her shoulders shook once before she stilled.

After long seconds, she pulled away. She'd stopped crying, letting her anger save her from a full breakdown, and her fury flashed in her eyes. "No point cleaning up now. I'd rather get to the cops and lay a complaint. Eddie and Craig should pray the police grab them first because when I get my hands on them, I'm not sure I'll have full control."

A surge of pride flashed through Matt. His warrior woman. "I'll hold them down for you," he promised.

CHAPTER 30

EDDIE WALSH BETTER WATCH OUT!

MATT SET A RAPID pace during their trek to the Walsh property, but Ada didn't complain. Every muscle throbbed. It didn't matter because the determination to best Eddie and Craig drove her. Grope her when she was helpless, would he?

"The first opportunity I get, I'm gonna kick Eddie Walsh in the balls." Her words sounded bloodthirsty, and she didn't care.

In front of her, Matt stopped. "I know you hate him."

"What sort of man molests women in the first place? To do it when she's restrained and helpless is a hundred times worse. I don't even understand what I've done to him or to Craig to attract this level of harassment. I've racked my brain, and nothing makes sense."

"Not the time for this discussion. Once we have the cops on their tail, we'll take a breather and go from there."

"Sherry is so nice. Well, usually. Evidently Sherry told Craig to drown Archie, but he dumped him instead. *Poor Archie.* Normally she's friendly and considerate and very popular. One or two people are mean-spirited behind her back, which I put down to jealousy. All I wanted was to run my business and make a profit. A comfortable country life. It was what Greg wanted, what we both strove for. I wanted to shove our success in my in-laws' faces because they were horrid to Greg. Yet all along, Greg's parents and it appears the Walsh family have worked to make me fail. I don't get it. What is this? Tall poppy syndrome. No, that can't be right," she muttered. "I haven't succeeded, not yet, because everyone keeps slapping me down."

"Ada."

"I wish I understood why."

"Ada," Matt repeated. "You're pissed. I understand but we have a mission. I offered to go by myself because it'd be quicker, but you insisted on coming with me. Please, button those gorgeous lips of yours and focus. We're almost at the Walshes' house, and the last thing we need is to alert anyone who might be at home."

"Sorry." Ada made a zipping motion across her mouth.

Matt's gaze was searching as if he didn't trust her to remain silent. A few seconds later, he continued along the stock track. Ada fell into step, chastened because he was right.

Matt halted on the ridge above the Walsh property, and Ada stopped beside him, heartened to see the empty driveway.

"What sort of vehicle does Sherry drive?" Matt asked, pitching his voice low.

"A red sedan."

"Do you know if she parks in the garage?"

"With the stuff they had stacked in there, I doubt they could fit a vehicle." Ada kept her gaze on the house.

"Excellent point." Matt scanned the house and its surroundings for several beats longer. "Looks empty, but we'll keep behind cover as much as possible."

"How will we get inside? If they've locked the doors, I mean."

"Eddie and Craig had no compunction in breaking into your home. Surely you're not feeling squeamish about doing the same?"

"But Sherry..." Ada trailed off. "You're right, but it may not be an issue. Or it wouldn't have been until we had the spate of burglaries."

Matt started down the hill in a zigzag fashion. Each time

he slipped out of the cover of the trees, he paused first to check the house. Ada followed his example, copying his cautious approach. At the last tree, the bush gave way to an expanse of green lawn.

"Have you been inside the house? Do you know where the phone is?"

"Sherry has a landline in the kitchen, and I think they have an extension in their bedroom."

"Okay, which side of the house is the kitchen? And the bedrooms?"

"They have an open-plan kitchen and dining room, plus a lounge. There is also a more formal lounge where Sherry holds meetings or entertains visitors when she wants to make an impression. The formal lounge is gorgeous since it has views over the bush and the Moewai river. The guest bathroom is first along the passage, and the bedrooms are at the far end of the house."

"Excellent. Is there an entrance to the kitchen?"

"Head to the right."

Matt shifted in that direction. "Keep close. No talking."

Ada rolled her eyes at his back. She followed, taking care of her footing while scanning the open areas around the house. The birds were tweeting, and a cow mooed from a paddock on the far side of the house.

When they reached the brick building, Matt cocked

his head. Ada couldn't hear anything to alarm her. Matt ghosted around the edge of the house toward the kitchen door. He peered through a window while Ada paused, trusting him to keep them safe.

"Wait here," he ordered.

Anxiety slithered through her as Matt tried the door. Her breath hissed out when it opened, and he slipped inside and disappeared. What the heck? Surely he didn't intend to leave her loitering here. The door creaked open farther, and Matt stuck his head outside. He signaled her before ducking out of sight. Ada scrambled to the entrance and stepped inside. It was deathly quiet apart from the tick of a clock.

"Had a quick look," he said against her ear. "No one is home. Let's make this quick. You ring the cops, and I'll keep watch."

"Should I ring Moewai or Eketāhuna?"

"Second thought, ring Dillon or Josh and get them to contact the cops. Tell them once we leave here, we'll make our way toward town."

Ada beelined to the phone. "Crap. Do you know the number?"

Matt rattled it off without taking his gaze off the view outside the window.

"Yeah." Dillon's deep voice sounded cautious even in

that tiny soundbite.

"It's Ada. I'm with Matt."

"Where are you? Why aren't you answering your phone?"

"No talking. Let me finish," she said when Dillon barked out more questions. "Eddie and Craig jumped us at my place. They tied us up and locked us in my shed after destroying our phones."

"Where are you ringing from?"

"The Walsh property. No one is home, and we broke into their house to use the phone. As soon as we hang up, Matt and I will walk toward town."

"We're on our way. Josh," Dillon called. "We're moving out. The cops picked up Bart, and I understand he's being helpful in their inquiries."

"Tell them they should arrest Craig and Eddie if they see them. Not only did they bash around Matt and me and tie us up, but they also trashed my house. I want them charged."

"One more thing," Dillon said. "Those two detectives who dragged you to the Moewai cop shop intend to arrest you for Ralph Dawson's murder."

Ada felt her mouth fall open. "But I didn't do it."

"Bart says there is proof you committed the crime."

"What sort of proof?" Ada demanded, her voice

growing louder.

"Whatever it is, it was enough to convince the cops you murdered him."

"I was with Matt for the entire weekend."

"There is something else," Dillon said after a brief hesitation.

"What?" Ada snapped. What could be worse than getting arrested for murder?

"The cops are looking at your husband's murder with the view to charging you for that too. From what my friend said, you didn't have an alibi, and you found the body."

Ada's knees almost gave out on her, and she gripped the countertop to remain upright. "I didn't kill him either."

"Hang tight. Josh and I are on the way. Make for the signpost at the start of Moewai. I recall a rest area with a picnic table. We'll park and wait for you to come to us. That way, we won't miss each other."

"Fine," Ada snapped and hung up.

"What's wrong?" Matt asked, concern etched into his handsome features.

"The cops have uncovered fresh evidence that purportedly points to me as Ralph Dawson's murderer. They're also taking another look at Greg's death. They think I killed him too."

"Crap, I'm sorry," Matt said. "Anyone who knows you

won't believe you're capable."

"Well, evidently, there are many people who imagine I killed Ralph and Greg."

Matt left the window and embraced her. "Not me."

But his faith wasn't enough. Proving her innocence was going to cost money for lawyers and legal fees. The thud of a car door jerked them apart. Matt darted to the window and peeked outside.

"Crap," he muttered, his gaze scanning the room.

A furious feminine shout galvanized them to action. Ada flinched while Matt grasped her hand and dragged her to the pantry. He flung open the door and thrust her inside. Matt squeezed in behind her and shut the door.

A tremble spread through Ada, and Matt must've felt it because he held her tighter and whispered against her ear. "She didn't see us."

But what if Sherry discovered them? Ada's cheeks flushed at the thought. There wasn't a single suitable reason for her and Matt to be hiding inside Sherry's kitchen pantry.

"Bloody stupid man," Sherry muttered and slammed the door.

Ada flinched again, even as her brows rose at the vindictive tone of Sherry's voice. She'd never heard her friend speak with anything but politeness and reason.

Something crashed into the wall right near the pantry. It smashed on the floor, and the pantry door almost flew open. It would've if Matt hadn't grabbed the knob from the inside. Another crash sounded, farther away this time.

"Why is she so angry? I've never heard her lose her temper." Ada fell silent when Sherry's shouts came closer.

"Stupid bastard. I told him. I bloody told him, but he thought he knew better."

Smash!

Ada's heart thudded against her ribcage, and she jumped when something crashed into the pantry door. A cry escaped her, but Matt's hand slapped across her mouth, not an instant too soon. Heck, had she given them away?

More crashes and bangs exploded in the kitchen. Some very close. The noise ceased without warning, and Ada realized the ringing wasn't in her head but was the telephone. She held her breath and attempted to make as little sound as possible.

"You what?" Sherry roared. "Never mind. Take the back roads, and we'll meet at the usual place." She paused. "I can't believe you were so stupid. It's that bloody cat scenario again. Just once, I wish you'd follow my orders." Another pause. "I'm coming now. Don't leave until we can speak."

The handpiece of the phone crashed down, and another

missile struck the wall to the right of the pantry. Ada closed her eyes and prayed for this to end.

The banging, along with intermittent crashes, continued for another ten minutes, and Ada focused on a different urge. She needed the restroom. She shifted from foot to foot.

"What's wrong?" Matt asked during a break in the din.

"I need to use the restroom."

Matt squeezed her shoulders in silent comfort. "If she doesn't leave soon, we'll try to sneak out. It sounded as if she's going somewhere."

The wait was endless before the exterior door slammed.

"Wait there," Matt said. "I'll make sure she's gone."

"I can't wait," Ada wailed, and she fled before Matt could object, taking in the carnage in the kitchen and the hall beyond. Sherry had grabbed everything sitting on the kitchen counter and fired it around the room. Ada flew to the restroom and locked the door after her. If Sherry were still here, she'd need to break down the door to deal with Ada's trespassing.

Ada took care of business and washed her hands in the small basin. A soft tap had her whirling and staring at the door in horror.

"Ada," came Matt's voice. "Sherry has gone. We should leave, in case she returns."

Ada unlocked the door and followed Matt through the kitchen and outside. "I don't understand. The Sherry I know never loses her temper."

"Maybe her family has pushed her to the limit?"

"Perhaps. She was responsible for Archie's dumping. I can't believe she'd treat a defenseless animal that way. I guess we should hustle. The rest area is a few kilometers from here."

"We'll follow the road for easier walking, but get ready to hide in the undergrowth if a vehicle heads our way."

"If I make it through today, I might sleep in tomorrow. My head is thudding."

"Mine too." Matt took her hand. "Once this is over, what do you say we go to Fiji for a week? Sun. Sea. A few drinks. Lots of sex."

"Sounds lovely," Ada said. "The last time I went on holiday was before Greg and I married. I traveled to the Gold Coast with three girlfriends. We had a ball."

"I was thinking of making it a honeymoon," Matt said, his tug on her hand insistent when Ada came to a dead halt.

"A honeymoon?"

"Ada, I want to marry you. We could get married in Fiji and relax afterward. Maybe ask Dillon and Josh if they want to come. My parents. Yours. Summer and Nikolai.

What do you say?"

"But I thought—even though you've told me before—that given my luck and the drama in my life, you'd change your mind and leave eventually."

"You were fine with that?" he growled.

"Not exactly, but if that was the only way I could have you, I thought I'd take what I could get." She paused, swallowed.

"I love you." Matt turned her to face him. "A future. That's what I want with you. I mentioned I have a short time left in the army, but I'm training rather than on active duty. Once my term is up, I'm leaving. You have your farm down here. What did you think when Josh and I asked about buying or using part of your land?"

"With the way my life has been running, I thought you'd leave again."

"Do you love me?"

Ada wrinkled her nose. "Yes. I didn't mean to, but you kept butting in and helping me. My liking for you turned into love."

"Do you not want to get married again? Is it your husband?"

"I miss him," Ada admitted. "But it has been years since he died. Greg wouldn't expect me to mourn him forever. He was a practical man. He'd want me to move on if I found the right man."

"Ada, will you marry me?"

"In Fiji?"

"If you want a big wedding, we can do that."

"Fiji sounds lovely. Nice and informal. I'll need to find someone to watch my farm and look after Archie."

"I'm sure someone will do that for us," Matt said. He took her hand and wove their fingers together. "Fiji, it is then. Soon," he added.

They rounded a corner in the road and halted. Up ahead, three police cars blocked the road and passage for Sherry's red car.

"She has a gun. Quick, into cover before she sees us." Matt directed Ada into the brush edging the tarmac. "Sherry is keeping the police busy. We'll wriggle through the fence and make our way through the paddock. If we're lucky, we'll creep past with no one noticing us."

"Sherry hates guns. She told me they frighten her."

"She lied since she's handling this one like a pro," Matt murmured.

As Ada watched from cover, Sherry waved her weapon. "Let me through! You have no right to stop me."

"Holding the police at gunpoint is a serious crime, Mrs. Walsh," a cop called.

Sherry's hand remained steady. Matt was right. Sherry's

behavior spoke of familiarity and confidence with weapons. Why had she lied?

"Ada," Matt spoke softly, controlling the carry of his voice. "Let the cops deal with Sherry. We should join forces with Josh and Dillon while we can."

Ada took care of her foot placement and followed Matt. She struggled through thick undergrowth with a minimum of noise. A gorse bush gouged her face, just missing her eyes. Her fingers came away bloody. Sighing, she navigated the vegetation as best she could.

A fraught half an hour later, they climbed a fence and arrived at the rest area to find Josh and Dillon waiting.

She slipped into the rear seat of the black SUV, and Matt climbed into the other side.

Dillon observed them through narrowed eyes. "You both look like crap. What happened?"

Matt ran through their story. Him getting winged, and Eddie and Craig holding them at gunpoint and locking them in Ada's shed. He mentioned Sherry and her weird behavior. "I don't know if it's a breakdown or if she's in shock, but she was holding off the police with a gun."

"We'll drive back to Eketāhuna," Dillon decided.

"Do the police still want me?" Ada asked.

"That's another reason to get out of here," Josh said as his brother reversed the vehicle and sped toward Moewai.

"We'll take the back roads," Dillon said. "Check in with my cop friend at Eketāhuna."

"You say the police want to question me about Greg's death? It's true I found him, but the police did tests. I had no gun residue on my hands. I'd rung the cops when I heard gunfire because we'd had problems with idiots stealing our sheep for meat. Townies coming to the country, looking for free food. When Greg didn't arrive home after checking on the lambing ewes, I searched for him. I found him and realized he was dead and rang the local police again."

Matt took her hand and squeezed in commiseration.

"Their experts tried to make a case against me, but they couldn't twist the facts to fit. As for Ralph Dawson, it's ludicrous to suspect I had an affair with him. I'd never become involved with a married man. Heck, I don't have time for an affair. You know how I've struggled to find the labor to help with my harvest."

"We'll speak with the cops," Josh said. "You have people on your side. A lawyer to make mincemeat of their arguments."

A fat lot of good that did when she had no money to pay said lawyer. Ada sat in the back of the vehicle, holding Matt's hand, and wondered what else could go wrong.

CHAPTER 31

POLICE STATION DRAMA

"Josh, ring Jeff Hoete and see if he can meet us at the police station. Give him a summary of the situation and what we've learned," Dillon said. "Tell him Matt and Ada have injuries, and we're stopping by our parents' house to doctor them up before we hit the police station."

Josh followed his brother's terse instructions, and Ada realized she was witnessing the army dynamics at work. Josh had told her he, Matt, and Dillon had been part of the same unit with Dillon, the leader.

She found Dillon a little scary and was glad he was on her side.

They pulled up at a house on the outskirts of Eketāhuna, and Dillon parked around the back before they exited the vehicle. Dillon's and Josh's mother met them at the rear door, which led into a home-style kitchen. A delicious savory scent wafted from a pot simmering on the stove. A family photo on the wall showed a teenage Dillon and Josh along with their sister and parents. The kitchen table was large and sturdy, and it was easy to imagine the family sitting around during breakfast or other meals.

"Dillon. Josh. Oh, you've brought friends. Come in," a woman said, her bright smile showing hints of Josh.

"I'll grab the first-aid kit." Josh disappeared down a hallway.

"Mum, this is our army friend, Frog—Matt—and his girlfriend, Ada. Ada has a farm in Moewai." Dillon pulled out a chair. "Sit," he directed Ada.

She pulled a face but sat as ordered, and Matt followed suit when Dillon yanked out a second chair.

Josh returned and dumped the first-aid kit on the kitchen table.

"Who's first?"

"Matt," Ada said at the same time Matt uttered her name.

"I'll take care of Ada," Mrs. Williams said. "That's a nasty scratch on your face, dear. Any other injuries?"

"My head is aching," Ada said. "Eddie hit me."

Mrs. Williams tsked. "Let me see. You have lovely thick hair. That probably helped save you a little." She kept her fingers gentle as she searched for a wound.

"Farther toward the front of my head. Yep. There." Ada grunted instead of crying out, as was her first instinct. Man, that hurt. She'd investigated the spot once they'd made it to the car. The lump had felt like a small mountain, but she figured it probably wasn't that bad.

"Josh, get Ada a glass of water and two headache tabs." Mrs. Williams spared a glance at Matt. "Better make that enough for two people. It's obvious Matt has a head injury too."

Neither Matt nor Dillon commented since they spoke in low voices, but Josh set a glass in front of Matt. Matt didn't hesitate to swallow the tablets along with a slug of water. Ada watched Dillon remove Matt's shirt. Blood stained the dressing she'd put on his upper arm, and she sucked in a hasty breath.

"Don't worry," Mrs. Williams chided. "These boys are tough. If Matt's wounds were bad enough for hospital treatment, Dillon would force him to go. My, that's an enormous lump on your noggin."

"I'm trying to tell myself it's not as big as I imagine."

Mrs. Williams reached for a cotton wool pad and a bottle of what smelled like antiseptic. It stung like a bitch, and she must've made a noise.

"Ada?" Matt said in a sharp voice.

"She's gonna be fine," Mrs. Williams assured him.

Ada wasn't so optimistic about that when Mrs. Williams turned her attention to her face. The antiseptic liquid burned her scratches, even though she tried not to act like a baby. When Mrs. Williams finished, she patted Ada's hand and shunted the headache tablets at her.

"Take those now. I'm sure I don't have to tell you if your headache persists, visit the doctor."

"Thank you, Mrs. Williams."

"I'll make a pot of tea," Mrs. Williams informed her sons, and her voice held a hint of challenge.

"Mum, we have to head to the police station," Josh protested.

"All the more reason to have something to eat," Mrs. Williams said. "I made a batch of shortbread yesterday. Only a fool turns down my shortbread."

"I'd love tea," Ada said in a firm voice. "Breakfast was ages ago."

"Ada is right," Dillon said. "No telling how long the cops will keep her. What time is Jeff free?"

"Not until this afternoon. It's his granddaughter's birthday party. She had a sleepover with her friends, and he was helping," Josh said.

"Sandwiches," Mrs. Williams suggested. "You have time."

It was almost two hours later when they drove to the police station. Jeff Hoete met them in the police car park, and they walked into the station together.

"Why are you at Eketāhuna station instead of the Moewai one?" the cop at the desk asked.

"We heard some local Moewai cops are in cahoots with the local criminals, and they're trying to smear Ms. Buckingham's reputation," Jeff Hoete said. "We want to have a fair hearing, which is why we came here."

The cop's eyes flashed. "That's a big allegation."

"We overheard the bad guys talking about their tame cops," Ada said sweetly. "I'll take my chances here."

"Fine, but we'll still contact Moewai because we don't know what the charges are against you."

Jeff Hoete bobbed his head in agreement. "That's fine, but they can conduct their questioning here. After that, we'll play the situation by ear."

"Wait in the interview room down the hall," the cop said, his tone abrupt. He picked up the phone and focused on the person on the other end of the call.

Ada hesitated, then crossed to Matt. "What are you going to do?"

"Wait for you."

"Go back to my place and get some rest."

His lips curved in a faint smile. "No, I'm staying with you."

Before she and her lawyer could walk to the interview room, the cop at the desk stopped them. "The Moewai cops want us to send you there."

Dillon picked up his phone and made a call while Matt protested this development.

"What happens if I refuse to go?"

"The Moewai cops have told me to detain you for the murder of Ralph Dawson," the cop said. "Wait there while I call a car around to take you to Moewai."

"What do I do?" Ada asked Jeff.

Jeff's mouth firmed. "I'm afraid you'll have to go with them. I'll follow and sit in with the interview."

A tall police officer appeared from out the back. "I'll take her to Moewai."

"Thanks," the cop at the desk replied. "Go with him. If you resist, we'll cuff you."

Ada gave a curt nod. She glanced at Matt, then at Josh and Dillon. Matt inclined his head and gave a quick smile of reassurance. She'd have to trust him. Heck, she did trust him, which was why she'd jumped into bed with him. She straightened her spine to prepare for the ordeal to come and followed the cop to the car.

The car park at the Moewai police station was busier than she'd ever seen before, with several police cars and half a dozen sedans.

Ada exited the vehicle when the Eketāhuna cop opened the rear door for her. He walked her into the station, but not before she noted Matt and the others had arrived. Another cop exited the building and spoke over his shoulder. He directed her inside and to an interview room. Jeff followed her into the police station, but Dillon, Matt, and Josh hung back to speak with the cop who'd delivered her to Moewai.

"Someone will be with you in a few minutes."

"Thank you," Jeff said. Once the door shut, he looked to Ada. "Tell me now. Do you have any idea what they have on you? Did you do it?"

"No!" Ada said in horror. "I loved my husband, and the last time I saw him, he was very much alive. As for the other man they're accusing me of murdering, what is my motivation? I work long hours and until Matt arrived and helped me, scarcely went out because I was too busy setting up my new business."

"All right. Have you—?" He ceased speaking when the door flew open, and the two detectives—Detectives George and Conway—entered.

They wore pleased expressions as if they'd cracked the

case.

"Ms. Buckingham, you've led us quite a chase," Detective George said.

They took seats and followed the same procedure as last time, advising her of her rights before announcing their names for the tape.

"Ms. Buckingham, we've discovered a cache of personal letters written by you to Ralph Dawson in which you express your undying love. The letters bear dates, and in the last one, it appears Mr. Dawson broke off your affair. You didn't take it well and threatened to kill him rather than let him return to his wife and child. What do you say to that?" Detective George asked.

"I say that is a lie. I never had an affair with the man, much less wrote him love letters. I've already told you this."

"They're in your writing. We executed a search warrant a few hours ago on your home. An expert compared the writing, and it is the same."

"Pardon?" Shock rippled through Ada. Her writing was atrocious, what some people called chicken scratch. It meant if she was sending a letter, she always wrote it on her laptop. She couldn't think what message they could've found to compare. "Eddie and Craig Walsh attacked me this morning and left me locked in my shed. Once I freed myself, I discovered they'd broken into my home. Craig Walsh is in trouble for falsifying loan documents and extorting money. I believe he lost his job. If I were you, I'd check with them and take samples of their handwriting. Also, I'm left-handed. My writing is terrible, which is why I seldom handwrite. It's easier for me to use my laptop and print documents." Certainty and truth rang in her voice, and she watched the two detectives share a glance.

"Ms. Buckingham, take me through finding your husband's body."

Ada gaped at Detective George. They truly believed she'd murdered Greg. Shrugging, she ran through what had happened and how she'd heard gunshots. When Greg had failed to return for breakfast, she'd gone looking for him.

"What would you say, Ms. Buckingham, if I told you we had a witness who saw you with a gun and they say you shot your husband?"

"First, I'd ask what they were drinking. Second, I'd ask if they needed glasses. Detective, I don't own a gun and have never shot one in my life. Greg owned a shotgun and used it to keep down the rabbit and possum populations. Not me. Also, your police tests showed no gun residue on my hands."

"Where is that shotgun?"

"Until the fire destroyed my house, it was in the gun safe. It burned along with the rest of the contents in my house. The fire investigators say it was arson. Another crime the police have never solved." Ada glared at the detectives.

"The police suspected you caused the fire."

"How?" Ada demanded. "I was in Auckland with my parents, attending my cousin's wedding."

"You could've paid someone to burn the house for you."

"You're an idiot. I lost everything in that fire apart from the suitcase of clothes I had with me for the weekend. Yes, I'd insured the property, but I didn't receive enough to rebuild a home of the same caliber."

The two detectives glanced at each other and turned back to her.

"Ada Buckingham, we are arresting you on suspicion of murder—"

A hard knock on the door interrupted the detective. Another police officer stuck his head in the door and gestured.

"Can't this wait?" Detective George snapped.

"No," the new arrival replied.

"Detective George and Detective Conroy are leaving the room. Tape stopped at 15:23."

As they left the interview room, a woman shrieked—the sound wild and ear-piercing. A chill shot down Ada's spine, and she glanced at her lawyer. He stood.

"I'll try to learn what's going on. This is more exciting than my previous plans," he added with a grin.

Ada rolled her eyes and sat back. She waited, drummed her fingers on the tabletop and waited some more.

Finally, Detective Conroy returned with her lawyer. Her lawyer winked at her, his expression smug.

"Ms. Buckingham, you are free to go," Detective Conroy said.

Ada gawked at him. "What?"

"You're free to go," he repeated with a snap in his voice.

"And?" her lawyer prompted.

"I am sorry for the distress caused during the interview," he choked out before striding from the interview room.

"What's happened?" Ada asked.

"Forensics showed the bullet that killed Ralph Dawson matched the one that killed your husband. You told me the police never found the weapon."

"Yes, that's correct."

Jeff grinned. "One of the older cops who worked your husband's case knows his weapons. He spotted the gun Mrs. Walsh was brandishing corresponded to what they knew of the murder weapon. The cops checked the bullets and noted they're similar, if not identical. They're conducting further tests, but it's a powerful reason to point the murder at someone in the Walsh family."

"Sherry?" Ada asked, shocked to the core.

"Perhaps," Jeff said. "It's up to the police to investigate further."

"What about the letters they told me about?" Ada asked.

"You did an excellent job of demolishing that thread of evidence. I get the impression someone has tried to frame you. Policemen have been questioning Bart Walsh for several hours. I believe the Eketāhuna police stopped Craig and Eddie in a roadblock, and they're about to question Sherry."

"I can't believe this."

"Me neither." Jeff grinned. "I was a little bored with retirement. Perhaps I can talk my wife into letting me do a few hours a week for those in the region who might benefit from my services. Yes," he mused. "That might work for both of us."

Jeff ushered Ada out of the interview room, and they came face-to-face with Sherry. Two police officers escorted her. One bore scratch marks on his face. Sherry sported handcuffs, and her normally immaculate hair was a rat's nest of tangles.

Ada's gaze met Sherry's, and for a long moment, it was as if Ada was staring through a tunnel. Sherry's eyes widened, and her nostrils flared.

"You!" she shouted, struggling against the police officers. Her skin turned a mottled red. "This is your fault. Things were fine until Eddie got a crush on you. You're nothing but a conniving bitch. You adopted that flea-bitten cat I ordered Craig to get rid of. You led on my son. Both my sons." Spittle formed at the corner of her mouth, and she fought, twisting and yanking at the officers, kicking them and pounding at them with her bound wrists. Obviously, they were trying not to hurt her, but she was making it difficult.

"I've never looked at your son the wrong way," Ada snapped, incensed by the accusation. "I kept to myself and worked hard."

"You flaunted your new man in front of him," Sherry said with another sneer. Her handcuffs rattled as she tried to claw Ada.

"Eddie stalked me and made my life difficult while your other son stole from me," Ada snapped. "I thought you were my friend, but I was sadly mistaken. Everything you get is your fault." Ada detoured around Sherry and her escorts and headed to the reception. She found Matt, Josh, and Dillon waiting for her.

"Everything okay?" Matt asked.

"It will be." Ada pressed herself against Matt and

sighed in contentment when his arms closed around her. "Eventually." She pushed away, far enough to stare up into his face. "There's a strong possibility that the gun we saw Sherry waving around is the same one that killed Greg."

"I know," he said.

"I can't believe all this time Sherry pretended to be my friend."

"From what we heard during her screaming demands to see her sons and husband, she has a chip on her shoulder."

"About what?" Ada demanded. "I always treated her as a friend."

Dillon and Josh stepped outside along with Jeff.

Matt steered her after them. "I get the impression Sherry had a challenging childhood. Her parents called her a gimp and didn't include her in family activities from what I heard. Her siblings took their parents' cue while the school kids mocked her for her limp."

"That sounds ghastly, but that doesn't give her the right to pass on her misery to others. I don't understand what they wanted from me."

Matt shrugged. "They've arrested Craig for stealing from you, and it appears he and Eddie were behind many of the farm machinery thefts."

"How do they know this?"

"The vehicle they were driving when the cops stopped

them was full of parts and two bags of cash. Eddie tried to tell the cops he'd purchased the parts for repairs, but Eddie and Craig had kept the number plates too."

"Why?"

"A trophy for each theft. They were leaving because they hated their mother for continually ordering them around and planning what they did and when."

"She was the brains behind the theft ring?" Ada asked, shocked once again.

"It appears that way."

"Wow. Small towns. This will set Moewai up for years of gossip."

Matt chuckled and guided her toward Dillon's vehicle. "Dillon is going to drop us off at home."

"That sounds fantastic," Ada said, and it did. A home she knew would be safe now that the Walsh family was in police custody, plus she'd have her man at her side. Couldn't get much better than that.

CHAPTER 32

SILVER LININGS

ADA AND MATT WAVED off Dillon and Josh.

Archie emerged from a flowering bush and trotted over to them with a meow. He wound around Ada's legs before bolting for her tiny house.

Matt opened the door, and Ada came to an abrupt halt. The upheaval in her home was worse than earlier. "The detectives told me they'd found letters purporting to be from me. I knew they'd searched my house, but I didn't expect them to leave such a mess."

"I'm sorry," Matt said.

Ada scowled at the open drawers and her possessions on the floor. She stalked to the bedroom and saw the chaos extended here with the covers of her bed yanked off and clothes strewn over the floor. Her best underwear.

"Bastards," Matt said. "We'll take photos before we start to tidy, and tomorrow, we'll file a complaint."

"I can get on board with that," Ada said through clenched teeth. "We'd better start on the bedroom because I won't be able to sleep in here without everything back in its place."

Matt took photos and let her get started while he wandered off to photograph the disarray in the rest of her home.

"What do you want me to do?" he asked.

"Start in the kitchen because we'll want to eat. I'm starving. We haven't eaten since Mrs. Williams fed us. Oh, we'd better feed Archie too. I'll work in here."

An hour later, she'd folded and sorted her clothes and changed the sheets. She strode out to help Matt and found her kitchen and lounge area almost normal.

"Thank you." She gave him a careful hug to avoid his ouchies. She opened her freezer and peered inside, relieved to find the contents untouched. "How does meat pie sound with mashed potato and peas?"

"Works for me," Matt said.

Ada set the pie on the counter and turned on the oven before she sank onto her couch and rested her head. "This was a horrid day. I ache. How is your arm?"

He kissed the top of her head. "On the plus side, the cops have caught the culprits, and your problems should settle."

"You'd hope," Ada said, her voice tart. "Now all I have to do is make a profit."

"You will." Matt spoke with confidence as he settled beside her and placed an arm around her shoulders. "Think of silver linings. That's what my father always told us. We have a huge one here."

"Oh?" Ada's brows rose. "What is that?"

"We met each other," he said simply. "I didn't know I was in the market for the perfect woman. A future. You are still going to marry me?"

"You sneaked up on me. I've become fond of you."

"How fond?"

Ada turned to meet his gaze, her lips curving upward. "I love you and can't wait to marry you."

Matt grinned. "Excellent answer. How long will the pie take to cook?"

"It's still frozen, so once the oven is to temperature around forty minutes."

"Plenty of time to show you how much I return the sentiment and to celebrate your freedom from harassment." Matt hauled her to her feet. "Put the pie on to cook. I'm taking you to bed."

With the timer on, Matt plucked her off her feet and carried her into the bedroom, his injuries not hampering him in the slightest. Their clothes melted away, and they fell to the bed in a tangle of limbs. Matt claimed her lips, and Ada clung, her contentment wrapping around her like a warm hug. Matt embraced and stroked her, and she returned each caress until they both gasped, their moves frenzied. He rolled on protection and slid into her, the thrust perfect and pleasurable and driving home the fact that Matt was hers. She was his, and they were perfect together.

Their passion rose in slow increments, despite their haste, and when her climax broke over her, she'd swear she heard Greg saying goodbye, felt his kiss on her forehead. Then she was back with Matt one hundred percent, holding his muscular body as he shuddered in pleasure. As they came back down from the blissful sensations, they kissed, their joining a promise for the future.

Matt and Ada together forever. He might've fallen for her, but she'd fallen equally hard, and she couldn't wait to walk into the future at his side.

CHAPTER 33

THE COURT CASE: SIX MONTHS LATER

"ALL STAND FOR THE judge," a man intoned.

Locals from Moewai and Eketāhuna packed the courthouse, the indistinct voices halting at the order. Everyone rose, and Ada sensed the intense curiosity swirling around the room. Apart from Greg's and Ralph's murders and the Walsh family's subsequent implosion, this case was the biggest thing to happen in the country region. The Walsh family had hurt many people during their spate of burglaries, and now everyone wanted to witness how low they'd fallen.

The locals sat, and after the judge's initial remarks, the rustling ceased.

The lawyer called Ada to the stand early, and as she

walked to the witness box, she glanced at Sherry. Her former friend wore a smart navy-blue dress. She'd arranged her long hair with strands plaited and pinned around her face, the rest flowing freely to her shoulders. But when Ada's gaze tangled with Sherry's, she received attitude and rudeness. The woman who she'd thought of as a friend sneered at her.

The lawyer started with straightforward questions, no doubt to settle Ada's nerves. Then the interrogation began in earnest.

"Can you describe what happened on the morning of your husband's death?"

Ada ran through the sequence of events of her hearing the gunshots and becoming worried when Greg didn't return for breakfast. She'd tried to call him, then after another hour, she'd gone looking for him. She'd discovered him lying near their stockyards, and it had been obvious he was dead.

"How did you know?"

"There was so much blood," Ada whispered. "No one can lose that much blood and still be alive."

"What did you do?" the lawyer asked.

"I rang the police. They came and later questioned me."

"Did you kill your husband?"

"No!" Ada snapped out. "I loved him. We were a great

team, and things were going well."

"Were you aware of anyone wanting to purchase your land? The land you and your husband owned?" the lawyer asked.

"Greg told me Bart Walsh had made a casual inquiry. He told Greg he'd made an offer to Greg's aunt, and she'd agreed to the sale. Greg didn't believe him because his aunt had always wanted the land to stay in the family."

"Did Bart Walsh offer to buy the land after your husband's death?"

"Yes, he approached me not long after Greg's funeral and asked if I intended to sell and return to the city. At that stage, I'd made no decisions and told him so."

"You agreed in principle to sell to Bart."

"No." She hesitated. "Should I wish to move, Greg's parents will take over the land. It's part of the conditions in Greg's aunt's will. I didn't tell Bart this."

"Why not?"

"I felt it was family business and not for public consumption." Ada's glance drifted to Sherry. Her former neighbor had lost weight during her time in jail, making her features sharper and more prominent and catlike. Sherry glowered back as if this entire situation was Ada's fault.

Ada straightened her spine and returned her focus to the

lawyer.

"How long have you known Sherry Walsh?"

"I met her the first week we moved into the property. She arrived at our house with a cake and stayed for a cup of tea. She was bright and bubbly. Friendly. I liked her. Sherry gave a lot of herself to the community. This made her popular."

"Did she get on with most people?"

"Yes, until the end, before her arrest, I'd never heard her say a nasty word about anyone."

"Her outbursts surprised you?"

"Yes, she shocked me, especially when she blamed me for everything that had happened. I had no idea she and her family wanted my land for illegal purposes."

"Objection," the opposition broke in.

Before her lawyer spoke again, Ada said, "I don't know why they wanted my land, and Sherry's behavior shocked me."

Her lawyer smiled. "Thank you."

More questions followed, and Ada answered them truthfully, making sure to phrase her answers carefully.

"Do you dislike Sherry?" her lawyer asked.

"No. She was my neighbor, and I thought my friend. She was always pleasant, and I acted in kind."

"What about Sherry's sons? Is it true you didn't like

them, and because Sherry was their mother, you talked about her behind her back?"

"Both Craig and Eddie Walsh asked me out at various times. I wasn't interested and politely told them no. When Eddie persisted, despite my rejection, our interactions became distasteful. I believe he and his brother spied on me and graffitied my property. They also decorated my fence with offal."

"Did you see them do this?" the lawyer asked.

"No, but when they locked my boyfriend and me in my shed, they told me they'd done these things. I had no reason to disbelieve them."

"That's a lie," Sherry shouted. "My sons would never do that."

"They stole my farm vehicle," a male voice called from the back.

The judge thumped his gavel. "Quiet in the court. If these outbursts persist, I will have you removed."

Everyone fell silent, and the questions continued: the loan debacle, the attack in the shed, the ransacking of her tiny house, the things she'd seen at Sherry and Bart's property. Ada answered each point.

The lawyer finished with Ada, and they called the next witness, a police officer.

Sherry's lawyer began questioning the man. "What

proof have you got that Sherry Walsh was the force behind the thefts that took place in Moewai and the surrounding district?"

"I have a written statement from her husband, Bart Walsh."

Sherry released an audible snort but ceased when the judge sent her a quelling glare over the top of his spectacles.

Other police officers gave evidence, presenting Sherry as the lynchpin and the brains behind the entire operation.

"Who shot Greg Buckingham?" the lawyer asked Bart when he took to the stand.

"Sherry," Bart said without hesitation.

Ada recoiled, gaping at Sherry even though she'd already known the woman was the criminal mastermind rather than Bart. Although the police had informed her of this early, Bart's confirmation was a punch to the gut. Murmurs flew from person to person, and Ada spotted Sherry's chin rise and the slight curve of her mouth.

Sherry *had* been in charge of the thefts, and she'd murdered Greg and Ralph Dawson. Ada wasn't the only one who noticed the pride in Sherry. Ada bit her bottom lip to halt her trembling protest. Deep-seated anger filled Ada, and she shook with it. Only Matt calmed her agitation, his fingers clasping hers, grounding her.

The lawyer continued. "Bart, you confessed while Craig

and Eddie confirmed their mother controlled the entire operation. They'd intended to leave Moewai and start afresh in the South Island. Is this correct?"

"Yes," Bart mumbled.

"Who shot Greg Buckingham?"

"My wife," Bart repeated his previous answer.

"Why?"

"He'd refused to sell his land. We wanted it because we could graze stolen cattle and get them away without risk of anyone seeing us. Greg appeared early one morning and took us by surprise. Sherry didn't normally come with us, but she had that morning. Greg accused us of theft and told us he was going to the cops. Sherry shot him, and we left."

Ada swallowed hard. Numbness filled her chest. Disbelief. Sherry... They'd walked away, leaving Greg like a piece of trash. The woman was a monster.

Matt's grip tightened on her hand, and she pressed closer, silently seeking comfort.

"Who shot Ralph Dawson?"

Bart glanced at his wife and seemed to shrink into himself at Sherry's glower. "Sherry," he whispered. "Sherry hated Ada and wanted to make her appear guilty of shooting both men."

The tightness in Ada's chest refused to loosen as the

lawyer guided the jury through the evidence of the bullets, the gun, and the related forensics.

Each successive trial day was an exercise in torture, but Ada turned up for each session, loyalty to Greg forcing her onward. One last task to complete—justice for Greg, then she could commit herself fully to Matt.

In a surprise twist, Sherry took the stand on the last day of the trial.

"Mrs. Walsh, your husband and sons have told the police you killed Greg Buckingham and Ralph Dawson. They have reiterated you were the brains behind the entire operation. What do you say to this?"

"It's a lie," Sherry snapped. "I'm the reason Craig and Eddie have succeeded in their careers. I pushed them to excel. Bart, too. My sons love me, and I love them in return."

"But that isn't true, is it, Mrs. Walsh?" the lawyer shouted above the resulting hubbub amongst those present in the courtroom. "Your sons have done a deal, too. Three family members assert you were in charge. Given your community position, you learned which families were away on holiday or at local functions. You gathered information and used this to mastermind the thefts."

The locals broke into conversation again. The judge banged his gavel to quell the outburst.

"Quiet in the court," a court official cried.

Sherry shrieked, "Pure fabrication."

The lawyer continued without hesitation. "We have statements from your family plus several from those who suffered a theft. Each has confirmed you gathered information in this way. You organized everything and shot two men who stood in your way."

Sherry's face twisted, full of malice, and underscored with pride. "Men are too stupid to pull off what I did. Too thick. Bart's useless at business and with money. I pinned my hopes on my sons, and everything was going well until they decided they'd do better on their own. They're idiots. The three of them."

"Why did you do it?" a man shouted from the rear.

"Because I could," Sherry screeched. "All my life, people have treated me as a poor cripple instead of seeing my potential. I'm smart. I'm talented. My limp doesn't define me. You're all the same," she sneered.

The judge banged his gavel. His face turned red as everyone ignored him. The locals lobbed shouts at Sherry. Insults.

Ada turned to Matt, who sat at her side as he had throughout the trial. "Sherry is an excellent organizer. Even without Bart's confirmation, I can see her masterminding this."

"Remove the accused from the court," the judge ordered.

"You're all stupid!" Sherry yelled. Two police officers shepherded her from the courtroom, one lifting her and practically running through the door. Sherry's indignation echoed for long moments before her screams and jeers no longer reached them.

"Order in the court," a court officer shouted above the laughter and the incensed comments regarding Sherry's outburst.

"This is the perfect time to adjourn for lunch," the judge said once silence fell.

"All rise!" the court officer shouted.

The jury rose and exited the courtroom while those in the gallery left in twos and threes. Ada followed Matt, Dillon, and Josh from the courtroom.

"She hasn't done herself any favors with her outburst," Dillon said.

"Superb entertainment, though," Josh added.

"She's arrogant," Matt said. "She wants to tell everyone of her cleverness and easy deception. The woman hates men."

"Was she always like this?" Josh asked.

"No." Ada considered Sherry's behavior. "She was always friendly and personable. The first woman to welcome newcomers to the district and popular with men and women. Everyone invited her to their homes and parties."

"It was a façade," Josh said. "Clever lady. She had everyone fooled."

"I hope the jury sees it the same way," Ada said.

The jury didn't take long to come to a decision, taking less than an hour before they filed back into the courtroom. The jury foreman stood.

"On the case of the murder of Greg Buckingham, guilty or not guilty," the court officer asked.

"Guilty," the foreman said.

"On the murder of Ralph Dawson, how do you find? Guilty or not guilty?"

"Guilty," the foreman said.

"On the multiple charges of theft, how do you find the accused?"

"Guilty," the foreman repeated.

Sherry released a furious cry that reminded Ada of a wounded wild animal. When she refused to fall silent, the judge ordered her from the courtroom again.

The court officer told everyone to stand, and the judge departed. The chatter grew as locals drifted outside. Ada plopped back on her seat, numb that she'd lived next door to a murderer. Yet, intense relief filled her too. Tears obscured her vision as grief for a man who had died too early tore through Ada.

"You okay, sweetheart?" Matt asked, his presence a haven.

"Numb, actually. I can't believe this is over."

"I love you," Matt said.

She gripped his hand. "I'm a lucky woman to have two such wonderful men in my life. Sometimes I miss Greg or think of him, but I'm with you one hundred percent."

"I know that too, sweetheart. You wouldn't be the woman you are now if it wasn't for Greg."

Ada sent him a tremulous smile. "It's time for us to take a holiday in Fiji."

"Yeah?"

"Yeah," Ada said, her smile more expansive this time.

Matt stood with a broad grin. "Ready to go?"

In response, Ada rose and followed him from the courthouse. They joined Josh and Dillon, who were waiting for them outside.

Matt clasped Ada's hand. "Ada and I are going to Fiji."

Josh's eyes narrowed. "When?"

"Yeah?" Alertness crossed Dillon's face.

"As soon as we can manage it," Matt said.

"You're not going without us," Josh stated. "I'm calling Ashley now. I don't care if she's in a meeting." He put his phone on speaker. "Ash?"

"Josh, now is not a good time. I'm on hold to speak to the US President."

"Matt and Ada are going to Fiji. Matt wants to know if we're going with them."

"Fiji," Ashley exclaimed.

Ada detected the rapid flip of pages.

"Ah, Mr. President." There was a brief pause. "Just one moment," Ashley said finally.

Ada felt her eyes widen while Josh winked at her.

The flipping of pages continued. "The tenth to the fourteenth is free. I'll pencil them out. Sorry about that, Mr. President," she said before Josh's phone clicked, and their call ended.

"We can go to Fiji on the tenth. Five days," Josh said in wonder. "Five days of sunshine, beaches, beers, and my babe."

"I'll contact the others," Dillon told Matt. "I'll get back to you tomorrow with numbers."

Ada glanced at the men, wondering at the conversation. Not one mention of a wedding. She shook her head and decided to ask Matt later. Now that the court case was over, she could step into the future with confidence. Josh and Matt wanted to purchase the Walshes' farm, and now that the bank had refunded her money, she had an extra cushion for her business.

She was confident of turning a profit within the will's time constraints, given the rent she'd received from Josh, Matt, and Dillon for the hill country. The records were with the accountant now, and although she thought she'd done it this year, he'd confirm the results in a week or two.

Life was sweet, and she'd started looking further into the future because, with Matt at her side, nothing scared her. Her soldier protected her, and she stood at his side, ready to do the same for him.

EPILOGUE

THREE WEEKS LATER, ON A FIJIAN BEACH

THE SUN SHONE OVERHEAD, bringing out a jewel-like sparkle in the fine white sand. Ada followed the waves with her eyes as they sounded a gentle whoosh of advance and retreat. A warm breeze rattled the nearby coconut palms while the floral scent of the air screamed tropical island.

Fiji. Her wedding day.

Ada stepped beneath a flower-decorated pagoda at The Ocean Resort Hotel, her hands linked with Matt's. She grinned, her gaze becoming enmeshed with Matt's as the tall Fijian marriage celebrant spoke in a deep voice and recited their wedding vows. Euphoria and excitement tugged at her, and she'd never been more certain of a decision.

"The rings," the marriage celebrant said.

Seconds later, Matt pushed a golden wedding band onto her finger, and she repeated the action, claiming him with her ring. *Mine*, she thought. *My man*. Happiness filled her, and she wondered if she might burst with anticipation and delight.

"I now pronounce you man and wife. You may kiss your bride."

Their friends cheered when the kiss continued for a long time.

"Hey!"

Matt pulled away from their kiss, and Ada grinned at her new sister-in-law, who'd been tapping on her brother's shoulder.

"You can save that for another time. I want to hug my new sister," Ashley said, her expression warm with a hint of mischief.

Matt grumbled, but love and respect reverberated between the siblings. Ada had liked Matt's mother and father too and was thrilled they'd made the trip to Fiji also. Ada's parents hadn't come, but she hadn't expected their support. After she'd married Greg against their wishes, they'd grown apart. She'd rung them and extended an invitation, but they'd declined. Matt's family made up for the lack, so she felt doubly blessed.

"Time for photos," Summer ordered.

Meeting Summer in person had been like finding another sister since the woman was a power, both funny and friendly, and Ada had enjoyed meeting Matt's friends and their wives. There was Nikolai, Summer's husband. Louie and Mac, and Jake and Sorrel.

They were all big men. Strong men, with their ex-army status and shared experiences binding them into a tight friendship. Ada might not have a welcoming family, but Matt's friends and family embraced her into their sphere.

Summer directed them onto the beach, where she snapped formal and informal shots of them and their friends. A group of local children stopped to watch, their smiles growing wider when Summer turned the camera on them. *"Bula,"* she called.

"Bula," came the chorused reply from the laughing children.

Once Summer finished taking photos, Ashley guided everyone inside.

"Bossy much?" Matt murmured in Ada's ear.

She grinned. "Wait until you see the feast Ash, your mother, and Summer have organized. I hope you're hungry."

"Not really," he said. "What I'd like to do is retire to our room and make love to my wife."

Ada snorted. "That's my preference, but we don't have a chance of that happening soon. I vote we celebrate with our friends and lounge around the pool or laze on the beach and save our private celebration for later. We have the rest of our lives."

Matt's expression softened, and he stole a kiss.

"Hey, enough of that," Josh said. "It's time for the toasts." His stomach let out a loud rumble. "And I'm hungry. This way. We've arranged for you to sing for Ada."

Matt chuckled. "This is payback for setting up you and Ashley. I stand by my plan to get the pair of you together. You love each other."

Ada grinned at Josh, having heard the story of Matt's sly maneuvering to get Josh into Ashley's life. A stalker with Ashley in their sights had provided the perfect excuse to give Josh a push.

"Maybe a little," Josh said. "Although mostly, I'm happy we're all here together to celebrate you finding this lovely lady and having the sense to keep her." He winked at Ada.

Ada enjoyed the toasts and the joking and teasing, but she teared up when Ashley stood to welcome her to the family.

"I love my big brother," Ashley told everyone. "Although he always thinks he knows better than me."

There were hoots at this.

"But I forgive him. He introduced me to Josh and, by extension, Summer, Nikolai, and our other friends. Now, he's gone one better and married a wonderful woman, one I'm proud to call sister. Please raise your glasses to Matt and Ada. To a long and fruitful marriage and excellent health. Matt and Ada."

"Matt and Ada," everyone repeated, lifting their glasses and drinking to their health.

They ate, drank, chattered, and laughed.

"It's time for singing," Josh called. "One song. That's all we'll manage to bear before our ears bleed. Go, Matt!"

The men smirked at each other and urged Matt to confer with the local guitarist.

"This should be fun," Ashley muttered. "You know they call my brother Frog because he used to entertain them at karaoke, and his singing was atrocious. I don't think they've persuaded him to sing since they've been home." Her smile turned mischievous. "You're about to learn why."

"Matt truly can't sing?" Ada asked. "Doesn't matter. I love him, faults and all."

"*Hmm.*" Ashley pressed her lips together.

The guitarist strummed his instrument, and Matt started singing "Love Me Tender". Josh, Dillon, Nikolai, and others had been grinning at each other, but their smiles faded fast. They straightened in their chairs and gaped as Matt continued singing with a gorgeous voice.

Ada glanced at Ashley in time to catch a wink.

"Matt is a talented singer," Ashley whispered.

"You never told Josh?"

"Where's the fun in that?" Ashley murmured.

Matt held the last note of the song, then blew a kiss at his friends.

"You can sing," Josh exclaimed.

"Yes," Matt agreed.

"Why?" Dillon demanded.

"The men needed light relief. I was happy to play the fool and lighten the tension." Matt made his way to Ada.

"That was lovely," she said.

Summer cackled, poking fun at her husband and her brothers.

Matt grinned. "I was saving that for a special moment."

Ada kissed his cheek. "They won't forget this. You'll need to watch yourself."

"Don't be sore losers," Summer said. "Let's go swimming."

They dispersed to change into swimsuits and walked onto the beach to enjoy the tropical breeze and sunshine.

Ada sat on a beach mat between Summer and Ashley.

The other women joined them while the men drifted down the beach and began a spirited game of football.

Ada smiled at Matt, tanned and sexy in his navy-blue swim shorts. Her husband. Tonight couldn't come fast enough, but she enjoyed the day and spent time with the other women. Today was such a contrast to her last wedding, which had been formal and stuffy because Greg's parents had wanted it that way.

Summer sat up suddenly, drawing Ada's attention. "I've had an idea. A brilliant one." Her gaze ran over the men before she turned to Ada with a dazzling smile. "Yes, Brilliant idea. The very best. Remind me to tell you later." She stood and ambled over to meet a sweaty Nikolai.

The men finished their game, and one by one, the couples wandered off to their rooms.

Matt came to her, holding out his hand to haul her to her feet. The hot, intense light in his gaze brought a flush of heat to her face.

"Ready?" he asked.

She nodded, and they walked hand-in-hand back to their room. Her phone beeped, signaling an incoming text. Ada released Matt's hand and pulled the cell from her bag. "Yes!"

"Good news?"

"It's official. The land is mine." She beamed at her new

husband.

"You made a profit?"

"Yes."

"We need to celebrate. Come shower with me," Matt suggested.

Ada grinned as Matt kicked off his shorts and turned on the water. She peeled off her clothes and joined him beneath the multitude of taps in the honeymoon suite. Matt's arms wrapped around her, and their lips met.

"I can't believe we're married," Matt whispered. "You've made me so happy."

Ada cupped his face and held his head still. She grinned up at him. "We're both blessed, husband."

Then they kissed, and passion bloomed. They finished their shower, but they didn't leave their room until late the next morning.

Married bliss.

· ❤ · ❤ · ❤ · ❤ · ❤ ·

WANT TO LEARN MORE about Summer's brilliant plan?

Not quite ready to let Matt and Ada go? Me neither. Subscribe to my newsletter and receive a copy of

Operation: Sensational Plan. Learn everything about Summer's sneakiness and the army boys' negotiations.

Go here: https://BookHip.com/VRKTLVP
to subscribe and receive your free bonus story.

About Author

USA Today bestselling author Shelley Munro lives in Auckland, the City of Sails, with her husband and a cheeky Jack Russell/mystery breed dog.

Typical New Zealanders, Shelley and her husband left home for their big OE soon after they married (translation of New Zealand speak - big overseas experience). A twelve-month-long adventure lengthened to six years of roaming the world. Enduring memories include being almost sat on by a mountain gorilla in Rwanda, lazing on white sandy beaches in India, whale watching in Alaska, searching for leprechauns in Ireland, and dealing with ghosts in an English pub.

While travel is still a big attraction, these days Shelley is most likely found in front of her computer following another love - that of writing stories of contemporary and paranormal romance and adventure. Other interests include watching rugby (strictly for research purposes), cycling, playing croquet and the ukelele, and curling up with an enjoyable book.

Visit Shelley at her Website

https://shelleymunro.com/

Join Shelley's Newsletter

https://shelleymunro.com/newsletter/

ALSO BY SHELLEY

Military Men
Innocent Next Door
Soldier with Benefits
Safeguarding Sorrel
Stranded with Ella
Josh's Fake Fiancee
Operation Flower Petal
Protecting the Bride

Friendship Chronicles
Secret Lovers
Reunited Lovers
Clandestine Lovers
Part-Time Lovers

Enemy Lovers

Maverick Lovers

Sports Lovers

Fancy Free

Protection

Romp

Buzz

Festive

Single Titles

One Night of Misbehavior

Playing to Win

Reformed Bad Girl

Milton Keynes UK
Ingram Content Group UK Ltd.
UKHW021936220724
445848UK00004B/80